THE GIRL FROM THE CHANNEL ISLANDS

THE GIRL FROM THE CHANNEL ISLANDS

JENNY LECOAT

THORNDIKE PRESS
A part of Gale, a Cengage Company

GALE
A Cengage Company

**LIBRARY OF CONGRESS CIP DATA ON FILE.
CATALOGUING IN PUBLICATION FOR THIS BOOK
IS AVAILABLE FROM THE LIBRARY OF CONGRESS.**

ISBN-13: 978-1-4328-8531-1 (hardcover alk. paper)

Published in 2021 by arrangement with Harlequin Books S.A.

Printed in Mexico
Print Number: 01   Print Year: 2021

For those courageous Channel Islanders
whose acts of kindness, resolution
and resistance under Occupation
saved the lives of others.

And for Gary.

This novel is based on true events. In 1940, young Hedwig Bercu, a Jewish girl who had recently escaped the Anschluss, found herself trapped on the tiny island of Jersey when Nazi Germany invaded the Channel Islands. The extraordinary story of Hedy's struggle for survival, including the role played by a serving officer of the occupying forces, was first documented almost sixty years later and is the foundation for this fictionalized account. Some names have been changed. For more background information, please see Acknowledgments.

ONE

Jersey, Channel Islands
Summer 1940

The sun's heat had begun to mellow, and the gulls were cruising for their final catch of the day when the siren sounded. Its wail climbed and fell, calling out over the jumbled slate roofs and church spires of the town, and across the patchwork of potato fields beyond. In St. Aubin's bay, where the waves lapped and fizzed on the sand, its warning finally reached Hedy's ears as she lay dozing by the sea wall, and woke her with a jolt.

Rising in slow motion, she scanned the sky. Now she could also hear a faint, tinny whine in the east. She tried to steady her breathing. Perhaps it was another false alarm? These warnings had become a daily event these past two weeks, each time the reconnaissance planes merely circling, then disappearing back out to sea with cameras crammed full of blurry images of main roads and harbor walls. But this time something was different. The engine sound contained a note of brutish intent, and now several tiny black dots were emerging in the distant blue. The whine became a hum, and the hum a strident drone. Then she knew. This was no reconnaissance mission. This was the start.

For days now, the islanders had watched the black smoke rise and mushroom on the French coast, felt the vibration of the distant blasts pulse through their bellies and rattle their bones. Women had spent hours counting and recounting the tinned foods in their larders, while the men squashed into banks to withdraw the family savings. Children had yelled their complaints as gas masks were forced over their heads. By then, all hope had vanished. There was no one here to deter the aggressors, nothing between them and their shimmering prize but flat blue water and an empty sky. And now the planes were on their way. Hedy could see them clearly now, still some distance away, but from the outline she guessed they were Stukas. Dive-bombers.

She spun around, looking for shelter. The nearest beachside café was almost a mile away. Stopping only to grab her wicker bag, she sprinted for the stone steps leading to the walkway above, and took them in three bounds. At the top she scoured the promenade; a hundred meters toward First Tower was a small seafront shelter. It contained nothing but a single wooden bench on each of its four exposed sides, but it would have to do. Hedy hurtled toward it, grazing her shin as she mistimed the leap onto the low plinth, and threw herself against the bench. A moment later she was joined by a panic-stricken young mother, probably not much older than herself, gripping a small white-faced boy by the wrist. By now the planes were over St. Helier harbor, one arcing across the bay toward them, the noise of the engine so thunderous that it drowned out the boy's screams as the woman pushed him to the ground. The violent rat-a-tat of machine-gun fire stung Hedy's ears as several bullets found the sea wall and zinged off in random directions. A second later, a distant explosion shook the shelter so hard Hedy thought the roof might collapse.

"Was that a bomb?" The woman's face was ashen beneath her tan.

"Yes. Near the harbor, I think."

The woman gave her a brief, confused look. It was the accent, Hedy knew — even in a moment like this it still set her apart,

11

marked her out as an alien. But the woman's attention quickly turned back to her child.

"Oh my God," she muttered, "what have we done? My husband said we should have evacuated when we had the chance." Her eyes fixed on the sky. "Do you think we should have gone?"

Hedy said nothing, but followed her companion's gaze upward. She thought about her employers, the Mitchells, staggering onto that filthy, inadequate cargo boat with their screaming child, and nothing but a change of underwear and a few provisions stuffed into a brown packing case. At this moment, with the aroma of burning aviation fuel in her nostrils, she would have given anything to be with them. Her knuckles turned yellow on the slatted bench. Corkscrews of charcoal smoke drifted across the bay, and she could hear the little boy beside her sobbing. Hedy swallowed hard and focused on the questions bouncing around her brain like a pinball. How long now before the Germans landed? Would they round people up, stand them in front of walls to be shot? If they came for her, then . . . ? There was no point finishing that thought. Anton, the only person on this island she could call a friend, would be powerless to help her. The shelter vibrated again, and she felt its fragility.

Hedy remained crouched silently, listening to the planes loop and dive and the crack of explosions a mile away, until at last the sound of the engines began to fade into the distance. An aging gentleman with disheveled white hair stumbled toward them, and stopped to peer into the shelter.

"The planes have gone," he called. "Try to get home as quickly as you can. It can't be long before they get here." Hedy's eyes fixed on his jacket, which was covered in dust and uneven patches of blood. "Don't worry, it's not mine," the man assured her. "Old fellow walking near the harbor took a bullet in the leg — we had to get him to the hospital."

"Are there many hurt? Or . . . ?" Hedy glanced toward the little boy, not wanting to finish the question.

"Some, yes." The man's voice faltered a little, and Hedy felt a surge of anguish. She pressed her fist to her lips and swallowed again before he continued: "They bombed a line of potato trucks waiting to unload at the harbor. I mean, for God's sake, what's the point of that?" He shook his head and gestured toward his destination. "Hurry now."

The man hastened away. Hedy hauled her

shaking body to its feet, wished the woman good luck and set off along the promenade toward the town, wondering how on earth she would get back to the Mitchells' — assuming the house was still there. She tried to hurry, but her skinny legs felt weak. She imagined Hemingway cowering beneath the sofa in the empty living room, his gray feline fur stiff with terror. Already she was half regretting disobeying Mr. Mitchell's instruction to have him put down. The animal's trusting eyes had melted her heart at the door of the vet's surgery. Now she wasn't even sure if she'd be able to feed herself, never mind a cat.

By the time she reached the outskirts of St. Helier town she could hear the bells of the ambulances and the random shouts of desperate men trying to work as a team. Smoke rose in perfect columns from boats and buildings in the windless summer evening; cars lay abandoned on the roads at odd angles. There were a few people about: some searching for the missing, some wandering aimlessly, and one old couple on a bench, sobbing. Hedy walked on, forcing herself to put one foot in front of the other, deliberately edging her mind toward reality. The seas around the island were probably already full of U-boats. Soon she would

14

once again be surrounded by those gray-green uniforms and hear the barking of orders. She pictured the bang on the door, Wehrmacht hands grabbing at her elbow, the house abandoned with dirty dishes still on the table. Anything was possible now. She recalled only too well the way the Germans had behaved in Vienna.

Especially toward Jews.

She pressed on, pushing her body weight forward, willing herself home. She needed to reach Hemingway and give him a hug.

"I have these. But might they get us into trouble?"

Anton stood in the doorway of his bedroom holding out a pair of once white, now gray, ribbed cotton underpants. Even from her seat by the window Hedy could see they had not been washed. She felt the tiniest smile creep around her lips at the word "trouble"; Anton could be so cautious sometimes, just as he could be absurdly optimistic at others. His face, like her own when she accidentally caught herself in the mirror, was pale with anxiety and exhaustion. Anton lived alone and Hedy suspected that he, too, had sat up for the last four nights, staring sleeplessly over deserted streets, counting down the curfewed hours

15

with fearful expectation.

"Too late to worry about that," Hedy replied. "And they said a white flag. They didn't specify what it should be made of. Look, everyone's doing it." They poked their heads out of the first-floor window into the sunshine. Below was a neat town street, lined with apartments built over shops and businesses, with doors that opened directly onto the pavement. Outside each window hung some kind of household fabric — an apron, a baby's nappy, an ancient undergarment. Defiance in the face of defeat. Anton nodded his agreement and Hedy, taking care to use only the tips of her fingers, took the underpants and tied them to the broom handle, then eased it out of the window, resting the brush end on a chair and weighting it down with a towel. As they did so, the sound of the vehicle engines swelled in their ears. "Here they come now," Hedy murmured.

The first car appeared at the end of the main street, clearly visible from their viewpoint — a smart open-topped Bentley filled with senior officers in full uniform. The second was a gleaming Daimler with several more. Behind them followed a dozen or so less impressive Fords and Morrises containing lower-ranked soldiers and a couple of motorcycles with sidecars at the rear — all stolen, Hedy supposed, from the garages of local residents, as the arriving military could hardly have had time to transport such vehicles from France. Even from up here, the delight on the Germans' faces was clearly visible. Presumably after months in the cold muddy fields of Europe, the creamy white beaches and tree-lined lanes of this picturesque island had come as a happy surprise to them, just as they once had to Hedy.

"Look at them." Anton's voice was thick with anger. "You'd think they'd conquered the whole of England, not a few British islands off St. Malo."

"For them it's the first step," Hedy muttered.

"We're not expected to salute them, are we?"

Hedy peered into the windows opposite. Behind every one stood morose local residents, staring with impotent hatred at their new masters. There had been no more bombs since Friday night, and the damage around the harbor and Weighbridge was already partly repaired, but everyone knew that today marked the true beginning of subjugation. Watching their captors arrive, the people willed their fury into the invaders' hearts, their sullenness their only defense.

Hedy shook her head. "They won't make us salute. They'll want to convince us how civilized they are — show the world how they intend to run Britain. What was it they said?" She picked up the leaflet from Anton's little table, and brushed away the dried granules of mud from the flower bed where it had landed. "Here it is: 'the liberty of peaceful inhabitants is solemnly guaranteed.' " She snorted. "We'll see how long that lasts."

Anton squeezed her shoulder for reassurance. She felt the warmth of his hand, her first physical contact with anyone since saying goodbye to the Mitchells' little girl, and had to chew the inside of her lip to keep the tears at bay. They stood like that for several moments, until the line of cars finally disappeared and the windows above the pavement began to close. There would be more soldiers, of course, in the coming days — many more — but the islanders had had their first glimpse of the enemy, enough for one day. Anton returned to his usual easy chair by the fireplace, carefully positioned to hide the torn linoleum beneath. It was a small, scrappy apartment, but it had a coziness far more comforting than her exemployers' sprawling, deserted house, and the smell from the bakery beneath made it homely. It was a place where she had always felt safe.

"There's no point thinking the worst," Anton said, reading her thoughts.

"All right for you." She slumped down on the only other chair and tucked one leg underneath her, as always. Her fingers fiddled constantly with the ribbon on her dress. "I'm so stupid! Why didn't I go to America when I had the chance?"

"You know why."

"I could have found the money somehow! I shouldn't have given up so easily."

Anton leaned forward in his chair. "Look, there are so few Jews left on the island — a dozen maybe? — it's probably not worth the Krauts seeking them out." He must have seen the cynicism in her eyes, for he went on: "I really don't think it will be as bad as it was in Vienna."

Hedy tossed her hair. "No? Even if you're right, even if they don't target my people, do you realize how vulnerable we'll be now? We're foreigners here, foreigners who speak German! We'll be caught in the cross fire."

"The Jersey people won't turn on us that way, they know exactly why we're here."

"Anton, they dragged you off to that

internment camp barely six weeks ago, just for being an enemy alien!"

"Only until they checked things out, then I was back home again. That's what I mean — people here are pretty reasonable."

"You Catholics!" Her voice sounded high and jagged. "You think the world is full of saints! You think the locals won't remember that the Austrians threw flowers and cheered when the Germans crossed our border?"

Anton pushed his mop of thick dark hair from his eyes and sat back in his chair. Despite her affection for him, it was one of Hedy's constant disappointments that Anton avoided arguments. It was partly a dislike of confrontation, partly a genuine desire not to cause unhappiness. Perhaps that was why she had never felt any romantic attraction toward him, despite all they had in common. How much more protected she might feel now, if things had been different between them.

Anton shifted in his chair, maneuvering to change the subject. "I must try to get some sleep tonight," he said eventually. "The bakery will reopen tomorrow. Mr. Reis reckons we'll be mobbed with people panic-buying, but I'm not so sure. I think most people will try to carry on as if it's a normal day."

Hedy gave a bitter laugh. "Oh yes, of course. Like you say, the shops will open, order of the Commandant. And we'll all go about our business like nothing's happened. That's what people do, isn't it? We'll hang up our blackout blinds and move our clocks forward an hour to fit German time. And we'll tell ourselves it'll all be fine." Her breath was coming in short gasps.

Anton moved toward her. "Hedy, don't."

"Everyone will walk around town, pretending we're not terrified of being arrested. And me, I'll sit around waiting to be packed off God knows where on the next boat. But you're right — apart from that, it'll be just like any normal day." The last words left her as a scream as she sank to her knees, the sobs jerking her body. "I can't take this, Anton, not again. Please, don't let them take me away."

Anton held her gently in his arms, muttering words of comfort, then passed her his handkerchief. Hedy cried into it for a full ten minutes while Anton made hot tea, and sat Hedy down in his own chair to drink it. Then he put Rachmaninov on the gramophone, and they both sat in a companionable stillness, listening to the soaring melodies until the sun began to dip. Hedy watched the sky above the rooftops turn from pale gold to pink, her thoughts in free fall. She thought about her parents back in Vienna, whose precious letters would no longer reach her. She thought about Roda, with her silver laugh and wild hair; how brave her sister had been, stuffing that envelope of schilling notes down her knickers as they pushed their old Steyr motorcar into thick, concealing undergrowth, two kilometers from the Swiss border. She wondered if Roda ever made it to Palestine. Then Hedy closed her eyes and dozed for a while. When she woke, Anton provided more tea and some stale macaroons he'd taken from the shop. He gave her a leftover tinned sardine to take back for Hemingway. Finally, as the sky grew royal blue, it was time for her to go.

"I'll get my jacket and walk you back," Anton said. "You shouldn't be out on the streets alone."

Hedy blew her nose and ran her fingers through her hair to push it back into shape. Tonight was a threshold, a time for putting things in order, for packing and storing away. Tomorrow she would buy a bolt for the front door. A large black steel one that would slide into its socket with a solid click. Metal was what she needed now.

Outside the window, the strongest, brightest stars were beginning to push through the darkness. As she stared at them, she thought of the protestors on the streets of Vienna, down on their hands and knees scrubbing pro-independence slogans from the pavements. The Krauts had laughed and pretended that the kicked-over pails and crushed fingers were an accident, and the chalk and paint eventually washed away. But the words and colors of the messages were burned into her memory forever, and the resolve never left those protestors' eyes.

Anton returned with his jacket. Hedy handed him back his handkerchief.

"Keep it."

Hedy shook her head. "No, thanks. I won't be needing it anymore."

The morning of 16 September, a day ringed in thick black ink on Hedy's calendar, dawned bright and clear, though a stiff breeze persisted from the direction of the harbor. The elements had been unpredictable in recent days; a fierce storm had blown in from the Atlantic straight into the Gulf of St. Malo, bringing sharp showers and a wind that whipped around the corners of the town's streets, blowing women's hats from their heads and catching the new swastika flag that now hung outside the town hall. Such squalls were unusual for the island's mild climate, not when the leaves were still green on the trees and the evenings were still so light. Yet Hedy had heard no one complain about it; perhaps because there were no longer any tourists to drive away, or perhaps because it seemed a fitting reflection of the island's new mass depression. Last night, when she had wandered by the sea wall of St. Aubin's bay watching German NCOs rolling out kilometers of barbed wire along the beach, it seemed to her that even the waves were receding quicker than before, as if they no longer wished to stay in this infected place.

Hedy pulled her cardigan a little tighter over her dress as she made her way toward the town's main shopping street, wondering why the purposeful rhythm of her heeled peep-toe sandals echoed so loudly as she hurried along the pavement — so much so that passersby turned to stare at her, seemingly affronted by the sound. Click-clacking into King Street, it slowly dawned on her that the volume was due to the disappearance of motorized traffic. Apart from occasional German vehicles, the streets of St. Helier were once more a maze of pedestrian streets, where every sharp noise bounced and ricocheted around the walls in a mimic

24

of bygone times. She made a mental note not to wear heels in public again. She had not spent the last weeks as a ghost in her own community, slipping into the streets occasionally to buy food or take some air, only to draw attention to herself now.

Still, she was grateful to have found a new apartment in the center of town, within easy reach of the shops and the covered market on Beresford Street. It was a big step down from the Mitchells' family home, but with that property now under legal stewardship, a chilly bedsitting room at the top of a town house was some kind of home, and better than getting stuck out in the country parishes. Already the shops had sold out of bicycles, and Hedy had spotted a few aging nags harnessed to tatty old Edwardian carts, piled up with produce from St. Mary and St. Martin, bringing steaming piles of horse dung back to the modern tarmac roads. Pretty soon, Hedy mused, the streets of Jersey would sound and smell like the streets of her childhood.

She checked her watch; it was a little after nine fifteen, giving her just enough time to buy new stockings before her appointment. This morning she'd chased Hemingway around the apartment with a newspaper after he'd clawed runs in her last pair, shouting at him that she wished she'd left him behind. Bare legs would simply not do — and certainly not today, when it was vital that she look and feel her very best. She hurried on toward De Gruchy's department store, passing several local housewives all wearing the same expression — a wary, hunted look of fearful expectation. Each of them quickened their pace as they passed groups of bantering German soldiers — scared to be so close to the enemy, afraid to run in case it should be misinterpreted. And there were scores, perhaps hundreds, of soldiers in the town now, browsing the shop windows and loafing in the parks. How the Reich could spare so many boats to transport them all, Hedy could only wonder. Crossing the road to avoid a boisterous group of off-duty privates sharing cigarettes and slapping each other's shoulders, she reached the store, pushed open the heavy glass door and made her way through the various elegant counters to the hosiery department.

"Excuse me?" Hedy tried to neutralize her accent as much as possible without sounding like a parody. "I would like to buy some stockings."

The assistant, a woman in her forties with hair in a topknot bun, inclined her head as she prepared her customer's bad news. "I'm sorry, madam, we're completely sold out."

Hedy glanced down at the display drawers under the counter's polished glass top, and saw that they were almost empty. "You have nothing in the back, perhaps?" She beamed a rictus smile, afraid this obvious approach might backfire, but the woman shook her head.

"Sorry, I can't help you." She leaned forward conspiratorially, her sickly floral perfume rising uninvited up Hedy's nostrils, and hissed: "It's them. They come in here all friendly, but look! Gone through the whole place like ruddy locusts — sending it all back to their families, see, 'cause they've had nothing in their shops for months. Winter coats, kitchen stuff, fabric, you name it. You tried to buy cheese this week? Can't get it for love nor money."

Hedy matched her low volume. "Can you not refuse to serve them?"

"This Jerry officer came in, said if we do, our managers will be thrown in prison. But where's the new stock going to come from, that's what I want to know? You see them down the harbor this week, sending all our Jersey Royals to France? What are we supposed to eat? Tell you what . . ." The woman's face brightened as an idea occurred to her, and her voice lowered even further. "You can have the stockings I'm wearing right now if you can get us a couple of pork chops by tonight? It's the old man's birthday and I've got nothing for him but a bit of leftover tripe."

Hedy stared at her, considering. The thought of putting on a strange woman's dirty stockings was unpleasant, but more dispiriting was the realization that even if she wanted to, she was in no position to strike that kind of deal. Only this morning she'd noticed that the butcher at the end of her road had stuck up a sign reading "Regular Customers Only." Special deals were doubtless available to friends and the favored in this insular little place, but Hedy had no such traction. She saw her future stretching ahead, an endless queue in which she was always at the back, getting what no one else wanted or nothing at all.

"Thank you. I appreciate the thought but I'll try elsewhere."

The assistant shrugged to indicate that Hedy was wasting her time. And so it proved to be. Voisins store, the haberdashers at the top end of town, even the funny little shop behind the market where the old ladies went for crossover pinafores and flannelette nightdresses all gave her the same story. By ten minutes to ten Hedy found herself defeated, heading toward her appointment with still naked legs, and her mother's disapproving voice ringing in her head, telling her that nice girls never went out like that.

As soon as she turned into the Royal Square, still bearing the giant white cross of surrender painted on its pink granite paving, she saw the crowd. A chaotic queue of men, snaking around the block into Church Street, huddled together in twos and threes, all shuffling their feet and muttering furtive expletives to each other as they waited to enter the makeshift records office set up in the library. It was, Hedy realized, the registration line for local men between eighteen and fifty-five — a manifestation of the Nazis' desire to list, classify and number, and a preparation for future identifications. From now on, the seeking out, hauling up and dispensation of Jersey people would be as easy as taking a memo from a pigeonhole. What was the English expression? Like shooting fish in a barrel. The wind blew again, and she shuddered.

From somewhere in the center of the crowd came shouts of anger. Hedy craned her neck to witness a young man in a flat cap gesticulating at two German privates, shouting that they had no right to treat law-abiding citizens this way. She watched the soldiers lead the man away, her heart thumping in her chest, and closed her eyes momentarily. Then she straightened her dress, swung away from the crowd and set off again without looking back. At the far end of the square she turned into Hill Street and, holding her head high, walked briskly into the Aliens Office.

Lieutenant Kurt Neumann dropped his duffel bag onto the waxed floor of his new quarters, and headed straight for the French windows at the end of the sunny room. He could already feel a grin spreading across his face, like a kid at his first funfair. What a view! If only he had a camera. The garden was gorgeous. Puffy white blooms of alamy roses and exotic seaside shrubs surrounded a neat lawn. At the end was an ornate iron gate, and beyond that — the sea. Or, to use the proper English word from his new dictionary, the seaside. This was not the ocean that Kurt was used to, that scary, churning plain that threatened to swallow ships and suck down soldiers. This was a sweep of sparkling sapphire, licking at a beach of ash-blond sand and bubbly black seaweed. It beckoned you into it, dared you to rip off your boots and run barefoot along its soft, welcoming shore. If he didn't have a deployment briefing in ten minutes, Kurt would have done exactly that, right now. He shook his head in wonder and gratitude at getting a posting here.

The Unterfeldwebel who'd collected them from the harbor a little after dawn had suggested a guided tour of the island before dropping each officer at his allocated billet. In the back of the gleaming Morris Eight convertible, Kurt's immediate neighbor, a Lieutenant Fischer who proudly mentioned three times that he was from Munich, spread a map over his knees and bombarded their driver with questions about geographical positions and plans for fortified defenses. But Kurt, apart from the odd nod of fake interest, simply sat back in the leather seat and looked around, happy to let the information wash over him. There was plenty of time for work later. Right now he wanted to absorb every detail.

The island, it seemed, was basically a rectangle. They drove first along St. Aubin's bay on the south side, past the quaint granite harbor with its bobbing fishing boats, and over the hill to St. Brelade where lush green vegetation tumbled down to a white sandy bay. The road took them up the west side with its vast beach and rolling dunes, then ten kilometers along the north coast, with its majestic cliffs and picture-postcard bays of blue-green water. On the east side, the terra-cotta moonscape of a barren rocky shore revealed itself as the tide slid out, and the glorious, centuries-old Mont Orgueil Castle rose skyward. At each bend in the winding roads, in every dip and under every arch of thick emerald foliage, Kurt felt a rush of excitement. But by now Fischer and the other officers were checking their watches, muttering about finding their billets and reporting in. Kurt nodded in agreement, while thinking how he'd like to return here with his old chum Helmut after the war; apparently there were plans afoot to turn all the Channel Islands into a high-class resort for the military when all this was over. They could stay at one of those big hotels on the Esplanade, hit the bars, meet some girls. They'd have a ball.

His billet turned out to be a pretty semi-detached house on the east side, in an area named Pontac Common. The interior smelled of polish and lavender, and had been decorated tastefully in muted floral patterns by its previous Jersey owners. Standing in the garden and looking out toward the sea, Kurt wondered where they were living now. The late summer sun warmed his face despite the chill wind, and bees buzzed among the flowers. Fischer, who was marked on the list as Kurt's new roommate, appeared through the French windows behind him, smiling in approval at the view.

"Some place, isn't it?"

"Beautiful," Kurt replied.

"Needs a lot of pulling into line, though. The whole garrison, I mean."

"Really?" Kurt noticed that he was wearing an Infantry Assault badge and a bronze Close Combat clasp.

"Public relations directive from Berlin." Fischer sniffed and stubbed out the end of a small cigar on the lawn. "There was a lot of cooperation with the local government in the first weeks — personally I think that sends out a bad message." Kurt nodded, wondering what that meant. "Apparently they've not even rounded up the Judenschweine yet."

Kurt dragged deeply on his cigarette, sensing that the fun part of the day was coming to a close. "Do they intend to?"

"They're being registered this week. Then we'll see." Fischer took in a huge lungful of sea air. "Yes. I reckon we can really do something with this place."

■ ■ ■

Hedy watched as Clifford Orange, Chief Aliens Officer of Jersey, arranged himself behind his desk, running his hands over the surface as if savoring its solidity. He was a middle-aged man with skin that bloomed and flaked around his cheeks; his hair was thinning but he sported a small mustache and eyebrows so heavy they looked like they might crawl away of their own accord. From the ceiling hung a chandelier, far too large for the room; the sun poured through the window and splashed off the gleaming floor. Beyond the pane, Hedy could see the trees in the town churchyard. She sat down on the upholstered chair in front of Orange's desk and folded her hands in her lap on top of her handbag, hoping it might convey conformity and obedience. She offered a small smile but Orange was already lost in the file laid out before him.

"So, Miss Bercu. Let me refresh my memory. You are twenty-one years old, you arrived in Jersey on the fifteenth of November 1938, and you currently reside at 28 New Street, correct?"

"That's correct, the top flat."

He glanced up at her with a curious look.

Hedy suspected it was her command of English that intrigued him. She wondered if he'd expected her to bark like a dog.

"When you arrived here you were in possession of a recent British visa in the name of Hedwig Bercu-Goldenberg, a foreigner's passport issued in Vienna the previous September, and a registration card recording your status as a Romanian national, issued in Vienna in May 1937 in the name of Hedwig Goldenberg." He put down the document and looked her in the eye. "Can you explain the variation in your nomenclature?"

"I think I have already explained: Bercu was my stepfather's name, and Goldenberg was my mother's."

"Your stepfather?"

"I don't know who my real father was. After I was born my mother married a Romanian, and I took his name."

Hedy swallowed at the end of the sentence and became painfully aware of a film of sweat on her upper lip. She had rehearsed this story a dozen times with Anton in her apartment, but saying it out loud in a formal environment felt different.

Orange removed his fountain pen from its holder and with great precision made a note on the document. "So, Goldenberg being a

Jewish name, you are in fact Jewish?"

"No."

Orange placed the cap back on his pen and laid it to one side, ensuring that it sat in perfect parallel with the blotter. "You're not Jewish?"

"I was raised a Protestant. My stepfather is Jewish and my mother adopted his religion when they married, but I have no Jewish blood." Hedy attempted the smile again but this time it wouldn't come. Every word of the lie grew like cotton wool in her mouth. Orange's eyes darted over her and she realized he was staring at her hair, which she had pinned up especially for today's interview. She knew its tawny blond color, a gift from her grandmother's side of the family, would be her greatest alibi today, particularly to someone like Orange who had probably only seen pictures of Jews in books. But now he seemed to be assessing its authenticity. Perhaps he had been told that all Jewish women wear wigs.

"You're telling me that your mother, whose name is Goldenberg, was in fact Protestant?"

"Yes." Her hands were now gripping her bag as if it might fly out of her lap at any moment.

Orange rose from his seat and walked over

to the window, gazing across at the Norman church tower in what he clearly hoped suggested a pose of judicious concentration.

"You see, Miss Bercu, I am in a most difficult position. I trust you understand the relationship between the Jersey authorities and the new German Field Command?"

"Not entirely."

Orange smoothed his mustache with his thumb and forefinger. "It is one, I fear, of immense delicacy. Jersey civil administration continues as before, but we must now accommodate and execute the orders of our new masters. And the Germans have requested that all Jews living within the Channel Islands must be registered separately from the remainder of the populace." He turned back to face her. "So you see I would be failing in my duty should I fail to register any Jewish persons with German Field Command."

Hedy tried to clear her throat surreptitiously before answering. "But I am not Jewish."

He sighed just loud enough to let her hear it. "If you'll forgive me, I find your explanation unconvincing in the light of the documented evidence. If you were somehow able to prove your heritage —"

"Why is it I who must provide proof? If

you don't believe me, is it not up to you, or the Germans, to provide proof that I am Jewish?" She stopped and bit her lip, remembering Anton's advice to placate, not provoke. In her lap, her nails dug into her palms.

Orange was glaring at her now, and returned to his seat as if to wrap things up. "On the contrary," he replied. "The Field Commandant's instructions state quite clearly that where any doubt exists, one should take the precautionary measure of classifying that person as Jewish."

Hedy took a deep breath. She sensed she had only seconds left. "Mr. Orange . . ." She was careful to pronounce the "g" softly in the French style, not hard like the English fruit. "I have seen in Vienna how the Germans treat the Jews. If you register me as a Jew, I will be watched constantly. I may be imprisoned, perhaps worse. You will be placing me in grave danger."

Orange frowned at her, a father disappointed in his errant child. "No active measures have been taken against Jewish citizens."

"That doesn't mean they are not planned."

"If you are so fearful of the Germans why did you not evacuate in June?"

"I would have done, if England had accepted my current visa status." She dabbed at her top lip with the back of her hand. "If you submit the information I have told you today, the Germans will accept your word. There is no reason why anyone should question my race status for the rest of this war." She raised her eyes to meet his, a final appeal. Orange looked from her face to her file and back again, before closing the file.

"I'm sorry, Miss Bercu, but given the information I have, it would be remiss of me not to classify you as Jewish by Romanian parentage within the current regulations. If I were to bypass the rules, and the Germans were to discover at some later date that I had done so, I could risk not just my own position but the whole relationship of cooperation between the Jersey Government and our occupiers, on which this island's security depends. I'm sure you understand." She continued to stare at him and, suddenly uncomfortable, Orange began to chatter on with false cheerfulness while shuffling his papers. "You really have nothing to worry about, you know. Whatever irregularities may have occurred in your home country, registration is simply a formality here, part of the German zeal for good administration. Those of us in government have found most of them perfectly reasonable and courteous. We simply have to play by their rules for the foreseeable future." She knew he was waiting for her to stand, but Hedy remained where she was, as if refusing to move from this chair might somehow alter the course of her destiny. "Anyway, I think that's all for today."

It was over. Hedy stood with difficulty, trying to recalibrate her new position. Her fate had now been sealed, her life transformed by the stroke of a pen. She glanced about her, noticing other things in the office — the brass banker's lamp set at a perfect forty-five-degree angle, the shelves of perfectly aligned alphabetical files on Jersey law. And in the furthest, dimmest corner, a globe on a stand, bearing a fine coating of dust, unturned in many months. She had never stood a chance.

Orange held out his hand for her to shake. "Good day, Miss Bercu."

Hedy stared at his hand without extending her own, then looked him straight in the eye.

"Fick dich selbst."

And she turned on her heel and left.

Two

1941

St. Ouen's bay on the west coast was the wildest, most dramatic side of the island. Five miles of pristine sand, curved into a perfect arc, provided an open graveyard for the foam-topped rollers that glided up the gulf from the Atlantic, rising and swelling before crashing onto the sand with the force of advancing tanks, blasting white spray into the air. The bay was broken only by rocky outcrops at each end, and La Rocco Tower half a mile out, a stubborn little edifice from the days of Napoleon still holding its own against the bay's strong currents. Hedy loved that little tower. This was her favorite place to walk, even though the bitter wind blew straight through the disintegrating fabric of her old woolen coat. And for want of proper glue, the sole of her left lace-up shoe, by now her only remaining pair, was trying to separate itself from the leather.

Spring had refused to appear this year. The sun that should by now be warming the soil, coaxing the flowers and tomatoes into premature season and injecting its unique, nutty flavor into the island's potatoes, glowed pale and watery. Hedy made her way along the path between the sharp blades of seagrass, feeling the penetrating sand grate between her toes. Behind the open spread of the beach, undulating sand dunes seeped into the gentle slopes of nearby farmland. If any Allied counterattack should come, it would surely be here. Little wonder that this bay was now the focus of Hitler's obsession with steel and concrete, shoring up his beloved Atlantic wall against a force he was certain was on its way. Feeling the vibration of distant trucks, Hedy turned to see a column of gray and khaki trundle its way up the Five Mile Road, weighed down with cargoes of metal and cement. Mines were being planted all along the shore, and new defenses were springing up from La Pulente in the south to Grosnez in the north, hulking gray towers with shadowy armament slits, squat concrete bunkers and gun emplacements. St. Ouen's would never look the same again.

The bus back to town was due in twenty minutes. Hedy considered a final stroll down to Le Braye slip, but decided against it; there was only one service today, and if she mistimed her return she knew she would not have the energy to run to catch it, nor to walk the six kilometers back to town. In recent months she had learned the role of fats in the human diet, and what happened when they were removed. Shivering, she stuffed her hands in her pockets, shuffled to the bus stop, grateful for the stone bench beside it, and slumped down, waiting for her breathing to return to normal. That was when she spotted the copy of yesterday's Evening Post lying on the grass behind the seat.

Hedy looked around in surprise, half expecting someone to appear and claim it. Newspaper could be used for kindling, stopping drafts or cleaning windows — discarding an entire edition was unthinkable, and the paper's owner must have been furious to discover its loss. Thrilled with her treasure, Hedy flicked through the eight dual-language pages, filled with orders and propaganda disguised as news. Later she could have fun scouring the columns for translation errors, the ones deliberately left in by the Jersey editors to let their readership know exactly which articles had been dictated. And she would read the exchange and mart columns too, even though Hedy had long ago exchanged any possession of any value she could afford to part with.

As she sat reading, her eyes caught the headline on page three: "THIRD ORDER relating to measures against Jews." The same proclamation had been printed the previous week. Hedy had no wish to read it again and tried to turn the page, but found herself drawn in by ghoulish fascination.

. . . shall be prohibited from carrying on the following economic activities:

(a) wholesale and retail trade;
(b) hotel and catering industry;
(c) insurance;
(d) navigation;
(e) dispatch and storage;
(f) travel agencies, organization of tours;
(g) guides;
(h) transport undertakings of all descriptions, including the hire of motor and other vehicles;
(i) banking and money exchange;

The list ran on to the bottom of the page, but Hedy folded the pages back together and stuffed the whole paper into her coat's inside pocket. Depressing as it was, in the end this latest order made no difference to her. No one would employ a Jew anyway, for fear of upsetting the Germans. Even her last job as a school cleaner was deemed too risky by the headmaster, who packed her off with a week's wages and some excuse about unsatisfactory toilets. For three months now she had lived on nothing but her meager savings and the charity of Anton, who saved every burnt crust in the bakery and often slipped her a few pennies to buy rations. But this morning as she wrapped up for her walk, she had noticed how the clothes hung loose on her body, and her skin, once creamy and lustrous, had become dry and sallow. This, she sometimes thought, was how it would end. The Germans weren't going to shoot her after all. They were just going to starve her to death.

The bus arrived, packed, and Hedy, having counted out the fare in small change, wriggled through and found a seat at the very back. Here she could take in the scenery without getting drawn into conversation. Too often she had seen people recoil at her accent, taking her for a German secretary or even a spy. Invisibility and silence were a simpler option these days. The bus pulled away up the hill and Hedy craned her neck to see La Rocco Tower disappear in the rear window, the water swirling and sucking at the rocks beneath.

At least tonight she had something to look forward to. Anton had offered to pay for her to go to West's cinema to see The Wizard of Oz, and although she had seen it six times since the picture house got stuck with it last year, it was a welcome change from another evening alone in her apartment. In the early days the cinema had sold mugs of cocoa in the interval, though nothing so lavish was available now. Hedy's stomach growled and her mouth watered at the memory, and for the rest of the journey she forced herself to count trucks of soldiers on the road ahead. Thinking about food achieved nothing but misery.

She alighted the bus at the Weighbridge and made her way to the cinema where the queue was already winding out of the building and down the street. It was always Jersey folk here, the Germans preferring films in their own language at the Forum picture house, though the field police sent down the occasional spy to keep an eye on events. Hedy searched the queue for Anton, and for a moment thought she had arrived before him. And then she saw. In the center of the queue, his tousled hair combed back into an impression of slickness, Anton was squashed tightly against a woman, a little older than himself, with a pale oval face and light blue eyes. Her black hair, worn in a homemade copy of a Greer Garson crop, made her look younger than her thirty-odd years, and a little vulnerable. She and Anton stood arm in arm, and Anton was laughing at something she'd said — a gurgling giggle Hedy hadn't heard in quite a while. Hedy felt a rush of curiosity. She had often seen Anton stare blushingly at pretty girls in parks and cafés, but he had never had the courage to ask anyone out before. Hedy edged toward them and waited.

Anton beamed and breathed in deeply as he always did before speaking in English. "Hedy, this is Dorothea. We met last week when she came to the bakery."

Dorothea ignored Hedy's outstretched hand and rushed at her cheek, her lips already pursed for a kiss. "Anton's told me so much about you," she gushed. "I know what good friends you are. I do hope we can be friends too."

The woman's fingernails, Hedy noticed, were bitten down to the quick, and her movements as fluttery as a baby bird. But the most startling thing was the strength of her Jersey accent, a twanging inflection Hedy had learned to recognize. Hedy

47

glanced at Anton, surprised by his choice of a local girl. She smiled at Dorothea. "I like your haircut."

Dorothea flushed with obvious pleasure. "Thanks, my mother does it. It's easier to manage like this when you can't buy shampoo." Hedy's hand went automatically to her own lank, papery locks. "You're from Vienna too?"

"I am, from Romania originally."

"And you're a Jew?"

Hedy took half a step back. Her eyes, bright with accusation, moved directly to Anton, but to her annoyance Anton's gaze never left Dorothea. Hedy peered ostentatiously around the queue, indicating that this wasn't a conversation for a public place. Eventually she answered quietly. "I am registered as a Jew, yes."

Dorothea, oblivious to Hedy's discomfort, shook her head with sympathy. "I think it's awful the way they're treating you. I don't know why Hitler hates Jews so much. How are you supposed to manage if you're not allowed to work?" Hedy felt suddenly aware of her frayed coat and gaping shoe. But then an idea lit up Dorothea's face. "I tell you what I saw the other day — an advert for translators."

48

"Translators?" Hedy stared at her, confused.

"That new transport compound the Germans are building at Millbrook? Apparently they want people who can speak English and German to work in the offices. You should apply. Your English is wonderful!" she added with a broad smile.

Hedy's mouth opened and shut, at a loss how to reply. She turned to Anton for a reaction but her friend, finally aware of the brewing storm, had developed a fascination with his own feet. A painful silence expanded in the space between them, until Hedy cleared her throat and spoke deliberately slowly. "You are suggesting that I, a Jewish girl, apply for a job in a German office?"

"They're probably desperate," Dorothea replied, as if dispensing a compliment. "Not many local people speak German — well, it's such a hard language, isn't it? The advert said the pay was good too."

At that moment a boy in a maroon uniform far too big for him pushed open the doors to the cinema, and Anton stepped forward.

"You said you needed the Ladies', Dory? Go ahead and I'll get the tickets."

Dorothea gave him a loud kiss on the

49

cheek and hurried off. Anton checked she was out of earshot before turning to Hedy, looking like a child awaiting the cane. "Please don't judge her, Hedy," he muttered in German. "She's got a heart of gold. She's just not very worldly."

"Anton, what are you playing at?" Hedy's voice came out as a hiss. "Telling my business to a total stranger?"

"It just came out — we've shared a lot of things this week. Don't worry, she's completely trustworthy."

"You hardly know her! In any case, she's an islander — she'll get labeled a Jerrybag going out with you."

Anton refused to meet her gaze. "She knows I'm not German."

"Let's not have that discussion again! Good God, Anton, did you hear what she said to me? Does she even know what this war is about? She's a shoyte!" Hedy shifted to try to force herself into Anton's eye line but he continued to glance about him, intent on everything but her.

"Lots of people are having to work for the Germans now, whether they want to or not. In your position it might be worth considering."

"My position?" Hedy glared at him. "My position is, those bastards drove us from our homeland and view me as no better than an animal! And you're saying I should help them with their administration?"

"I'm saying you need money." Anton's voice was quiet but steady. "Hedy, you're my friend. I worry about you. I want to help you but every week it gets harder. What Dorothea is suggesting might be a practical solution . . ." He reached out for her arm.

She brushed his hand away. "So this is how we behave now? We just accept what's happened — make friends with the Krauts?" She threw her arms in the air, exasperated. "I can't believe you're taking her side. Or that you're even interested in a woman like that. You know what?" She tugged her coat a little tighter around her. "I'm going home. I don't want to see the stupid Wizard of Oz anyway." And turning so that Anton would not see the hurt in her eyes, she stomped off. When she finally found the courage to glance back, the queue had disappeared into the cinema.

The concrete steps of the house were badly cracked, and the communal door beneath the once ornate portico was so swollen from rain and lack of paint that it barely closed. Hedy slunk into the building and began the long climb up the wide, unlit staircase to

51

her apartment. She heard the creak of dry, ancient wood as she stepped slowly onto each step, and felt as if the sound were coming from within her. Resentment mixed with acid in her empty stomach and ripped at the lining. How would she fill her evening now? The BBC news at nine o'clock, with more depressing reports of Allied defeats in North Africa? Climb into bed with Hemingway and a library book, pull the heavy curtain that separated her "bedroom" area, and close out the world for a few hours? Her spirits sank at the thought. She knew she'd been hasty walking off like that. That idiotic, petulant temper from her father's side. But it was too late now.

On the first floor she heard the predictable scrape of Mrs. Le Couteur's door as it opened an inch, saw one droopy eye peering out from the darkness. In her first weeks here Hedy used to call out a greeting to her neighbor to reassure her, hoping that it might allay the old widow's suspicions and perhaps build a little trust between them. But Hedy had never received more than a grunt in reply, and after she found the pensioner in the downstairs hallway holding Hedy's mail up to the light to assess the contents, Hedy had given up. Now she ignored the old bat as she passed by, and heard the door click shut again as she continued her steady ascent to the top floor.

The apartment was gloomy, with only the last gray fingers of dusk throwing a little light onto the linoleum. It was bitterly cold. Hemingway padded across to greet her, and Hedy picked him up and held him close, glad of his warm silkiness on her face. But quickly realizing there was no food about her body, the ungrateful beast wriggled out of her arms and returned to his basket in front of the fireplace. He sniffed at the empty grate, throwing her hopeful looks.

"Some chance," Hedy muttered, pulling down the blackout blind. Then, with a slow, reluctant stretch, she took one of the precious candles from the box under the sink. They had cost most of her remaining savings on the black market, and she'd meticulously nicked the wax of each one with a knife, limiting her nightly usage. No Hanukkah ceremony this year. Taking a match from the box on the windowsill, she struck it carefully so that it would light first time without splitting. The wick flared and she placed her hands around its small gold flame.

Now the chill of the room began to bite, bringing with it a crowd of righteous justifications for her stormy departure. She had a right, did she not, to feel upset at Anton's carelessness? Betraying his only friend, in the face of such meshugaas — from a woman he'd only just met! Might be worth considering? This, from the man who complained when he was forced to serve German soldiers in the bakery? If there was one thing she'd always admired about Anton it was his moral compass. Had he just tossed it aside for the sake of a pretty face?

On the tiny stove was a milk saucepan containing the last inch of the cabbage and swede soup she had cooked the day before. The smell of it hung in the air like sour washing. For a moment she debated leaving it for breakfast, but hunger, as always, beat common sense, and soon she was scooping it greedily into her mouth, swallowing faster than was good for her. She sucked hard on the tin spoon to get the last drops, licked the inside of the saucepan until she could taste nothing but metal, and slumped down onto the wooden chair at the little table, staring into the flickering flame. Then, even as she told herself it was a bad idea, she pulled open the shallow drawer tucked beneath the table and slid her hand in, feeling around till she found the small bundle of papers. Drawing the candle closer, she unfurled the thin sheets and sifted through to the last letter, dated April 1940 — exactly a year ago.

"Our darling daughter," it began in her mother's spidery hand. Several vacuous and suspiciously cheery sentences about the lovely weather and the helpful neighbors followed. And finally, the darkly coded final paragraph: "But there is talk of us going on a holiday." Hedy stared back at the flame. Not once in all their years of marriage had her parents ever discussed going on holiday. She closed her eyes and conjured up her mother, warming her hands by the old kitchen range. She thought of Roda — ebony-haired, giggling Roda, posed as she always was in Hedy's mind in a broad sun hat and holding a long pole, tilling the soil on some Palestinian kibbutz. After a while Hedy smoothed down the sheet of paper and returned it to its bundle and its drawer, this time locking it with its small metal key. Reading these letters never brought comfort, any more than recipe books killed hunger pangs. Not for a month would she read those again.

She sat back in her seat but the image of Roda persisted. Roda who had flirted with the German guards when they were questioned that night near the Swiss border, laughing coquettishly over her shoulder to avoid showing her papers, winking at some grinning Nazi to get across the border. Hedy had brimmed over with admiration for her that night. Roda would do whatever she had to in order to survive. She was too bright, too plucky to do anything else.

Hedy, you're my friend. I worry about you.

Very slowly, as if to pull a trick on herself, Hedy eased the copy of the Evening Post from her pocket. She opened it on the table and flicked through the pages, this time ignoring the Jewish order and speeding through to the classifieds at the back. It was there, on page seven, a box advertisement.

Wanted: translators fluent in both English and German for office work at NSKK Transportgruppe West, Staffel Vt. Excellent rates. Applications in writing by 15th May.

She read it again, then a third time. The room was perfectly silent, and the only light came from the candle flame and its yellow reflection in Hemingway's staring, questioning eyes. The rent was due on Friday. Once paid, she would have nothing left to buy her rations. A burning pain crept across her chest as she tore around the edges of the advertisement and placed the little rectangle of paper on the table. The room was still cold, but she realized she was sweating.

"Private? This one's ready."

The NCO approached with a clipboard and jotted down the registration plate of the Opel Blitz truck. He then offered the document for signature, and tore off the copy. "Shall I bring the next one through, Lieutenant?"

"No, I'm going to break for lunch. Give me half an hour." Wiping his greasy hands on a piece of rag, Kurt Neumann stretched his aching back, slicked his hair back into place and headed for the officers' mess. Rabbit stew on the menu today. Proper stew, with mashed potatoes! This time last year he was living on tins of Fleischkonserve (remembering it still made him belch a little) and that awful rye bread that broke your teeth. His tummy rumbled in happy anticipation.

Crossing the compound, Kurt coughed to clear the dust from his throat. The fine, pale powder of Lager Hühnlein got into everything — clothes, eyes, even socks. That was what you got for throwing up such a vast, sprawling complex in a few short weeks. The scale of the place was impressive, with rows of prefabricated administration huts, material storage units and fortified pathways for heavy vehicles to run in and out all day. From here, according to Field Command, "the greatest construction of fortifications the world had ever seen" would be planned and implemented.

Privately, Kurt found the whole concept a bit daft. After all, if Churchill wanted to take back these islands by force, wouldn't he have done it by now? Why pour so much money and energy into ruining beautiful scenery? But Kurt knew better than to voice such thoughts to fellow officers — and certainly not around fanatics like Fischer at his billet, or the employees at this place. The Organisation Todt, or "OT" as the military engineering section was known, was dominated by a real bunch of reprobates — very different from the professional, disciplined guys he'd served with in France. At mealtimes they sat in tight groups, chain-smoking and laughing too hard at jokes he found cruel. On one occasion he'd seen a local lad, a kid with a funny walk who was employed to clean out the latrines, kicked in the groin by an OT officer for some apparent disrespect. Kurt had felt sickened by the incident, but hadn't reported it. He told himself there was no point, as no action would be taken. As Helmut had cautioned him all through their schooldays, better to keep your head down when there was nothing to gain. And apart from the OT thugs, he enjoyed his work here. Supervising the work of the mechanics, ticking off inspection lists, signing off the imported trucks — these were all jobs he could do in his sleep. A little fiddling with the Buick engines, a little paperwork — hardly the front line. He could almost be back at engineering college.

There was a queue at the mess hut, so he decided to have a smoke and wait it out. Leaning against the wall of a storage hut, he tapped a Gauloise, his new favorite brand, from a pack in his pocket, and was about to light it when what he saw made him stop, the flame of his lighter still flickering in the breeze. A pale, skinny girl with tawny blond hair was standing between two of the admin blocks, looking around her in some confusion. Her hair was neatly pinned up, but despite the warmth of the day she wore a shabby wool coat and shoes that looked as if they'd seen better days. She looked anxious, and she clearly needed a good meal, but what struck him most were her eyes. They were the large, frightened eyes of a woodland creature, yet there was a hint of defiance there too. He was about to ask if she needed assistance when she spoke first.

"Excuse me, I'm looking for OT Feldwebel Schulz in Block Seven?"

Kurt smiled, surprised. "You're German?"

She shook her head. "From Austria. I'm here for" — she hesitated, as if the words hurt her mouth — "for the translator's job."

He couldn't stop staring at those eyes. They were the color of the sea in Rozel bay. "Block Seven is the next hut on the left. Here, let me show you."

"No, thank you." Her voice contained the chill of compulsory courtesy. "I can find my own way." Kurt watched her walk across the uneven terrain, her figure swaying as she moved, not taking his eyes off her for a second until she turned the corner and disappeared.

An hour later, his belly now full of rabbit stew, Kurt was passing the entrance to Block Seven with a stack of signed dockets, when he saw the girl again. This time she was leaving the hut, and as she did so she shook hands with a pudgy little man with wire-rimmed glasses whom Kurt assumed to be Schulz. It was an odd, perfunctory handshake, as if neither of them wanted to partake in it, and both wanted it over as soon as possible. Kurt watched the girl as she walked down the path toward the barbed-wire boundary and the exit gate, then he called Schulz over.

"OT Feldwebel?" The man nodded. Kurt towered over him. "That young woman — she was here for the translator's job, yes?"

"Yes, Lieutenant."

"Are you taking her on?"

Schulz squirmed a little. "No choice I'm afraid, sir. She's fluent in both languages. We've had so few applicants."

"I don't understand. Is there a problem?"

Schulz blinked very quickly as if someone had kicked sand in his face, and scratched the end of his nose. "Not at all, sir. I'm sure she will prove entirely acceptable." Kurt sensed that Schulz was holding something back, but couldn't be bothered to pursue it. His attention was still half on the girl's disappearing figure, so he smiled vaguely and indicated Schulz could go. Then, still holding the dockets in his hand, he felt a surge of curiosity that pressed him forward. At least, that's what he told himself afterward.

Checking that no one was watching, he crept down the path after the girl, taking care to keep his distance. Reaching the gate, she turned left down the narrow country lane beyond. Throwing the guards a quick salute, Kurt strolled out of the compound after her. Still keeping well back — after all, if she turned to question him what would he say? — he followed the girl to the next bend. There, what he saw made him step back and press himself into the steep grass verge for fear of intruding on this private moment.

The girl was leaning on a rusty iron gate leading to a neighboring farm, her forearms resting on its top bar. He couldn't see her expression, but the droop of her slender shoulders suggested intense sadness, even despair. She raised one pale, slight hand to her face and wiped her cheeks. With the other hand she pulled out the pins at the back of her neck until her hair fell in soft curls, then she threw back her head to loosen it further, carefully bunched the pins together and placed them in the pocket of her coat. Kurt watched, transfixed, scarcely breathing, afraid she might turn and see him, while at the same time wishing that she would. But the girl didn't turn around; she continued to stand perfectly still, leaning on the gate and staring out across the field before her, as if taking in the scents and perfumes of the surrounding country-side. The breeze caught her hair and the edges of her coat, redrawing her silhouette, and Kurt fancied that she had closed her eyes. Then, as a flight of swallows moved across the sky above her, she leaned forward over the gate and vomited hard into the field below.

Town was busier than usual, perhaps due to the morning rumors of French cheeses on sale in the covered market. Hedy stood on the corner, watching housewives hurry past with half-empty shopping bags, and cyclists with rubber tubing for tires swerving to avoid potholes. She looked about her, trying to make up her mind. Anton's apartment was a short walk to her right, but if she turned left toward New Street she would be home in eight minutes. She had a strong urge to race back to her apartment, feel the comfort of Hemingway's purring on her belly. But she knew this chill between her and Anton had stretched on for too long, and it was time to end it. Today, especially, she craved Anton's easy company and optimistic reassurance. She turned to the right and felt her footsteps quicken as she neared the shop. Without knocking, she pushed open the side door to the flat and started up the stairs. But what she heard next froze her in her tracks.

"In through the nose, out through the mouth . . . slowly now." The voice — male, filled with authority — drifted toward her on the stale air that smelled of must and flour. Hedy's stomach tightened as she continued on tiptoe, trying to identify the speaker. It certainly wasn't Anton, nor was it his boss Mr. Reis. She tried not to make a sound, hesitating as she reached the top.

"Anton?" The apartment door was ajar, and she pressed on it until it swung wide enough for her to see inside. Sitting upright in the center of the room on a wooden chair was Dorothea, her eyes closed in concentration, her breaths quick and shallow, her brunette crop sticking to her forehead. She was holding her hands together in front of her as if in prayer, and her chest jumped with a persistent cough. On her right, his hand resting reassuringly on her shoulder, was Anton, and on her left stood a short middle-aged gentleman with gray flecks around the temples and round horn-rimmed spectacles. The man turned to nod at Hedy before turning back to his charge. Hedy looked from one to the other in confusion, till she spotted the large leather bag, partly open, and the stethoscope peeping out from beneath the gentleman's flannel jacket.

Anton's eyes flicked toward her. "Dory had an asthma attack."

A shameful burst of irritation flared immediately. What was this woman doing here, if she was ill? And why was she relying on Anton, when she surely had family of her own? But taking in her clay-colored skin and the beads of sweat around the forehead, Hedy pushed her other feelings down. An empty stomach, Albert Einstein once advised, was not a good political adviser.

"Fortunately," Anton was saying, "Doctor Maine was willing to come here from the hospital."

"Are you all right?" Hedy asked. Dorothea opened her eyes for a moment and acknowledged Hedy's question with a desultory waggle of her fingers. "What caused this?"

"She was upset." Anton gave a little shake of his head, warning Hedy not to pursue it further. Hedy tentatively placed her bag down on the table, unsure if she should stay, while the doctor continued to listen to Dorothea's lungs through his stethoscope. Finally he straightened up.

"You must try to avoid situations that make you anxious, Miss Le Brocq. Prevention is better than cure, yes?" His voice, which had the Jersey lilt to it, was honeyed and kind, though cracked with tiredness. The bags under his eyes reminded Hedy of her uncle Otto, and when he turned to include her in his smile she found herself smiling back. "Stocks of epinephrine are low, like everything else," he continued. "We may not be able to get it at all in a couple of months. There are a few home treatments that can help — mustard oil, ginger — but I doubt you'll find those in the shops these days. Try to get her to the hospital if it happens again. House calls are becoming limited to absolute emergencies."

"I thought doctors were allowed private cars?" Anton asked.

"Yes, but our fuel allocation is less than two gallons a week. That can mean difficult choices sometimes." He scribbled out a bill in a chaotic hand and gave it to Anton, who looked at it with surprise. The doctor waved his hand. "What can money buy you now? A loaf from your delightful Austrian bakery will more than cover it. Good day to you all." And with that he collected his bag and slipped quietly from the room, leaving a faint smell of cigarette smoke. To her surprise, Hedy found herself a little saddened by his exit.

Anton went to the sink in the corner to get Dorothea a glass of water. Hedy followed him, speaking softly in German. "So what happened?"

Anton kept his eyes on the running tap, but answered in German too. "Her stepfather found out about me and threw her out of the house. Dory's going to live with her grandmother for a while until things calm down." He caught her eye for a split second. "Please don't say I told you so."

"Fine, I won't say it."

Anton shut off the tap and turned toward her. "I'm sorry, but I like her. And she likes me. What should I do? Dump her to please everyone else?"

Hedy reached out to touch his arm. "You've only known her a few weeks. Is it really worth this much trouble?"

"It's only trouble if you choose to see it that way. Her family will come around eventually. Like Dory says, if it makes us happy, it must be right."

"And what if the Germans force you into the army?"

"I'm classed as a food producer, so that won't happen. Unless the war drags on." He shrugged to indicate there was nothing more to say, then took the water to Dorothea and held the glass to her mouth. Dorothea sipped it slowly, keeping her hand on his. Hedy stayed by the sink, watching the two of them, listening to Dorothea's shallow, grainy breaths. The window was open, and the grubby lace curtain blew up a little in the breeze. Somewhere outside, a mother shouted at a crying child.

Anton broke the moment, speaking deliberately in English. "How come you're in your best dress?"

Hedy hesitated, reluctant to share her big news now. But Anton would find out soon enough anyway. "I got that translator's job at Lager Hühnlein." She watched their astonished faces for a moment before adding, "You were right — they were desperate."

Anton smiled for the first time. "But that's wonderful. Dory, did you hear that?"

Dorothea nodded and took her deepest breath yet to reply. "That's great news, Hedy. I knew it would work out for you." She smiled with real warmth, and at that moment Hedy realized that, probably thanks to Anton's diplomacy, Dorothea had no idea of the upset she'd caused that first night.

"If I had any other choice . . ." Hedy stopped. Such rationales, even from her own lips, sounded hollow and pathetic.

"Some acorn coffee?" Anton gesticulated toward his little stove.

Hedy shook her head. "Another time maybe — you've got enough on your hands." The remark prickled with resentment, and she saw the hurt in his eyes, instantly wished she could take it back.

"Well, I'm really pleased for you, Hedy. Come to the bakery soon and tell me all about it."

The child outside the window was wailing now, and the room seemed stifling. Hedy felt a sudden need for fresh air. She forced herself to smile. "All right, I will. Bye."

On her way down the stairs, she heard him call after her: "You've done the right thing, you know."

But Hedy pretended not to hear.

The clock on the back wall read four: the predictable aching hour, when the strain of sitting hunched over her ancient Adler typewriter since early morning produced a shot of hot pain behind her left shoulder blade, and the pressure required to hammer down the stiff keys burned her tendons.

Hedy sat back on her rickety wooden chair and took a moment to stretch her back and massage her throbbing wrists. She wondered if the other girls in the office suffered the same way. Those big blowsy Bavarians, imported from the Fatherland to type and file all week, and screw their soldier boyfriends all weekend. If they shared her pain, they never showed it. Hedy gazed up at the narrow window of the hut, the shafts of sunlight taunting her with their promise of a glorious afternoon beyond. The room was airless, its fluorescent lights flickering pointlessly even on a bright day like this, and from her neighbor Derek, a sallow, nervous youth who was one of the only other non-Germans in her block, emanated a perpetual smell of mold. Hedy suspected it was because, like her, he had nowhere to dry wet laundry. She suspected she probably smelled the same. If so, she didn't care. Let them smell her. Aware of the sweeping gaze of Frau Vogt, the block supervisor, she took another list of German building company bids and stuffed a translation form into the Adler's roller.

Today was Saturday, the end of her first month in the office, and it was payday. She hoped that collecting the small brown envelope might lift her crushed spirits. The job itself was undemanding — translation of correspondence, payrolls, allocations — and the wages were decent. But the misery of it weighed heavier than even she had expected. The long hours, the dust, the stuffiness, the exhausting one-hour walk twice a day on so little food — all that was bad enough. But a conscience, it transpired, could not be assuaged or scrubbed clean. Each morning she watched as the trucks, filled with dead-eyed mercenaries, rumbled off to their construction sites to reinforce antitank walls and build new airport runways, knowing that she was now a part of it. Survival, it seemed, was an expensive business for the soul.

Schulz, whose eyebrows had almost shot out of his head when he'd first seen the red "J" on her identity card, had allocated her a desk in the farthest, dimmest corner of the hut, clearly anxious that her racial status might cause a riot. But it soon became clear that senior OT staff were keeping Hedy's classification to themselves. For that at least, Hedy was grateful. Those vapid Aryan typists, who stared right through her as if she were made of paper, would doubtless be far less passive in the shadowy pathways between the work huts, should they discover the truth. She accepted her corner seat without complaint, kept her head down and got through her work with speed and minimal speech — though here, at least, her accent acted as a cover, rather than a liability. She ate alone in the canteen, made no eye contact. Other than her supervisor, and occasionally Derek when he ran out of something, she drew no attention from anyone. Were it not for the perfectly formed dollop of saliva that, with vengeful secrecy, she spat onto the floor of the latrines on every visit, she might not have been there at all.

The only exception was the German lieutenant she had met on the day of her interview. They had passed each other on the footpaths several times, and each time he greeted her with a broad smile and some small courtesy in German. She replied with a mumbled hello, knowing that a word interpreted as inappropriate or disrespectful could mean dismissal. But there was an unexpected warmth in those eyes, almost a mischievous twinkle, that she liked. And secretly, when she had gone through an entire week without one meaningful conversation, she quite looked forward to these fleeting moments of normality. Strange what tricks loneliness could play on the mind.

Just as she pulled her finished sheet from the roller, Vogt, a pinched woman with exceptionally long, yellowing fingernails, approached Hedy's desk. On it she placed her wage packet, followed by a list of names and addresses and a bundle of petrol coupons. "Allocation lists," she squawked in her strangled, parrot-like voice. "To be done this afternoon. Coupons are for immediate dispatch. When you have completed each list, place the recipient's form and the appropriate number of coupons in the sealed brown envelope."

"Does each recipient get the same number of coupons each week?"

"No. If fuel stocks are low, they may receive fewer."

"And is that information provided on the form?"

"No explanation is required. The difference will be compensated to them the next week, or when stocks recover."

Hedy nodded and began to fill in the forms as requested, but her mind scattered with a dangerous thought. If recipients had no idea how many coupons to expect each week, then she could, in theory, allocate any number she chose, and pocket the rest. Her heart began to hammer in her chest. Petrol coupons were worth a fortune and could be exchanged for anything. Every week she saw black market meat, eggs and sugar sneaked across market stalls, at prices even her new wages wouldn't meet. This could be her key to that magic kingdom. But what if the forms were checked before dispatch? Gray, irregular shapes appeared on her paperwork, and she realized her palms were sweating.

She tried to focus, think clearly. Getting caught was unthinkable. Theft of German property had sent plenty of islanders to jail — as a Jew, it would mean deportation. But still her mind danced and dived, picturing not just the prize, but the satisfaction. Scoring a point. Getting one over. She breathed in and out slowly and deeply, while observing the other employees from beneath her brows.

Over the next hour she watched each worker take their paperwork to the front desk and place the coupons in the collection boxes. Each time, the copies of the documents were stamped by an administrator and piled high on Vogt's desk like a layer cake, but at no point did anyone bother to check them. Hedy calculated that so long as the correct amount of coupon bundles were counted in the stockroom, no one would be any the wiser. And even if some delivery driver complained about a reduced allowance, there was no way anyone could trace the variation back to her.

At ten minutes to six she still hadn't made up her mind. By now she was fighting to control her trembling fingers. Then, as the large hand on the clock eased almost to the twelve, she saw Vogt turn away to deal with a pile of signatures. Hedy picked up a form for an Irish construction company with an allowance of thirty coupons, and rolled it into the Adler. With rivulets of sweat tickling her armpits, she typed the number twenty-five in the box, at the same time slipping five coupons into the inside pocket of her coat, which hung on the back of her chair. No one, she was certain, had seen her. As the end-of-shift bell shrieked on the wall, she stood up, delivered her remaining forms and envelopes to Vogt's desk, and walked out of the hut at a regular pace.

The evening was golden, with the sun still high in the sky and a gentle breeze on the air. She barely needed her coat, but she didn't dare remove it now; anyway, over-dressing on this semistarved island was commonplace these days and no one gave her a second look. The dust particles stuck in her eyes and throat, and her heart was pounding, but she looked straight ahead and continued walking. She told herself this was destiny. The ease of this opportunity was surely the hand of fate, as if the universe was forcing her to take this chance to even the score. She moved with the flow of work-ers down the slope toward the south gate, her booty nestled securely next to her heart. Bodies jostled and pushed past her in their eagerness to get home. She maneuvered her way through them, making sure she kept her footing firm on the path. She was almost at the gate. She was almost free. Then she felt the hand on her shoulder.

Turning, she saw his face close to hers. For a second all she saw was the uniform and thought she might pass out.

"Hedy, isn't it? Kurt Neumann, remember? We met the day you were hired." He must have seen the color drain from her face because he added quickly, "Don't worry. This isn't about work — I'm not even part of the OT. I wanted to ask you a favor."

She stared at him, half expecting the coupons to come to life, burst through her coat and hurl themselves into his face. She breathed in slowly, trying to get a grip of herself. "Yes?"

"I know you're one of our translators. I have this article from the American Journal of Science, about the future of the motorcar, and I was wondering if you might translate it for me?" Hedy opened her mouth but no sound came out. "I do speak English, but I know yours is far better than mine! I'd be happy to pay you, or I could thank you by buying you a drink sometime. Maybe dinner?" He smiled, and it was an authentic smile — warm, full of optimism and ideas. It made the crow's-feet around his eyes crease up. His teeth were white and even. Hedy sensed that the acid swirling in her stomach was rising up.

"Dinner?"

"Look, I understand," he assured her. "If you don't want to be seen in public with a German officer. But we do have access to our own stores. I could bring food to your home. Do you like cheese?"

"Cheese?" She cursed herself. This kind of panicked reaction was exactly how she would be caught.

"Or whatever you like. No funny business, I promise. I was in the Deutsche Jungenschaft, you know. Perfect manners." He gave a little laugh, inviting her to join in. Hedy wrenched her facial muscles into a laughing position. "So what do you say?"

"Sure." She felt the space around her shift and blur. Her only conscious thought was that this man clearly did not know that she was Jewish. Every particle of her body was screaming at her to get away. In her peripheral vision, she was scouting the exits.

"Great. Well, I'll put the article on your desk and you let me know what night is good for you, all right? See you."

Another brilliant smile and he was gone. Hedy turned and continued down the path out of the compound. Her legs seemed to swing weightlessly beneath her, and the lane swam unseen in front of her eyes. She hardly exhaled until she reached the main road, and for the remainder of her journey home she had to stop several times to catch her breath at the roadside. Not until she was back in her apartment was she able to take stock of what had happened. As the reality sank in, she began to laugh, a frightening cackle of hysteria that sent Hemingway scurrying under the bed, and forced her to sit down at the table. For several minutes she wondered if she would ever stop.

With a shaking hand, she pulled the coupons from her inside pocket and stared at them. She had got away with it. And aside from her own fear, there was no reason why she shouldn't get away with it again. Perhaps every week. She felt a flush of pride. She had swindled her overlords, scored a victory. No longer a collaborator, she was now a resistance fighter. Hiding in plain sight within the snake pit, trickling poison into their nest, throwing a V-sign to the entire German nation.

There was just one problem. She appeared to have invited a German officer to her home for dinner.

THREE

Anton's apartment was as clean and neat as Hedy had ever seen it. Every surface had been scrubbed with hot water and there was even an eggcup of daisies and buttercups on the table. Two places were set with chipped plates and old tin cutlery, and a pot of cabbage and swede stew bubbled away on the single electric ring. Hedy stirred the pot with a bent metal spoon, wishing that Anton owned a wooden one. If she'd known there wasn't one in either of the drawers of his little dresser, she would have brought her own from home, and saved the ends of her fingers from blisters. She turned the heat down just as Anton burst through the door of the apartment, his hands stuffed into his jacket pockets and an uneasy look in his eyes. Hedy wiped her hands on a ragged tea towel.

"Forget something?"

"I need something to read while I'm sitting down there." He took a Stefan Zweig novel from the half dozen books on the shelf and shifted it from palm to palm. "How long do you think the Kraut will stay?"

"Couple of hours at the most. Thank you again for offering to do this. I really didn't want him coming to my place."

"Are you sure you want to go through with it?" Anton's face was taut with concern.

"If I bail out now he could get angry, say that I led him on. And I don't want to give him any reason to get suspicious."

"But what if he, you know . . ."

"If anything happens I'll stamp on the floor, or scream. But it won't. He's not like that." The words left her mouth easily; she realized that she meant it, and wondered why.

"So long as he doesn't find out you're Jewish. What if he wants to see you again?"

"He won't. I plan to bore him to death. You know I can do it." They exchanged a small smile across the room, but Anton still looked unsettled.

"And you're certain he has no idea about the coupons?" Hedy shook her head with confidence. "I still think you're crazy. Stealing right under their noses . . ."

"It's only trouble if you choose to see it that way." She left a deliberate beat, waiting

80

for Anton to get the reference. "How is Dorothea? Still at her grandmother's?"

Anton pursed his lips a little, but let it go. "Yes, for the moment."

"No more asthma attacks?"

"No, thank God. What will you do with the coupons? Sell them?"

Hedy couldn't help a little grin of triumph. "I thought about it. But I've decided to give them to Doctor Maine."

The gawping expression on Anton's face was just as she'd imagined it. "Give them?"

"Then it becomes an act of pure resistance, not just petty theft or selfishness. It's an atonement, for taking wages from the Krauts. My own personal mitzvah."

Anton shook his head. "Maybe our faiths aren't so far apart after all." He waved his novel. "I'll be just downstairs."

Hedy listened to Anton's clumping footsteps heading down to the bakery. She straightened the table settings, pulled the two paper sheets of the translated article from her bag, and laid them out. Turning off the electric ring, she smoothed her skirt and fiddled with the buttons of her blouse. A violent churning in her stomach caused her to burp ferociously.

At six, she went to the window from which she and Anton had waved their makeshift

81

white flag almost a year ago, and peered out. Neumann, holding a canvas bag, was making his way up the road. He saw her face and smiled. Hedy gestured to him to come up, and a few seconds later he was standing at Anton's door, a sheepish grin on his face. Hedy did her best to smile back, though the sight of a man in full German uniform in Anton's familiar little apartment was overwhelming. She stood aside to avoid any physical contact as she ushered him inside. He hovered near the door politely, as if wary of looking too much at home; his dark blond hair was slicked back with some kind of oil, his eyes bright with childlike excitement. After bidding each other good evening, they stood awkwardly in silence.

Eventually Neumann gestured to the sheets of paper on the table. "Is this my translation?" Hedy nodded. "Thank you, I will read it when I get home tonight. You have excellent handwriting."

"May I see what you brought?"

Neumann was already lifting his bag onto the table and unbuckling the flap. From it he pulled two small plucked chickens, a Camembert cheese, a large white loaf, a packet of real French coffee, a bar of plain chocolate and two bottles of Bordeaux. Hedy gazed at the display, feeling the drool rise in her mouth.

"This is for you of course — not to be shared with me," Kurt assured her.

"Thank you, Lieutenant," Hedy replied. She had made a promise to herself to be polite at all times.

"Call me Kurt, please."

Hedy scooped up the provisions, leaving only the wine and bread on the table, and stuffed it all into one of Anton's cupboards, shutting the door as if to pretend none of it existed. She gestured to him to sit, and dished the meager vegetables into mismatched bowls. Kurt opened the wine and poured a little into chipped cups, they both mumbled a toast to the end of the war, and Hedy cut the bread with a knife. Then they sat eating in silence. Hedy mopped up every morsel of the stew with the delicious bread crusts. She had forgotten what real bread could taste like. Once or twice she glanced up at him and caught him watching her eat, but she was too hungry to find it disturbing.

Eventually Kurt made a polite inquiry about her early life in Austria; Hedy answered in the fewest words possible, pretending that her move to Jersey had been due to a job opportunity. And how did she like working at Lager Hühnlein? Hedy

83

replied that she liked it well enough, although the dust was sometimes irksome. A half hour dragged by, stumbling and uncomfortable, the conversation bumping awkwardly along, like a plane that couldn't take off. Hedy sipped her wine at a snail's pace. It was months since she'd drunk alcohol and a loosened tongue was the last thing she needed now. When Kurt spoke of his passion for American cars, Hedy drew him out on the subject, calculating correctly that the topic would occupy a good few minutes. But eventually he drained his second wine, and placed the cup down with intention.

"Hedy, I don't wish to be rude, but I would prefer not to spend this evening discussing the Ford motor company."

She rose to her feet and began clearing the table. "So what would you prefer to talk about?"

The German shifted on his wooden chair, trying to assume a pose of relaxation. "I'd just like us to get to know each other."

She lowered the crockery into the sink, keeping her back to him. "There's nothing special about me. There are plenty of German girls at the compound who would prove far more interesting, I'm sure." She bit her lip as soon as she'd said it, knowing he wouldn't miss the dig. She was right.

"You know, not all Germans, even in the military, are the master-race enthusiasts Hitler would like you to believe."

"Really?" She rubbed at the dirty bowls with her fingers so she didn't have to look at him. "I thought that was one of the main reasons for your country going to war. Do you not consider yourself superior to Slavs? Or Jews?" She glanced up into the shard of broken mirror that Anton kept above the kitchen sink for shaving, and saw that her cheeks were flushed. She must have drunk too much wine after all; this was a suicidal path.

"Can I tell you something in confidence?" Kurt replied. Hedy said nothing, which he seemed to take as consent. "Between you and me, I believe Hitler attacks those groups to elevate his own position — they're nothing but scapegoats. Personally I've never had a problem with any Russian or Jewish person." She heard him give a small sigh. "Look, would you sit down for a minute? It's hard talking to someone's back." Hedy dried her hands and sat back down on the edge of her chair. "Thank you." He leaned so close to her that she could see those tiny crow's-feet around his eyes. His breath smelled of the soft red wine. "You know, Hedy, I'm not a military man. When I was a little boy, all I ever wanted to be was an engineer. I did my apprenticeship in a shipyard, and then one day, my company was told we had to make tank engines instead of trawlers, and we all had to wear this." He indicated his gabardine wool tunic, unbuttoned at the top. "Next thing I know, we're at war and I'm servicing Panzers. Men my age had no choice."

"So you just . . . accepted it?"

"It was that or prison. Sometimes when a force is that strong, it's pointless, arrogant even, to think you can fight it. Like King Canute, the king who drowned because he believed he could stop the waves just by the power of his own command? You know that story?"

She sniffed. "Everyone knows that story. And that version is wrong anyway. Canute didn't drown, and he wasn't trying to stop the tide."

"He wasn't?"

"Canute was a good king. He was trying to prove to his egotistical nobility that no man can challenge the power of God, even a monarch. It was a gesture of humility." She fought the urge to move back to the sink. She felt too exposed here, too close to him.

Kurt was laughing. He had a beautiful

laugh. "Well, I guess I learned something today." He smiled, inviting one in return; she refused it. "All I'm saying is, I didn't choose to do this, or to be here. I really didn't have any option."

"So in your view you share no responsibility for what your country is doing, or the pain you are causing?" The words seemed to tumble out of her mouth.

"What I'm trying to say is —"

"What about the people I saw in Vienna, being put on trucks and driven away?"

He reached across the table, and for a second she thought he was reaching for her, but his hand went toward the wine bottle, which he emptied into his cup. "I agree with you that's wrong." He took a long swig. "Moving people around like cattle, it's cruel and unnecessary. But they'll be put on good farmland, among their own kind."

"Farmland? You think they're moving the . . . those people to farms?" The wine was mixing with her fury; the fountain was now unstoppable, her earlier promises of caution and courtesy forgotten. "Most of them have never been heard of again! You're telling me they weren't taken to some forest and shot?"

"A lot of those stories are propaganda." There was irritation in his voice now. "You think the Allies aren't capable of that? What did you hear about us before we came here? I bet you were told we'd rape the women and eat babies alive! Of course there are stupid, ignorant people on my side, as there are on yours. But that doesn't mean we're all the same."

Hedy rose to her feet, and to her alarm, he did too. He was a good head taller, and she realized that one blow could knock her unconscious. She heard a door bang somewhere below and wondered if Anton was preparing to sprint up the stairs. Yet still her mouth ran on. "Why should I believe that? You wear the uniform of a Nazi, you accept the pay of the Nazis, you carry out the orders of the Nazis. What else are you but a Nazi?"

He stared at her with an expression she couldn't fathom. It wasn't the anger or contempt she'd expected, it looked more like disappointment. He raised his arm, and for a second Hedy thought the blow was coming, but he just picked up his canvas bag from the table and threw it over his shoulder.

"And you?" he barked. "You are an Austrian; we are technically countrymen. You work for the same people as me, you take their wages. You invite me here to get your hands on my food, but you continue to treat me like an enemy. And you know . . . ?" He pulled his cap down tightly on his head. "If you lump an entire race together, and believe every person is the same — then you're no better than Hitler."

Hedy stared at him. Her hands were trembling but she managed to keep her voice steady. "I think you'd better go."

"All right." He moved toward the door then turned back. "You know, despite everything, I would like us to be friends."

"Thank you for the food." She tried to hold her chin high, determined not to show weakness.

Kurt looked despondent, but merely shrugged. "Thank you for the translation, and for dinner." And then he was gone. Hedy stood for a moment, her hand on the table for support, as Anton rushed in, his face full of anxiety, and put a tentative arm around her.

"It's all right. He's gone."

"I shouted at him." Her whole body was shaking now.

"Don't worry. He won't report it. How would it make him look, complaining that he'd been upset by a young girl? He won't say anything."

Hedy nodded but the trembling continued. It went on long after Anton opened the second bottle of wine, poured her a large cupful and insisted she drink it while she reported the night's events to him. She was still unsteady and a little nauseous when, having thanked Anton for everything, she scurried home, the precious groceries wrapped in newspaper under her old coat, and gratefully pulled the bolt across the door of her apartment. Lighting the stub of a candle, she breathed deeply and tried to talk herself down. Maybe she was simply shocked by her own rashness, speaking to a German officer that way? Or it could be a reaction to the unaccustomed alcohol. She drank cold water from her kitchen tap. Perhaps she was a little ashamed. Behaving that way to a man who, after all, had been kind to her and treated her like a human being.

It was at three in the morning, when the dream woke her, that she knew the lie was starting to crack. A dream of such sexual charge that it drew sweat from every part of her and tossed her blankets from the bed. Kurt's hands on her body, his lips on her mouth, her hips arcing up to meet him.

In the shadowy darkness of her apartment, Hemingway arched his spine and hissed at her.

■ ■ ■ ■

"I hear they're finally confiscating the Judenschweine wireless sets." Fischer shoved the gear stick into third with ludicrous force, causing a grinding in complaint. Kurt winced at the sound. "Can't believe it's taken them this long. I mean, if anyone's going to transmit information to the British mainland it's those devious little kikes, right? Should have been a priority."

Kurt gave a vague nod, but kept his eyes fixed on the world outside. The day was warm with a cloudless sky. Fishing boats bobbed in the harbor, and on the far side of the quay the outline of Elizabeth Castle sprawled in the bay. The best policy for these morning journeys, he'd discovered, was to focus on the landscape. At first Kurt had found Fischer's daily diatribes amusing — in fact Kurt had rather enjoyed lobbing in new statistics and arguments, watching his colleague's face grow pink and sweaty. But now the guy just got on his nerves. And Fischer drove the staff car as if he were breaking a wild stallion, speeding up to stop signs and slamming on the brakes at the last minute. Kurt mentally ran through the other guys in his billet, wondering if anyone else could give him a ride to work. He'd ask around tonight.

This morning was even worse than usual, because in the back seat was the odious Geheime Feldpolizei operative, Erich Wildgrube. At least, secret police was what everyone assumed him to be: the man studiously avoided direct questions. He was forever hanging around the barracks and social clubs, pumping out a stream of questions disguised as casual curiosity. His piggy eyes swiveled constantly, and he always wore a leather trench coat, felt Alpine hat and a musky cologne that turned Kurt's stomach. Kurt could never figure out why someone whose entire job depended on anonymity deliberately drew so much attention to himself. Kurt didn't trust Wildgrube further than he could piss.

Fischer was pointing to a large white V-sign that had been painted on a granite wall. "And there's another thing. Have you seen how many of those have appeared around town? God knows where they're getting the paint." He shook his head in bewilderment at the islanders' persistence.

Wildgrube leaned forward, his whiny, girlish voice cutting through the sound of the engine. "It's pure insubordination. Needs to be clamped down hard, or the rot spreads.

Don't you think, Neumann?" A whiff of cologne brought Kurt's breakfast partway up his gullet.

"Sure," Kurt replied. "Nothing spreads like rot."

There was no reply, and Kurt wondered if he'd overplayed his hand. But they were now approaching Millbrook, his drop-off point, and with relief Kurt hopped out, giving the roof a double bang to imply cheeriness, and jogged into the compound. With luck, there'd be a nice long list of jobs for him today. A full schedule meant no time to think about Fischer, Wildgrube or even — well, no point going back to that one now.

In fact, it turned out to be a swine of a day. His entire morning was taken up with some misaligned pistons on the crankshaft of a Horch 108 that caused him to miss lunch, and he spent the afternoon chasing a bundle of dockets his junior mechanic had put in the wrong pigeonhole. By the time six o'clock came, Kurt was hot and grubby, and decided that tonight he would try out the new officers' club in town. He usually avoided those places — the sight of the young French whores depressed him. But there was always a decent stock of the local apple brandy and enough friendly faces to take his mind off things. He was just about

93

to shout to his NCO engineer for a lift home when he saw her.

She was leaving Block Seven, wearing the same clothes she always wore — those tatty lace-up shoes and, for some strange reason, a heavy winter coat that was falling to pieces. She walked with an even, deliberate step, and her hair rippled gold in the breeze. Kurt slowed, wondering whether to hold back and let her pass through the exit gate first. They hadn't spoken since that awful night, even though he'd seen her at a distance several times and pictured their next encounter more often than he'd like to admit. He'd thought about apologizing, but what was the point? He'd not really done anything wrong. And if she hated all Germans as much as she claimed, it was a loser from the start. Best to put it down to experience and move on — plenty more fish in the sea. Except that none of the others seemed to interest him. And he had fallen asleep every night with Hedy's green eyes imprinted on his memory.

Kurt pushed back his shoulders. No more of this schoolboy creeping around, he would clear the air once and for all. He walked purposefully in her direction. Hedy turned, as if sensing his approach, and then something extraordinary happened. To Kurt's

94

astonishment, she smiled at him. It was the first full, true smile he'd had from her, and the effect on his heart rate was a shock. He responded with a grin of his own, hoping his partial erection wouldn't be obvious in his uniform trousers. Pushing through the crowd of employees toward her, Kurt felt a surge of optimism, possibilities flooding in, lifting him. As he drew breath to speak, a harsh German voice shouted from behind him, "What is this? To whom do these belong?"

Kurt turned. Behind him stood OT Feldwebel Schulz, who, in his right hand, held a bundle of ten petrol coupons, now covered in mud and footprints. His nervous, blinking eyes scanned the crowd, evidently expecting a reply. Kurt looked around too, then his gaze landed on Hedy. The color had drained from her face and her hand was sliding into her coat toward her inside pocket. She fumbled around inside but her hand emerged, empty. At that moment, their eyes locked, and Kurt understood everything. Then, as if hearing another person's voice somewhere in the distance, he heard his own.

"Yes, they belong to me. Thank you, I must have dropped them."

From that second, everyone seemed to

95

move a little more slowly, and when Kurt recalled it later, it seemed as if the events were lit by bright floodlights, like a film set. Hedy stared at him in pure disbelief. Kurt forced his eyes away from hers as Schulz marched toward him.

"Why were these in your possession, Lieutenant? Do you have an allocation?" The evening sun was catching Schulz's glasses, giving him the appearance of a blind robot.

Kurt thought fast. "Actually, no. I got them from one of the drivers in exchange for tobacco."

"Which driver, sir?" Schulz shifted to his other foot, embarrassed by the inappropriateness of the situation.

"I don't know — there's scores of those guys. They all look the same to me. Is this a problem?"

"Yes, Lieutenant, indeed it is." Schulz's cheeks were flushed red. "This represents an illegal transaction of Reich property! Officers are meant to set an example." His voice dropped an octave. "I'm sorry, sir, but I will have to report this."

Kurt felt a trickle of sweat run down his back. "Come on, Henrik, seriously? It's just a few coupons — everyone does it."

"Perhaps so, sir, but you have admitted

it." Schulz hung his head, clearly not relishing his duty. "I must talk to my superior. Please be in my office in thirty minutes." And he stomped off, stuffing the evidence into his top pocket.

The onlookers began to disperse, murmuring quietly among themselves. Kurt forced himself to wait several seconds before glancing back to Hedy. Her face still registered incredulity but there was something else there now, a nameless emotion that turned Kurt's insides to caramel. She looked as if she were about to say something, but Kurt warned her off with the tiniest shake of his head and a wink. He spun on his foot and walked back toward his cubbyhole office. He looked back only once, and was glad to see that Hedy had already gone.

The military police arrived within an hour. A little after eight, Kurt was escorted to a Black Maria where one of the two MPs opened the door for him and offered him a cigarette for the journey. Kurt blew perfect smoke rings through the rear bars of the van as he watched Lager Hühnlein disappear behind them. What he still couldn't figure out was why, at that moment, he felt more at peace than he had in months.

"Two weeks?"

"That's what all the typists are saying. Apparently they want to make an example of him."

Anton pulled a face. "Mr. Reis's neighbor was in the Jersey section last month for black market trading. I hear that jail's pretty grim."

"Better than being sent to France, I suppose. I would take him some food, but —"

"No!" Anton put his hand toward her, the index finger raised. "You stay away, or you'll make them suspicious. And I think you ought to look for another job."

Hedy sat back on her haunches, watching Anton wiggle his homemade fishing line deep under the rock. It was an ingenious contraption: a coat hook tied to a length of old hose, partially braced with a length of broken broom handle. Ormers, even small lobsters, could be pried from these gloomy depths if you were lucky.

"You know as well I do, I wouldn't get another job."

"But you need to protect yourself. What if Neumann finds it too tough in there, and decides to tell them the truth?"

Hedy blinked in the glare of the white sky, and peered across the lunar wilderness of rocks and shining pools toward La Roque beach. They were a long way out, and the people on the distant shore were no more than colored dots. One of them was Dorothea, waiting by the sea wall for their return.

"If he was going to rat on me he would have done it by now." Hedy hoped her tone sounded pragmatic.

"Maybe, but what kind of reward will he want when he comes out? He obviously likes you, and now he has information on you. He could take advantage." Anton's probing was becoming more frantic, as if he could taste the seafood meal lurking just out of reach. Still nothing moved in the pool except minuscule, transparent fish, no longer than a fingernail, shooting through the water in a thousand directions, and a few shore crabs, smaller than silver sixpences, scuttling over the sandy floor to the shelter of the next stone. Such tiny creatures, Hedy thought, with no defense system; their only hope was concealment. She stood to stretch her legs.

"So what should I do? If I leave now, that would look more suspicious. And my address is on record — if he wants to blackmail me, I can't stop him." She wiped the film of sweat from her top lip and fiddled with the strip of torn curtain fabric she had wrapped around her hair for a scarf. The day was hot, and every nerve in her body felt too near the surface of her skin. "How long do we have before the tide turns?"

"Twenty minutes, if that. Then we have to head straight back." Anton checked the watch in his pocket. "Dorothea says it comes in really fast down here. This island has one of the biggest tides in Europe, about twelve meters — it's really powerful."

Hedy nodded. "All right, then let's at least try to get some limpets. No point going home empty-handed."

She headed for a patch of jagged rocks, on the far side of the gully, and crouched down out of the sun. Taking her improvised chisel — a piece of slate stolen from a building site in town — she chipped at the dull yellow pyramids on the shadowy underside of the rock, until a few fell into her basket. Anton chose a different clump of rocks to work on, and for a while there was no sound but scraping and the breath of their exertions. Above them rose the silhouette of the ancient Seymour Tower, a memorial to other wars and older struggles. Hedy glanced at her friend a few times, but his eyes stayed on his work. Soon their fingers

100

were numb and their knuckles bleeding from the barnacled rock. They had twenty-seven limpets between them, barely enough for a snack.

Anton gave a weary sigh. "Let's call it a day. Don't want to take any chances." They began their slow journey back toward the shore, slipping and staggering on the wet rocks, grasping at each other to steady themselves.

As the silence lengthened, Hedy reached for a safe topic. "So what were the main headlines on the BBC last night?"

"Germans are closing in on Leningrad. If the Russians can't stop them and Roosevelt doesn't step in soon, this might all be over by Christmas." He stopped, drew a tiny pouch of tobacco from his pocket and rolled the slimmest cigarette he could. "Does this mean you handed your wireless in?"

Hedy nodded. "If I didn't surrender it, they'd only search my apartment. No point taking stupid chances."

"And I trust all this has brought an end to your petrol coupon business too?"

"I'm not a fool, Anton." Then she added: "Although if I'd known the seam on my pocket had come loose, none of this would have happened."

"What about Doctor Maine?"

"I feel bad for him. But there are plenty of black marketeers he can go to."

The rocks flattened out as they moved toward the shore, and now they were crunching on drying seaweed. Hedy looked up and made out the slim figure of Dorothea sitting on an old blanket by the sea wall, her legs tucked neatly to the side beneath her homemade skirt, waving at them. Hedy let slip a sigh she intended to be inaudible, but Anton's frown told her that it wasn't. He rolled the limpets around the basket in his hand before turning to look at her.

"There's a freshwater tap over by the slipway — I'm going to go and rinse these off. I'll be a few minutes. You go and keep Dorothea company." Hedy met his eyes and saw determination. "Go on. I won't be long."

It was a standoff, and Hedy knew it. Feeling like a schoolgirl, she shuffled through the dry sand of the upper shore. Dorothea shifted herself along the blanket and patted the space next to her feet. "How did you get on?"

"Not so good. Twenty-seven limpets."

Dorothea laughed. "Don't worry. I can put them in a potato pie; they'll still give some flavor. Ah, look, you grazed your hand!" She took a small lacy handkerchief

102

from her bag and dabbed at Hedy's knuckles before Hedy had a chance to decline.
"It's a messy business, low-water fishing.
But worth it, if you come away with some
supper. Hey, look what I got today." She
pulled a small black tube from her bag and
twisted it to reveal a stub of pink lipstick.
"It belonged to my grandmother; she said I
could keep it. Would you like to use it?"

Hedy craned her neck for Anton, who was
still messing about by the slipway. "No,
thanks."

"Sure? It's Coty. A good one. And I bet
it's your color."

"Honestly." Hedy bent down to brush her
bare legs with her fingers. The coarse grains
were clinging to her damp feet and shins,
making her skin itch. She yearned to follow
Anton to the water tap to rinse it off, but
understood that abandoning her post was
not an option. She was about to ask a polite
question about Dorothea's family when
Dorothea casually remarked, "Anton tells
me they put your lieutenant in prison?"

Hedy stared at her, dumbstruck. In the
corner of her vision, she could see Anton
making his way back toward them. She
wanted to slap him.

"Anton told you?"

"Of course. I think it's so romantic,"

Dorothea trilled. "It's like a movie — going to prison to save the woman you love."

Hedy's skin felt as if it was crawling with insects. Her voice came out tight and loud. "It's nothing like that! Why would you say that? He felt sorry for me, that's all."

Dorothea's face became childlike. "Hedy, I'm sorry if I've offended you. But . . . it's a big gesture to make out of pity. Are you sure that's all it was?"

"I don't know why he did it! Perhaps he felt bad for upsetting me the night we ate together. But really, you think I would have a romance with a Nazi officer?" The words seemed to hang and twist in the air, and she could feel the blood pumping to her cheeks.

At that moment Anton's shadow loomed over them. The basket of wet limpets hung loose in his fingers, dripping onto the sand. "What's this?"

Hedy stood up, glaring at him with all the outrage she could muster. "Dorothea seems to think there is some kind of love affair going on between me and Lieutenant Neumann. Where on earth would she get such an idea?"

Anton pushed sand with his foot. "I'm sure no one is suggesting any such thing. How about we all go back to town and find somewhere to get a cold drink?"

"No, I'm sorry, I'm not feeling so good. I need to go home." It was true. She needed to find some shade. She needed to get this sand off her, clean herself, cool down, calm down.

Dorothea held out the basket of limpets. "At least take your share."

Hedy pushed it back. "I can't eat them anyway. They're not kosher."

"I think some things shouldn't matter in wartime." Dorothea's voice was oddly calm, and when Hedy looked up she saw that the woman was staring at her with a disconcerting intensity. "Hedy, you know you can trust me, don't you?"

"I'm not sure who I can trust anymore."

She turned and walked briskly across the beach to the slipway, scrambling onto it with difficulty. At the tap she ran cold water over her legs and only then, struggling to get her shoes onto her damp feet, did she look back. Anton was sitting with his knees pulled up, rubbing his eyes and head in the slow rhythm of exhaustion. But Dorothea was still looking at Hedy, the blue of her eyes glinting in the afternoon sun.

The thin column of light angling in through the high barred window lit up Wildgrube's oiled hair like a brightly jeweled cap. Together with his earnest expression, he looked like a commedia dell'arte character, and Kurt had to suppress a smirk. Wildgrube stood with his feet neatly together, as if on parade, looking down at him.

"Of all the people I might suspect of something like this, Kurt, it would never have been you."

Kurt drew deep on the cigarette Wildgrube had given him, and watched the smoke drift through the sunbeam. The wooden bench under his backside was slightly damp and full of splinters, and he still hadn't got used to the smell of shit and piss in this place. But he was damned if he was going to give this idiot the satisfaction. He shrugged, as if he didn't understand what the fuss was about. He'd got rather good at that shrug over the last few days.

"To be honest, Erich . . ." He watched Wildgrube flinch a little at the use of his Christian name. Two can play at that game, Kurt thought. "I knew it was against the rules, but I never saw it as a serious issue. I mean, half the guys I know have some kind of deal going on the side. I hear the head of the secret police has quite a little business going with one of the local butchers."

Wildgrube's lips pressed together to hold in a remark, and Kurt detected the smallest twitch in his left eye.

"You are misinformed, my friend," Wildgrube replied. "Black marketeering takes valuable supplies out of circulation, causes hardship and risks insurgence among the civilian population. It is viewed very dimly." He turned and did a strange little walk up and down the narrow cell while he composed his next sentence. Kurt took another long drag on his cigarette. "I am still shocked that you, a respected officer, would so casually flout these rules, knowing the damage it would do to your reputation. You are fortunate that the Russian campaign is progressing so rapidly, otherwise you might find yourself leaving this jail and being put on a plane to the Eastern Front."

Kurt sucked the last dregs of his cigarette and stubbed it out on the floor of the cell, grinding it into the cold black stone. He felt a weight lift. A fortnight in this hellhole he could cope with, even losing his leave was a price worth paying. But the possibility of a transfer east had kept him awake every night since this began. In those long, dark hours he'd found himself questioning his motives and coming up with no real answers. Sure, saving a pretty girl from prison was a noble thing to do, but if it meant dying on the Pripet Marshes? And for what? He'd only been given one tiny indication that she felt anything for him at all — in that single split second in the compound when she'd looked at him with thankfulness and . . . Affection? Bemusement? Pity, that he was prepared to behave like such a sap? Yet he'd carried that treasure of a moment in his head ever since, and promised himself that no matter what punishment was handed down, he would not betray her. Whether that made him Don Quixote or the biggest fool in the Wehrmacht he still wasn't sure. He only knew that he wanted to see her again, as soon as possible.

Kurt hauled himself up from the bench, pleased that Wildgrube was so much shorter than him, and gave the policeman a friendly pat on the arm. "You're absolutely right, Erich. And believe me, this is the only lesson I'll need. I assure you I'll be a good boy from now on."

Wildgrube's eyes narrowed a little. "It is not a question of being a 'good boy.' It is about maintaining the right attitude toward our great Reich and our beloved Führer."

"Of course."

They stood like that for what felt a long time, neither wanting to break first. Eventually Wildgrube gave a loud sniff and banged on the door for the guard to release him. As he turned to bid Kurt farewell, Kurt saw the trace of a smile around his thin mouth.

"When they let you out, come and find me. We'll have a drink together — put all this behind us, yes?"

"Sounds good."

Kurt watched the door slam shut and heard the footsteps disappear down the corridor, until the only sound remaining was the groaning of a sick prisoner in a neighboring cell. He sat on his bench and leaned back, watching the sunbeam catch new bumps and cracks in the wall as it crept upward, and his thoughts turned to King Canute.

The leaves on the trees in Parade Gardens were turning yellow and brown, and bulbous, rain-filled clouds scuttled across the sky. It was almost September. As Hedy made her way past the Don Memorial, several bored off-duty German soldiers lolled on the granite plinth or leaned on the replica cannons, smoking French cigarettes and chatting. There was a louche, tainted quality about them. One of them gave a low whistle as she passed, and she turned her head away in disgust.

The café was on York Street, close to the General Hospital. It was a dim, inconspicuous little place with a faded awning above the window and a brown interior made darker by heavy lace curtains. A perfect venue for her meeting. The door pinged as she pushed it open. She was relieved to find the place empty, except for the bored-looking waitress and one old lady in a window seat, eking out a cup of bramble tea and staring blankly at passersby. Hedy tucked herself behind a table at the rear, ordered a cup of carrot coffee and settled down to wait.

Five minutes later, the bell rang again and Hedy looked up. He was standing in the doorway, wearing a long brown raincoat and an old homburg, his eyes darting around to seek her out, while taking care not to make direct contact. He shuffled to the table next to hers and sat down, pretending to study the menu. Hedy sipped her drink and kept her gaze on the window. She heard him order a glass of milk from the waitress, his voice noticeably strained and weary, then heard the rustle of his newspaper. Hedy waited until the waitress had gone into the back larder to get the milk jug, pulled a small package from her bag, stretched across and deftly placed it on his table. She sat back, cup in hand.

With equal nimbleness, Doctor Maine

took the slim bundle and slipped it into his coat pocket. Only then did they allow themselves the smallest exchange of smiles, an acknowledgment of a transaction well done. But in that fleeting moment, Hedy saw that the shadows beneath his eyes were darker than ever, and the hair around his temples grayer than before. And she knew that she'd been right not to tell him about the events at Lager Hühnlein, just as she'd been right not to tell Anton that she had no intention of giving up her theft of petrol coupons. Everyone was under enough strain, already living with too much fear and uncertainty, without the anxiety of knowing other people's secrets. Occupation was making enigmas of them all.

Hedy drained what was left in her cup, left the correct money on the table and slipped quietly back onto the street. She felt pleased with herself, admiring of her own courage and fortitude, and tried to connect with the feeling, to record it in her memory. Because she knew that this might be the last time she could feel such an undiluted emotion. From now on, if today turned out as she planned, every future achievement would be weighed against shanda and found wanting.

The previous night she had lain awake in

her bed, so afraid of the darkness and her own thoughts that she let the remains of a precious candle burn right down to its end. The flame had flickered in the drafty room, throwing shadows and shapes onto the curtain, but she'd barely seen them. Instead, she saw her mother bent over, weeping and inconsolable, and her father in the raging temper of his life. She saw Roda, staring with incomprehension at a sister she no longer knew, and Anton with his head in his hands, just as he had looked that day at the beach. But what she saw most was Kurt, and that tiny wink that had communicated so much. The picture was already fraying with repetition, but it sent a pulse of long-ing through her. She ached to touch herself, but guilt kept her hands above the blanket in the cool damp air. She closed her eyes and turned over, burying her face in the pil-low. But there she found nothing but Ger-man soldiers marching down Grabenstrasse and SS guards kicking at the curled-up bundle of an elderly Jewish neighbor as he lay dying on the street. Each time, the im-age was dispersed by Kurt's smiling face pushing its way to the fore. And as her bat-tered windup alarm clock showed three o'clock, she let her resolve slip away, and her hand slipped down beneath the blankets to silence her body's throbbing demands.

By the time Hedy reached Newgate Street, her heart was thumping. She turned into the narrow, deserted road, aware of her own footsteps on the cobbles. Halfway down, a dimpled metal door was set into the imposing granite wall; a large metal ring served as a knocker, and beneath it was a small sliding hatch. Hedy edged past the door and stood waiting on the opposite side of the street, in the shadow of the prison walls. Spots of water began to polka dot the cobbles, and as the rain grew heavier it seeped into her hair and shoulders, but still she waited, silent and motionless.

Finally, the door opened. Kurt, wearing his uniform tunic and cap, and carrying a paper parcel of his belongings, stepped out into the street. She watched him lift his eyes to the sky and breathe deeply, then he turned and saw her. For a moment she feared what she saw was anger. But the smile came again. Relieved, she returned it. She raised her finger to her lips, then walked toward him.

"Twenty meters behind," she whispered, "no closer."

Kurt nodded.

Hedy began walking back to the main road. Now and then she glanced over her shoulder or made some excuse to turn, and saw that he was still following. They walked, so intimate in their distance, up to the Parade and through the slender streets of town cottages and business premises, until they reached New Street and Hedy's front door. Hedy climbed the steps and slipped inside, pausing only a second to see the distant figure of Kurt at the end of the road, measuring his steps to control his speed. Leaving the door ajar, she climbed the two staircases to her apartment, thankful that Mrs. Le Couteur's door remained firmly closed. Her key turned in the lock just as she heard the tread of Kurt's footstep at the bottom, and she hurried inside. Standing quite still in the center of the tiny room, she breathed heavily, steam rising off her coat, streaks of wet hair stuck to her forehead. The room reeked of last night's boiled vegetables — hers or a neighbor's, she couldn't be sure. She heard him coming up the stairs. Hemingway, sensing danger, ran under the bed and stayed there. Then Kurt was standing in the doorway, looking directly at her, trying to get the measure of the situation. He pulled the door behind him and took off his cap.

For a moment, neither of them moved. Hedy had no sense of his thoughts. He took a step toward her, then another, and reached out his arms. Hedy felt herself melt into him. His lips, which tasted faintly of stale tobacco, were on hers, and he was kissing her with a tender ferocity that sent desire shooting through her body, his hands pushing through her hair and feeling for the back of her neck, squeezing her arms and shoulders, reaching down toward her breasts. Hedy reached out one last time for her conscience, but rules and certainty were already gone, and longing dragged her toward a pit of pleasure. By the time her dress was on the floor she couldn't have told you her own name.

FOUR

The open truck was crammed with soldiers — perhaps twenty-five, thirty. As it sped by, churning up dust and fallen leaves, and blurring the uniforms into a smear of greenish gray, Hedy pressed herself against the hedgerow, taking care to keep her face buried in her scarf. The truck rumbled on toward the bend in the lane, but before it turned she caught the face of one young private, pale and vacant, staring out toward the headland. Hardly more than a schoolboy, his eyes were glazed, his lips pressed together as if to hold back some imminent torrent. From beneath the brim of her old felt hat, Hedy watched his features smudge, then disappear, before she slipped down the footpath that led to the sea.

In tiny Belcroute bay the waves slapped rhythmically at the water's edge. The tide was still coming in; soon the glassy rock pools would disappear in gushes of silvery water, absorbed back into the ocean. Hedy clambered over the slimy rocks, leaving her hands free to break any slip, steering well clear of the flat areas of the beach where mines might be laid. She looked for the line of discarded seaweed on the shingle, and was relieved to see the ragged marker lay a good two meters beyond the low sea wall. Soon the spring tides would swell the flow, trapping any careless visitor and forcing them to scrabble up to the steep woodland above. But today she would be safe.

Edging around the corner where the foliage still grew thick, she threw a quick glance over her shoulder to make sure no one was following. Then, reaching the familiar gap between the rocks she had come to view as her own, she crouched down and snuggled into the gap, making sure to keep her back tight against the slab so that no one walking on the pathway above could peer over and see her. The breeze was stiff, but the sun still held a little warmth, and its position told her it was around midday. She pulled off her hat and made herself comfortable, knowing she wouldn't have long to wait.

So far, November had been a harsh month. The bread ration had been cut again. There were rumors circulating about further restrictions to the gas supply. And the arrival of more German troops from France, hundred after hundred swarming off boats in St. Helier harbor, had caused a collective wave of despair through the community. What were all these soldiers for? What would they do here? It could only mean more orders and new harassments. Still, sitting here with the sun's rays on her eyelids, and no sound except the lapping water, there was no denying an old, familiar sensation rising in her chest. It was happiness. She'd almost forgotten it. Resting her head back, she smiled as the feeling flowed down her arms and pooled in her fingertips. She breathed it in, letting her thoughts drift.

Then, as always, came the payback. The sinking chill of fear and guilt.

It had been like this right from the first day — that rainy afternoon in her apartment, with the thin light bleeding through the skylight onto their naked bodies, the two of them still and exhausted on the counterpane. They had stayed for hours squashed together on her tiny bed, sharing confessions of their first stirrings of attraction and waiting for darkness to fall so that he could slip away unseen. That was when it began in earnest. This psychotic pendulum of joy and self-hatred punching it out in her solar plexus — random fits of laughter as she walked to work, and frantic crying in the early hours. It was exhausting — but not the worst part. The worst was the one constant emotion that never truly went away, but bubbled under the surface all day and night. The terror.

Several times she was seconds away from blurting out the truth. Two tiny words, she often told herself, and it would be over. Two words: "I'm Jewish." It wouldn't have been so dangerous, right at the start. She could have dismissed his anger with a shrug — did he really not know? Was it her fault that he, an officer, didn't know the employee background of his own compound? And if he'd raged and yelled, stomped about her apartment in indignant haste to find his clothes, she'd have gambled that he could never tell anyone, for fear of retaliation. It would have been simple.

But she didn't tell him. Not that day, nor the next time, nor any of the wild, furtive encounters they had shared since. As her affection for him grew, so did the fear of his disapproval. After a while she became crazy enough to think she might never need to tell him. She dreamed up a universe in which the issue would simply never come up. Until one day, months or years in the future — this part she left deliberately vague — he would turn to her over a meal in a pavement café, smile, sip a glass of wine and say, "By the way, you never mentioned . . ." But alone in her bed, Hedy knew it was already too late.

A low whistle from the other side of the rocks snapped her eyes open. A few seconds later, Kurt's loping figure appeared around the outcrop. She watched him climb toward her, his long limbs moving with grace and confidence, until he dropped down close to her and steadied himself. She waited for those crinkly eyes to find her, holding out her arms toward him. Then he was on top of her, embracing her, kissing her long and hard, murmuring that she looked beautiful and how he'd missed her in their days apart. As they squeezed together between the rocks, he opened his canvas bag to reveal half a loaf, some tiny French apples and a few tomatoes. She snuggled into the space beneath his left arm, and for a while they ate their lunch in silence.

Finally Kurt wiped his mouth with the back of his hand. "You hear about Sidi Rezegh?" Hedy shook her head. "Afrika Korps crushed the British 7th Armoured Division. If we take Malta, it could all be over in a few months." Hedy stared down at the last hemisphere of tomato in her palm, letting him pick up on her silence, and felt his twitch of regret. "I'm sorry. But that's what we both want, right? For this to be over?"

"What about the Eastern Front?"

"Still gridlocked. The snow must have arrived by now. God knows what it must be like for those poor bastards. I just hope Helmut's not out there." He caught her questioning look. "My best mate since we were kids, he's like a brother. He's in the Panzers now." He peered at her, his head on one side. "Hedy, why don't you have a wireless? All the other locals have one."

Hedy threw the piece of tomato into her mouth and chewed longer than was necessary, trying to remember the correct lie. "I told you, mine broke. You can't buy them anymore."

"Maybe I could get hold of one, use my contacts? Then I could listen to the BBC news with you. More accurate than the rubbish we have to listen to."

She touched his knee. "Thanks, but I don't want you spending that kind of money. I can get the news from you, or Anton."

"Ah, the famous Anton. Are you ever going to let me meet him?" Hedy threw him

121

the wry look that bagged up a dozen previous conversations, but Kurt merely shrugged. "If he's that good a friend, he'll understand, surely? And isn't he in the same position, dating that local girl?"

"You'll meet him one of these days. You ever hear from Helmut?" Her tactic was blatant and she knew he'd spotted it, but he let it slide.

"One letter in the summer, most of it censored. Don't even know where he is. I worry about him." He threw his apple core into the rocks and turned to face her. "When can I come to your apartment again? I mean, this is great, but" — he slipped his hand down to her breast, his thumb gently circling her nipple — "I miss you."

Hedy felt her sex ache in response, but she could also hear distant voices further along the headland path. She pushed his hand up toward her neck.

"I miss you too, but it's too risky here."

That smile again. She could smell the apple on his breath, the oil he used on his hair, and she fought the urge to place his hand back where it had been.

Kurt pushed himself up on one elbow. "I really don't think you need to be so cautious. At least two of the officers in my house are seeing island women. And it's not like you're a Jersey girl anyway."

"That's the point. The locals are already suspicious of me, with my nationality and my accent. I could be labeled a spy, kicked out of my apartment. I have to be doubly careful." Sensing his disappointment, she continued quickly. "Mrs. Le Couteur's cough sounds better, though. If she's well enough to go to her sister's on Friday, you can come over then."

He nodded. "I'll make sure I see my friend at the supply store and get" — to Hedy's delight he blushed slightly — "what we need. Oh, and I almost forgot — a present for you." He reached into his pocket and pulled out a bar of Stollwerck chocolate.

Hedy gasped at the sight of the smart blue wrapper with its familiar curly brand script, holding it like a baby bird in the palm of her hand. "How did you know this used to be my favorite? You want to share it now?"

"No, it's for you. I can get more next week. Save it till you really need it." He turned his face toward the sun. "I love this spot. How long before the spring tides?"

"About ten days."

"And then this beach will be cut off completely?"

"Water will come right up to the wall — perhaps over the top with a storm tide." She sensed the question in his eyes. "That's when the wind and tide rise together, and force the sea levels up. I saw one here a couple of years ago. It was frightening."

He took her hand in his and closed his fingers around it. "We'll have to find another meeting place. Be too easy to get trapped here."

Hedy merely nodded, put her head on his shoulder and let the low autumn sun melt her thoughts away.

"Swedes, swedes, beautiful swedes,
We sing the praises of dear old swedes,
Oh yes, they're just all right,
They fill you up till you're blown up tight,
Swedes, swedes, succulent swedes,
They're all a fellow needs,
We all adore 'em, give us some more of
   'em,
Beautiful, beautiful swedes."

The five singers, chaotically costumed in various remnants from the Green Room Club's prewar wardrobe chest, conducted the crowd with lusty enthusiasm. Chains of clasped hands formed along each row of seats, a forest of swaying arms silhouetted against the stage, while eager faces turned to each other, chuckling at the silliness of it all.

Hedy, holding tight to Anton on her right and a white-haired old lady on her left, sang as loudly as she could, giggling between breaths. This had been a great idea after all. She'd hesitated last night about accepting Anton's spare ticket, mainly because she'd been hoping that Kurt might be free this afternoon. But after she found Kurt's note in the pocket of her coat, saying that he'd been called to some local authorities meeting, she'd decided that a trip to the theater might be a nice distraction. Now she wondered why she'd not been before. The pretty Victorian Opera House, with its gold trim and laurel moldings, reminded her of her local theater in Vienna, where her father had taken her to matinees as a child. That smell of polished wood and dusty old velvet, the mood of expectation . . . And so what if she recognized the lead actor from the stall in the fish market, or that the stage was lit by three car headlights fixed in the orchestra pit and powered from car batteries in the wings? What did it matter that the curtain had to rise at four, so that people from the country parishes could get home in time for curfew? Here, there was color and song and escape, and for once the bubbling dread was

125

firmly caged.

She leaned across to shout in Anton's ear, "Isn't this wonderful?"

Anton smiled, but Hedy saw that there was nothing behind it. He looked distant, remote. Now that she thought about it, Anton had been in a strange mood since they'd met earlier that afternoon. The volume of her singing dropped a little, and she began slipping her friend sly little looks. Leaning back to glance at Dorothea on Anton's far side, she scanned for signs of argument or sulking. But Dorothea was grinning at the stage with wide, unblinking eyes, singing her heart out along with the rest. If there was trouble in paradise, Dorothea was clearly not aware of it.

The thick red curtains swung across to announce the intermission, and with a clatter of lifting seats the audience began to file out to the bars and lavatories. Hedy leaned across her two companions. "Shall we get something to drink?"

Anton wrinkled his nose. "They won't have any real tea or coffee."

"No, but I saw a sign on the way in that they have the best parsnip coffee in town! Come on, my treat?"

Dorothea glanced between the two of

them with bush-baby eyes. "You mean both of us?"

Hedy felt a flutter of embarrassment. She'd been trying for weeks now to be more friendly toward Dorothea. The romance had showed no sign of fading, and knowing she needed to make an effort for Anton's sake, she'd showered Dorothea with inquiries about her health, her grandmother, even her machinist job at the Summerland factory. But the woman's obsession with old movie magazines and endless chatter about hairstyles made for poor conversation, and her persistent girlish snickering, at things that really weren't that funny, set Hedy's nerves on edge. Until now she'd been confident that she'd kept her irritation hidden, but Dorothea's remark revealed that Hedy's tight, impatient smiles had concealed nothing. Now she'd have to repair the damage.

"Of course both of you! Come on, or we won't have time to get served."

The three of them shuffled out of the auditorium and down the stairs to the tiny theater bar, where they joined the long line of ragged locals queuing for whatever paltry fare was on offer. Everyone was so used to queuing these days, it hardly raised a comment anymore. Hedy opened her bag to find her purse, but Anton placed his hand over it.

"Don't be silly. I don't really expect you to pay."

Hedy bridled. "Why not? I'm earning now. And after all the times you've paid for me —"

"It's all right — put your purse away." His voice had an edge to it.

"Anton, what's wrong? You've been grumpy since we got here." She looked to Dorothea for agreement, but Dorothea ignored her. Hedy had noticed that Dorothea, like Anton, was wary of any form of conflict.

"I'm fine, I'm just tired."

"Ah, poor old Anton." Hedy leaned into his ear and began to sing an old lullaby in a melodic whisper: "Schlaf, Kindlein, schlaf! Der Vater hüt't die Schaf, die Mutter schütttelt's Bäume lein . . ."

Anton yanked himself away. His scowl was so fierce Hedy took a step backward. "Hedy, for goodness' sake! You want to get us beaten up?" He wiped his ear with his fingers as if to remove the melody. "You think I'm in a strange mood, what's wrong with you lately? You've been acting like you were drunk or something, these last few weeks."

"I was only teasing you, that's all!"

"No, it's more than that. Something is going on with you."

Hedy felt the blood rise to her cheeks. She hoped he would put it down to the stuffiness of the bar, which suddenly felt overwhelming. "I'm just trying to stay cheerful! Wouldn't hurt you to try it. Everyone's tired, everyone's hungry, but what's the use in complaining? Dorothea, don't you think so?"

But Dorothea was staring at her as if she'd just worked out the last clue in the crossword. "I know what it is! It's that lieutenant, isn't it? Have you seen him again?"

The air grew hotter. Hedy prayed her voice was still working. "What?"

"That's it, isn't it? What was his name — Kurt?"

She knew her only option was to attack, though her cheeks were aflame now.

"For goodness' sake, Dorothea, not this again!"

"I'm right, aren't I? You've seen him."

At that moment, Hedy hated her. Treating it like some schoolgirl joke behind the bicycle sheds! How could the woman not grasp the severity of this? An elderly couple carrying chipped teacups bumped into the three of them as they pushed their way back through the crowd. The old man muttered an apology, but Hedy barely acknowledged him. She took a deep steadying breath. "I told you, I met him that once when he came out of prison, to thank him. That's all."

"You've not seen him since?" Anton asked.

"Why would I?"

"Because you really like him? Same as he likes you?" Dorothea's face was full of eagerness and concern, with no hint of judgment. Hedy almost envied her naivete.

"I don't know what goes on in that head of yours, Dorothea, but you really don't know me at all. And can you please not say things like this in a public place? Go back to your seats — I'll queue for the drinks."

But Anton was still pawing for an argument. "You two sit down — I'll get them."

"Anton, for the last time, I said I'll pay." Hedy reached for her purse again.

"And I said put your money away!" He pushed at the bag, which slipped from Hedy's arm, falling to the floor with a thud and sprawling the contents across the pink carpet. Each of them looked down to see the intimate story laid out beneath them. Hedy's leather purse, a Christmas gift to her from the Mitchells before the war; a lace handkerchief bought from the local market in happier times; and a half-eaten bar of

Stollwerck chocolate, still in its bright blue wrapper.

For a moment none of them spoke. They simply stared down at the chocolate as though it were a hand grenade. The queue for the counter moved forward; two women in battered straw hats behind them, realizing that Anton's trio had no intention of following, shrugged and maneuvered in front of them.

Hedy lifted her eyes to meet Anton's and saw the anger.

"And I suppose" — his voice had steel within it — "I suppose you bought this down the market?"

Involuntarily, Hedy put a hand to her cheek, leaving Dorothea to scrabble on the ground for the spilled items. "I got it from a secretary at work." The phrase swung in the air like frozen washing, stiff and wrongly shaped.

"I don't believe you." Anton had never before said those words to her. "You told me you never speak to anyone there. And yes, your face is crimson."

Hedy felt the wall start to crumble. She didn't have the strength for this, not with him. It came out as a whisper. "Anton, I'm sorry. I should have told you. But . . ."

Dorothea was instantly at her side, placing the bag back on her arm, putting one hand around Hedy's shoulder while the other stroked her hair. "Hedy, don't apologize! No one can help who they fall in love with. And it's no different from me and Anton."

Hedy kept her eyes fixed on Anton, whose face was setting with controlled fury. His voice stayed low. "It's totally different. Have you told him?"

"Told him?"

"Don't play games. Have you?"

"I . . . no."

Anton shook his head. At the counter, the straw-hatted women were telling the girl serving them about the best recipe for carrot jam. The clink of teaspoons being placed into cups was suddenly ear-splitting.

"All that talk at the start . . . how you hated them, how scared you were! I did everything I could to protect you. And now this!" Hedy gazed down at the carpet. The patch in front of her was reduced to a bald, stringy trellis of fibers, scuffed apart by thousands of footsteps over the decades. "Do you want to be imprisoned, maybe deported? Is that what you want?"

Dorothea's hand was still in her hair. Hedy wanted to smack it away but dared not draw any more attention.

"Don't be cruel to her, Anton. It's not her fault," whispered Dorothea.

But Anton was buttoning his jacket and retying the scarf around his neck. "Actually, it is. Are you coming with me or staying here?"

Dorothea cast a pained look at Hedy, but Hedy nodded at her to go. With a final squeeze of Hedy's arm, Dorothea followed Anton out of the bar. Hedy heard their feet on the staircase, her eyes still determinedly on the carpet, then at a slow, measured pace she made her own way out of the theater by another exit. With luck, she would just manage to get home before the tears began.

Low sunbeams streamed in through the vast arched window at the end of the council chamber, bouncing off the polished table and lighting up the medals pinned on the German's chest. The reflection was so bright that Kurt, directly opposite, was forced to sit back in his seat to avoid being dazzled. Why a mere administrator like Doctor Wilhelm Casper, who looked as if he had spent the entire Great War in a variety of offices and wouldn't know one end of a rifle from the other, should have such an impressive array of decorations, Kurt could only speculate. He glanced at the twenty or so other faces around the table to see if anyone else shared his skepticism, but the other German faces all displayed taut little smiles, while the Jersey heads were slumped despondently over their paperwork. The only other person Kurt recognized was a baby-faced lance corporal called Manfred, who he had recently met on a reconnaissance trip to one of the new north coast bunkers. A fellow Dresdner SC fan, Kurt had found Manfred friendly and curious out in the field. But here, under the gaze of the great and the good, Manfred kept his head down over his notebook, barely acknowledging Kurt's presence.

Kurt cast a wistful look at the bare boughs of the birch tree outside the window as they bounced in the wind against the evening sky, and suppressed a sigh. He didn't even know why he'd been summoned to this stupid meeting. The subject he was here to advise on — the adaptation of the local airport to accommodate new Luftwaffe fighters — was listed on the agenda as "Other Business Time Permitting," and as it was now nearing six, it was obvious that his presence was a total waste of time. He could have been with Hedy today. Saturday was usually a good day to avoid her neighbors, with many of them out queuing at the market or visiting family. They could be tucked up in that tiny bed together right now. He felt a surge of resentment as his mind drifted to the mossy scent of her hair, the softness of her fingers, that supple, responsive body.

It was more than that now, though. Of course he'd had girlfriends back home — a couple he'd been quite keen on at the time — but what he'd felt in recent weeks, this new depth of emotion, genuinely shocked him. He found himself thinking about her all the time, wanting to share any interesting moment of the day, longing to hear her voice. It was affecting his attitude to his colleagues too. In the kitchen of his billet, he would often hear the other officers laughing as they swapped stories about some girl they had flirted with, or fucked in the back of the clubhouse. They would slap each other's knees in boyish congratulation over some brunette who had given them head in the back of a car for a kilo of fish, one crowing that he'd had both mother and daughter in return for 200 French cigarettes. Kurt had never felt comfortable around this kind of talk, but now he found it positively distasteful. More than that, it baffled him. What satisfaction lay there? What challenge, what discovery? Sure, at the start it was lust that

had driven him toward Hedy. But now . . .
now it was that internal darkness that kept
him coming back for more. The mix of
anger and sadness in her eyes that masked a
mystery so complex it frightened him. How
could a woman give her body to him with
such abandon yet simultaneously hide so
much? Like a fisherman at the end of the
day who has caught only minnows, but
knows that great, fat fish still swim beneath
the surface, Kurt couldn't drag himself
away.

"Some additional fuel restrictions," Doctor Casper was droning through his inter-
preter, a slight, bespectacled young man
who could have passed for Casper's own
son. "From next week gas will only be available between seven a.m. and two thirty
p.m., and between five thirty and nine p.m.
And Field Command wishes to procure the
contents of the island's current wood stores.
We will, of course, be happy to negotiate a
settlement on an amicable basis."

A new voice piped up: "That firewood is
needed by the local population for heating
and cooking. What if we do not wish to
negotiate?"

Kurt turned his attention back to the table
to see who had spoken. A tired Jerseyman
with thinning gray hair and wire-rimmed

spectacles, who Kurt understood to be the local councillor for labor issues, was glaring at Casper with ill-disguised contempt.

Casper merely shrugged. "Then, Mr. Le Quesne, we will take it anyway. Field Command must place the needs of the island garrison before the needs of . . . Einheimische." Casper wiped his dry lips with his fingers as if the word "locals" had caused an unpleasant taste. "We also require that the contents of your greenhouses be placed at the disposal of the military."

Kurt looked down at the papers before him, careful to keep his expression neutral. Inwardly, he flinched. Every day for months now he'd listened to his colleague Fischer bleat on about the idiocy of the local Superior Council members — these dumb provincials, with their stubborn refusal to accept the natural, common-sense orders of their masters, and their rustic small-mindedness that prevented them from helping themselves. Even Kurt himself, watching Hedy eke out her meager vegetables for the week, had privately wondered if these shortages had more to do with the failings of local agricultural policy than Field Command's interference. Yet here was the new governor stealing food from the locals and not even bothering to lie about it.

"Oh, I think we fully understand the status of the 'locals,' Doctor Casper," Le Quesne chipped back, undimmed. "Your imprisonment of my messenger boy, whose stammer prevented him from apologizing when he brushed against a German officer on the street, made that crystal clear. As has your latest measure — ordering us to seize the proceeds of all Jewish businesses."

Kurt looked to Casper, wondering if this would result in a sharp rebuke or something worse, when another Jersey voice rang out from the far end of the table. It came from a flaky-skinned fellow sporting a mustache and heavy eyebrows.

"I don't believe, Mr. Le Quesne," the newcomer chimed in nasal tones, "that deliberate antagonism will serve anyone here. Last year, you yourself were one of the strongest advocates of the Jersey Superior Council retaining civil authority, that we might act as a bridge of communication, so to speak, between our German visitors and the local population. On that basis, implementation of Doctor Casper's wishes is both our duty and obligation." The speaker turned to Casper and offered him a simpering smile that turned Kurt's stomach.

"I am grateful," Casper replied with a nod, "to Chief Aliens Officer Mr. Clifford Orange for his pragmatic and courteous response. And as time is running on, I believe, on that basis we should conclude."

Casper snapped his folder together, as did his uniformed minions, and rose to his feet. Kurt, grateful for the release, but with his anger still churning, followed the line of obedient uniforms out of the chamber and toward the grand marble stairs of the council building. As they made their way down the steps, he found himself next to Manfred.

Kurt greeted him with a pat on the shoulder. "Hey, Manfred, what did you make of that?" He was careful to keep his voice under the level of communal chatter.

Manfred looked up at him, apparently taken aback to be addressed by a senior officer. "Sir? You mean the meeting?"

"Did you know that we were requisitioning food from the locals to feed the garrison?"

Manfred nodded. Kurt spotted a tic in the boy's eye. "Not surprising, I guess, sir. Our being here has pretty much doubled the population. Only so much they can bring over from France."

"Doesn't really fit with the promise we made, though, does it? About guaranteeing their liberty." Manfred gave no reply, but threw Kurt a tortured look.

"You don't have a view on this?"

"No, sir."

"I thought you wanted to make Oberge-freiter next year?" Kurt pressed him. "If you want to climb the ladder, you have to express an opinion occasionally."

"Yes sir, but . . ."

Sensing his discomfort, Kurt waited for the rest of the contingent to move on before taking Manfred to one side. In the pink reflected glow of the giant swastika flag that hung in the entrance, Kurt took his remaining tobacco from his breast pocket and offered Manfred a hand-rolled cigarette, which the youth happily accepted.

Kurt waited for him to take a deep drag. "But what?"

It was Manfred's turn to lower his voice. "Lieutenant, you're a good guy, sir. I — I admire you, you know? But if people know I've had this kind of conversation with you —"

Kurt raised an eyebrow. "Because of that petrol coupon business?"

"Lieutenant Fischer, he says we need to be careful who we mix with. And that guy with the hat . . ."

"Erich Wildgrube?"

"Yes, him. He drops in at all the barracks,

talks about watching out for the bad apples."

"So much for paying for your mistake and moving on."

"See, sir, my family depends on my wages." Manfred took another deep drag on the precious tobacco, holding it down before he spoke. "Making Obergefreiter is important. They need me to do well, you understand? If it was down to me . . ."

"Don't apologize. You run along. And, Manfred? Don't worry — this conversation never happened, okay?"

Kurt slapped the lad on the shoulder and pushed him toward the door, giving it a moment before he followed. He'd suspected as much, but the confirmation hurt. Fucking Fischer, fucking Wildgrube. Fucking pointless rules and mindless fucking loyalties. He stepped out into the chilly darkness and set off toward the coast road, deciding that the long walk back to Pontac Common would do him good. But his mind continued to bounce from one ugly image to the next. German soldiers loading up barrows from the greenhouses of local farmers. Wildgrube's ugly, pasty face with those furtive little eyes. But mainly Kurt kept thinking of King Canute, sitting stubbornly on his throne, gasping for air between the

crashing waves as the tide moved unceas-
ingly toward him.

The paraffin lamps around the shop gave
off an eerie blue glow, throwing strange,
looming shadows on the tiled walls. From
the darkness of the street, the empty display
window revealed the story within, like
watching a movie on a screen. At the rear,
Anton, in his white apron and pillbox
baker's cap, moved effortlessly around the
room, sweeping the floor and wiping down
surfaces in a series of methodical arcs, while
at the front counter the ebullient Mr. Reis,
visibly slimmer these days, was patiently
explaining to the last customer of the day
that he had nothing left to sell her at any
price. Even from her viewpoint on the
bench across the street, Hedy could see the
woman's desperation as she waved a pair of
children's shoes in front of him, pleading
for a bartering deal on the burnt rejects she
hoped lay under the counter. But the old
man continued to pacify her, smiling apolo-
getically and patting her hand, until eventually she nodded and let herself out through
the shop door, shuffling down the road with
her shopping bag swinging empty at her
side.
The freezing seat penetrated the thin

142

fabric of her coat as Hedy shifted her sitting position. She watched Mr. Reis close the door behind the customer and pull the bolts across — three of them now, due to the recent nighttime raids on food premises — and turn the sign to "Closed." Ten more minutes, and Anton would be upstairs in his apartment. She decided to give it fifteen before she followed him up there; give him time to shake off the bakery dust and feel a little more conversational. Assuming, of course, that he let her in at all.

Her breath came in unsteady little pants as she climbed the stairs. The door to the flat was ajar and she could hear Anton padding around, no doubt trying to figure out what kind of evening meal was possible. As she neared his apartment door, his voice from within took her by surprise.

"Come in, Hedy. I know it's you."

Hedy slunk in, leaving the door open, staying close to the wall. "How did you know?"

"You were sitting on that bench for half an hour. I'm not blind!"

"Can we talk?"

"Yes, but Dory will be here in ten minutes."

Hedy tiptoed across the floor and took her old seat by the window, one leg tucked under her body as always. It was months

143

since she'd been here. How long ago it seemed, cooking that meal for Kurt in this very room.

"You must be freezing. I'm afraid I've nothing much to offer you," Anton continued. "But I can warm some water for you? Maybe with a spoonful of sugar beet syrup?"

Hedy nodded her gratitude, and Anton busied himself in the kitchen area.

"How'd you make the syrup?"

"Skin a turnip and boil it for hours." Anton banged the tap above the sink with the flat of his hand to get it to work properly. "But you didn't come to talk about that, did you?"

Hedy clenched her fists and stared at the back of her hands as she spoke. "I want to apologize. I understand why you're angry. I'm angry with myself. Me and Kurt . . . it was the last thing I wanted to happen, but . . ."

Anton continued to fiddle with pots and matches. "Is it serious?"

"Nothing's been said, exactly, but . . . I really care about him. And I think he feels the same."

"Well, that's something, I suppose." He looked at her properly for the first time. "Sorry I lost my temper. But you're like a sister to me. And the fact that you lied for

144

so long —"

"I was ashamed. And I also wanted to protect you. The less people know, the less trouble they can get into — sometimes it's safer to lie." She rubbed her forehead with the palm of her hand. "And I seem to be getting rather good at it."

"What do you mean? Anything else I ought to know?"

A short silence. To hell with it, she thought. "I'm still stealing coupons for Doctor Maine."

His face was a picture. "What?"

"Actually, I never stopped. I still meet him every week to deliver them. Kurt doesn't know. No one does."

Another silence endured, longer than the first. Then, to her relief he broke it with a grin of disbelief. "For God's sake, Hedy. Do you have a death wish or something?"

"Apparently." A manic giggle escaped from her nose; she attempted to sniff it back up. "Papa always said I never made things easy for myself. But I don't think even he could have imagined this." Another giggle leaked out. "Stealing from my enemy during the day, and sleeping with him at night. I know . . . I must be out of my mind."

The chuckle fizzed between them for a moment, faded. Anton put down the matches. "You have to tell Kurt — I mean, about your race classification. He will find out eventually."

"I'm seeing him tomorrow. I'm going to tell him then."

"And you're prepared for him to end it? Because he'll have to, if he wants to protect himself."

"I know." She got up, crossed over to Anton and gave him a hug. "Thank you. I'm so sorry, Anton. Sometimes I don't know what I'd do without you." But as she spoke the words, she felt a stiffness, a retreat. "What did I say?"

"I haven't been entirely honest with you, either."

The water in the tiny saucepan began to boil but neither of them moved.

Hedy's first thought was that Dorothea was pregnant. "Tell me?"

"I've been drafted."

Hedy's stomach seemed to drop into a lower space. "You mean . . ."

"Letter arrived that day we went to the Opera House. I've not even told Dory yet. I'll be signed up in a few weeks, assigned local duties. After that, who knows? Way things are going, it could be the Eastern Front."

She felt light-headed. Her hand instinc-

146

tively reached out to grasp the countertop and steady herself. "But you're a food producer. You're classed as an essential worker."

"Obviously they've decided they need soldiers more."

Hedy felt her throat closing. She blinked hard but the tears leaked out anyway. "But it's not fair! You're not German!"

"We're both technically German citizens now."

"But you . . . you might . . ."

"Might not come back? Of course. But if I refuse, they'll shoot me anyway."

"Who would shoot you? What's happened?"

Hedy and Anton both whipped around to see Dorothea standing in the doorway, her eyes wide with fear; her grandmother's coat swamped her tiny frame, making her look even more vulnerable. Anton moved quickly toward her and enveloped her in his arms.

"I've had my orders to join the Wehrmacht. I'm so sorry, Dory."

Dorothea let out a howl of despair, burying her face in his chest. "No! No, I need you here! What if you get hurt or killed? I can't bear it!"

Hedy hung back, embarrassed to be a witness to such an intimate moment, yet sensing that to leave now would be as bad. She could hear Dorothea's breaths becoming shorter and wheezier, and tried to recall what Maine's advice had been in the event of another attack. Her eyes darted to Anton's store cupboard, wondering if it contained any mustard. But what happened next pushed any such thoughts from her head.

"I know, and I want to make sure you'll be protected, whatever the future holds," Anton was saying. "That's why today I got this." He reached into his trouser pocket and pulled out a small box. As he opened it, Hedy could just make out the glint of something shiny. "It's not new, of course — it belonged to Mr. Reis's aunt. But it's small, so I think it might fit you. The stone is an opal, I think." Taking Dorothea's hand, he stared into her stunned, tearstained face. "Dorothea, will you marry me?"

Dorothea clapped both hands to her mouth to muffle another cry, this one mixed with joy. "Oh, Anton! Of course I will!" She flung her arms around his skinny body, clinging so hard his spine made a faint cracking sound. They both turned toward Hedy.

"You hear that, Hedy? She said yes! We're getting married!"

Hedy looked from one to the other as they hugged, kissed each other long on the lips, then hugged again. Her throat was still full of rocks from Anton's first news; events were now turning to quicksand beneath her feet. She saw Dorothea's beaming, tear-streaked face and felt a surge of pity and loss, though who it was for, she couldn't say. Eventually she gained enough control to croak out the compulsory sentences: "Congratulations, I'm so happy for you both. Everything will work out, I know it."

She'd been mistaken, she thought, as she gathered up her coat and bag, wished them luck and hurried down the narrow stairs toward the street. She wasn't getting any better at lying at all.

Pulling her scarf tighter around her neck, Hedy perched on one of the granite bollards placed along the quay for boat anchorage, and knocked her feet together to get the blood flowing. The icy gusts from the ocean beyond rippled the black water around the fishing boats. The locals called this little marina, tucked away at the back of the main port, the French Harbour. This had been her idea for a meeting place this evening — quiet but not secluded, private enough for the conversation she planned, but public enough to summon help if things should turn ugly. The road here from the town was lined with harbor warehouses, hulking great slabs with ribbed doors that roared like engines as they were rolled up and down. Behind her rose the vast, impenetrable walls of Fort Regent, raised by Royal Engineers over a century before. This was a charmless, transient place where no one ever lingered, but simply did whatever job needed to be done and moved on. Appropriate, then, for her task today: deliver her message and walk off into the darkness.

All day long, typing reports in that soulless crate of an office, she had played out this moment in her mind, feeling the dread rise. Yet what, exactly, was she dreading? Perhaps he would fly into a rage, but in all these weeks she'd never seen anything to suggest that was likely. Kurt could, in theory, report her to the authorities; miscegenation was unquestionably a sackable offense, and who knew what he might be driven to in desperation. But the fear that nudged persistently, like a rubber band twanging on her wrist, was the anticipation of her own future: months, maybe years, trapped in this island prison, without Kurt for comfort. The secret meetings, the softness of his hand on hers, his kindly questions about her day — they were all that had made the last months bearable. But she had promised Anton, and she knew herself that to stretch this out any further was suicidal. It had to be tonight.

Suddenly she heard a strange sound some distance away — a collective shuffling and heavy breathing, like a herd of small animals. It was getting closer. Anxious, she stood and peered down the road that led back to the Weighbridge and main harbor. In the fragments of remaining light she could just make out an approaching group of people. It wasn't a troop of German soldiers, whose rapping boots could be heard for miles, but there were guards at the fore, wearing the uniform of the Organisation Todt. Then, as they came closer, she saw it. Lumbering toward her was a stinking cloud of broken humanity. Skeletal, shaven-headed men, some old beyond their years, some no more than boys, shuffling along in a frightened pack, their eyes on the ground to avoid those of their guards, who grinned as they swung their rubber truncheons for any imagined offense. Despite the cold, the prisoners were dressed in nothing but rags, their feet bound only in cloth. Several had visible injuries, many others the obvious stains of shit and vomit. As one

151

sharp breeze brought the smell of them into Hedy's nostrils, the bile rose in her throat until she retched. She wanted to turn away, in horror or respect, but could not.

The guards drove their victims on at a quick pace; as they passed by, not one raised his face to look at her; they simply stumbled on, saving every gram of energy for the march ahead. Hedy was so shocked that she hardly noticed Kurt approaching from the opposite direction.

"Did you see that?"

Kurt nodded. "Slave laborers, for the defense construction. Third boatful this week. It's hideous."

"But did you see them? They're half dead already! How can anyone treat human beings that way?" She searched for Kurt's eyes in the gloom, and realized his focus was miles away. Anger erupted inside her. "This is what your people are doing in the name of your superior race! Can you still tell me you don't feel responsible? Do you still think this is nothing to do with you?"

"It's about all of us!" His voice was cracked and sour, a tone she'd never heard before. "You think this stupid fucking war doesn't touch everyone? All our lives will be ruined by this, all of us!"

Hedy stared, stunned, canceling a dozen

questions in her head. She reached out and touched his arm. It was all it took. Kurt sank back onto the granite bollard, made a small choking sound and began to weep. She stood silent for a moment, then slowly put her arms around him and cradled his head on her chest. His sobs shook his body while he tried to get control of himself. When at last he spoke it came in forced, intermittent bursts. "Had a letter from Helmut's mother. His unit was attacked by Russian planes. Some of them made it, but —"

"But?"

"Helmut's tank took a direct hit."

Hedy pulled his head closer to her. "Oh, Kurt, no! Are they certain?"

He nodded. "They identified him by his dog tag." The sobbing began in earnest again. "The last time I saw him, he told me to take care of myself. He told me!"

Hedy said nothing, but continued to hold him, stroking that soft, dark blond hair. She thought again of her parents, perhaps still sitting around that kitchen stove, more likely rounded up onto some truck and driven God knows where. She felt his grief blend with her own, and twist painfully in her chest.

"It's all right, Kurt, it's all right. I'm here.

I'm here."

They stayed there on the frozen quay for what seemed like hours, until Kurt pulled away and stood up straight, brushing the tears from his face.

"I'm sorry. I feel a little better now."

Hedy nodded. "We all need to cry sometimes."

"So what was it you wanted to tell me?"

"Me?"

"You said in your note that you needed to talk to me about something important. It sounded serious."

She looked out across the glistening black water, at the shadowy shapes of the boats. How she'd love to climb into one now and sail away into the void, swallowed up by the darkness. Her voice was tiny. "Yes . . ."

"Well, let me say something first. It's something I've wanted to get out in the open before, for a long time, but I wasn't sure you . . ." She held her breath, half anticipating a question. Did he already know? Perhaps someone at work had said something. His hands reached for her face. "Anyway, tonight I have to say it. Hedy, I love you. I have done since the start. I'm still not sure if you feel the same, but I know this is it for me. I always want us to be together. So it's up to you now." She pressed herself even closer to him, letting herself melt into his body. The buttons of his uniform dug through her coat into her flesh. Her face ached with the contortions of emotion, and she could feel her heart hammering. "So, now it's your turn. What did you want to say?"

Hedy screwed up her eyes. For the first time in years, she wished for a true faith. A faith like her mother's, one that brought the gift of guidance. Yet she already knew what she had to do. Even now, it was not too late. She just had to push her emotions aside, drag common sense back in. Find the kind of strength the rabbis used to talk about, the kind her sister Roda could summon at will. She pulled back to look at him and placed her frozen hand on his face.

"I wanted to tell you . . . that I love you too."

He grinned, and kissed her with passion and tenderness. Afterward, she tried to recall her feelings at that moment — shame, relief, anger? But all she could remember was the pleasure of that kiss.

FIVE

The atmosphere on the street was tangible,
Kurt thought, as he strode along St. Saviours Road in the pink glow of the afternoon
sun. In two weeks it would be Christmas. A
novel kind of holiday this year, one without
turkeys, trees, nuts or even presents for most
of the kids. It would be little better in
Germany, he was sure, but that brought no
comfort here. If you stretched out your
hand into the cold, still air, you could rub
the bitterness between your thumb and
forefinger and feel its grit. The "ghosts"
whom other officers often spoke of — the
glass-eyed, unseeing locals who had for
months ignored every German on the street
as if they were invisible — now stared
directly at Kurt as he walked by. Some
exuded pure hatred, some just the gloating
anticipation that the end was near. It was
now "only a matter of time" they muttered
to themselves or to each other on street

corners, just loud enough for passing soldiers to hear. The game had changed; the tide had turned. The Yanks were in.

Poor fools, Kurt thought. Yes, Pearl Harbor had swung the compass around. But with the Americans focused on the Pacific Theater, it couldn't possibly have much effect in Europe for at least a year, probably more. All this meant was a longer, greater, more destructive war, with no guarantee of victory on either side. And for what? The questioning voices that had whispered to Kurt for months were now shouting so loudly they were waking him in the early hours, leaving him staring at the ceiling while Fischer snored peacefully in the bed beside him. What the hell were they all doing here? Parading around this island in their ridiculous uniforms, torturing foreign prisoners, tormenting the locals with cold and hunger. Just yesterday the senior OT officer had lectured the compound staff on the importance of pride in their great nationalist work. The schedule was vital, he told them, for the security and success of the Fatherland. The same day, Kurt had received Helmut's last letter, dated two weeks before his death. Inside he felt something taking shape, an icy crystal of disgust. He thought of Hedy, the only light in his life, and felt grateful that he'd kept his promise to keep their relationship private. At first he'd thought her obsession with secrecy tiresome, creeping around and inventing stories to satisfy his colleagues' questions. But now, with the locals' attitude shifting, he saw the sense in it.

A twisting murmuration of starlings filled the bright winter sky, and he smiled at the thought of the evening to come. Hedy's nosy downstairs neighbor was away at her sister's, and he was off duty till tomorrow morning. As he passed a forlorn little group of children, singing "Away In A Manger" outside an unrelenting house, he felt a rush of Christmas cheer and goodwill, and flipped two coins into their cloth cap. Turning into New Street, he began the final stretch toward Hedy's building; he imagined her standing by her tiny stove, stirring a pot, and quickened his pace in excitement.

So lost was he in his thoughts that when he first heard the voice he didn't realize it was aimed at him. Only when the shout of "Leutnant!" became "Leutnant Neumann!" did Kurt turn to see the figure on the other side of the street. Wildgrube raised his silly Alpine hat in a greeting as he hurried across the road. Kurt tried his best to smile but suspected the result was unconvincing.

"Good evening, Lieutenant." Wildgrube's voice sounded even more whiny and high-pitched than usual. "And where, may I ask, are you headed this fine afternoon?"

Kurt stared at him, trying to remain expressionless. Was this a coincidence, or was the guy actually following him? If so, for how long? Kurt's immediate concern, though, was that he was no more than ten meters from Hedy's front door.

"Actually, I was just taking a stroll." It sounded fake and Kurt knew it.

Wildgrube's smile was stretched to breaking point but his eyes were empty. "Really? Around here?" He looked about him with theatrical puzzlement. "Hardly the most scenic choice!"

"I thought I might head up to Vallée des Vaux — it's about fifteen minutes that way. Still green up there this time of year. Have you been?"

The policeman corrected the angle of his hat as he replaced it on his head. "I confess I have not. I did not know that you were such a keen walker?"

Kurt kept his expression friendly, doing a dozen lightning calculations in his head. If Wildgrube had followed him all the way from his billet, he must be receiving information on Kurt's movements. Had he

159

received a tip-off of some kind, and if so, from whom? Fischer was the most likely candidate; he had hardly spoken to Kurt for weeks following Kurt's prison sentence, and he and Wildgrube were definitely chummy. But Kurt was always discreet around Fischer, and it was doubtful the Nazi had anything specific to report. Kurt's guess was that this was a simple fishing expedition.

He smoothed back his hair to indicate composure. "Keeps me out of trouble." He hoped Wildgrube would appreciate the self-deprecating reference, but the spy's expression didn't change. If Kurt was going to throw him permanently off the scent, he was going to have to come up with something good. "All right, Erich, you've got me. I'm not planning to walk up Vallée des Vaux . . ." He tried to look suitably embarrassed. "I heard there was a new 'officers' club,' over on Rouge Boullion. One of the guys in my house went last week, came back with some stories! I thought I might stop by."

At this, Wildgrube smiled properly, with intent. The effect was rather chilling. "Ah! You are looking for some female company, perhaps? The kind whose company is, let's say, reliable in its outcome?"

"Exactly." Kurt forced out a laugh. "Like I said, you got me."

Wildgrube joined in his laughter. "You don't have to be embarrassed about such natural needs, Lieutenant! Tell you what — I wouldn't mind checking out the place myself. Would you mind signing me in?"

Frustration rose in Kurt's gullet and threatened to choke him. The trap had snapped shut — any lie he told now would be too obvious, and he had no doubt Wildgrube would follow him anyway. Now he would be stuck with this reptile for the rest of the night, while Hedy waited alone up there, confused and disappointed. He longed to glance up at her window to throw her some explanatory look. But he kept his eyes firmly fixed on Wildgrube's face and, accepting his fate, pulled the plug.

"Sure, if you like."

"Great. After we both get laid I will buy you a nice Scotch whisky. How about that? It will be a chance for us to get to know each other better."

Kurt's brain continued to whir as they set off up the road. Perhaps there was an advantage to this nightmare. If Wildgrube still had Kurt marked as a potential trouble-maker, this was Kurt's chance to allay suspicions, maybe even soften him up for information in the future. He planned the evening out in his mind — he'd been through enough of these nights back home to know how it would go. Wildgrube would knock back a couple of whiskies then make a big deal of picking the "best" woman in the place. Meanwhile, Kurt would cover his tracks with the youngest, most vulnerable kid he could find, and pay her for a half-hour conversation about her family, tipping her enough to buy any lies he required later. He and Wildgrube would drink the rest of the night away, while Kurt threw in a few remarks about his previous "foolishness" for good measure. That way, the night would at least be an investment. It was the thought of not being able to let Hedy know that hurt the most.

Only when they were a good twenty meters past Hedy's door did Kurt make the excuse of retying his bootlace in order to sneak a glance up at her window. He had barely a second to take it in, but swore he saw her at the edge of the attic pane, peeping down into the street. Not daring to make even the smallest sign, he took a deep breath before rejoining Wildgrube for the short walk to the officers' club and the miserable young whores who waited for them.

"Maybe a little tighter around the waist?

I'm so skinny now — well, who isn't these days! I don't want it to hang off me or I'll look like I'm wearing an old sack!"

Dorothea giggled and pulled the dress tighter on her body, indicating to Hedy where the fabric should sit.

Hedy, squinting with concentration, pulled the darts a little further out and pushed the pins into place. "Like that?"

Dorothea stepped down from the chair and stood back, craning her neck to try to view the dress from different angles. Hedy took the tiny vanity mirror from her dressing table and held it up for her, wishing that her landlord provided a full-length mirror as part of the furnishings.

"That's much better. I love the texture of this dimity, don't you? I mean, it would have been lovely to have something new . . ."

Hedy obediently rubbed the fabric between her fingers. "Yes, but no one expects new clothes these days, even for a wedding. Anton's borrowing a suit from Mr. Reis's son, isn't he?"

"I know." Dorothea sighed. "It's just . . . you know how you always planned your wedding, dreamed about what you would wear, right from when you were a little girl?" Hedy raised her brows as if in agreement, even though it was a topic she'd never

163

given a moment's thought. "I even used to walk my dolly down the hallway to 'Here Comes The Bride,' with an old lace curtain draped over her head! Still, this is a lovely dress. And I think with that little white hat . . ." She twirled herself around Hedy's apartment, her head flicking back for approval.

Hedy opted for a stock response. "You'll look lovely. Anton will be proud of you. But you should probably take it off now — it's like an icebox in here. And you don't want to get it dirty before the big day."

Dorothea unzipped herself at the side and wriggled out of the dress, trying to avoid the pins, babbling as she did so. "Still can't believe I spotted that hat in the exchange adverts. I mean, what are the chances of the perfect hat popping up just this week? Well worth a bar of soap and an old bedsheet! Now all I need is gloves to match, but that's probably overoptimistic."

Hedy sneaked a glance at Dorothea's pale, bony body beneath her slip, wondering how much of it Anton had seen and what he would think of it. She wondered if that was how she looked to Kurt; perhaps it was fortunate not having a proper mirror after all. "And listen, Hedy, I wanted to say thank you for doing this. I loved making things before we had to trade the Singer, but I've never been much good at hand-sewing. My grandmother would have helped if she could, of course, but her eyesight is so poor now. Then I thought of you, and when Anton told me you'd volunteered, I was just . . . well, it means a lot to me."

Hedy, avoiding Dorothea's eyes, knelt on the floor and placed the pins back in their old tobacco tin one at a time. She knew what her mother would call her at this moment — a Farshtinkiner, a louse. Only three days earlier, Hedy had visited Anton at the bakery. She'd gone on the excuse of returning a borrowed book, but in truth intended to talk to him about this marriage, perhaps even persuade him not to go through with it. She'd even maneuvered him into the privacy of the bakery's backyard, away from prying ears. If she could just make him see that he had only proposed through guilt, through a fear of leaving Dorothea without a widow's pension . . . Surely he would understand this was no basis for a marriage?

Of course, the conversation had never got that far. No sooner had Anton closed the outer door, he had badgered her about Kurt, demanding to know what had happened — had she told him the truth? How had he reacted, were they still together?

Hedy rushed headlong into a passionate defense of her procrastination: if Anton had only seen Kurt that night! The man was broken, and it would have been inhuman to pile on so much grief in one day. And she'd honestly intended to tell him at their next meeting, if only Kurt had not been followed by that dreadful secret police officer. But she would tell him the truth the next day, she swore, or at least the day after. And as her mouth sprayed its pitiful nonsense, she watched Anton nod wearily, his hair and lashes covered in fine gray flour, too stooped and exhausted by his impending conscription to argue. She knew he saw right through her. Overwhelmed by her own hypocrisy and spinelessness, Hedy had hurried from the bakery without bringing up the wedding at all, guiltily agreeing over her shoulder to help in any way she could. She'd slouched home, comparing the open, straightforward girl she'd been at school with the selfish, scheming reflection that now jumped out at her from dark shop windows. This infected boil of lies and self-delusion swelled a little more each day, contaminating people who were supposed to love each other, poisoning her own soul. She cursed this stupid, pointless war.

She looked up at Dorothea and forced a

smile. "You're welcome. I just hope I do a good enough job."

"I know you will. And you must come round for supper at the new house. Did I tell you about the place Anton's found for us on West Park Avenue?"

"You did."

"The rent's a bit steep, but it's got the prettiest fireplace in the front room and a sweet little yard at the back."

"And brass knobs on all the doors," Hedy chipped in, hoping she'd take the hint.

Oblivious, Dorothea slipped her shoes back on and wriggled into her old woolen dress. "I can't wait to be Mrs. Anton Weber! Now, here's your invitation." She pulled a homemade card from her bag, cut from some old packaging and painted in what looked like whitewash.

Hedy read the text, handwritten in pen and ink: Dorothea Le Brocq and Anton Weber request the pleasure of Hedy and Kurt at the States of Jersey Register Office, followed by a reception at 7 West Park Avenue.

"I know how sensitive you are about your relationship," Dorothea added, "but it would be wonderful if you wanted to bring him."

Hedy shook her head. "I'm sorry, it's just

not possible. Kurt and I can't be seen together in public."

Dorothea reached out for her hand. Her fingers were like ice. "But you've been courting for months now, and we've still not met him! What if he just came to the reception at our place? No one there would judge you."

Hedy reread the card. "I thought you wanted the reception at the Pierson pub?"

Dorothea kept her eyes and fingers on the buttons of her dress, even though it seemed to Hedy that she had already finished buttoning it. "We were, but it seemed a waste of money for just five or six of us."

"Five or six? But what about your family, friends?"

"Well, Nana will come to the ceremony, of course!" The false brightness splintered in her voice. "But she won't have the stamina for the reception too. And Mr. Reis has to run the shop. So it's just you and Kurt, Doctor Maine if he's free — and I'm hoping my schoolfriend Sandy will come, if her dad agrees."

"But your parents?" Hedy felt a wave of pity.

"We're honestly happy with a small do. It'll save us trying to scrape together food for lots of people."

Hedy watched Dorothea fold up her wedding dress with ritualistic care, stroking the fabric as if it were a kitten, placing it in a neat bundle on Hedy's table. She continued to touch it, as if the garment held some magic power she didn't quite understand, yet believed in utterly. Once more, Hedy wondered what she was really thinking. The woman seemed almost ethereal at times, a spirit from another world. But when she spoke again her voice was stronger. "We just want our best friends there, that's all that matters!" She patted the bundle down and managed a big, generous grin. "So, you see, there's no reason why Kurt shouldn't come."

Hedy decided the safest course was to let the subject drop. "Thank you. I'll think about it."

Dorothea pulled on her coat, arranged her hat and headed for the door. "Thanks again for this, Hedy. If there's ever anything I can do for you in return . . ."

Hedy hesitated. She had, in actual fact, been brewing an idea for several weeks, but was still unsure if she wanted to ask such a huge favor of this ditsy girl. Deciding that this was not the right time, she was about to say no, when Dorothea, evidently detecting something in her body language, stopped with her hand still on the door latch. Hedy found herself pinned by those intense eyes glinting from the other side of the room.

"What is it? Tell me?" said Dorothea.

"It's nothing. At least, it can wait till after the wedding." Hemingway rubbed himself against her leg, as if prompting Hedy to ask the question.

"Please, Hedy. Anything?"

"Well, it's just that . . . I've heard nothing from my parents in twenty months, nor they from me. They can't even receive mail in Vienna, being Jewish."

Dorothea shook her head. "It's so unfair."

"But I have an old school friend, Elke, who I think still lives there. If I use a false name and I'm careful what I say, I think I can slip a letter into the franking pile at work. But what I need is a safe return address . . ."

"So how can I help?"

Hedy suppressed a sigh, and reminded herself that Dorothea was doing her best to be helpful. "I was wondering if I could write care of your new house?"

Dorothea blossomed. "Oh, of course! Use our address by all means."

Hedy nodded. "Thank you. It's a . . . what is the English phrase? A long shot. But it's

170

all I have." It was Hedy's turn to pat the wedding dress. "I'd better be getting on with this."

Dorothea waved goodbye with her fingertips, the way a child waves to its mother, as she let herself out the door, and Hedy heard the fading sound of her feet skipping down the stairs and the humming of the wedding march in her high, frail voice. Hedy picked the dress up from the table to plan her work, wondering, with an unsettled feeling, how long that voice would be a significant sound in her life.

The day was cold and monochrome, but the wind had dropped and the bulbous flint-colored clouds were still clinging to their rain. Hedy stepped as lightly as she could across the Royal Square, walking carefully so as not to disturb the ancient glue on the sole of her shoe, and enjoying the sensation of wearing stockings for the first time in months. She had been saving them for weeks, for just such a special occasion. Of course Kurt must have bought them on the black market, and they must have cost him an absurd amount of money, which made her feel both guilty and delighted. She wore the same old crepe dress and the same old cardigan she wore for every event other than

171

work, but the slippery thrill she felt when her legs brushed together did give a sense of occasion to the day.

She was unsure which door led to the registrar's office, but as she turned the corner by the town church, the crowd on the steps led her straight to it. Hedy watched as a family party gathered on the steps. The bride was a local lass of no more than seventeen, with an empire line dress that Hedy was pretty sure was designed to hide the middle trimester of pregnancy. Holding her hand, wearing a suit he'd probably had since school and an expression of pure misery, was a spotty youth, hemmed in between a surly, stocky man Hedy took for the bride's father and his slit-mouthed wife in a tight floral dress. A shotgun wedding if ever Hedy had seen one — yet the steps were crowded with siblings, aunts and cousins, kissing the bride and clucking around, glad of the excuse to break their grim, daily routine with a family celebration.

Hedy squeezed past them and into the building, following the signs until she found the waiting area. She found herself in a vapid charmless space, despite its gleaming oak floor, and only a stone's throw away from the Aliens Office where she'd been interviewed by Orange, over a year ago. It had the same smell of wood and musty papers, and oozed municipality, bringing to mind shuffling queues for permits and bored secretaries smashing down on staplers. Two wedding parties sprawled over the plain benches against the wall, laughing and chatting excitedly. On the third bench sat Anton and Doctor Maine, silent and expressionless.

Hedy stood in the doorway for a moment, taking in the two of them. Doctor Maine was in his Sunday best, but she could plainly see the scruffy old shoes beneath his flannel trousers. He looked abandoned, somehow, almost derelict, his skin dry and sallow. She had never found out how old he actually was. Younger than his face suggested, she was sure of that. But they had agreed early on to keep conversations, and especially personal details, to a minimum: it was unwise to be seen chatting together too regularly, and safer to remain in ignorance in case either of them should ever be caught. All Hedy knew from their snippets of conversation was that his wife was effectively an invalid, and that he had very little in his life beyond his work. On several occasions, when Kurt brought Hedy little treats of tobacco or fresh rabbit meat from the German stores, she had passed on what she could to the doctor, knowing that he had no access to such luxuries. He never asked questions, just smiled with gratitude and tucked the contraband away in his medical bag before hobbling away up the road. She had never heard him complain about anything. Abandoning caution just this once, she leaned across to kiss his cheek.

"How are you, Doctor Maine?"

"I'm well, my dear. And please, call me Oliver."

Hedy sat down between them, pulling her coat down over her knees to hide the two moth holes in her dress, and turned to Anton. His suit was oversized, but it was a quality cut in dark charcoal gray, and with the sprig of wild cyclamen in his buttonhole, and his roguish hair beaten down with the last of Mr. Reis's Brylcreem, he looked genuinely handsome. Hedy gave him her broadest grin.

"You look very smart." She brushed his shoulders, feeling the subtle padding of his jacket beneath her fingers.

"Thanks. Is Dory here yet?"

"Don't worry, she's on her way! Remember she's bringing her grandmother. I imagine she can't walk very fast." She trawled her mind for a safe topic of conversation. "Is Dorothea's friend coming? Sandy, is it?"

"Apparently not. Will Kurt be joining us later?"

She opted to keep it simple: "I'm afraid he couldn't get the time off."

Anton shrugged. "More sherry for us, then."

They sat waiting in silence. In the unusual warmth of the crowded room Hedy's eyelids began to droop, and her mind drifted to the last wedding she'd been to, around five years earlier. Her cousin, draped in white lace over satin, swirling through the local hall; the melodies of the klezmer band; the thunder of three score pairs of feet on the dance floor. Otto had told his favorite joke about the tailor while his wife pretended to scold him, and her parents had danced together as if they were teenagers. Hedy opened her eyes, found herself staring at the lattice windows and the naked branches of the trees in the churchyard, and stifled a sigh.

Moments later, Dorothea arrived, resplendent in her fitted dress and hat. She was accompanied by her grandmother, a bird of a woman with gnarled arthritic hands, but with the same look of wilful determination that Hedy recognized well. Dorothea's eyes glistened with excitement behind the bird-cage net that hung across her face, painstakingly arranged to look like a casual draping. She hugged her husband-to-be, then took Hedy's hands in hers and squeezed hard.

"It means everything that you're here today," she whispered.

A small, neat official approached them with a clipboard. "Le Brocq-Weber party?" His voice was clear and traveled easily, and he pronounced Anton's surname with an excessive German accent. Hedy glanced around, and saw every pair of eyes across the waiting room slowly turn toward the three of them. Adults pulled children closer, older locals made a clucking sound with their tongues, and heads bowed together, muttering at a volume too low to hear, but Hedy knew what the content was. And without any doubt at all, it contained the word "Jerrybag." She glanced at Dorothea to see if she had noticed, but the bride-to-be was fiddling with the buttons on her gloves and grinning at everyone in her party.

"Shall we go in?"

The five of them pressed into the little ceremony room, fitted with nothing but a few chairs, a plain blue rug and heavy oak desk. Before the Occupation there would no doubt have been beautiful arrangements of flowers set around the room, and perhaps a musician in the corner playing harp or guitar. Both Dorothea's grandmother and Doctor Maine hurried toward the seats at the very front, as if to give the impression of an enthusiastic throng. Almost before everyone was settled, the registrar began reading from his book, and Anton and Dorothea were muttering the few essential phrases as instructed. Anton slipped onto her finger a slim gold band — a sacrifice that Hedy knew had cost him his last warm sweater ("I'll be in uniform in a few weeks anyway" he'd pointed out with a shrug). And then it was over. Anton and Dorothea kissed each other self-consciously, and her grandmother applauded the happy couple, though it was barely audible in her soft cotton gloves. The five of them traipsed out of the room and into the street, where the old lady threw some homemade confetti made from the ripped pages of Dorothea's movie magazines, and everyone laughed for no reason, and stood looking at each other on the chilly gray pavement.

"Well," Anton volunteered eventually, "I suppose that's that. Shall we go?"

Kurt's feet ached; they filled his boots like throbbing weights as he dragged them up the pathway toward the door of his billet. He could feel each toe, swollen and stinking, in the thick wool of his socks — socks that hadn't been washed in at least four days. All he wanted in the world at that moment was a bowl of warm water and a chair. He wasn't even bothered about lunch, or the fact that he'd forgotten to go to the officers' supply store for more tobacco. Nothing mattered now except to get his damn feet into the open air and give them a good soak.

For three days solid now he'd been working seventeen-hour days, arriving at the compound at first light and returning to Pontac Common long after the evening meal had been cleared away. Yet still new orders continued to clog up his pigeonhole. In recent weeks the stream of foreign workers had become a flood, causing construction activity around the coast to rocket, and, exponentially, the orders for trucks to more than double. Trucks for material transportation, trucks for moving men from one site to another, trucks for tools and cooking utensils and food supplies — the last of which Kurt suspected was for the OT guards, rather than the poor devils toiling under them. More manpower at the compound had been promised, but had not yet arrived, and last night, sick with exhaustion, Kurt had announced that he would be taking Saturday afternoon and evening off, and if Field Command had anything to say about it they could take it up with him on Monday morning. Now he had one overriding hope — that either the kitchen or his own shared room would be peacefully empty, and that he could spend the next few hours on his backside, feeling water swirl around his toes and reading a trashy novel.

As he pushed the door of the little house, he knew instantly that his first wish was not to be granted. Loud voices and the smell of French cigarettes poured from the kitchen, where three officers were engaged in a highly competitive game of auction rummy. As he headed for the stairs Kurt shook his head, musing at the odd, pointless ways young soldiers found to fritter away their free time. But of course, he considered, he was hardly planning to use the afternoon any more productively. Remembering where he should have been, he felt a niggle of annoyance. He adored Hedy, no question. But dear Lord, she could be an irritating little tyke at times.

It had been a fractious, difficult evening at her apartment last week, resulting in the closest they had come to an argument since their first date. Kurt had spotted the home-made wedding invitation propped up on Hedy's dressing table, and questioned her deliberate avoidance of the whole topic. Surely, he argued, this was the ideal day to meet everyone? Wouldn't it be rude to refuse? Hedy, who was frying up some chicken livers he'd brought her on the little electric ring, and had been in a splendid mood till that moment, immediately went on the defensive. They'd had this discussion a hundred times! Secrecy was paramount, as Kurt knew, so why was he even contemplating the idea? It was such an overreaction that Kurt became instantly irritated, and got hold of the argument like a puppy with a slipper.

"I understand you wouldn't want me at the ceremony," he protested, scattering cutlery on the table with unnecessary force. "But if the reception literally consists of the happy couple, you and your doctor friend, in a private house, I really don't see the problem."

"Someone might see you coming in."

"Someone might see me coming here! You know I'm always careful. And Anton will be a Wehrmacht soldier himself in a few weeks' time."

"Exactly. They've got enough problems with Dorothea's family boycotting the whole day, without us adding to it."

"Surely that would make them even keener to see a friendly face! Are you ashamed of me or something?"

"Of course not." She sounded genuine, but he noticed she kept her attention on the chicken livers.

"Then what's this really about?"

But he never did get a satisfactory answer, and later he'd found the invitation torn up in her rubbish bin. Lying awake later that night, listening to Hedy's soft snores beside him, Kurt decided that it was some kind of psychological block she had developed. She'd overthought this meeting with her friends, building it up in her mind until it became an unassailable mountain. As soon as the wedding was over, Kurt decided to confront it. After all, some day in the not-too-distant future, it would be him and Hedy toasting their future together. They'd never actually discussed it, but given their mutual feelings it seemed inevitable. What kind of wedding would they have, if she couldn't come to terms with the fact that he'd been forcibly conscripted into this damn army?

The thin afternoon light seeped through

181

the landing window as he plodded up the stairs toward his room, his lumpen feet feeling like sacks of coal on the treads. In his mind, he struck bargains with some imagined deity, promising all kinds of generous behavior in the week ahead, if he could just get a few hours to himself. But as he pushed the door open, the first thing he saw was Fischer sitting at the little writing desk, files and papers piled in front of him. Kurt did little to hide his frustration, and by the look on Fischer's face the disappointment was mutual. Pulling off his boots with a sigh of relief, Kurt hurled himself onto his bed without speaking for several minutes, wondering whether he had the energy to fill the china bowl on the washstand, but eventually he felt compelled to be polite.

"Are they making you take the office home with you now?"

"Idiots in there don't even know how to calculate a percentage," Fischer snapped back. Kurt suppressed a smirk. Fischer had been transferred from agriculture to one of the internal security departments a fortnight earlier, a change Kurt assumed would suit him perfectly, but the man had been in a filthy mood ever since.

"Percentages of what?"

"Payments from Jew undertakings, as laid

out in the fifth order. Ninety percent of proceeds to the Jersey Department of Finance and Economics, ten percent to the General Commissioner for the Jewish Question. I mean, how hard is that?"

Kurt hauled himself to his feet and shuffled over to the washstand. Yes, there was water in the jug — it was cold, but the thought of going downstairs to heat it up was too grueling. He poured some into the bowl and shuffled back to his bed.

"There can't be many cases to check, though, surely? I mean, there's only a handful of Jews on the island?"

"Quite enough," Fischer spat from the side of his mouth, "to cause problems. All have to be accounted for, whether they own businesses or not. Little rats get everywhere. You know they've even got one of them working for us?"

Kurt pulled off his socks, noting with some glee Fischer's wrinkling nose as the pungent smell reached his nostrils, and plunged his feet into the water. Immediately he wished he'd made the journey downstairs for hot — this was not the sensation he wanted at all. "Who's that, then?" He was barely listening. Since his conversation with Manfred a few weeks back, Kurt had decided to let Fischer's regular rants go in one ear and out the other.

"Some Jew bitch in your compound, working as a translator. Bercu?" He flipped a sheaf of paper. "Yes, Hedwig Bercu. Good job the other employees don't know what she is, there'd be a riot. I mean what kind of message does that send, putting one of them on our own payroll?"

Kurt sat very still. The sensation of the icy water around his feet seemed to be spreading, as if the cold was moving up through his legs and into his chest. "Did you say Hedwig Bercu?"

Fischer nodded. "Why? You know her?"

Kurt felt his head shaking, though he didn't recall trying to move it. "No . . . Heard the name perhaps." Fischer's eyes were on his face, curious, searching. "Are you sure she's a Jew?"

"It's on her identity card, signed off at the local Aliens Office!" Fischer sniffed with irritation and turned back to his papers, though Kurt sensed he was still being watched. "Too bloody soft, this administration. I'd have had the lot of them on a boat the first week . . ." His voice became fainter, turned into white noise.

Very slowly Kurt removed one foot, then the other, from the bowl of water. Two foot-shaped dark patches formed on the rug next to his bed. His feet were no longer painful, but his heart was banging in his chest and he felt a little queasy. After what he hoped was an acceptable pause, he stood up.

"I'll leave you in peace. Got something I need to do."

It was a sweet little house, Hedy thought, as the four of them trooped up West Park Avenue, self-conscious in their best clothes, chattering gaily to keep embarrassment at bay. Not a fancy property, but a good location, and you could see the blue of St. Aubin's bay from the end of the road. It formed part of a terrace, a well-kept row of Victorian villas on the western edge of town, with bays at the front and attractive arched windows on the upper floors, highlighted with decorative stones in contrasting colors. Anton had done well to find a place like this, and on a private's wages; no wonder Dorothea was so excited about it.

Anton opened the door with a flourish, and made a big comedic fuss about lifting Dorothea over the threshold, even though he could probably have lifted her tiny frame one-handed.

Giggling like a child, Dorothea beckoned Hedy and Doctor Maine inside from the hallway. "Come in, come in. My grandmother gave us a bottle of sherry that's almost three-quarters full! Anton, we can get to use those new glasses Hedy gave us!"

Hedy winced, thinking of the two uninspiring glasses she had found in the exchange adverts in the Post, which were certainly not designed for sherry. But she and the doctor trooped in behind them, both making the requisite oohs and aahs as they entered the small formal sitting room at the front of the house. Hedy's first impression was that it was remarkably tidy, but she quickly realized that it was, in fact, just very empty. There was nothing on the walls but a patterned paper from the turn of the century; the only seats were two simple wooden chairs and a green baize foldaway table designed for playing cards. Doctor Maine offered one seat to Dorothea, and Hedy insisted the doctor take the other, making herself as comfortable as she could on the bare floorboards and trying to look as if this was the most natural position in the world, while praying that the rough wood beneath her legs wouldn't make runs in her precious new nylons.

Anton came in carrying the bottle of sherry, the new glasses and two chipped teacups Hedy recognized from his old apartment, and proceeded to pour everyone a drink. Dorothea apologized for the cold and promised that it would warm up once they got a fire going. The little group leaned in to clink their vessels together.

"To the happy couple," Doctor Maine volunteered. "May your life together be long and joyful." Hedy took a sip and threw Dorothea a nervous look, hoping that the irony of the toast, indeed the entire day, wouldn't tip her into tears. But the bride was grinning from ear to ear, her head perpetually tipping against Anton's jacket and her fingers constantly wiggling to touch some part of him. She was thoroughly relishing every second of the occasion.

"I just wish we could have taken some photographs," she burbled, "but we plan to go to Scott's and have some taken in the next few days. I mean, you must have a reminder of the happiest day of your life, mustn't you?"

"And guess what?" Anton volunteered. "Mr. Reis's family saved some of their ration for us. We've got some delicious Pont-l'Evêque cheese with enough bread to make toast. And Dory's grandmother has made us a delicious caraway seed cake. So we can celebrate in style."

"I'll get some plates from the kitchen," said Dorothea, draining her sherry glass.

"No, let me," Hedy chipped in, eager to get her rapidly chilling body off the freezing floor, and even more eager to eat. "A bride on her wedding day should do nothing but sit and look beautiful! I'm sure I can find everything." She pulled herself up and started toward the kitchen.

That was when it came. A loud rat-a-tat-tat on the front door. Not the cautious, friendly knock of a curious neighbor, but the determined, righteous hammering of one who expects to be admitted. For a second, everyone froze. Dorothea's smile vanished, replaced by a look of bewilderment. Hedy looked anxiously toward Anton, knowing that he, too, suspected one of Dorothea's family might show up to cause trouble. Handing his teacup of sherry to his bride, he marched quickly into the hallway with the stance of someone expecting a fight, while the three of them sat very still, listening. The visitor spoke before Anton could get a word out, and as he did so, Hedy's stomach lurched.

"I'm sorry to interrupt your party, but I must speak to Hedy at once." Seeing the color drain from her face, Doctor Maine and Dorothea both gaped at Hedy, while they all waited for the next sentence. "I am Kurt Neumann. Could you get her for me,

188

please?"

Hedy stumbled into the hallway. Kurt, in uniform, was standing on the doorstep. For some reason he seemed taller than usual. Hedy's voice came out as a croak. "I thought you had to work today?"

"May we speak in private?"

His formality terrified her. But somewhere inside she already knew the reason, and from the look of him, Anton did too.

Anton gestured to the end of the hallway. "Please, be my guest."

Hedy walked down the hall into the unfamiliar kitchen, hearing Kurt's footsteps directly behind her but not daring to turn and look at his face. They found themselves in a dull, chilly little room with black-and-green checked linoleum, and a gas water heater over a deep ceramic sink. The gas supply was currently on, and Hedy could hear the sputtering of the tiny flame inside the white metal cylinder. Strange, she thought, the rooms in which your life changes forever are never the places you would imagine. She positioned herself by a small leaf table covered with a chenille tablecloth, and forced herself to face him, though she kept her eyeline firmly on his knees.

"What is it?" The question was insulting

189

and she knew it.

"Fischer says your registration card classifies you as Jewish. Is it true? Are you?"

Even now — and she marveled at her own idiocy — part of her was still preparing to continue the lie. She thought about the story she had used at the Aliens Office about her surname being inherited and having no Jewish blood, and almost began to tell it again. But when she opened her mouth, nothing came out. In that second she realized she was exhausted by the pretense, sick of the imagined scenarios. Whatever was about to happen, it was better that it was now.

"Yes." Her body began to tremble. She tried to calm herself by picking at the tassels of the tablecloth, twisting them between her fingers. Still she couldn't bring herself to look at his face, but the bewilderment in his voice told her everything.

"I told you that very first evening that I didn't believe in any of that master-race nonsense." He paused, selecting and rejecting various sentences. "Since I've been here, witnessed what's happened, that feeling has only grown stronger. And you knew that." Another pause. "So after all we've been through together the last few months, all that we've said . . ." He fell silent. The sputtering of the gas flame filled the painfully empty space. "I've only got one question: why? Why didn't you tell me?"

Hedy had assembled three of the tassels, and began to plait them. She remembered how she used to plait Roda's hair in her bedroom, finishing it off with a silken bow.

"I wanted to. But I left it too long. I didn't know how you'd react."

He gave a snort of disbelief. "For heaven's sake, Hedy! I spent two weeks in that stinking jail for you! But apparently" — his arms rose in exasperation then dropped back to his sides, lifeless — "apparently that meant nothing."

"Of course it did . . . does . . . it means everything. I'd have been arrested if it wasn't for you."

"Yet you still thought I was capable of turning against you?"

Hedy began another plait, then returned to the first. She could feel the fabric start to fray in her fingers. Soon that section would be completely bald.

"I know it's hard to understand, but you don't know what it's like to be picked out, hated by everyone."

"Try walking down King Street in full Wehrmacht uniform —"

"It's not the same! When the Anschluss

191

came, I saw people turn on us. People who'd been friends for years, who we thought we trusted. Hiding becomes an instinct. I hated lying to you, but . . ." With a supreme effort, she lifted her eyes. The hurt she saw was shocking. "I'm sorry. I was just . . . scared."

"But this wasn't just about you. You've put me in danger too, without my knowledge, or consent."

"I know."

For a long moment he said nothing. Then his features softened and he took a step toward her, stretching out his hand to touch her fingers with the ends of his own. She let go of the tassels as she felt the softness of his skin.

"Hedy, I would never do anything to hurt you."

She bit her lip, a chastised child sent into a corner. Her logic of the last few months was disintegrating, and suddenly seemed ridiculous. This war had driven out every gram of trust she once had. "You mean it?"

"I swear."

The ball of anxiety in her stomach began to unravel and she felt a swell of optimism. "I know that now." She reached out her other hand, but as she did so, he released her and pulled his arm backward. Instantly, something shifted in the space between them. The room grew colder, tiny icicles seemed to form within her bones.

"Yes, I think you do. But it's too late."

The icicles broke into every organ. It was hard to catch her breath. "Why?"

"If you can hide something so important for so long, treat me like the enemy, compromise my safety . . ." He shrugged, drained. "Without trust, there's no point going on."

Hedy could hear her teeth grinding in her head. Her jaw felt stiff. "I said I'm sorry . . . and I mean it."

Kurt shook his head. "I know . . . and I believe you. But it makes no difference."

It was too much. Every nerve in her now felt raw and exposed. A wall rose up, high and protective. "That's an excuse. You just don't want to risk being with me, now that you know. You're scared you'll be charged with Rassenschande, lose your commission and be packed off to the Russian Front."

His face changed at that moment. She could feel the fury.

"You know damn well that's not true. I'd have willingly taken that chance." He turned and walked back toward the kitchen door. "You know that first night, when you were angry with me? Called me a coward for getting swept along by the Nazi machine? I've thought a lot about that. I'd actually decided you were right. But now . . . now I think you're the coward. Goodbye, Hedy."

She heard his footsteps in the hallway, his mumbled apology to Anton and Dorothea for spoiling their day, and the sound of the front door slamming shut. Just at that moment, the gentle popping of the gas light in the cylinder fizzled out.

The last thing she recalled was Anton's concerned voice asking if she was all right, the soft swish of her body sliding down the wall onto her haunches, and the gasping of her lungs as she dropped her head onto her arms and sobbed.

SIX

1942

There was sleet in the air. Fine feathery specks whirled in corkscrews, then vanished into dark spots as they landed on the pavement. Every person shuffling along the street, bundled against the wind in threadbare old coats hunted down from cobwebbed attics, kept their chins on their chests and elbows tucked close to their bodies, occasionally releasing a hand to brush away the frozen flecks. How sad, Hedy thought, that something so fragile and beautiful could cause such pain; her fingers, gripped around the straps of her battered handbag, were now a cruel, livid purple, and stinging as if her skin had been torn away.

She hesitated at the junction, considering a detour via Rimington's, the fruit seller at the top of King Street — a rumor had gone around her building last night that some early rhubarb had been spotted in the town. But a diversion that way would mean coming back past the Aliens Office, and after last month's encounter Hedy decided she would prefer to miss out altogether than clap eyes on that hated place. She walked on, trying to push the memory of that meeting from her mind, but anger brought it bouncing back. The officiousness of the assistant registrar, and his imperviousness to her obvious distress as she'd showed him the brief official note she'd been handed by Feldwebel Schulz the day before.

You are instructed that all registered Jews are requested to attend an interview with German Field Command at College House. Jews must present themselves at the address below at the earliest opportunity.

No reason, no explanation. Hedy had rushed down to the bureau in the faint hope that they might offer some kind of strategy or information. But the registrar had merely scratched his head, shrugged and said that if the Germans wished to see her, she'd be advised to comply. Hedy had thanked him in a tone bordering on sarcasm and walked out, already resolute that she would do no such thing. She tamped her anxiety down, telling herself that given the mere handful of Jews involved, the implementation of the order might be postponed, perhaps eventually overlooked. But hope and optimism were scarce commodities right now. Since Anton's wedding, each day had become a tunnel of sludge to be trudged through, each waking dawn another plunge into numbness. Most mornings, the sheer effort of climbing out of bed seemed insurmountable.

It was three months now, thirteen whole weeks, since she'd spoken with Kurt. She'd seen his gangly figure once or twice across the compound, talking with mechanics or carrying boxes of parts from one hut to another, but she'd never got close enough to see his face, or hear his voice. He was probably staying out of her way, keeping close to the motor block and eating only in the officers' mess. She told herself it was for the best, the right thing for both of them in the end, but her body argued violently every night, and she'd wake from dreams with her arms wrapped around a damp pillow. She had been lonely, desperately so, in that first year of Occupation, but this — this was a whole new realm of misery. Now she understood what they meant by a broken heart.

She had tried, in the first days, to shift the blame. Kurt, Clifford Orange, Hitler, anyone but herself. But curled up in a bawling heap on the floor of her apartment, the truth had oozed out of every pitiful argument and drowned such nonsense. Kurt was right. When it came to the tough decisions, she was the coward. She had had a thousand opportunities to tell him in those early days, but found a thousand and one reasons to avoid it. She had let down not just him, but her family, her entire faith. And now she was paying the price. She spent her days at her typewriter, producing meaningless reports, avoiding eye contact with everyone around her, and her evenings alone, reading whatever books were left on the sparse shelves of the library, and watching the windows of her neighbors turn black one by one until the town sat in darkness. Once or twice she caught herself wondering if it mattered what happened to her anymore; if they wished to imprison or shoot her, let them do it. But thoughts of her distant, scattered family kept her going. And today, at least, she had a clear and meaningful purpose. She wrapped her scarf a little tighter and turned down toward the harbor and the distant crowds.

The boat was packed. Every meter of rail,

every tiny patch of deck contained four or five soldiers squashed together, beans in a tin, leaning, loafing or waving to others on the quay. Others continued to stream up the gangplank, an endless caterpillar of hunched, reluctant men. The quayside, too, swarmed with people: Wehrmacht officers rubbed shoulders with local bobbies, Jersey dockers with secret police. Up above, pale faces leapt out from the mud-green uniforms, most of them smoking or staring out to sea. A few were visibly distressed, clearly in no doubt where they were headed now. Despite the best attempts of the Nazi propaganda machine, facts had filtered through even to the lowliest troops, through coded letters, snippets of BBC news, whispers of military personnel from France. The stories had torn through the troops like a flash fire — the disaster of the Battle of Moscow, entire divisions wiped out by the Red Army and the blizzards. Now these young men knew they were being ripped from the cushiest post in Western Europe to be dumped into a frozen hell. Some young Germans were said to have committed suicide on receiving their new orders.

Hedy spotted Dorothea first, not far from the gangplank, and fought her way through. Dorothea was dressed in an elegant black coat of her grandmother's which, although it had seen better days, suited the drama of the occasion, and a navy scarf tied over her cropped hair made her skin look even whiter than usual. She was standing in front of Anton, her eyes bloodshot and teary, staring at him as if trying to burn every detail of him into her memory. Anton himself stood tall and square-shouldered in his uniform, exclaiming some proud defiance to the world. It was the first time Hedy had seen him in full Wehrmacht attire, and it made her shudder.

Anton noticed her and pressed his lips together in an attempt at a smile. "You made it. I'm glad."

"Of course. So . . . this is it." The banality of her remark embarrassed her, but her mind felt fogged, devoid of anything useful. "Do you know how long the crossing is?"

Anton shrugged. "No idea."

Hedy could see that Dorothea was shaking. Her breath was thick and wheezy; Hedy wondered what they would do if she had an asthma attack right here in the open. "How are you bearing up, Dorothea?"

Dorothea tried to smile, but her lips trembled, preparing for a cloudburst.

Anton kissed her on the cheek and squeezed her arm. "Darling, would you just give us a moment? I promise it won't take long."

Dorothea nodded meekly and drifted away toward the harbor wall, using the opportunity to squash a lace hankie into her eyes. Hedy stood silent, waiting, already knowing what Anton was going to say.

"Hedy, I need you to promise you'll look after her." He was reaching for her hand, grabbing at it, crushing it in both his own. "Her grandmother is so frail, she may not last the year, and there's no sign of Dory's parents relenting on this marriage. She's stronger than she seems, but there's only so much she can take."

Hedy opened and closed her mouth, searching for the right words. "I'll try, Anton, really. But I'm not sure that I —"

"I'm not asking you to love her like I do, I'm just asking you to look out for her. You're not far away, you could drop in on your way home from work, just check on her, you know?" His grip on her hand increased, and she felt sure she heard a bone crack. "She'll look out for you too, of course. You're both on your own now." He bit his lip so hard that it turned white. "If there was anything I could do to change this . . ."

Hedy closed her eyes. It was too much,

201

this sadness. How was anyone supposed to bear this weight, this endless avalanche of misery? She felt the desperation of Anton's grasp, and knew there was only one answer she could give. "Of course I'll take care of Dorothea, Anton. I promise."

Her words seemed to soothe him, and with a final squeeze he released her hand. "Nothing from Kurt, I suppose?"

"There won't be. It's over." Saying the words aloud opened dangerous gates, and she swallowed hard. This was no time to fall apart, she owed Anton that, and she wouldn't want to give the Germans the satisfaction. She raised her chin. "Don't worry, we'll be all right. You take care of yourself."

Anton beckoned to Dorothea who flew back to his side and buried her face in his shoulder. Just then a raucous shout came from down the quay: "Letzter Aufruf! Alle an Bord! Schnell!" There was a forceful thrust of people toward the gangway, and for a moment the three of them were carried along with it. Hedy grasped Anton's arm and kissed his cheek, then Dorothea pressed her lips to his, her arms so tight around his neck Hedy feared she would damage him. Then Anton was lost inside the mud-green caterpillar, the great flow of despair rippling up to the decks above, and Hedy and Dorothea were left standing on the quayside, waving at a peach-colored dot they knew to be Anton's face, their own features twisted into parodies of smiles. They remained there, shivering on the cobbles, as ropes were unwound and heavy chains thrown, watching as the vessel slowly maneuvered out of its mooring toward the harbor mouth and the open sea, and for once Dorothea said nothing.

When at last there was nothing to watch, they turned to each other. Hedy reached out and placed a hand on Dorothea's arm, knowing that this was her first call of duty. "Would you like to go and find somewhere warm for a cup of something?"

Dorothea dabbed her eyes with her sodden hankie. "Thank you, Hedy, that's sweet of you. But no, I just want to go home." She turned, then spun back, digging deep into her pocket. "I'm sorry, I almost forgot. This came for you yesterday." She pressed an envelope into Hedy's hand, then went on her way, walking slowly up the quayside, her black coat billowing in the wind, looking for all the world like the tragic heroine in the final scene of a romantic movie.

Holding the note out of sight, below the

level of her desk, Hedy read it again. It was a small cream-colored sheet, smaller than a regular letter, already crumpled from constant folding. In the top corner a round, circular rubber stamp read "Le Comité international de la Croix-Rouge, Genève." And there, at the bottom, were the permissible twenty-five words that had imprinted themselves on Hedy's mind forever.

Hope all well. Your mother and father departed January, holiday. Return date uncertain. Sent love. No news Roda or others. Moving, no further letters. Elke.

Hedy sat back in her chair, let her eyes drift around the office. Luck was on her side this morning; Supervisor Vogt was busy at her desk with some administrative catastrophe, real or imagined. And the clatter of typewriters — that exasperating din and the overture to so many persistent headaches — today became a comforting noise that helped to shut out the rest of the world. With quiet, deft movements, Hedy refolded the letter, returned it to her handbag on the back of her chair, and held a materials quality translation in front of her face, frowning, to give the impression that she was dealing with something of great complexity and importance.

It had been such a chance, writing to Elke. It was years since they'd seen each other — Hedy wasn't even sure that the family was still at the same address — and it carried a huge risk that her old school chum might betray her or her parents. They had been close once, but who knew what transformations people had undergone since the start of this insanity? Elke might have been in the Bund Deutscher Mädel by now. But somehow, Hedy's letter had reached her, and Elke had found the courage and means to reply.

Holiday. Her mother must, at some point, have used that word with Elke to describe deportation, and Elke had repeated it, knowing Hedy would understand. Now, each time she closed her eyes, she saw an open truck, crowds of Jews being pushed aboard, the butts of Karabiner rifles poking the soft flesh of their backs. She saw her parents, exhausted and terrified, huddled together on someone else's packing case, hugging what possessions they could carry in their arms. And then the long, petrifying journey to . . . at that point, her mind shut down. There was only so much horror any mind could absorb, she supposed, and she was currently at her limit.

The clock indicated it was almost lunchtime. She'd had no breakfast, but in her current state she couldn't think about eating. From the moment she'd opened her eyes that morning, knowing what she had to do, acid had forced its way into her gullet, generating waves of sickness. But weeks had passed since Dorothea had handed her the envelope on the dockside, and over many sleepless nights she had exhausted every other option. Seeing Vogt still bent over her desk, Hedy placed her bag over her arm and slipped silently from the room as if making an early dash for the canteen, ignoring the irritated looks of the Bavarians who were still key-smashing at their desks.

Out in the fresh spring sunshine, she hurried down the dusty, uneven paths toward the officers' mess. Fifty meters before the entrance was a small patch of scrubby grass, which gave a clear view down toward the mechanical yards. Pretending to fiddle with her shoelace, she waited there for several moments, half praying that she hadn't already missed him, half wishing that he wouldn't show up at all. Then she saw him. That unmistakable outline, that walk — and there, there was the bubbling laugh she knew so well. Not as deep and throaty as she'd heard in the past — this one was a little on the tight side as he responded politely to some colleague's joke — but the memory of it made her smile. At that moment he saw her, and she watched his entire body react, a tiny backward rearing such as a horse might make with a bad rider. She stood still, staring, hoping that he would understand from her expression alone. And sure enough, a second later Kurt made excuses to the men he was with, and began to walk toward her.

At first, the proximity of him almost wiped her mission from her mind. If anything, he looked taller, more handsome; he had lost a little weight, but that faint scent of sweat and engine oil punched her into the past, and those eyes pinned her to the spot. He said nothing, but stood before her expectantly. It was impossible to guess what he was thinking.

"I have a favor to ask you." The words finally tripped out, and she kept her eyes fixed on his, anticipating a refusal. But what came back was a friendly nod, an encouragement to continue; he must have known this was important for her to approach him so brazenly. "I received this." She took the Red Cross letter from her bag and handed it to him, taking care not to let their hands touch. The paths were now thronged with people on their way to lunch, and Hedy glanced anxiously about as Kurt read it, wondering if she should have picked a more private place. But most people seemed to be fixed on getting to the canteen, eager to get to their one reliable meal of the day, and passed the two of them without interest.

Kurt handed the letter back to her. "You think they've been taken away to some ghetto or prison?"

"I don't think there's any doubt. They might already have been shot."

"I'm sorry, Hedy, really I am." The kindness in his voice pricked her defenses and she had to drive her nails into her palm to focus her mind. "But what do you want me to do?"

"I just want to know . . . ." Her voice was shaky; she could hear the cracks in it. "I just want to know where they were taken, what's happened to them."

"But how can I help?"

"I thought perhaps you might have some contacts out east, maybe someone in Berlin who could check the records . . . ." Now that her thoughts were words, they suddenly sounded ridiculous. It was obvious that Kurt wouldn't know any more than she did. Afraid he would think this was all an excuse to strike up a conversation or perhaps something more, she added: "I know it's unlikely, but I'm desperate. And I have no one else." She saw it then — that old look of affection, the look that had once calmed her fears and made the whole world seem bearable. To her shame, she felt a tear pop out and roll toward her mouth. To add to the agony, he reached out his hand and, with his index finger, brushed it gently away.

"I can't guarantee anything, and it may take a while. But I'll do my best. I promise." The affection faded then, replaced with something between sadness and disappointment.

Hedy wiped away another tear and tried to stand up straight. "Thank you. I'm still in Block Seven. You can find me there any day."

She turned and walked quickly back to her block, unable to bear the idea of sitting in that canteen surrounded by people. She would work through her lunch hour, hammering out those reports until six o'clock, fingers thumping the keys, head filled with nothing but quantities of cement and addresses of delivery companies. She wouldn't make eye contact with Vogt, or her neighbor Derek, or give any of them the opportunity to notice her. After that she would hurry home, rush through her meager meal and climb into bed at the earliest opportunity. There, she would bury her face in the pillow so that no one in the surrounding apartments would hear her. And then she would weep and howl like a wounded animal into the early hours of the morning.

"But why? Why are you making us do this?"

Dorothea's voice rang out over the clatter and hubbub of the room. Her eyes were wide with innocent confusion. Hedy glanced nervously at the German private behind the makeshift table, as he grabbed Dorothea's Bush wireless set and pushed it along the surface toward the rising bank of radio sets at the end. For a moment Hedy feared the soldier might retaliate, but she quickly realized that the look on his face wasn't aggression but incomprehension. The man didn't speak English.

"Dorothea, just walk away," Hedy muttered, at the same time checking out the number of other armed Germans in the room and the position of the exits. "He doesn't understand you. And I want to get out of here."

In fact, Hedy hadn't wanted to come to the parish hall at all. It was a nest of German soldiers, festooned with swastikas, and being among it made her skin crawl. But when the announcement of the radio confiscation had been made in the evening paper the previous week, Dorothea had come straight round to see her, begging Hedy to help her deliver the bulky device with its heavy wooden surround. Remembering her promise to Anton, Hedy had no choice but to agree.

She looked around. The room was packed with furious, murmuring Jersey folk, slamming their beloved family wirelesses on the tabletop, snatching their paper receipts from the Germans' hands with flushed, bitter faces. The idea that they would be returned at the end of the war was so pitiful a lie, it was almost funny — everyone knew that these highly desirable items would be packed onto a boat headed for the Continent by this afternoon, and that all of them would be gracing the drawing rooms of Nazi Party officers by the start of next week. Meanwhile, the locals would now be completely shut off from the real war, dependent solely on the risible misinformation of the German-controlled press. Hedy, already without a wireless for over a year, had grown used to the pressing silence of the long evenings without music or human voices. But her regular visits to Dorothea's to listen

211

to the BBC were a vital link to the world, even if she did have to spend much of the time pointing out the locations on Dorothea's ancient atlas. This new level of isolation frightened her as much as anyone.

Eager to get back to the anonymity of the street, Hedy pulled at Dorothea's arm. But Dorothea was still facing down the soldier. "I think you understand enough," Dorothea was saying. "I would just like to know what good you think this will do."

Hedy stared at her charge, baffled. The woman had never so much as contradicted Anton in public (or, Hedy suspected, in private) yet here she was, fearlessly accosting an enemy soldier. Hedy looked around to see a second German, heavily-built and with a rifle slung low across his chest, craning his neck to watch the exchange from the far side of the room. One signal from the first, Hedy knew, and they would both be arrested. Arriving here this morning, they had already seen one local man dragged off following a scuffle in the queue that flowed out onto the pavement.

This time Hedy's grip was more forceful. "I mean it, we need to leave now."

Her heart leapt as she felt a hand upon her back, pushing her away from the table and toward the exit. Dorothea, she realized, was being similarly propelled. There was a good deal of strength behind the pressure, so much so that she was halfway across the floor before she managed to turn and see the cause. To her relief, it was a weary-looking, gray-haired gentleman with thinning hair and wire-rimmed spectacles, wearing a fixed but beatific smile.

"I can answer your questions, ladies, but I suggest you don't pursue the matter here." His voice was as tired as his appearance suggested, but Hedy recognized the inflections of a Jersey accent, similar to Doctor Maine's. He continued to drive them forward until they were all standing on the pavement, squinting in the bright sunshine after the gloom of the parish hall.

There, he turned to them and offered his hand. "Deputy Ned Le Quesne, pleased to meet you." Hedy and Dorothea both returned the gesture. The name meant nothing to Hedy but Dorothea was peering at him with curiosity.

"From the States?" Dorothea asked.

"States Labour Department, for my sins." He smiled but Hedy sensed there was some truth to the apology. "I'm sorry if I appear unchivalrous, but I didn't want you to get into trouble. I'm afraid Jerry have been quite forceful about this latest nonsense;

213

there have already been a number of arrests."

"I just want to know why. Why are they taking our radios away?" Dorothea pressed him.

Le Quesne glanced over his shoulder and encouraged them a little further down the road. "Simple revenge, I fear. The tide of the war has turned in recent weeks. So they hope to punish us and, at the same time, keep the truth from us to destroy morale. But we shan't let that happen, shall we?"

Hedy glanced back at the parish hall, where two youths were arguing with a German private, drawing attention from other soldiers. A woman in her sixties, emerging onto the pavement, was weeping on her husband's shoulder.

"We certainly won't!" Dorothea was shaking the old man's hand. "And I say my prayers for our troops every night." Hedy drew a breath at the disingenuous irony of this remark, but the Deputy was already bidding them good day and heading back toward the parish hall.

Dorothea turned to her. "Thank you so much for your help, Hedy. I couldn't have carried that here on my own. Would you like to come over this evening? I've got enough potatoes to make vegetable rissoles, if you have a couple of carrots you can share?"

Hedy hesitated. The BBC news and the discussions that followed it were the only thing that had made recent visits to West Park Avenue bearable, as they kept Dorothea off the subject of movie stars or, worse, how much she missed Anton. The thought of an evening with nothing but conversation between them was a grim prospect. But her promise to her old friend kept tapping her on the shoulder.

"Thank you — maybe just for an hour." She protected her eyes with her hand as she looked upward into the blue, feeling the warmth of the sun burning her skin. "It's hard, the first night without your radio. I remember."

"Oh, we can still listen to the news." Dorothea's tone was bright.

"I don't understand?"

"I handed in my wireless, just as they asked. I just didn't hand in the one in the attic." She beamed as she tripped lightly along the road in the direction of the park, leaving Hedy watching her, astonished.

"Same again?" Kurt, with a broad smile, raised two fingers toward the skinny, bored waitress. "This brandy is excellent. I might see if I can get myself a bottle at the stores."

Wildgrube knocked back the dregs of his own glass — his fourth large one tonight by Kurt's reckoning — and licked his lips in agreement. Even in the muted light of the club, Kurt could see that his face was starting to flush, the puce-colored streaks echoing the heavily applied rouge of the club hookers. Already his gestures were becoming expansive, and his watery eyes danced around, taking in the latest batch of Normandy whores, enthralled by his own sense of well-being. Kurt suspected that he didn't receive many social invitations.

"Now, my father" — Wildgrube took a drag on his cigarette and continued as if Kurt hadn't spoken — "worked in a factory. No interest in his appearance. Used to clip my ear when I spent my money on quality shirts and decent shoes, called me a little fairy." He threw his head back and laughed uproariously. Kurt mirrored the laugh precisely, at the same time using the moment to empty most of his own brandy into the aspidistra on the ledge behind his shoulder. "But look at me now! Just these cuffs alone . . ." He displayed the crisp white cuffs of his shirt as if modeling them for sale. "Always pressed to perfection. I tell you, the housekeeper at our billet — ugly as a bulldog, but my God can she iron a shirt! And her stews are pretty good too!" He patted his belly and laughed again.

Kurt pretended to take a sip from his nearly empty glass, thinking that the woman probably pissed heartily into every dish she served him. He glanced at the clock — seven thirty. It was the fourth time he had brought Wildgrube to the club in three weeks, and experience told him that by eight he should be able to push him in any direction he wanted. The tricky part was catching him in the golden moments between professional discretion and passing out.

Kurt's first invitation to join him on a "boys' night out" — a phrase Kurt had picked deliberately, knowing that it would appeal to the spy's ego — had been met with skepticism. Wildgrube possessed the bullied child's instinct for knowing when anyone was looking down on him, and Kurt had to work hard to convince him that the whole thing wasn't some practical joke. But Kurt knew that, whatever reservations or suspicions Wildgrube might have about him, they would eventually drown under the weight of curiosity and desperation for approval. On the first three occasions Kurt had played it safe, keeping the conversation to German architecture and what cup size created the best female figure, while also dropping in meaningless titbits about himself and the others in his billet. But Kurt was beginning to assess Wildgrube's powerlessness and indiscretion around booze. How the man had risen through the ranks with such an obvious flaw was baffling, but then, Kurt thought, on that basis how would you explain Göring? In any case, Kurt sensed that tonight, if he could get the levels of enjoyment just right, he could move in for the kill. And Wildgrube appeared to be having a whale of a time.

"This is wonderful. I love this place."

Kurt nodded. "Good to get away from the hoi polloi, spend time with your own kind. Not that I'm in your strata, Erich. Access all areas, cozy chats with all the big boys — am I right?"

Wildgrube shrugged, lapping it up. "I know a lot of people. Not just here."

Kurt twirled his glass in his fingers. "You mean, in Berlin?"

"Oh yes. Got friends there who've done very well for themselves. Inner circle, you know?" Then his manicured hand brushed away the topic like an imaginary fly. "How often do you come here on an average week?"

Kurt thought quickly, aware that his

218

answer could well be checked later for accuracy. "Not too often. Don't want to make a pig of myself!"

Wildgrube laughed hard and slapped his thigh. "You see that one?" He pointed to a young blonde of around seventeen, wearing a tight flimsy dress and tossing her hair in an obvious bid for sales. Kurt wondered if her mother knew where she was and what she was doing. "That's the one I'm having later. Fantastic little arse, don't you think?" He leaned toward Kurt, conspiratorial. "Though I have heard that some of the new ones are not that clean. Might just tit-fuck her to be safe — don't want to catch a dose of something."

The waitress put down two new glasses with a wide, artificial smile. Kurt raised his toward Wildgrube's for a toast, and heard the glass almost crack as Wildgrube went in too hard.

Kurt decided it was time to change tack. "So tell me, Erich, how's it going in your department?" He let the term hang in the air, vague enough to be interpreted as ignorance. "Who's giving you trouble at the moment?"

Wildgrube blew dismissive air through his thin lips. "Ah, you know. The usual suspects. Black marketeers. Dumb Einheimische who think they're Rosa Luxemburg. You know, some of the laborers we brought over have escaped from their compounds? Turns out some of the locals are actually hiding them in their homes!" He knocked back half the brandy in a single gulp. "Serve them right if they get raped or robbed, stupid fuckers."

"And how are things back home? Is it true the Führer's planning a new offensive against the Soviets?"

Wildgrube tapped the side of his nose to indicate that Kurt had overstepped the mark. Kurt, realizing his mistake, held up one palm and turned his head away, as if deferring to a greater power. But the next moment Wildgrube was pulling back to the forbidden path, prudence swirling in the bottom of his glass. "Big man's doing great work there. Of course, the best stuff is hush-hush."

"I'll drink to that." Kurt held up his glass again, and once more Wildgrube drained his own in one. Kurt leaned in and glanced ostentatiously around him, deliberately whipping up a sense of drama. "But come on, give me a clue at least? Something to do with the Jews, am I right?"

Wildgrube wagged his finger, with a look a parent might give a naughty child they're about to forgive. "You're a bugger, Neumann! Of course it's the damn Jews. Finally found a solution. Bloody clever too. But" — all the fingers went up now, suggesting a barrier that could not be crossed — "I can say no more. Tell me . . ." He beckoned Kurt in further. "These pretty little bitches. Which one is yours?"

Kurt grinned, pretending to be entranced by the game, and cast a slow, thoughtful gaze around the room. The decor in the club was gaudy, a collection of gold-plated light fittings and red velvet armchairs that probably looked ghastly in daylight. Everywhere he looked drunken officers and grim-faced, malnourished women sprawled. In the far corner, Fischer was sitting with some of his hardline cronies, playing some kind of drinking game with a pack of cards. Dear God, Kurt thought, why was he even putting himself through this, for a woman he'd sworn never to see again? Images of Hedy floated through his mind. That soft mouth and those sea-green eyes; her startled expression when he entered a room; the smile that sank softly into a pillow. The last months without her had been the most unhappy he could remember. A dozen times he'd walked from his billet all the way to New Street and stood outside her building, waiting for a glimpse of pale skin or tawny hair at the window. Once he had even got as far as the door. Each time, a prickling resistance — pride, perhaps a sense of betrayal — held him back. But the thought of being with any other woman left him limp and dispirited.

Wildgrube was waiting for his answer, his tongue lolling at the side of his mouth like a raw clam. At random, Kurt picked out a tall, willowy brunette draped across the end of the bar. "That one."

Wildgrube laughed again. He would laugh at anything now. "Ah, you like them tall and dark? For me, has to be a blonde. Nice Aryan girl." He picked up Kurt's brandy, mistaking it for his own, and finished that too. "Soon that'll be all that's left, you'll see! They'll get all the scum in the end. Every one of them."

Kurt sensed the door was opening, and warned himself not to push too hard for fear it might slam again. At the same time, he knew he didn't have too long — Wildgrube was so drunk now that he could barely make segues between his own sentences. "Let's hope so, eh? Won't be easy, mind."

Wildgrube scoffed. "Shooting fish in a barrel. They don't know, see. No idea where they're headed, what they're walking into."

His speech was slurring now. "SS chum showed me some photos last time I was home. Genius — way they pack them in, nice and easy."

Kurt kept his body perfectly still. "Pack them in?"

Wildgrube gave a smile that Kurt would remember for years afterward. "That's the beauty of it." He cocked his head to Kurt, telling him to come a little closer. "Keep this to yourself, now — this is just between us, understand?"

Hedy was fast asleep when the banging started. Her first response was rage. So many nights recently she had lain awake until the dawn chorus began around four, dragging herself to work in a state of exhaustion. Tonight was the one night she had actually managed to drop off at a reasonable hour, and now some idiot . . . For a few seconds she thought it was coming from one of the other apartments. Then she realized it was coming all the way from the communal street door. Someone was demanding entry, and someone — probably Mrs. Le Couteur — was opening it. Hedy spun around to the clock: almost three. Now she was upright in bed, her ears pricked like a wild animal. Pictures of German soldiers with arrest warrants swam in her mind. Grabbing a woolen cardigan from the chair, she jumped out of bed and ran to the apartment door, pressing her ear against it. That was when she heard the footsteps on the stairs and the familiar voice: "Hedy? Hedy, please, I know you're in there."

With her heart almost jumping out of her chest, Hedy pulled back the bolts and threw open the door. Outside, the hallway felt shockingly black and drafty. Kurt stood swaying on the landing, his hair sticking up at strange angles, a wild expression on his face. As soon as he saw her he threw himself into her arms, knocking her backward several steps. Cautiously she placed her arms around him and somehow manhandled him across the threshold.

"Kurt, what's happened? What are you doing here?" His face was buried in her neck now, and it sounded as if he was crying. Hedy disentangled herself and managed to get a firm grip on his arm. She pulled him into the apartment and steered him toward the chair by the table, where he slumped as if he hadn't sat down for a week. She could smell the alcohol on him, strong and sour. She raised the blackout blind to relieve the intensity of the darkness, then sat down next to him.

"Tell me what's happened."

He looked up at her, the moonlight from the window lighting one side of his features. She could see that he was crazy with booze-heightened emotion, but as he stared at her he seemed to sober up, and with one gentle hand pushed the hair back from her face the way he had when they were lovers.

"Hedy, I am so sorry."

"For what?" Her mind was spinning with awful possibilities.

"I didn't believe you, didn't believe any of it. Thought it was just stories. I didn't think people could really behave that way."

"Like what? What are you talking about?"

"I honestly thought . . . they said it was farmland. Just relocation. I didn't know. I swear to you I didn't know."

And then it began to tumble out — the facts that Wildgrube had confided, and the connections Kurt had put together for himself. The secret plans, the liquidation of the ghettos, the burning of synagogues with Jews locked inside, the roundups, the "special" cattle trucks, the purpose-built extermination camps. The separation of men and women at the gates, the classification of prisoners, the removal of belongings, the overalls, the forced labor, the trickery of the fake showers, the chambers piled up with bodies.

Hedy sat in silence beside him as the phrases kept coming, sometimes choking him, sometimes spewing out in a bilious stream. The words landed on her like burning tacks, blistering her skin. Crematoria . . . chimneys . . . gas. As the words became pictures, and the pictures a reality, she began to lean away from him. She wanted to hit him in the mouth to shut him up, to stop this knowledge from reaching her brain, to punish him for being one of them. And at the same time she wanted to hold him, and tell him that he couldn't have known — who could ever know something so inhuman, so incomprehensible? As Kurt ranted on, she felt herself growing smaller, shrinking down like Alice in Wonderland. By the time he got to her parents, confessing that if they had been transported they were probably already dead, she was a speck of humanity on the vast expanse of the earth, tiny and inconsequential.

Slowly, in small sputtering fits, he reached the end of his story and fell into a deep, brooding silence. Hedy rose slowly, staggered across to the sink and vomited for several minutes, clinging to the porcelain, feeling the wet streaks on her face, but too numb to move. Eventually she hauled herself up, rinsed out her mouth and dragged herself to the bed. Kurt moved slowly to join her, and they sat, wordless, staring at nothing but the shafts of moonlight arcing their way across Hedy's pillows. Then, as Hedy remembered it, she must have fallen asleep for a few moments, because when she stirred, the moonbeams had been replaced by a dim leaden light in the distant sky, returning outlines of furniture in the bedroom and hints of color to their skin. Somewhere outside, the first birds began to call to each other.

Kurt put his hand on her knee. "Tomorrow I'm going to walk into College House with my Walther P38 and take out the Field Commander."

"Don't be stupid."

"I mean it. I have to do something. You were right: I've been a part of this, I'm responsible. I have to find some way to atone for what we've done."

"You'd be dead before he hit the floor."

Kurt shook his head. "Doesn't matter what happens to me."

"It would do no good. Berlin would just send someone else."

"Then I'll go to Berlin, take out the lot of them. I have to do something, Hedy, I have to make this better. And somehow I have to win your forgiveness."

Hedy felt a surge of tenderness. She took his face in her hands. "Kurt, listen. That stuff I said months ago — I was just angry. You're not responsible for what they're doing. You said yourself, you had no choice, no more than Anton. And you have to stop talking like this. No suicidal mutiny on this little island is going to save a single Jew."

"But I have to do something . . ." His voice was growing weaker, like a child.

"You already did, Kurt, don't you see? You saved me! But for you, I'd have been sent to one of those camps!" She gripped him harder, her fingers pressing the blood from his face. "That's not war, that's not hatred — it's goodness, it's love! That's who you are!"

He placed his hands on her shoulders, and a calm seemed to descend on him. "Then let's fight them — both of us! I don't know how exactly, but we can try, can't we? If we've got each other, then we've both got a chance. Maybe we can get out of this alive, together. Please, Hedy?"

She looked at him, knowing that he meant it, and in her gut she felt something lift. It was hope, and possibility. She breathed in deeply, and whispered, "I've never stopped

228

stealing petrol coupons."

He stared for a moment, as if she'd spoken in another language, full of incomprehension. Then he started to laugh. "You never stopped stealing coupons? You never stopped?" She could feel the tension seeping from his body, until he became helpless with laughter and fell onto his back, pulling her on top of him. "Oh, Hedy, I'm so proud of you! I love you so much!"

He pulled her body toward him then, and kissed her with an intensity that melted her, that stirred a sense of life within all this destruction, and soon their two bodies merged, rolling back and forth across the mattress as the dawn pushed through the tiny attic window.

SEVEN

It was a spring tide. The ocean had been dragged so far out of Belcroute bay that the shingle gave way to gleaming, rarely exposed sand at the water's edge. Blurred, shadowy outlines of rocks could now be seen beneath the calm turquoise water. Like sharks, Hedy thought, lying in wait beneath the surface. The morning was hot and clear, but she shivered anyway. As if reading her mind, Kurt extended his arm and pulled her into his body a little tighter. With a sigh, she leaned into him and rested her head on his shoulder.

It was the kind of day that summer tourists would have embraced just a few years ago. Then, there would have been women in swimsuits lounging on the magnolia sands around the corner in St. Brelade's bay, and children splashing each other in the shallows. There would have been ice creams and blankets, and the air would have been pierced by excited shouts. Now, it was hard to find any sliver of coast free from mines and barbed wire. And these days, Hedy found it hard to look at such fortifications.

Since the night of Kurt's revelations, she found many sights painful. High stone walls, bars on windows, the small train that ran along the front of St. Aubin's bay to transport building materials. Children crying, people coughing. The hiss of a gas heater. Everything she saw and touched projected her into the horror. She saw the tiny square of sky through the vent in the boxcars used to transport them. She reeled back as the doors opened and the limp bodies were disgorged, smelled the shit on the floors and heard the clank of the door as the bolts sealed her inside. And she would think of her mama and papa, the same people who had cuddled and sung to her, washed her hands at the kitchen tap while she stood on a stool, and she couldn't put the two halves together. How was it possible that this had happened to them? To anyone?

She had faked an illness for a week to stay home from work, knowing she couldn't trust herself around the Germans. Kurt had waited for Doctor Maine outside the hospital and acquired a sick note for Hedy to give to the compound authorities, as well as a prescription for a small bottle of brandy. For six days she had lain on her bed, watching the sun appear and disappear in the skylight above, wondering if she, too, would die, not much caring either way. But on the sixth day she felt hungry, ate a little vegetable soup, and poured a bowl of water to wash herself all over, grateful for the sensation of the sponge against her skin. If she was the only one of her family left, she considered, she carried a responsibility now. She needed to stand up straight again, get a grip on herself. She forced herself to do some dishes, buy her rations — and even, the next week, return to work. And as the days grew longer and warmer, honeying her skin and melting the frozen tundra beneath it, she began to perceive a future again. Because now she was no longer on her own. She and Kurt were finally, properly together.

Over a long, intense evening, crouched in this very spot among the rocks and huddled against the wind, they had formulated the basis of their new relationship, consisting of three heartfelt promises. First, that both of them would carry on with their lives as if nothing had happened — although in reality they would do every little thing they could to wreck the system while they waited for their deliverance. Second, they would repeat nothing to anyone of what they had learned; a leak of such sensitive information could too easily be traced back to Kurt's conversation with Wildgrube, and the consequences could snowball quickly. Plus, with letters from Anton so few and infrequent, there was no point in upsetting Dorothea any further.

Their last undertaking proved a little more complicated. Kurt insisted that Hedy needed to move — too many neighbors in the New Street building would be aware of Kurt's nocturnal visit, making future contact there risky. Hedy, sick of the stairs and Mrs. Le Couteur's (now quite blatant) snooping, willingly agreed. But a trawl through the rentals column in the Post revealed no affordable apartments within walking distance of Hedy's work; every town property was now filled with soldiers or local farming families kicked off their land in the early months of Occupation. For several days Hedy had scoured the library notice board and the scant offerings of the rental agency, but found nothing.

Once again, it was Doctor Maine who came to the rescue. Without even inquiring why Hedy needed such help, the doctor pushed a note through her letterbox, informing her that a patient of his on Pierson

Road had died, and that the woman's son was giving notice on her apartment that week. Hedy was there within an hour. It was a small, dingy basement, close to Anton and Dorothea's house, with a distinct smell of mold; the only view was people's feet as they passed on the road outside, and the no-pets rule meant leaving Hemingway behind. But it was cheap and convenient, furnished with a double bed, and the spivvy-looking landlord seemed happy to take her money without references. Hedy thrust the first fortnight's rent into his hand before he had time to reconsider. The next day she fed Hemingway his last meal, stroked his little gray head, pinned a note to his collar, and left him outside the door of the new lady tenant who was always stroking him in the hallway. Then she took her old wicker bag stuffed only with a few garments, a toothbrush and her parents' beloved letters, and moved into her new life.

Now she and Kurt met as often as schedules and security allowed. They used hidden locations such as Belcroute or, on occasion, Hedy's new apartment, Kurt slipping in with his own key after dark and sneaking away early before he was missed at his billet. Neither of them ever joked about the excitement of the subterfuge. Both knew it was far too serious for that.

Hedy shuffled a little closer to him as they squashed together on the pebbles between the jagged boulders, and squeezed his hand. "Did you manage to find out any more about getting a crystal radio set?"

Kurt nodded. "That radio and gramophone shop near Anton's old flat? Apparently the owner makes them for people in the back room. But there's a waiting list, and I suspect he only helps people he knows."

Hedy pushed her bare toes into the tiny warm stones at her feet. "Guess I'll have to carry on relying on Dorothea."

"I'm so sick of the nonsense the RRG puts out." Kurt picked up a pebble and threw it down the beach where it bounced on the shingle. "They're still reporting the Pacific like Midway never happened. And as for what's going on in the east . . ." An image of Anton squatting in some dugout flashed in Hedy's brain. She quickly pushed it away. "It's ludicrous — everyone knows it's all lies. Even Colonel Knackfuss has a radio in his office for listening to the BBC." He picked up another pebble, but Hedy, mindful of the footpaths above them, gently took it from him. "The Yanks are hammering our cities. At this rate there'll be nothing left by the end." He turned to her with an ironic smile. "I'm starting to think Sydney might be a good place for us, afterward. Can't get much further away than that!"

Hedy forced a smile in return. As wonderful as it was to be with Kurt again, talk of a future beyond the war still frightened her. He dropped a lot of such references into the conversation, mentioning the style of house he'd like to live in, or a boy's name he particularly liked. No doubt Kurt thought it showed confidence and commitment; he was certain that in a postwar world, mixed marriages would be lawful, perhaps even encouraged. Hedy kept her own thoughts private: that laws don't change people's minds, and that the hatred between Jews and Germans would likely last for generations. Nor did she mention that this new world terrified her, that she dreaded an Austria where her family no longer existed and the neighborhoods of her childhood had been razed. To Hedy, the coming years seemed so fraught with danger and complexity that she blocked the idea out. Surviving each day, each week, was as much as she could manage right now.

She shivered again and changed the subject. "Remember that peg-leg fisherman Oliver Maine told me about?"

"The one who sells black market fish?"

"I found his mooring the other day, near some steps at the English harbor. Bought a mackerel before the German inspectors arrived to take his catch."

"A whole mackerel? Lucky you!"

"Oliver says the guy's building a boat in secret, somewhere out at Fauvic. When the time's right, he plans to use it to escape."

Kurt wrinkled his nose. "Have to be some boat to reach England from here. If he heads for the French coast, he'll be shot before he's landed."

"Still, it shows you people are fighting back. And the mackerel was delicious — I'll go back again next week."

Kurt pushed the hair from her face. "Take care. This new Jewish curfew . . ."

Hedy dismissed the comment with a wave of her hand, even though the same anxiety had kept her awake on many nights. "I keep an eye on the time. Anyway, I'm an insurgent now, aren't I?"

Kurt laughed. "I nearly forgot." He rummaged in his pocket, drew out a bundle of paper Reichmarks and pressed them into her hand. "There you go. Resistance wages."

Hedy pulled a face. "I don't like taking money from you."

"I told you, this is for both of us — for

emergencies. Are you keeping it somewhere safe?"

"Behind that loose skirting board by the bed."

"First rule of revolution: always have a stash of money you can access quickly." He grinned, and Hedy saluted to join in the game. Perhaps Kurt was right — perhaps a little self-delusion was no bad thing for the spirit. She tucked the money away in her bag, and when she turned back Kurt was still watching her.

"Look at you! You are so gorgeous. Can I come over this evening?"

"If the coast is clear. Come the long way around, through the park — make sure you're not followed."

He nodded, placing his other arm around her. "I'm always careful. Now give me a kiss."

She didn't need to be asked twice.

The café was tiny, with a dark interior, chipped paint and grubby curtains. The air was filled with the scent of charred vegetables, the only food that had been cooked here for many months, and the tablecloths had long ago been scrapped for lack of any detergent to wash them in. Pictures of happier times, poorly painted (by the proprietor, Hedy suspected), hung on the walls under thick layers of dust. As usual, it was empty, the owners presumably keeping the place running as a reason to get out of bed in the morning, rather than to provide a meaningful service. But it was a useful private space, away from prying eyes. Hedy took a corner seat, asked for any kind of hot drink they could provide — they all tasted the same anyway, no matter what you called them — and waited for the doctor to arrive.

Fifteen minutes later, her drink cooled and stewed in its cup, the shop door pinged and Maine shuffled in, lifting his heavy doctor's bag over the backs of the chairs as he pushed his way through the tables. He glanced around to choose an appropriate seat, but Hedy caught his eye and gestured for him to sit at her table, as the elderly woman at the counter — probably the owner's mother — had such poor eyesight she barely knew who she was serving. He slumped onto the seat opposite, placed his bag on the floor and smiled. "Good day, my dear, and how are you?"

"Mustn't grumble." She had recently learned the phrase from listening to local women in the covered market, and now liked to drop it into conversation whenever she got the chance. Checking that the old lady's attention was elsewhere, she slid the envelope of petrol coupons across the table. "And yourself?"

"A little tired, but aren't we all? How is your friend?"

A code had evolved between them over the months: "your friend" meant Dorothea, "your other friend" meant Anton, and "your additional friend" referred to Kurt. They also referred to the petrol coupons, on the rare occasion they needed to, as postcards.

Hedy pulled a face to indicate she was giving only part of the story. "I saw her yesterday. I think the stress of her situation is affecting her." She patted her chest to clarify her point, and the doctor nodded. In fact, Hedy had stayed at Dorothea's house for an hour after the end of the news bulletin the previous night, alarmed by her enduring cough and the disturbing bluish shade of her lips. In recent weeks Dorothea's health had noticeably declined, worsened by a poor diet and her anxiety about Anton. She often said herself that she dreaded another winter under Occupation. Yet she often seemed more focused on her movie scrapbooks than the details of the BBC reports, and Hedy often had to repeat the salient points to her after the broadcast. In truth, Hedy was finding the role of guardian increasingly testing;

it certainly involved a lot more than popping around every few days to make sure she had food in the cupboard.

Maine reached into his bag, drawing out a tiny jar of pale flakes. "Grated ginger," he muttered, pushing the jar across the table toward her. "From a patient of mine. It's far from fresh, but she can sprinkle a little on her evening meal. Or add it to a chest rub, if she can find any oils." He gave a wry smile. "Six years' medical training, and I'm reduced to dispensing folk treatments like some old peasant woman."

Hedy reached across for the jar, letting her fingers cover his for a moment. She remembered how, at their first meeting, he had reminded her of her uncle Otto. Otto was likely dead now, caught up in the same net as her parents, and this man was probably the only person left of that generation who she trusted. She wished she could just climb into his lap and have him sing her a lullaby.

"Thank you. I don't know what we would do without you."

Maine smiled with a rare vulnerability, revealing the gratitude of a man who received few compliments. He was on the edge of a reply when the room was filled with a violent rushing noise, and the café

241

door flew open. Their hands sprung instantly apart, and each of them pinned themselves back in their seats. All eyes were on this sudden, alarming intruder.

"You got any water there? Give us a glass, would you? I've a terrible thirst."

The man was tall and well built, his thickset features pulled into a scowl, his rusty hair unkempt. His voice was deep and powerful, and Hedy knew at once that he had an accent, though she did not know then that it was Irish. The man stomped up to the counter, where the old lady quietly poured him a glass of water and watched him down it in one go, as if huge men burst into the place every day demanding drinks.

The envelope of coupons, Hedy realized, was still sitting on the table. She glanced up at the doctor, indicating that he should put it out of sight, when she realized that Maine was turning in his seat, trying to keep his face out of the newcomer's eyeline. Hedy felt a rising panic; something frightening was happening, but she wasn't sure what. At that moment the man at the counter looked toward their table and peered at Maine's face, seeking out the features.

"The doctor, is it?" Hedy's stomach somersaulted. "Fintan Quinn — you patched up my mate down the hospital two weeks back, after that fall, remember?"

Maine smiled at Quinn. Hedy wondered if it looked as unconvincing to its recipient as it did to her. She pulled the envelope back to her side of the table and dropped it into her lap, out of sight.

"Indeed. Is he recovering well?"

"Ah, sure. He's back on the job, good as new now."

Quinn helped himself to another glass of water while Hedy's mind galloped on. If that was the extent of their relationship, there was no need to panic. All the man had seen was a doctor he barely knew, sitting in a café with a young woman. She breathed deeply, scoffing at herself — some resistance fighter she was, panicking at every passing remark. But what the man said next almost stopped her heart.

"And you — you work up at Lager Hühn-lein, don't you?"

Hedy turned to Quinn and nodded, calculating that an obvious lie could backfire. Now she could see his face full on, it did look vaguely familiar. Yes, she had seen him driving trucks of cement and girders in and out of the compound, his arm casually draped from the window, that blank, ruddy face perusing the site. He stood out from the other mercenaries because of that rumbling voice and wild ginger hair. Hedy gave him a cool, courteous smile, hoping to hit the sweet spot between encouragement and hostility.

"That's right."

"Thought I recognized you. Never forget a face."

The man downed the second glass then turned and headed for the door, giving them both a small American-style salute with two fingers as he passed. Then he was out the door as rapidly as he'd entered.

Hedy and Maine stared at each other for several moments, communicating only through nervous glances. As soon as the old lady disappeared into the back, Hedy pressed the coupon envelope into Maine's hands. She leaned forward to whisper across the table. "You think he saw anything?"

Maine shook his head. "What could he see? It's just an envelope."

Hedy sat back and nodded, breathing out for what felt like the first time in several minutes. "It's just that we've been linked together, by someone who can identify both of us . . ."

Maine leaned in, his turn now to cover her hand. "My dear Hedy, from what I saw of those gentlemen at the hospital, I don't believe they'd even be interested. All any of them cared about was how quickly the chap could get back to work, so that they didn't miss a day's pay."

"But if he were to find out about . . . me." She was careful to observe their unwritten rule, never to say the word "Jewish" in public. "You know they deported those women from Guernsey a few weeks ago?" She bit her lip, wishing she could tell him all she knew of their probable fate.

He patted her fingers. "You have cause to be careful, and I know you always are. But you have enough real worries, without inventing new ones."

Hedy nodded, forcing a smile, vowing that the next time she saw the peg-leg fisherman she would buy an extra mackerel for the doctor and his wife. "You're right. This bloody war, it's making me so edgy. But perhaps a different venue next week?"

"That would be sensible, I think. You want to leave first? I'm not on call till four."

Hedy paid the woman for her drink and slipped out into the cobbled street, trying to shake off the sense of anxiety that had planted itself in her stomach. It was a warm afternoon, and as she reached the park the sun on her skin felt like treacle. She tossed her hair a little and instructed herself to relax, to live a little in the moment. After all, she had done good work today. The coupons would enable Maine to reach dozens of sick people in the parishes. She was expanding her contacts to acquire food supplies — and tomorrow night she would see Kurt again. There was still much to feel thankful for, she reminded herself, as she slipped silently through the backstreets of St. Helier, passing the swastika flags and soldiers without a second glance.

Kurt shifted uncomfortably on the wooden bench, eyeing the other officers nearby. All were smoking or engaged in stilted, distracted conversations. It was a high-ranking affair, to be sure — no one under the rank of lieutenant, and a generous sprinkling of captains. It was clear that none of them knew why they had been summoned today, and equally clear that this was something big. The sun, strikingly warm for September, poured through the casement windows of College House, turning the gray stone corridor into a slow-bake oven; several of the older officers had already turned an unhealthy shade of puce. Much longer stuck here, Kurt thought, and Berlin might have to replace the entire Field Command.

He looked around the grand interior with its ancient flagstones and crafted wood trim, the perfect example of the British Victorian boarding school it had been before the war, and tried to imagine snotty-faced boys tumbling through these hallways. Where were those kids now? Probably stuffed in some prefabricated wooden hut, compulsory German grammars perched on their knees. This place must have seemed a daunting enough environment to a young lad; now, inhabited by the uniformed pen pushers of the Field Command, it reminded Kurt of a hive, and the buzzing, claustrophobic cells around a queen bee.

On the far side of the room he spotted Fischer, deep in some private conversation with an administrator. Fischer had been chummy with Kurt lately, apologizing for the mess in his half of their shared room, and offering Kurt a substantial amount of the cigarettes his brother had sent from Germany. But there was a coldness beneath the camaraderie, and Kurt was aware that conversations at the billet often ended abruptly when he entered a room. Kurt knew Fischer's game but continued to ignore it. If Wildgrube and his gorillas chose to spy on him from time to time, he'd just have to make sure he gave them nothing to see; he was scrupulous now about looking over his shoulder. And the way things were going on the Continent, they could all be out of here within six months.

A uniformed lackey emerged from a wooden double door and waved them forward. Kurt followed the crowd into the large meeting room, finding a space to stand at the back with a decent view of the senior commanders around the table. The windows here were even larger, the stuffy heat even more unbearable. Whatever this news was, Kurt thought, let it be delivered quickly.

Colonel Knackfuss himself was seated at the center of the table. Kurt stared at the man's stiff decorative collar, biting into his craggy neck, and the tiny scabs at the side of his head where some barber had shaved the stubble growth with excessive speed. The officers arranged themselves around the room as the colonel's deep-set eyes remained fixed on the paperwork before him, evidently glad of the extra time to prepare his statement. Then silence fell, and Knackfuss's rasping tones rang out.

"I summoned you here today because the Swiss Government has recently asked the German High Command to consider an exchange of prisoners of war. As you may be aware, several thousand German citizens are currently interned in Persia by order of the British." A lightning exchange of con-

248

fused looks pinged around the room. What did this have to do with the administration of the Channel Islands? "One year ago," Knackfuss continued, "when the internment first came to light, an order was issued that, in retaliation, Feldkommandantur 515 should immediately deport all British residents not born within the Channel Islands, at a ratio of ten to one for those held in Persia." The silence deepened as minds began to turn over, unraveling the significance. Kurt sensed that a number of people in the room had actually stopped breathing. "This order was never enacted. In January of this year I made known my objections to 319 Infantry: it is my view that the British-born islanders serve as a shield to attacking Allied forces, and that such a deportation would create additional defensive problems, including potential resistance. However . . ." Knackfuss shuffled the papers before him, as if it might somehow alter what was typed upon them. "However, the new applications of the Swiss have brought this situation to the attention of the Führer, who is displeased that previous orders were ignored. Berlin now insists that the deportations be carried out as directed: that is, all British subjects without permanent residence, and all British men between the ages of sixteen and seventy born on the British mainland, along with their families, be sent forthwith to internment camps in Germany."

Knackfuss lowered his papers and scanned the room, giving his officers permission to react. A low rumble of muttering rolled through the room. Several heads had dropped in anticipation of what the next weeks would involve, others maintained expressions of cautious neutrality. Fischer, Kurt noticed, was one of those glaring at Knackfuss, clearly incensed that one so senior should question the Führer's orders. The heat of the room fizzed in Kurt's bones and made him nauseous. He tried to think of mountain streams and glasses brimming with ice cubes.

"We calculate that the number of islanders affected," Knackfuss went on, "amounts to approximately two thousand, around one in twenty of the population. The announcement will be made in the Evening Post on the fifteenth, that is, in five days' time, with the first deportations taking place the following day." The muttering grew louder. Kurt heard distinct phrases such as "twenty-four hours?" and "got to be kidding!" bubbling up in pockets around him. Knackfuss, aware of the disturbance, raised his own volume against it. "This will present significant challenges, but gives us the advantage of surprise. The less time people are given to organize their personal affairs, the less opportunity they will have for opposition."

He gazed around the room — making mental notes, Kurt suspected, of the less forgiving faces and to whom they belonged. Fischer had now arranged his own visage into a model of impartiality; Kurt made a feeble attempt to copy it, but when he caught his reflection in the window, he just looked mildly deranged. "There may well be resistance," Knackfuss continued, "but this order comes from the Führer himself with the highest priority, and no exceptions can be made. I need not tell you that this remains highly classified information until it is publicly released, and that no mention of this will be made outside this room, other than to those within Field Command involved in the practical arrangements. That is all. Heil Hitler."

A forest of hands rose in salute, and then Knackfuss was gone, whisked away to some private office deep within the building. The explosion of conversation went off like a bazooka. Kurt muttered something to his neighbor about making a telephone call, and slid silently from the room, down the grand corridor and out through the nearest exit.

As he trotted down Mont Millais toward the town, the queasiness persisted. He looked at each local he passed — ordinary men and women going about their daily business, heading home on lunch breaks, shopping or pushing prams. How many of them would have their lives turned inside out within a few days? How many kids and elderly people would not survive the journey? How many more would perish in internment camps? But Kurt knew full well the real reason for his churning stomach. This order meant that all pretense of reasonable behavior from his administration was now finished. If Berlin was prepared to treat British subjects with this degree of contempt, a new sweep of foreign nationals and Jews would likely follow. He would have to see Hedy tonight and warn her. They would need to stash more money behind the skirting, and he would suggest she keep a bag packed at all times.

The sun was burning the skin on his face, cooking his body through the thick wool of his tunic. It was already far too hot for September. But the distant high clouds were static, and the stillness in the air promised an even hotter night to come.

It was a noise Hedy had never heard before

in these streets. A cacophony of singing, wailing and roars of defiance, individual voices occasionally cutting through the hubbub and rising to the surface. Somewhere to her right was a rousing chorus of the song she had heard sung in public houses in the months before the Occupation, "There'll Always Be An England." To her left came the anguished high-pitched cries of a woman and her children. On Commercial Street a group of men had gathered in an ominous, illegal group of ten or twelve, yelling and gesticulating to the world at large. Pushing her way past them and the milling crowds blocking the thoroughfare, Hedy grabbed hold of Dorothea's hand for security as they pressed on toward the harbor.

As the narrow street gave onto the open expanse of the Weighbridge, the sight stopped both of them dead. Hundreds of people in small groups, standing or collapsed on their haunches, all of them bundled in layers of clothes far too hot for the day's searing heat. Each clutched a battered packing case, or a roll of blankets tied up with string. Grim-faced men herded their families; their wilting, red-faced wives dispensed fragments of scorched swede to their hungry young, while older children bounced screaming toddlers to no avail.

Wherever she looked Hedy could see people hugging each other. Many were weeping. Families, neighbors, work colleagues — people who had all considered themselves locals until the previous night, when a sharp rap on the door and a sheaf of papers had brutally delivered a different interpretation. Women who had escaped the order ran to friends and in-laws who had not, pressing into their hands whatever treasures had been found at the back of the store cupboard — a tin of tunny fish, a couple of undersized apples. Men sweating in their winter coats thrashed out hurried deals with pals and neighbors over the upkeep of properties, custody of businesses, care or disposal of family pets. The scene formed a gray, raucous mural of despair.

Hedy turned to Dorothea to see her hand clasped to her mouth. "I didn't believe it till now. How can they do this?" Dorothea looked around, searching. "I have to find her."

Hedy followed her gaze over the sea of heads. "I'm not sure you'll be able to find anyone in this crowd."

"I have to try."

They tiptoed through the chaos, stepping over legs, children and belongings, peering into assembled groups. The sun was now reaching its height, and Hedy yearned for shade.

Suddenly Dorothea gave a shout. "That's her! Over there!" She pointed to a small group sitting in a semicircle on the ground near the bottom end of Commercial Buildings. "Sandy? Sandy, it's me!" Hedy found herself dragged along by Dorothea's fierce grip, bumping into people and stumbling over luggage, until they reached the family group. One of them was a woman of Dorothea's age, with striking dark hair and olive eyes, a winter coat tucked under her bottom as a cushion. Next to her, a man Hedy assumed to be her father, sporting ruddy cheeks and a booming voice, was engaged in an intense conversation with another gentleman. As they drew near, Hedy realized that the second man was the deputy they had met on the day of the wireless collection.

"But why have the Jersey States allowed this to happen?" the father was shouting. "We've lived in the island for thirty years, Le Quesne, do we have no rights?"

The deputy's eyelids were heavy, as if the simple challenge of wakefulness was too much for his aging body. "We have done everything in our power. We refused to serve the notices, but the Germans dragged parish officials from their homes and ordered them on pain of imprisonment."

"You're supposed to protect us. It's a damned disgrace."

Le Quesne trudged off, only to be accosted by another furious deportee.

Dorothea threw her arms around her friend. "Sandy! I had to come to say goodbye. Do you have any idea where they're sending you?"

"All we know is that it's some camp in Germany," the woman replied. The phrase turned Hedy's stomach. "They only told us last night." She looked composed, but Hedy could sense the turmoil underneath.

Dorothea took a small jar of sugar from her bag and pressed it into Sandy's hand. "I've been saving this for something important. I want you to have it."

Sandy smiled with gratitude, but her father immediately stepped forward. "We don't need anything from your sort, thank you."

"Daddy, please!" Sandy jumped in, but the old man pushed himself in between her and Dorothea.

"You're married to one of them — you're on their side. You stay away from my daughter. Go on, clear off."

Seeing the hurt on Dorothea's face, Hedy

took hold of her elbow to draw her away. But to her surprise Dorothea drew herself up. "I may love a man in the German army but I know whose side I'm on, thank you very much." She reached out and squeezed Sandy's hand. "Take care of yourself, my love."

She turned on her heel and walked away. Hedy hurried after her, knowing she could lose her in a moment. "That was brave."

Dorothea shrugged. "It's not the first time. Won't be the last." Then she stopped, her head on one side. "Listen — there are people down there singing the national anthem." It was true. "God Save The King" was now plainly audible from a large group over by the quay. "Let's go and join them."

"I don't think that's a good idea. The Jerries are jumpy today, they could start shooting."

But Dorothea shook her head. "Let them. These are my people. I'll not let them be packed off to God knows where without letting them know how I feel about it." She marched off in the direction of the quay.

Hedy hesitated, half wanting to go home, half feeling that she should support Dorothea. Duty finally forced her on, but as she traipsed along behind Dorothea's purposeful figure, she felt a twinge of admiration.

The island community had already spat this woman out as trash, yet here she was defending them. Anton had been right, Hedy reflected, about her good heart.

The two of them picked their way through the crowd until they reached the quayside and the improvised choir of locals, self-consciously attaching themselves to the edge of the throng. As a scrappy version of "Keep The Home Fires Burning" started up, Dorothea joined in, tentative at first, then belting it out with gusto. She sang as if it were the last song of her life, her usual wheezing temporarily vanished. Hedy, looking around for soldiers and spies, timidly mimed along. The song ended and was immediately replaced with "We'll Meet Again." Then another, noisier version of the national anthem, and a somewhat chaotic rendition of "Run, Rabbit, Run." Minutes turned into hours, and as the Germans continued to stare vacantly above the heads of the rebels, Hedy, finally familiar with the words and tunes, let her voice ring out and reverberate in her chest in a way she had forgotten it could. Now and then she and Dorothea would turn, in the middle of a phrase, and grin at each other.

The sun slowly arced around to the west, and as it did so the mass of people and the baked paving stones beneath their feet intensified the heat of the day, shimmering off the quayside in distorted waves. By the time the first boat began to board, the Germans' rifles were primed and aimed at the crowd, ready to stop any last-minute rebellion. The singers' voices, hoarse as they were, grew louder and more defiant. And at that moment Hedy was struck by a single, powerful certainty. Kurt's suspicions were right: everything that had happened in the last two years had simply been a rehearsal. The real Occupation was only now beginning — a new, bitter wind was blowing in. Soon, perhaps sooner than anyone imagined, everything was going to change. At that moment and with great clarity, Hedy understood that she was no more than a cork bobbing on the surface of the harbor, waiting to see where the current would take her.

She took a deep breath and bellowed out the final chorus of "Pack Up Your Troubles," and her voice traveled out across the water and into the void.

EIGHT

The clock on the wall showed 5:55. Hedy
tore the last sheet from her typewriter and
placed it on the pile of finished reports. She
scanned the room, noting the position of
every staff member, calculating their precise
stage of departure; she knew all their habits
well enough by now. Bruna, the tall girl
from Munich who always brushed her hair
for two minutes before leaving, presumably
to impress her endless succession of boyfriends. Rosamund, Miss Vogt's pinch-
lipped favorite, who always lingered by the
supervisor's desk in the hope of soliciting a
compliment on her day's work. Smelly
Derek with his stench of mold, who fussed
over his station each night before putting
on his jacket, obsessed with leaving everything perfectly tidy. It was vital that Hedy
chose exactly the right moment to transfer
the petrol coupons from her desk to her

coat, just when everyone was distracted. Pretending to look for something in her bag, she waited for her moment. Then, as Derek bent over to tuck the dust cover under his machine, Hedy moved, deftly slipping the coupons into her inside pocket. Another sweep of the room told her that, as usual, no one had noticed. Projecting an air of calm indifference, she took her bag from the back of her chair, collected her coat, and strolled out into the dusty exterior of the compound.

Walking toward the exit gate she kept her eyes ahead of her, as always. It was rare for her to catch a glimpse of Kurt at this time of day — normally he was over in the warehouses, doing the last stocktake of the day — but they had long ago agreed that they should never be seen speaking to each other at work. On the occasions when they did pass each other on the pathways, both of them would look the other way or, in Kurt's case, manufacture a conversation with a colleague as a sleight of hand. Hedy had never trusted anyone at Lager Hühnlein, but now she viewed everyone as a potential enemy. People could be seen whispering in quiet corners of the canteen, in the shadows of filing cabinets or outside toilet cubicles — rumors about spies and collaborators, about imminent Allied raids and possible German reprisals. It was impossible to separate cynical German employees, who genuinely wouldn't have cared if you stole an entire desk from under their noses, from secret police operatives snooping for information. Even harder to tell the difference between resistance-minded locals and those who would sell their own grandmothers for a cash reward. The only safe option was to keep your mouth shut at all times and, if asked anything, profess complete ignorance.

Last year's fears of a new, more repressive phase had proved all too correct. Paranoia was now the default mood of the German authorities. Rations had been cut for several months as "punishment" for the sinking of German ships, and a number of local people, including a recalcitrant canon, had been sent to punishment camps for listening to the BBC news. Worst of all had been the announcement made one cold, wet day in the early spring that, in retaliation for an abortive British commando raid on the sister island of Sark, a further two hundred islanders were to be deported. Neither Hedy nor Kurt needed to be told that this latest seizure would be certain to include the few remaining Jews.

Frantic, they discussed options. The Jersey authorities, Hedy asserted, would be useless; she adamantly refused Kurt's suggestion to interfere on her behalf, arguing that it would be sure to arouse suspicion and put them both in greater danger. Finally, in desperation, Hedy approached Feldwebel Schulz, who sulkily agreed that in the light of her work at the compound and the difficulty of replacing German-speaking employees, he would request an exception be made in her case. It seemed a meager hope. For three weeks she had lived in dread, her nights tormented with fitful sleep, her days broken by stomach cramps and diarrhea. Several times Kurt delivered news of another Jewish arrest or disappearance (clearly some had gone into hiding with friends, a dangerous solution in Hedy's view), always reassuring her that the longer she escaped attention, the more optimistic they could be. Other individuals, he pointed out, were being deliberately overlooked if Field Command deemed it expedient to do so. But his pallor, and the way his fingers trembled as he lifted a cup to his lips, gave his real feelings away.

No formal decision was ever announced. But by the fourth week, with arrests petering out, they began to suspect that this particular storm had passed. Perhaps Schulz's request had been accepted, or maybe Hedy's refusal to attend the College House interview the previous year had caused her name to drop off a list. Whatever the reason, it seemed that, for now, life could return to whatever currently passed for normality. Till the next time.

By the summer, she and Kurt felt sufficiently confident to return to their tiny acts of sabotage. Shut away in the privacy of Hedy's flat, they would entertain each other with their stories: of how Hedy had deliberately placed over seventy audit sheets in the wrong files, a mistake impossible to trace back but which took two hours for the administrators of Block Three to correct. Or how Kurt had purposely ignored the faulty wiring connections of a young mechanic in his charge, causing the truck to break down on its first girder delivery of the morning. They never fooled themselves that such actions made any real difference, but the laughter they shared in repeating them had a caustic edge to it, and stoked their yearning for revenge.

On nights like that, their lovemaking often had a cold, urgent undercurrent, as if sex was the one channel where their rage could be safely expressed. At other times the boyish gentleness of Kurt's touch brought Hedy to tears. She felt shame for ever doubting him. Never had she known anyone so kind, so utterly himself. She loved his attempts to supplement her weekly supplies with whatever he could bargain for at the military stores, the way he gleefully passed on any news of in-fighting or incompetence in the local administration. Best of all were the times he was able to create an excuse at his billet and stay the whole night. Then they would have long whispered conversations into the early hours, reflecting on how Hitler had risen to power and how Europe might prevent such collective delusion ever recurring. Because, as summer turned to autumn, bringing with it the fall of Italy, they became ever more optimistic that the Allies would win. All they had to do, Kurt reminded her, was survive, and see the end. Worn down by his certainty, and recognizing how many bullets had already been dodged, Hedy had recently begun to believe that some kind of future might be possible.

The sky was darkening as she set off down her usual route, following the lane toward the main road, then along St. Aubin's road toward First Tower. Her new secondhand coat, a successful barter made by Kurt for some French candy, was a vast improvement on her old one, which had worn away to threads and buttons, but constant undernourishment meant she always felt the cold. Her mouth watered at the thought of the small piece of fish she had purchased at huge expense from her friendly fisherman the previous day. She'd also managed to save a swede and a few potatoes from the previous week, and Kurt had given her a small candle he'd stolen from his billet. Tonight she would eat like a queen.

She was just passing the arched gate of the old Sun Works tea-packing factory when a hand on her shoulder caused her to cry out. Spinning around, her first reaction was relief that she saw no uniform. Then, as she caught a proper view of the man's face beneath his cap in the half-light, relief was quickly replaced by fear. She recognized him even before he began to speak, the strength of the accent jerking Hedy straight back to the café where she and Doctor Maine had sat over a year ago.

"I know about your little sideline. Do us a deal and I'll say nothing about it."

Hedy swallowed, her mind racing. Quinn, that was the fellow's name. Was he talking about the coupons? How could he possibly know? Was he bluffing? She tried to arrange her face in a way that suggested innocence and confusion. "I don't know what you mean."

The Irishman now had a tight grip on her arm. Hedy glanced about but there was no one else on the street. He had chosen his moment carefully, and at that second she realized he had probably followed her all the way from work.

"You know. Those petrol coupons, the ones you've been filching away."

Hedy's heart sank. Had Quinn spoken to someone in her office? Had someone there seen her after all? Did he know there were coupons in her pocket right now? She decided it was worth one last throw of the dice. "I don't understand."

The grip of his hand tightened, his fingers now biting through her coat and hurting her skinny arm. "I think you do. You get them for your doctor friend."

Hedy felt the blood drain from her head. "Nonsense."

He squeezed her harder and Hedy whimpered. "I'm not stupid. My girlfriend knows there's coupons going missing from your office." Bruna, Hedy thought. Bruna, that Bavarian bitch, whose romantic interests were clearly now stretching beyond the German NCOs to include OT employees. "Then I remembered — you and the doc together that time. I knew there was something going on. Guilt written all over you."

"That's ridiculous." It sounded like a lie.

Quinn smirked. "Don't worry. I'm saying nothing. All I want is a cut. Couple of coupons a week and your secret's safe."

Hedy stood as still as she could, hoping that a lack of resistance would calm him, quickly trying to calculate the best way out. She could give him two of the coupons right now and get away from him, which was what her body was begging her to do. But she reminded herself he was a mercenary. The man had no loyalties, and any fool could see where this kind of blackmail would lead. Two coupons today, ten next week, a hundred the week after. Either she would be caught by Vogt, or she'd fail to deliver and Quinn would betray her anyway. Her only chance was to close this down now.

"I'm sorry, but you've made a mistake." She looked him straight in the eye, rebellious. "I'm just a translator. I don't steal. I've nothing to give you."

Quinn stared at her with impotent impatience. Clearly he had not envisaged this reaction and was at a loss where to take it now. Hedy could hear the blood pumping in her ears, and fought to keep her thinking clear. If she was right, Bruna's accusation was likely based on suspicion rather than certainty. And it had often occurred to Hedy that other people within the office were probably stealing too. If Quinn took Hedy's word now, perhaps he would walk away and try his luck elsewhere. For a moment she thought she sensed a retreat. Then fury blasted from him. "You've got some nerve for a Kraut bitch, you know that? Well, they're all going to know about you now, and you'll be sorry. You'll see how sorry."

Hedy felt his clutch release, then he was gone as quickly as he'd arrived, bounding up the road toward First Tower in a loping run. Hedy leaned back against the painted wooden gates of the factory, unable to stand unsupported. Rivulets of sweat ran down her chest between her breasts, though she was cold and shaking. All thoughts of home and dinner had now evaporated. There was only one coherent thought in her mind. It was all over.

She sewed the final stitch, cut the cotton with her teeth and held the coat up in the dim light of the apartment to examine it. It was good workmanship — her mother would have been proud. Provided you didn't feel or press the hem, no one would ever guess there were items concealed there:

her toothbrush (impossible to replace now, and the thought of not brushing her teeth, even with the crushed cuttlefish "toothpaste" of recent months, repelled her); the bundle of notes from behind the skirting board, finally stepping up to its rightful role; her mother's precious letters. She shook the coat a little — as she hoped, nothing moved or called attention to itself. She considered taking the small bag of essentials she kept packed, at Kurt's insistence, under her bed. But she quickly realized that the risk of walking through town with such an item, inviting searches and questions, was too great. In any case, she needed to remain as small and unobtrusive as possible.

She remembered herself and Roda preparing to escape across the Swiss border all those years ago, and tried to recall everything her sister had said. "Money for bribes" — that had been her mantra. Anything else could be acquired later. It was funny really, Hedy mused; everyone in the family always thought of Hedy as the sensible, hardheaded one and Roda the romantic one who would fuss over girlish possessions and crack under pressure. But it was Roda who organized, chivvied and made all the harsh decisions, even volunteering to drive them through the mountains on those treacherous roads. Now it was Hedy's turn to show what she was made of.

The knock on the door froze her to the spot. Could Quinn have raised the alarm in the few hours since his threat? She searched for the small tear in the curtain fabric that allowed her to peek out without being seen, and pressed her eye to it. Dorothea. She leaned back against the bedstead, wondering whether to answer, weighing up the pros and cons of speaking to Dorothea today. Then she moved quickly to the door.

"I just wanted to tell you," Dorothea began, chattering before she was across the threshold, "an old friend of Anton's told me today that there's been a shipment of French cheese. Of course the Jerries have taken most of it, but there'll be a little on sale in the market tomorrow if you get there first thing." She beamed at Hedy, so proud of her news, so childishly hopeful of gratitude.

"Thank you. But I won't be able to get to the market tomorrow."

"If I take your ration card, maybe I can get some for you?"

Hedy looked at those innocent, pale eyes. She knew she was about to break her promise to Anton, and felt a tug of remorse, but it was too late. The decision was made.

"Dorothea, I'm sorry, but I have to go away for a while."

"Go away? What do you mean?"

"Something's happened. They're going to find out I've been stealing petrol coupons."

Dorothea's mouth fell open. "You're still doing that?"

Hedy nodded. "And I can't take the chance. If I stay here, I'll be arrested and deported."

"You want to come over to my house?"

To her own surprise, Hedy gave a little snort of laughter. "I need to go a little further than that."

Dorothea slumped into the only chair, her face even whiter than usual. "Is Kurt going to help you?"

Hedy hesitated, considering a lie. But she already knew she was going to need Dorothea's help. "Kurt doesn't know. I haven't told him."

Dorothea's eyes grew wider with each second. "Doesn't know? Hedy, you can't just vanish!" She shook her head in disbelief. "Kurt loves you. And you love him. Don't you?"

"Which is exactly why I have to do it this way." Hedy moved around the room, tidying the books, pulling the bed covers straight, trying to keep her hands occupied.

"Kurt has a record for coupon theft already. Once they know about this, they could easily connect us. God knows what they'd do to him."

To her embarrassment, she could see Dorothea was starting to cry.

"No, this is all wrong. Where will you go?"

"I have a plan. But I can't tell you. It's better no one knows — in case they question you."

"You're not going to try and get off the island?" Dorothea's breath was becoming wheezy.

Hedy made a scoffing sound and turned her face away. "That would be foolish and dangerous."

"You can't do this alone!"

"It's all taken care of."

"Doctor Maine? Is he helping you?"

"No!" Hedy was shocked at the volume of her own voice. "He's to know nothing about this. That way, if they question him, they can't prove he was involved in any of it." She wiped her cold sweating brow with the back of her hand. "It will only be for a while, till things settle down."

At this point Dorothea broke down completely and buried her face in her hands. Hedy watched her cry, too distracted to reach out, too scared to shed any tears herself. Then she crouched down beside her to get Dorothea's full attention. "I need you to do something for me." Hedy took the sheet of paper she had spent so long writing out on her last precious sheet of writing paper, folded several times for want of an envelope. "Please give this to Kurt. I don't want to leave it in the apartment in case someone else finds it first."

Dorothea took the note and pressed it to her rasping chest. "Of course. But, Hedy, are you sure? Whatever you have planned, it sounds dangerous."

"Doing nothing will be worse." Hedy pulled on her coat and buttoned it up to the neck. "I'm really sorry."

"For what?" Dorothea looked genuinely confused.

"For dragging you into this. For leaving you on your own."

"Oh, Hedy, don't worry about me." Her voice had a new steeliness. "Just take care of yourself, for God's sake."

Hedy put her hands in her pockets to pull the coat more tightly around herself, feeling the weight of its new additions in the hem. Her voice wobbled a little as she forced out her reply: "Of course. Don't worry, it's all going to be fine."

■ ■ ■

He was just emerging from his tiny office when he saw them. A group of six or seven female employees — typists, he assumed — were gathered on the pathway from the canteen, talking with great animation. Their heads were bobbing together as if discussing something very important, but the way they kept glancing over their shoulders to check who was listening suggested that it was also rather shameful. Some gossip about a boyfriend, Kurt supposed. Perhaps a pregnancy? He knew, through an overheard conversation at his billet, that Fischer had just been through a similar panic with his married girlfriend, and had felt a twinge of smugness that he and Hedy were always so careful. Eager to show how uninterested he was, Kurt stepped off the path and gave the women a wide berth. But just as he passed them, a German phrase jumped out at him.

"At least you weren't in her block! Who knows what I might have caught!"

Kurt tried to dismiss it, but something told him that he needed to hear more. Deliberately dropping a couple of the files he was carrying, he bent down and began to shuffle them back together. He didn't have to wait long.

"What's the management playing at anyway, employing Jews? I hope they find the bitch and shoot her."

Slowly Kurt rose and sauntered toward them. Unsure how else to approach it, he decided to pull rank.

"Ladies, you're blocking the path. What's so important that you have to stand around here gossiping?"

The tallest of the group, with blond hair worn in a single plait, stepped forward. "Sorry, Lieutenant, but we've just found out that there was a Jew working in Block Seven. Apparently she's been stealing petrol coupons."

Kurt gave a little cough to cover his involuntary gasp. "Really? And where is she now?"

"No one knows, sir. She hasn't been in for two days. It's not right, though, sir."

"It's scandalous," chipped in a pug-nosed brunette. "People have been sitting next to her all this time and never knew. I think we should have been told."

Kurt looked at them, their angry, contorted faces scowling in unison, then turned and marched quickly in the direction of Block Seven. His heart was beating so fast he felt sick. Could it be true? How had she been caught? And how come he hadn't heard about it? Arriving at the hut, he opened the door and scanned the room, but saw only a handful of secretaries working through their lunch hour. Hedy's coat was not on the rack.

Without waiting to give notice to anyone, he dumped the files on a colleague, pulled on his tunic and ran from the compound, jogging the two miles to her apartment, arriving soaked and gasping at her door. Shouting Hedy's name, he wiggled his key frantically in the slot until he managed to get inside. The apartment was deserted. The bed was neatly made, a few garments still hung in the cupboard, and for a few terrible moments Kurt was certain that she had already been arrested. But then he took some deep breaths and began to look around. Her toothbrush was missing, the drawer where she kept her parents' letters was empty. With trembling hands he got on all fours and pulled the loose skirting away from the wall — the Reichmarks, too, were gone. He gasped with relief — clearly this was a planned escape. But where the hell had she gone?

Only when he reached Dorothea's house, and was greeted with her anxious, pallid face and Hedy's note, moistened by Dorothea's sweating hand, did the panic begin to return.

"I'm sorry, Kurt," Dorothea muttered. "I tried to make her tell me, but she thinks it's safer for us not to know." She stood before him, arms crossed over her chest against the chill, looking up at him, wide-eyed. He placed his hand on the foot of the hall banister for support and read the note again. He had already read it three times, but could not accept that it told him nothing.

My darling Kurt,

They know about the coupons. I have to disappear. I wanted nothing more than to see this out with you, but I won't risk your life along with mine. I don't want to be a coward this time. Perhaps, if the fates are willing, we will find each other again when this is all over. I love you more than anything. Take care of yourself.

Hedy

Kurt sank down onto the stairs, rubbing his eyes and pushing strands of hair back from his face. He had to work out all the possibilities, eliminate them one at a time, but all he could think about were those eyes — that brooding darkness behind the green, the very quality that had drawn him to her. Always secrets, thoughts that were never expressed, even to him. It was obvious now that this was something she must have plotted months ago, a premeditated plan for just this kind of eventuality. He cursed himself for not seeing it earlier, for not forcing her to open up. At least the fact that she had taken her few treasured possessions probably ruled out suicide.

He turned back to Dorothea. "She said Maine is not helping her?"

"She was very clear that she didn't want to involve him. Said this way he would be safe."

"But she has no one else here, no one!" He thought for a minute. "What about Anton's old boss?"

"Mr. Reis? I don't think she's seen him for months. Anyway, I heard he was in the hospital."

"But who else would she trust enough to shelter her?"

"Kurt, I think she may try to escape the island altogether."

His stomach lurched. "She wouldn't be that crazy, would she?"

"When I asked her, she agreed it was

stupid and dangerous. But I noticed that she blushed a little, and she wouldn't look at me."

Kurt hauled himself to his feet and began to pace. "She could get herself shot just for being on the beach! And what would she do? Stow away on some boat? She knows there's no sea traffic to England."

Dorothea nodded. "The only place she could reach is the French coast. And what good would that do?"

A small electric charge fired in his head. "The French coast?"

"Yes?"

Kurt's heart began to hammer again. "I think I might know where she's gone. But I need to hurry."

Dorothea asked no further questions but merely nodded. "I still have Anton's old bicycle hidden in the larder . . ."

Hedy woke with a jump, astonished that she had been asleep. She tried to stretch out her legs but they had grown numb with stillness and cold; she could no longer feel her toes at all. The smell of wet wood and paint was in her nostrils. Pulling her coat tighter around her, she peered into the darkness, trying to identify the unfamiliar shapes: the tools hanging on nails, the ropes on hooks.

Rising above her, filling three-quarters of the space with its bulk and forcing her into one small corner, was the hull of a wooden boat. Through the ventilation window near the roof, the crescent moon shone a perfect rhombus of silver light onto the rough splintered wall; she pressed her ear against it, and heard the distant waves creeping their way up the beach in sucks and splashes. She guessed it must be four or five in the morning — only another hour or two to wait.

Crunching, uneven footsteps on the shingle forced her upright, breathless. A moment later the door shuddered open, and she recognized the stocky silhouette with heavy whiskers around the chin, and the soft, gruff voice.

"Ça va?"

"Bien."

She watched the fisherman's dark figure limp into the hut and move around the hull, checking each section with his fingertips. Jean-Paul's limited English and Hedy's meager smattering of French restricted conversations to single words and gestures. They knew virtually nothing of each other, and Hedy felt far from ready to trust him; when she had produced her precious bundle of Reichmarks for payment, he'd snatched at it with an eagerness that alarmed her. But certainty was a luxury she could no longer afford. All that she had managed to glean, in her months of buying Jean-Paul's mackerel at the harborside, was that his wife had died a year or so earlier, and that for some reason he held the Germans responsible for her death. The look of disgust on his face and the voluminous, aggressive spitting that accompanied the recounting of his tale told Hedy all she needed to know: the fisherman hated the Jerries and felt he had little left to lose.

She wondered now if she had ever, truly, expected the plan to get this far. The notion of using this mythical, illegal boat for her own ends had popped into her mind the moment she'd heard about it, but at the time it was only a fantasy. Then, during those long, tortured weeks waiting to know if she would escape deportation, it had mutated into something possible, an emergency option should everything fall apart. Yet even then, in saner moments Hedy assumed the old man would laugh at her — tell her that the boat was not seaworthy, or that this "escape plan" was just a joke, a good story for the harbor taverns once the war was over.

Two nights ago, he had stared cynically at

her when she showed up at his mooring at dusk, attempting to explain her objective with random French words and bad mime. He probably thought she was working for the enemy, because he merely grunted, hobbling about the deck of his fishing vessel on his wooden leg and gesturing for her to push off. Only when she wrote down the sum she intended to pay did he seem to take the idea seriously. Half an hour later, after painful, repetitive communications and a great deal of staring out to sea, Jean-Paul, as she now knew him, spat thoughtfully onto the deck of his fishing boat and offered his hand to shake.

The first stages of the escape were clear in her mind, thanks to the old man's scribblings on scraps of newspaper. She would hide in the boathouse, tucked away down a lane on scrubland at Fauvic beach — an area known to be light on patrols and surveillance. Just before dawn, when the tide was high enough to launch, Jean-Paul would guide his vessel carefully around the rocks, then row them out to a safe distance before starting the outboard engine. Fourteen miles to the east — storms, riptides and patrols permitting — they would reach a quiet cove south of Portbail on the French coast just as darkness fell in the late afternoon. But here the plan grew vague and, if Hedy thought about it too much, quite preposterous. It was likely she would have to swim to shore, in darkness and freezing water, a task she knew might be beyond her. Then she would have to hide out in barns and outhouses around the German-occupied village for several days until she could find someone to help her. After that, her only idea was somehow to make contact with the French Resistance, who would help to get her over the border to Switzerland.

But crouched in the dark corner of the boathouse, it all seemed frighteningly remote, and Hedy tried not to look that far ahead. Instead, she told herself for the hundredth time that here, on this tiny occupied rock, discovery and death were a certainty, and at least this way she stood a chance. Her stomach rumbled, and she sighed, wondering when she might eat again. Kurt's smiling face came to mind and drew an embryonic sob to her throat, but she pushed the image away. She had done the right thing, the only loving thing she could. Now the decision was made, the money spent, there was nothing to do but sit here and wait for the rising tide.

Kurt could feel the muscles in his thighs

begin to ache as he pushed the pedals harder. He'd convinced himself in recent months that he'd remained fairly fit even on his restricted diet, but this journey was telling otherwise. The rusty state of this ancient bicycle and the improvised tires made from an old garden hose were certainly no help. His lungs burned, begging for more oxygen, as he pumped his way up the St. Clements road. By his calculation of the tides, he had half an hour — assuming he was even going to the right place. But as soon as he'd remembered Hedy's story of the fisherman and his secret boat, he knew it was his best and only chance. The sky in front of him was just starting to turn cyan blue above the rooftops as he cycled east. She would be out to sea long before the sun brought its full strength. Stopping was not an option.

As he cycled, adrenaline inflated his anger. Why, why would she do this, when she could have come straight to him? An attempt like this was suicide — surely she had to see that? But even in his fury, he recognized her calculations and understood. Her stubborn, stupid independence made him want to scoop her up.

He pressed on up La Rue de Fauvic, passing tiny granite cottages. Beyond them he

285

could just make out the open fields. Ahead lay a dark expanse that he prayed was the sea. He must be close now. Arriving at a T-junction, he peered through the emergent half-light to see, on the far side, a track running on ahead. It had to lead down to the beach — he could feel the wind and smell the salt in his nostrils. Looking in every direction to make sure he hadn't been spotted, he summoned the last of his energy to pedal across the tarmac road and onto the rough earth track, horribly aware of the sound of the wheels in the thick silence. As the track came to an end and the sea rose up to meet him, he dismounted and threw the bike to one side. He ran the last few yards and peered over the sea wall, then, spotting a break indicating a set of steps, hurried down them.

He scanned the beach to his left and right. The tide was high; waves were breaking rhythmically on the shore, hiding every rock and boulder beneath. His heart began to calm and the blood roar in his ears eased. But it had all been for nothing. The whole area was completely deserted. If Hedy ever was here, he was too late. And wherever she and her fisherman were now, there was nothing he could do to save them. A pain spread in his chest as he pictured the remainder of the war without her. He saw her bloated body washed up on the beach, or lying in woods with a bullet in her back. He stood staring at the horizon for several moments, rooted in misery.

A sound further down the shore drew his eyes to the south. In the semigloom he peered in its direction until he made out a shape — a bulky gray form that seemed to be moving at the water's edge. He staggered toward it, his brain finally making sense of it; now he could see the open wooden boat, with what looked like a small engine at the stern. He stumbled on, tripping over rocks, slipping on seaweed. Yes, there were two figures, pushing it into the water — both short, slight. And one of them . . .

"Hedy!"

His voice echoed across the beach. Both figures froze. He could see her clearly now, the shape of her shoulders and the way her body was leaning. The person with her, an old man, jumped back from the boat and raised his hands as if expecting to be shot. Kurt continued to lurch toward them till he was no more than five meters away, then stopped. Hedy was staring at him, white and shaking with fear and cold. As a child, Kurt had once entered the shed in Helmut's garden to find Helmut's father on a chair, about to put a noose around his neck; the expression on Hedy's face now was identical. For a moment no one moved, unsure where this would go.

"Kurt, I'm sorry." She was clinging to the edge of the boat, either to support the boat or herself, Kurt wasn't sure. The boat was bouncing furiously in the surf, rolling with each incoming surge. "I have to do this alone."

"No." Kurt spoke in English and deliberately kept his voice low and steady — the worst outcome now would be some kind of fracas. It seemed that the fisherman wasn't armed, but Kurt had no idea what the guy was capable of, and in this state of mind he wasn't sure about Hedy either. "Hedy, this won't work. There are patrols out there. You won't get out of island waters." He gesticulated at the little vessel; it looked pretty professional for something built in a shed with no proper materials, but a glance told him all he needed to know. "Even if this reached France, you'd never make it past the beach."

"I have to try. If I stay I'll be sent to a camp." Her voice was choked with terror.

"Hedy, listen, please. I know you're afraid. But we can find an answer." He remained quite still, keeping his focus on the two of them. If they decided to jump into the boat and start rowing, Kurt knew he probably wouldn't have the strength to pull it back. The fisherman, realizing Kurt was unarmed, had now dropped his hands and was hanging firmly onto the other side of the hull. He was looking from Kurt to Hedy, waiting to see what the next move would be. In the incipient pale gold of the horizon, Kurt could now see the man's face — he seemed to be chewing slowly on some unseen root or tobacco, and beneath the leathered skin and whiskers his expression indicated he might be willing to put up a fight, if only to save his profit.

Kurt turned his attention back to Hedy, who had begun to buckle from the center, as if someone had taken out an air stopper.

Her voice dropped to a whisper. "It's the only way."

"No. There's another, better way. Hedy, I'll keep you safe, I promise. But please, if you do one thing for me in your life, do not get in that boat."

Hedy looked from him to the fisherman. She turned her head to look out across the bay, gazing at the navy-blue line of the horizon against the rapidly lightening sky. At that moment, to Kurt's relief, he could see reality descend, the recognition of the futility of it all. As her hopes drained away, she let go of the boat and swayed for a few seconds, then toppled backward into the shallow water, arms flailing, head struggling to get above the surface. Kurt ran to her, hauling her sodden body from the water and held her, both of them trembling. Hedy was now weeping openly, while the fisherman stood silently by, staring at them with a blank expression, his jaw still moving as he chewed away, the boat beneath his hands bobbing up and down on the morning waves.

Hedy peeped through the hole in the curtain. It was almost dark, and the wind was picking up — she could hear it blowing through the high trees on Westmount.

"Make sure to weigh everything down properly," Kurt reminded her. "And be careful that no one sees you coming back. Is everything packed?"

Hedy peered into the wicker bag containing the clothes and personal effects that would travel with her. Everything she owned was in that bag, except for her coat that lay across her bedstead, still damp around the cuffs and hem. She hadn't had the heart to open it up and see what remained of her parents' letters, but suspected they were now papier-mâché. She would slit the hem open to retrieve her toothbrush later.

"Yes, that's everything. It's almost time. What will you do?"

"I'm going to go through the apartment, make sure there's nothing here that leaves any clues. What about the key?"

"Push it through the letterbox when you leave," Hedy instructed. "We won't be coming back." She covered her mouth to stop a nervous belch. Acid swirled painfully in her empty stomach, but it wasn't food she craved, it was a cigarette. At that moment she would have traded anything for a quality smoke. But neither she nor Kurt had any tobacco left, and anyway, in her current state it would probably make her sick. She slipped on her coat, shivering as the damp sections touched her skin, then picked up the small pile of clothes they had chosen carefully together: a cotton shirt, a scraggy V-necked pullover, a tweed skirt and a battered pair of ladies shoes Kurt had bought at great expense from a black marketeer. She shoved the clothes down the front of the coat and buttoned it up, holding the items in place with one hand. "I'll be as quick as I can."

"Be very, very careful."

She slipped out of the apartment, and

began her journey down Pierson Road, one hand pressed to her chest to keep her little stash safe. The street, unsurprisingly so close to curfew, was deserted. She had to move quickly, silently; remembering the young deer that used to wander in the forests around Vienna, she tried to imitate their delicate footsteps. What luck, she thought bitterly, that she was now the same weight she had been at thirteen. Breathing hard, she hurried across the Esplanade and toward the seafront, her head constantly turning, her eyes darting to every flicker of light or perceived movement. Thank heaven there was barely any moon tonight, and a fair cover of cloud.

She reached the seafront, stepping delicately across the small railway track the Germans had laid last year to transport their building materials, and made her way to the steps leading down to the beach. After a last check for patrols, she began her descent. The stone risers were too high for comfort, and she had to take extra care not to slip — a tumble and a broken ankle now would put an end to everything. Finally she reached the beach. A few meters down the shore on either side were fences of barbed wire and signs declaring mines, but there was enough space around her for the plan to work. With her breath coming in thick, nervous pants, she pulled the clothes out of the coat and laid them on the sand. It seemed criminal to throw such items away, and for a moment she wondered about keeping the pullover. But she reminded herself that she had to make this look realistic. This was a piece of theater, and as such needed some level of sacrifice. Folding them into a neat pile, she took the carefully worded note from her pocket and placed it on top. Searching around for the largest stone she could find, she picked it up and placed it on the note. Then she stood back to assess her work, knowing that she had only one chance to get this right.

Out in the bay the sweeper light of a sea patrol swung across the black water. She thought about Jean-Paul, counting his money in the dark corner of some tavern. Her last sight of him had been his stooped, hardy body hauling the boat back to its secret boathouse, perhaps unwilling to attempt the journey alone, or perhaps just deciding to postpone his adventure for another day. She hoped one day he'd make it, but understood that she would probably never know. He was part of the world she was leaving behind.

She had resisted Kurt's idea for several

hours. Not because she thought staging her suicide an implausible idea — many islanders had been driven to it in the last couple of years, and she had more reason than most. It was more that in a small, heavily guarded community, permanent concealment seemed impossible. And could she even survive such a life? Whatever hardships she had faced up till now would seem like nothing. How long would it last? A year, two? Five, six, seven? The numbers spun in her head, meaningless, terrifying. But she had no other option. Kurt was right: if actual disappearance was out of the question, an illusion of it was the next best thing.

Taking a last look at the picture story she had created, she tiptoed back up the steps to the seafront and across the main road. She hurried past what had once been the People's Park, now the headquarters of the Organisation Todt, walking as quickly as her legs could carry her, looking around her all the time. At the same time, she couldn't help but enjoy that fresh air and savor the scent of the ocean and the evergreens. She took in the glory of the stars, the majesty of the cumulus clouds scudding across the sky, and tried to imprint it on her mind. It would be a long time before she saw all this again.

She reached the narrow entrance to the

alleyway that ran behind the terraced back-yards of West Park Avenue and, with one final confirmation that no one was watching, scuttled down the passage until she reached the gate of number seven. Lifting the wooden latch, she let herself into the yard, crossed quickly to the back door and tapped four times as arranged. It opened immediately and Hedy stepped inside, shivering with cold and fear. Kurt was already standing in the kitchen, his features tight with anticipation. Dorothea hugged her briefly, then, without a word, closed the door and pulled across the heavy black bolt.

NINE

Kurt stood in the hallway of his billet, listening hard. Fortunately — or unfortunately, depending how one looked at it — this was a creaky old house, and every footstep on the upper floors could be heard downstairs. Other officers were moving around, padding across their rooms, crossing to the bathroom, closing doors. This was a useful time of day, he figured, when those on night shift had already left, and the rest of his colleagues were taking advantage of this break to wash, write letters home or snooze on their beds. In about fifteen minutes Fischer and the rest would pile downstairs for their evening meal, prepared by housekeeper Mrs. Mezec, a local woman who came in daily to collect laundry and cook for the officers. Evidently she was a cousin of the original residents who had evacuated in 1940, and considered this a way to keep an eye on the place. She only spoke if absolutely necessary, and pocketed her wages each Friday with a sullen nod. Most of the officers ignored her or made tasteless jokes about how grateful she'd be for their attentions. Kurt often sniffed his dinner before eating it, knowing full well what revenge he would take in her shoes.

Strolling into the kitchen with what Kurt hoped looked like casual interest in tonight's menu, he found Mrs. Mezec stirring a pot on the stove, and smiled at her. She acknowledged him without anything resembling a greeting. Kurt adjusted the chairs around the kitchen table, as if preparing for a dinner party, then sat down.

"What is dinner tonight, Mrs. Mezec?"

"Pork stew."

Kurt nodded with enthusiasm, wondering which poor local farmer had had their valuable porcine asset grabbed by soldiers and loaded onto a pickup. Still, this meant there were likely to be further cuts of meat in the larder. Hedy had refused pork in the early days, but any such cultural taboos had long been discarded.

"Sounds delicious. Oh, by the way, the window in the bathroom is jamming again. Would you mind taking a look at it, please?"

She turned to him with a look that could sour milk. "I'm not a handyman."

Kurt beamed at her. "Of course not, but you have a . . . what is the English word . . . a knack."

Mrs. Mezec laid down the wooden spoon in her hand and, without trying to hide the roll of her eyes, shuffled out of the kitchen to see to it. Kurt leapt up and opened the larder door, taking care to place a finger on the ball catch to prevent it making a pinging sound. It was dim inside, but as he suspected, a decent-sized leg of pork lay on the back shelf, covered by a sheet of muslin. All Kurt needed was a sharp knife to hack a slice off the front. He was about to take one from the drawer when he heard footsteps on the stairs. Damn it — he would have to sneak down in the early hours to complete his mission. He moved quickly to the sink and pretended to be washing his hands.

"Evening, Neumann." Fischer was dressed smartly and smelled of scented soap. Where the hell he had got hold of something like that, Kurt could only guess. There were rumors that Fischer had now moved on from his pregnant married lover, and was now screwing the widow of some local aristocrat. "Waiting for dinner?"

"I am. I'm starving." Kurt kept his tone light and playful. "Good day?"

Fischer grunted and threw the local paper

298

onto the table. "Bloody waste of time. Had to attend the burial of those Allied seamen washed up on the beach. Bigwigs decided to send a guard of honor and a firing party, show 'respect.' I ask you, what's the point?" Indeed, Kurt thought, considering how we treat them while they're alive. But he kept his jovial expression pasted in place. Fischer gestured to the paper. "Think there's a photograph in there somewhere." Kurt obediently took the paper and leafed through it while Fischer droned on. "What sickens me is that the Allies are placing sea mines all around the islands, trying to stop our supplies coming across from France, but top brass still insist we doff our caps when we manage to blow them out of the water."

Kurt mumbled a passive agreement, but was no longer listening. There, in the middle of the paper, was a photograph of Hedy. It was a professional shot in a formal pose, and from her normal weight and creamy complexion he knew it must be an old one, presumably taken before the war. Perhaps she had had some portraits done as a gift to send to her family in Austria. Her hair, thick and lustrous, was swept back from her face; those eyes he knew so well were looking up toward something or someone to the right of the camera; and there was both a trace of a smile and a sense of sadness in her expression. But what drew Kurt's gaze was the text above it in German, and the same lines in English below:

Notice
The German authorities are looking for Miss Hedwig Bercu (see photograph), typist, of no nationality, 24 years of age, formerly residing at West Park, 1 Canon Tower. She has been missing from her residence since November 4th, 1943, and has evaded the German authorities. Any person who knows the whereabouts of Miss Bercu is requested to get in touch with the Feldkommandantur 515, who will treat any information with the strictest confidence. Anyone concealing Miss Bercu or aiding her in any other manner makes himself liable to punishment.

It was signed by the Field Commander, with today's date.

Kurt read and reread the notice. Of course, he'd been expecting this. It was ten days since Hedy had effectively vanished from the outside world, and despite her efforts, it wouldn't have taken the secret police long to trace her address once they decided to find her. What was worrying, though, was that the notice mentioned nothing about a suicide. Had they not found the clothes and the note? Did they not believe it? Or was not mentioning it here some kind of trap? He glanced toward Fischer, wondering if the Nazi had deliberately led Kurt to the paper, knowing he would see the photograph. Perhaps this was all an elaborate ruse to gauge his reaction. Kurt's mind was still grabbing at possibilities when he realized Fischer was still talking to him.

"Don't you think?"

"Hmm?"

"I'm saying, next time we should just chuck the bodies in a hole and be done with it. Either that or burn them for fuel. Damn freezing in this house!" Fischer laughed at his own joke.

Kurt thought about the crematoria at the camps and imagined punching Fischer across the kitchen. Instead, he folded up the paper and smiled. "Yes, it is. You know, an engineer friend of mine got hold of a load of logs last week. I'll pop over there, see if he'll sell us a couple." He held up the newspaper, opting for a double bluff. "Mind if I borrow this? There's a picture in here of that missing Jew — this guy lives near the compound, maybe he's seen something."

Fischer, giving nothing away, merely nodded. Kurt walked into the hall, took his greatcoat from the peg, and slipped quietly out into the night. If he jogged some of the way he could be at West Park Avenue in thirty minutes.

"Okay, I am going to knock now." Hedy laid her ten cards on the table.

Dorothea leaned over to look at them, and her face creased a little with embarrassment. "You need at least three for a run, Hedy."

"I have three — Queen, King, Ace?"

"But Ace is low in this game, remember?" Dorothea sat back in her chair with the kind of bright smile you'd give a child. "Never mind, let's deal again. You've almost got it."

"Do you mind if we stop?" Hedy heard the tightness in her own voice. "I'm a little tired."

It was a feeble excuse, but the thought of sitting at this table any longer, playing yet another round of this pointless game, set off a rising panic that was becoming all too familiar in recent days. As usual, it was accompanied by sweating, breathlessness and a barely controlled desire to run out into the street. It was all she could do to stay in her chair. Dorothea collected the cards and tucked them back into their pack.

"You're right, we've been playing for hours. Shall I see what we've got in the larder for dinner?"

Hedy stared at her new housemate, mystified by her stoicism. As if they might open the larder door and find shelves groaning with cold chicken and homemade tarts, and it were merely a matter of deciding what accompaniments to serve. Her unrelenting cheeriness, the determined avoidance of any alarming thought or memory, baffled Hedy; once or twice she'd actually wondered if Dorothea was quite right in the head. Just the other night, Dorothea had pulled the wireless from the cupboard under the stairs, and they had crouched in the doorway listening to the BBC news at the lowest possible volume, poised to thrust it back into its hiding place at a second's notice should anyone knock on the door. The news was depressing, the main headline being the Allied defeat in the Dodecanese. Yet at the end of the broadcast, Dorothea packed the wireless away and returned immediately to her movie scrapbooks, humming a jolly American big-band tune to herself, as if none of it had really touched her. The melody sawed at Hedy's nerves like cheese wire as she tried to occupy herself looking up the island of Leros in Dorothea's old atlas.

Hedy also noticed that Dorothea had begun to duck any mention of Anton, although Hedy had seen her kiss his photograph on her way up to bed. Hedy was only allowed to mention his name in the context of the past, and even then only happy memories were acceptable. Any talk of local trouble was closed down too, whether it was last week's night-bombing raids that almost shattered the windows, or public notices about the salt shortage. Conversely Dorothea would drag her adored movie stars into any conversation, as she did the imagined lives of the knitted dolls she kept on her bedroom windowsill. She introduced them to Hedy one by one, explaining the stories behind their names, and gazing into their expressionless woolen eyes as if she could read their thoughts. Sometimes Hedy looked at this overgrown, delusional kid and had to remind herself that this was the same woman who had bellowed patriotic songs into the faces of hostile Germans at the quayside.

She realized that Dorothea was waiting for an answer to her question.

"Of course," Hedy replied, "let's take a look."

When Kurt had first suggested Dorothea's

house as a hideout, Hedy had dismissed the idea. For one, she was certain Dorothea would never agree to such a dangerous arrangement on a permanent basis. And she would go crazy, she pointed out, finding Dorothea's company difficult enough over a couple of hours.

But Kurt had put up irrefutable arguments. Practically no one on this island could link the two of them, as they'd only been seen in public together a handful of times. Neither of them had any friends who might drop by or ask awkward questions, and with Anton away there was plenty of space. In any case, what alternatives did they have?

Dorothea said yes. She hadn't hesitated for a second, even when Kurt had spelled out the risks to her quite openly. On the night of Hedy's arrival, she seemed excited by the idea of a houseguest, flitting from room to room finding spare blankets for the old single mattress she and Kurt had hauled into the attic space through the tiny hatch. Beneath the eaves she had pushed back old packing cases and ancient, moldering rugs to create a bed area, and placed up there a precious candle in a holder and a few books to read. Hedy could move freely around the house during the day, so long as she stayed away from the windows. Should anyone unexpected come to the door, a carefully placed dresser beneath the attic hatch and a short hook-on ladder would enable Hedy to climb into her hiding space and have the cover back within half a minute.

Hedy concentrated all her efforts into trying to feel grateful, but the reality of her new imprisonment was already taking its toll. Her new sleeping arrangements, despite her host's best efforts, were a particular torture. The pitch black when she blew out the candle was a nightmare; every settling sound of the house manifested as the scurry of a mouse or rat, and locating a precious match to allay her fear was nigh impossible. Hedy had taken to sleeping in her clothes as the space was so cold, and calls of nature either risked a catastrophe with a bucket or simply had to be ignored till daylight. She had started napping in the front room during the day to compensate for her sleepless nights, but was jolted awake by every footstep or raised voice on the street outside. For the first time, Hedy was starting to feel more anxious about the condition of her mind than of her body. A sense of obligation and gratitude kept such thoughts buried, and in any case she didn't want Dorothea fussing over her any more than she already did. But knowing that the one thing that would calm her would be a stroll in the fresh air, knowing that even this simple pleasure was now out of bounds, made her want to curl up into a ball and scream.

There was also the unsolvable issue of food. As Hedy's ration card could no longer be used, they were now forced to survive on a single ration, plus whatever extras Kurt could provide on the days he made it to the house. The two women were now as dependent on him as Kurt was reliant on their sense and security. Sometimes, in her fitful afternoon naps, Hedy dreamed of a three-stick tripod, bound with twine and trembling on a wasteland, whipped by a wind that threatened to send it flying into pieces. Then she would wake with a shout, and when Dorothea asked if she was all right, would pretend it was a childhood dream of monsters. She never knew if Dorothea believed her, but no further questions ever came.

The coded knock at the back door alerted them both. Checking at the kitchen window, Dorothea nodded that it was Kurt and hurriedly let him in. Hedy ran to him and hugged him, fighting disappointment when she saw he was carrying nothing more substantial than an evening paper.

"I'm sorry," Kurt said, reading her thoughts. "Fischer came down at the crucial moment. But I'll try and get down to the kitchen later tonight. I thought you should see this."

He showed her the notice in the newspaper. Hedy read it several times and stared at the picture. It had been taken in 1939, and the physical changes in four years shocked her; she wondered if Kurt was thinking the same thing. She folded the paper and handed it back.

"We knew this was coming. Maybe they haven't found the clothes and the note yet. It's not like people are using the beaches."

"Maybe."

"Can you stay a while?"

Kurt shook his head, despondent. "I'm meant to be out getting logs. I need to get back." He stroked her face with his fingers. "Do you have enough food tonight?"

Hedy made a titanic effort to smile. "We'll manage. Don't worry."

Kurt kissed her lightly on the lips then slipped out into the darkness of the alleyway and was gone again. Hedy felt a strong urge to weep, but choked it down. Dorothea's fingers fluttered on the back of Hedy's neck in an attempt to comfort her before propelling her toward the larder.

She opened the door. "Right, then — what do we have here? How about a nice mashed swede with a boiled potato?"

"But there's barely enough for one."

Dorothea laughed pointlessly. "You boil the water and I'll cut the swede up, all right?" While Hedy ran freezing water into a pan, Dorothea took the vegetable and began to slice it on a wooden board, her hands pushing the knife expertly through the flesh, softly humming to herself a melody that Hedy vaguely recognized. She turned to Hedy. "You know that one?"

Hedy forced herself to answer. "It's from a movie, I think?"

"Top Hat — Fred Astaire and Ginger Rogers. It won the best song of 1935. Did you see the film?"

"I don't remember."

The phrases from the newspaper notice were running through Hedy's mind. Missing from her residence . . . evaded the German authorities . . . concealing Miss Bercu . . . liable to punishment . . . Dorothea's knife kept disappearing into the swede, the slices falling one after the other, helpless against the gleaming metal. Over and over the blade sawed its way through the pale flesh. Hedy felt bile rise in her throat and realized that even tonight's meager meal may be beyond her.

"Did you know," Dorothea was saying, "that Ginger Rogers had to fight the director to wear that dress? You know, the beautiful one with all the feathers? But she won, and it looks amazing, the most beautiful gown in any movie. When we've had dinner, I'll show you a picture. And I'll show you some of the other gowns of hers. She's got such style, don't you think? Would you like that?"

Hedy heard her own voice from the end of a long tunnel, as she forced out the smallest smile and replied, "Yes. Yes, that would be fun."

Kurt stood still on the pathway, his eyes skyward. All over the compound, workers had stopped to do the same, transfixed. The plane, clearly visible in the blue winter sky, climbed then dived, displaying its RAF roundel to the world. Antiaircraft guns could be heard firing at it from every direction, and when smoke began to pour from its rear end, there was a gasp as everyone thought it had been hit. Kurt held his breath, waiting for the plane to tumble toward them, taking out houses and civilians in its path. But the plane turned to climb again, and the letter "V" began to form in smoke in the sky.

The muttering around the compound grew to a full-throated hum as questions were thrown, one to another. Was it the beginning of a daylight raid, or just a warning of worse to come? Then, when the plane shut down its smoke and sped away northward toward the English coast, most agreed it was probably a Christmas message of support for the islanders from Mr. Churchill. Good for him, Kurt thought to himself, though an airdrop of food parcels would have brought these people a lot more joy.

He turned to head back to the metal lean-to where the latest collection of pickups were awaiting repairs. That was when he saw him. He would know that hat anywhere, perched idiotically to one side, bobbing through the crowd. And when those piggy eyes found Kurt and crinkled in a fake smile, Kurt knew immediately that this was not a social visit. Deciding that it was safer to take the lead, Kurt approached him with his hand held out.

"Erich, how are you? It's been a while."

Wildgrube's clammy hand slithered out to shake his own. "It certainly has. A long while."

Instantly, Kurt realized his mistake. Following that hideous night in the officers' club, Kurt had felt far too angry to face the man again in a social situation. Frankly, he didn't trust himself not to have one too many drinks and say something stupid, maybe even start a fight. He'd effectively dumped Wildgrube as a drinking partner, always coming up with excuses whenever Wildgrube suggested another "boys' night" or boozing session. Apart from a birthday party Wildgrube had thrown for himself, to which Kurt had reluctantly shown up for half an hour, their recent encounters had been limited to official engagements, or bumping into each other in town. It was obvious now that Wildgrube felt slighted, and would take his revenge.

Kurt could have kicked himself for not seeing this one coming. He offered his warmest smile. "So what can I do for you?"

Wildgrube pulled a small booklet from his inside pocket, flicking through it till he came to the right page. Kurt could see that it was a book of portrait photographs — people of interest to the secret police. He shoved it under Kurt's nose. "This girl. You know her?"

Kurt didn't need to look, but made a show of peering at it. It was the photograph of Hedy that had appeared in the local paper.

His blood began to pump, but his mind spoke to him softly — how he behaved in the next minute could change the entire course of his life.

"I saw that photograph in the Post a couple of weeks back. She's gone missing, hasn't she?" He looked back to Wildgrube, and saw that the man's eyes had never left his own.

"She has. Does she look familiar to you?"

Kurt thought fast, trying to calculate how much Wildgrube already knew, feeling the man's hot, sour breath on his face.

"A little." He groped in his memory for what he had previously admitted, trying to recall the content of numerous conversations. "Is this the Jew who was given a job here?" Wildgrube gave the tiniest nod. "She doesn't look Jewish, actually. Maybe that's how the mistake occurred — someone forgot to check her papers."

"But you remember her?"

"From around the compound."

"Nothing else?"

"Afraid not."

Wildgrube took back the booklet and tucked it into his pocket. Kurt knew from the twitch at the corner of the policeman's mouth that he had an ace to play, and was enjoying the anticipation of pulling it out.

What a tragic little bastard, Kurt thought, getting his kicks in life from cat-and-mouse games like this.

Wildgrube made the most of his moment, dragging it out until the last possible second. "Unfortunately, Lieutenant, that does not fit with what other people have told me. OT Feldwebel Schulz recalls quite clearly that when she came here for her job interview two years ago, you showed quite an interest in her. He remembers that you followed her down to the gate as she left."

Jesus, Kurt thought, how did these people remember such details? Did they have nothing better to think about?

"Well, if Schulz remembers that, I probably did. To be fair, she's pretty cute . . . If you didn't know," he added quickly.

"And other people here recall that you have been seen talking to each other on several occasions."

Kurt stalled. They had been so careful in recent months. And of course Wildgrube could be lying. But there were other times, before he knew the whole picture, before he became conscious of security . . .

"I might have spoken to her once or twice. But to be honest, Erich" — Kurt tried to grin, uncertain he could pull off — "I talk to a lot of girls. I mean, I don't take notes!"

314

He chuckled, but Wildgrube's expression did not change.

"Are you aware that this woman was stealing petrol coupons for some considerable time?"

Kurt blew air between his lips with some force. "So it's true. I heard the secretaries gossiping about it. You caught her?"

"We have sufficient grounds for her arrest."

"And that's why she went missing?" Kurt girded himself, waiting.

"No doubt. Now this vermin is loose, unaccounted for. And her interest in petrol coupons does, I'm afraid, create a strong connection to you."

Kurt breathed in. Attack was his only option now. "Damn it, Erich, will you never let this go? I made one mistake, years ago, and served my time for it. Half the employees are pilfering something! Am I to be linked to everyone you catch for the rest of my time here?"

Wildgrube stared at him, emotionless. "So you know nothing about this woman or where she might be?"

"Why on earth would I?" He threw up his hands in exasperation. "But the size of this island, I wouldn't have thought she'd be hard to find."

"That's the interesting thing." Wildgrube readjusted his Alpine hat to an even more ridiculous angle. "We found a pile of clothes on the beach, with a suicide note written in her own hand — we checked it against examples in the office."

"Well, there you go. That answers your question, doesn't it?"

"It would, it would. Except for one thing. You are aware of the tidal system around these islands?" Kurt gave a neutral shrug, even though he knew exactly where this was going. "It is one of the largest tidal ranges in the world. As we have seen from the bombing of ships in the vicinity, the bodies invariably end up on the island shores. Just last week a storm tide threw up all sorts of debris. Yet, no body has been reported. Not one sighting, after a month."

"Maybe she weighted herself down, or the body hit a mine."

"Perhaps. Or perhaps the whole 'suicide' is a ruse and she is still somewhere on the island. If so, we will find her, and both she, and anyone assisting her, will be dealt with appropriately." Wildgrube brushed imaginary fluff from his coat and lifted his hat. "Good to talk to you again, Kurt. Thank you for your help in this matter. We shall speak again, I'm sure." And, with a ludicrous

316

little bow, he puttered off into the crowd. Kurt watched the hat dip and weave away. One word spun around and around his brain like a mantra. Scheisse . . . scheisse . . . scheisse.

It was Christmas Eve. The distant sound of carolers could be heard across the park, and doors up and down the street banged throughout the day as housewives scurried into town and back, sniffing out every shop rumored to have festive treats in store. Most returned empty-handed. The small patches of sky visible at the top of the windows were already the color of slate, sucking the color out of the chimneys and rooftops; somewhere, beyond the clouds, the sun was preparing to set.

Hedy sat with her chin on her knees, hugging her shins for warmth, and wriggled to get comfortable. No fat reserves, she'd recently discovered, meant that sitting for long periods, even with a cushion, was a painful experience. But what else could she do? She had spent the afternoon wandering aimlessly from room to empty room, searching for the balance between warming up and burning calories, but last night even climbing the stairs to the attic had left her panting and dizzy. Her weakness frightened her. What if there was an emergency that meant she needed to run? What if she got really sick? Approaching Doctor Maine for any kind of treatment would mean drawing him into this conspiracy. So far, no further arrests had been reported in connection with her case, implying that either Quinn had kept Maine's name out of it, or that the Germans had chosen not to pursue a useful individual based on hearsay. Dorothea told Hedy she thought she'd seen Maine leaving the hospital two weeks before, though it was dark and she couldn't be certain. Hedy had desperately hoped that she was right.

She looked at the calendar on the wall — a homemade affair made from movie magazine cuttings, the dates marked out in stubby pencil. Images of Christmases in Vienna floated across her mind — the lights in the squares, the creaking, laden stalls of produce in the market. Though the family had never celebrated it at home, she'd always loved the atmosphere on the streets, soaking up the excitement of Christian friends and neighbors. One year, Roda had been given a huge box of yellow and pink bonbons by an admirer. She wondered what Roda was doing today — if she were still alive.

She had been living in Dorothea's house

for a little over six weeks now. For every seven days, they had between them two ounces of margarine, seven ounces of flour, three of sugar, four ounces of meat, plus four and a half pounds of bread. Tea was a flavor barely remembered. Salt was now impossible to obtain unless you could get access to seawater. Each Friday, Dorothea burst eagerly through the door, beaming all over her pallid little face, and laid the week's fare on the kitchen table. For a few moments they rejoiced as they devoured an acceptable lunch — perhaps a slice of tongue to go with a crust of tasteless Occupation bread, or a scrap of imported mutton that could be stewed into an edible form with some potatoes. Then they would force themselves to stash the rest of the goods in the larder, and eke out their supplies for the days to come. Kurt still brought whatever he could, but knowing that he was under surveillance, his visits were currently reduced to once or twice a week, often empty-handed. Last Sunday he stayed no more than ten minutes, giving Hedy only the briefest hug and kiss on the forehead; sometimes she wondered if that particular deprivation wasn't the most painful of all.

Hours drifted by. It was now completely dark outside, and cold in the house. Hedy didn't dare to light a fire; there was so little wood left, and in any case it would have been reckless to display any signs of life while Dorothea was absent. She compromised by lighting the paraffin lamp. From next door came the sound of festive merriment — numerous voices raised in excitement. Hedy tried to remember what it was like to have raucous, carefree fun like that.

When the hands of the clock reached eight, she felt her anxiety rise. Dorothea never stayed out this late in the evening, even when she visited her ailing grandmother. She had left at lunchtime, muttering something about visiting a cousin in St. Martin's. It had struck Hedy as odd at the time — Dorothea had never mentioned this cousin before, and it was out of character for her to be so evasive about her movements. Hedy guessed that she was up to something, but was sensible enough, or cowardly enough, not to ask.

Eight thirty. Hedy began to wonder what she'd do if Dorothea didn't come back. There was no telephone, and anyway, who would she ring? There was no means of finding anything out; she couldn't even go out and buy a newspaper. She would be dependent on Kurt's next visit, not just for information but for her next meal. As the minutes ticked by, her anxiety grew, and it took every shred of self-discipline not to pull back the curtains and peer out into the dark, deserted street.

Suddenly she heard the clip-clop of a horse's hooves and the grind of heavy cart wheels. Horses rarely came down this street, and never at this time. Hedy rose from her seat and, taking the paraffin lamp with her, moved to the doorway between the sitting room and hallway, breathing heavily. From outside came bizarre sounds — scraping, banging and the grunts of people straining to move heavy objects. And then, another noise — a high-pitched screech that sounded like . . . No, Hedy told herself, she was imagining it. It couldn't possibly be . . . ?

The front door flew open and the noise crashed into the house like a double-decker bus. Squealing, gasping and clattering. Hedy gaped, astonished, as Dorothea slammed the front door behind her and pressed herself against it, a mixture of panic and triumph on her face. At the same time Hedy let out a shriek as something at knee-height brushed quickly past her legs. Her eyes followed the squealing sound that accompanied the shape, and there it was, careering down the hallway toward the kitchen — a young pig. She stared at Dorothea, too shocked to speak.

Dorothea's voice was shrill with excitement. "Quickly! Trap it in the kitchen!" Breathless, she pushed Hedy toward the kitchen door. "I was going to bring it round the back, but I was afraid it might escape up the alleyway. We have to kill it before the neighbors hear."

Hedy looked from Dorothea to the pig, which was now careering around the kitchen in panicky circles, looking for a way out.

"You can't be serious. Neither of us knows how to butcher a pig." She pressed herself against the wall, half expecting the animal to attack her. A familiar sentence from her childhood was running through her head: "And the pig, because it has a cloven hoof that is completely split, but will not regurgitate its cud; it is unclean for you. You shall not eat of their flesh, and you shall not touch their carcasses; they are unclean for you." She had long abandoned kosher rules — pork being one of the only meats occasionally available on the island — but killing it herself? That was an entirely different matter.

But Dorothea had a glint in her eye Hedy had never seen before. "We can do it, between us. We can use this." Dorothea began rummaging through an old wooden crate in the hallway, which she used for storing old newspapers, as Hedy looked anxiously toward the animal, now headbutting the walls in its desperation to escape. From the bottom of the pile of papers, Dorothea produced a slim, flat item that, in the dimness, Hedy could barely make out. Only when Dorothea undid the catch and pulled it from its sheath did Hedy realize she was holding a knife, about twenty centimeters long with a clean, gleaming blade. "Anton left it with me when he went away, in case I should ever need it. It's sharp enough." She held it out to Hedy like a prize.

Hedy put her hand on the wall to steady herself, scarcely believing this was happening. She was aghast at this stranger before her, a crazed, fearless fireball who stashed forbidden weapons and murdered wild animals in her own kitchen. "No, Dorothea, I can't! I can't even touch it. Really!"

Dorothea placed her hand on Hedy's arm, gentle but firm. "I can't do this alone. You have to help me." Hedy's head continued to shake, but Dorothea's grip grew tighter. "I mean it. If just one neighbor gets wind of this, they could call the Germans down here." She listened for a moment, hearing the revelries next door. "They're having a party — perfect. Come on!"

She walked purposefully into the kitchen, stuffing the blade down the front of her brassiere. The pig became even more agitated. Its trotters were clattering on the kitchen floor like a satanic tap dance. Hedy could see the hairs on its leathery skin, make out the pink moistness of its snout. She wanted to scream, but Dorothea's voice was calm. "Keep that door closed, or it'll get loose in the house. Get the old tin bath, the one that's meant for the firewood — that should be big enough."

Too frightened to disobey, Hedy maneuvered herself toward the larder, making sure not to turn her back on the animal. She groped in the dark for the container on the larder floor and grabbed the end of it, hauling it noisily from the cupboard and skidding it across the kitchen floor with her foot.

"Good. Now we just have to catch the bugger!" Dorothea hissed. Hedy held the lamp a little higher. "Just keep thinking about the pork steaks we'll have! Right . . . I'm going to try and trap it in this corner. Copy me, keep moving forward." Dorothea opened her arms and made some low whooping noises to encourage the pig backward into the far corner. Placing the lamp on the side — the last thing they needed now was to be plunged into total darkness — Hedy extended her arms and moved forward too, creating a pincer movement between the two of them. The squealing grew louder, and Hedy longed to close her eyes and shut it all out, but her eyes remained fixed on their terrified prey. As she got close, Dorothea dropped to her knees and grabbed the pig by its middle, forcing its backside into the corner.

"Grab its front legs, Hedy, quickly!" Her tone was so urgent that Hedy did as she was told, thrashing with her arms to find the animal's legs, turning her face to the side in terror of being bitten, until she managed to grab one and then the other. Dorothea somehow managed to turn herself around until she had got a proper grip of its back end and lifted the animal by its rear legs. "Get it into the bath, on its back! Try to hold it still while I cut its throat."

Hedy heard her own voice, shrill, half screaming: "I can't, I can't!"

"You can! It's only a wee one, it's not that strong. Now lift!"

With huge effort they managed to swing the struggling beast up and into the tin bath. Hedy fought to hold a pair of legs in each hand as the animal twisted and writhed. Suddenly there was a squirting noise and the smell of shit was in her nostrils. Hedy retched violently, knowing that actual vomit was not far behind.

"Quickly!" Dorothea was screaming herself now. Party or no party, the neighbors were going to hear something soon if they didn't finish this fast. Just then, Hedy saw Dorothea pull the sheath knife from her brassiere and slice it forcefully across the pig's throat. The squealing stopped instantly, but the thrashing grew worse.

"Again, again!" Hedy cried. "It's not dead!"

Dorothea pulled the knife free where it had got stuck in the flesh and slashed again. Immediately the flailing stopped, and the animal lay limp in the bath, half submerged in its blood and shit. Hedy rushed to the kitchen sink and vomited green bile and water, having nothing else in her stomach. By the time she turned back, Dorothea had hauled the animal up by the neck and slit its belly from top to bottom, spilling guts and organs into the disgusting soup beneath. Her hands and wrists were covered in blood and gore. When most of the blood had drained she let the carcass slip down, and looked toward Hedy with a look of overwhelming relief. Only then, hearing the wheezing in her breath and seeing the tears in Dorothea's eyes, did Hedy understand the superhuman effort it had taken her to accomplish this. Hedy moved toward her and squeezed her arm. "Well done. That was extraordinary."

Dorothea shut her eyes and shook her head. "Come on. We need to get this thing cleaned up — I'll bury the entrails in the park. Then . . ." She smiled. "Then we can make our Christmas dinner!"

Hedy moved the mouthful of pig's liver across her tongue, savoring it, letting the flavor transport her. She had already consumed one of the kidneys and a portion of its heart, but had saved the tastiest part till last. A little juice ran from the corner of her mouth and she saved it with her finger, pushing it back into her mouth. At that moment Dorothea did exactly the same, and both of them giggled like children. Hedy took another bite, astonished at herself. She had anticipated revulsion, or at least regret; the trauma of the slaughter, the nausea she'd felt scraping the filth from the carcass under the cold tap, the imagined horror of her mother. But right now she felt as if every cell within her body was bursting into life, like a wilting plant finally taking water. Singing still swelled and faded from the other side of the party wall, adding to the sense of celebration, and the light of the paraffin lamp danced on the wall above the table. Dorothea had opened a bottle of Beaujolais she had been saving for a special occasion — it was a little vinegary, but velvety on the tongue — and by the third sip Hedy could already feel its effect.

"What should we do with the rest of it?" Hedy wondered aloud, using a small crust of bread to mop the remains of the juice from her plate.

Dorothea shrugged. "Tomorrow we must skin it and cut it up. Then we can keep it in the attic where it's cold — sorry, I'll put it as far away from you as I can. Should last at least a week."

"What about the backyard?"

"Too dangerous. Someone might steal it, or a dog will get to it."

"Do you think we can get through it all in a week?"

"If we don't, we can trade it for eggs or fresh rabbits. There's still things you can get in the country parishes, if you know who to ask."

Hedy's chewing was interrupted by a mouthful of gristle, but she happily swallowed it anyway. "How did your cousin manage this? I thought the Germans accounted for every piglet born?"

"The farmers have their tricks. They'll sneak a sow into another pen while the Germans aren't looking, so it gets counted as a different pig — then the Jerries don't notice when one goes missing." She snorted laughter through her nose. "Apparently one farmer tied a bonnet on a pig and put it in his bed, told the Jerries it was his sick mother! They wouldn't even go in the room!"

Hedy burst out laughing, and they continued eating for a few more minutes until she piped up again: "I still don't understand why your cousin agreed to help us? I thought, apart from your grandmother, none of your family spoke to you anymore?"

Dorothea glanced down and hesitated a moment before replying. "He didn't want to help me, and he made it clear it's just this once. We won't be able to ask him for anything again."

"So why today? Because it's Christmas?"

Dorothea shook her head. "I told them Anton was dead."

Hedy sat back in her seat. "You lied to your own family?"

"I don't know that it is a lie."

"Dorothea!"

"I've heard nothing for months — Anton

may very well be dead."

Hedy felt a rush of pity. "You can't really think that? How do you carry on?"

Dorothea looked her straight in the eye. "I love Anton with all my heart, but we all have to face facts. God will find a path for me, for all of us, if it's his will."

Hedy shifted uncomfortably in her chair. "You still believe in God? After the last few years?"

Dorothea looked a little puzzled. "Of course." She turned her attention back to her plate, wiping the last specks of meat juice with a damp finger, wasting nothing. Hedy did the same, glancing up at Dorothea's face. There were dark rings beneath her eyes and flecks of gray at the sides of her jet-black hair. But she noticed a rigid set of her jaw and the pale lips that tightened when she was forced into an opinion or decision.

As Dorothea stood to collect the plates and take them to the sink, Hedy stopped her. "Is that why you agreed to shelter me here?"

Dorothea turned, the plates in her hand. "What do you mean?"

"Because you believe it's what God would want? That it's your duty?"

"I never thought about it like that."

"But you know what you're risking," Hedy pressed her. "What if Anton is still alive? He could be back in less than a year! You're both young, you'd have the rest of your lives together. Yet you've chosen to jeopardize all that for me."

Dorothea thought for a moment, then sat back down, placing the crockery on the table. "I didn't really think about any of that, to be honest. You're Anton's closest friend here, and you were in trouble. It was just the right thing to do."

Hedy shook her head. "I don't want to be responsible for anything happening to you. Kurt could find me another place."

"Don't talk daft." Dorothea put her arms around her. "You're far safer here. And I like the company." She began to pull away, anticipating Hedy's usual reluctance, but this time Hedy reached up and held her in the embrace.

"Thank you."

They stayed like that for a moment until the coded tap at the back door made them both jump. Dorothea hurried to open it, and Kurt, his collar turned up high for warmth and concealment, stepped lightly inside. Hedy, warmed by the wine and events of the day, ran to him and kissed him passionately, right in front of Dorothea. Both women gabbled at him for several minutes, talking over each other in their enthusiasm to tell the story of the pig's arrival, the drama of the slaughter, the wonderful meal.

Kurt listened to all of it before pushing back his hair with one hand and looking at both of them with a combination of admiration and horror. "If that cart had been stopped on the way over here, you'd have been arrested along with your cousin. Within a couple of days we'd all be in jail."

Dorothea nodded. "I know."

Kurt looked to Hedy for agreement, but Hedy shrugged. "Dorothea did this for us, Kurt. I think she's been incredibly brave."

Kurt raised the small glass of wine that Dorothea had poured for him. "You're right. To a merry Christmas, and a better one next year." Then he glanced awkwardly at Dorothea and back to Hedy, too embarrassed to be specific. "I won't be missed at my billet for a couple of hours . . ."

Without waiting to be asked, Dorothea gestured toward the hallway. "Use my bedroom — I need to clean the kitchen up anyway." Hedy blushed. But Dorothea made a shooing movement with her hands. "Go on, make the most of it. It's Christmas, after all."

Kurt nodded his thanks and took Hedy

by the hand, leading her toward the stairs. Halfway up, Hedy stopped and leaned over the banister. "Thank you. You're a good friend, Dory." She hesitated. "I believe Anton is still alive. And he'd be really proud of you." Then she followed Kurt up the stairs, feeling her body grow warm at the thought of him.

TEN

June 1944

"Hedy! Hedy, wake up!"

Hedy sat bolt upright on her mattress, almost banging her head on the rafter above, filled with panic before she was even properly conscious. In the slivers of morning light rising through the floor hatch, she could just make out Dorothea's features, and saw that she was smiling.

"What? What is it?"

"Listen. Can you hear them?"

Hedy sat perfectly still. The sound was outside — far away, but loud enough to penetrate the walls and windows. It was indisputably the throbbing drone of airplane engines. Not in ones and twos, as they were used to, but in dozens, perhaps scores. The noise was followed by another, louder and intermittent — the rat-a-tat-tat of antiaircraft fire. Hedy pushed the blankets off her legs and clambered across the rafters toward the hatch. "I want to see them."

Dorothea nodded and let herself down the ladder into the bedroom below, with Hedy following behind. They hurried to the window. Dorothea pulled back the blackout blind and the thin fabric curtain, and pressed her face to the window, her eyes skipping about to detect the movement of neighbors. Finding the backyards deserted, she beckoned Hedy toward her.

"Here . . ." She grabbed a small towel from her bed and handed it over. "Wrap this around your hair, as if you'd washed it. Then, if someone sees you, I can say it was me, and they made a mistake."

Hedy did as she was told, then, kneeling on the bed, pushed her face toward the window, looking out across the yard and onto the backs of the houses beyond. The long-forgotten colors of the outside world, even on this unseasonably cloudy day, set her senses alight — the emerald of the scrubby grass, the subtle blues and lilacs of the rain clouds! But the real excitement was in the distant sky. A squadron of planes, like a cluster of disciplined insects in rigid formation, was heading toward the French coast, followed by another, then another. She sat motionless for a moment, enthralled by the light, pattern and complexity, then dropped the curtains back.

"What time did this start?"

"A little while ago, and there's no sign of it stopping."

"So this is it? The Allied invasion?"

"I don't see how it can be anything else."

Hedy involuntarily clenched both fists and her teeth, emitting an impassioned growl. "Come on, come on! Let those bastards have it!" Then she saw the wince on Dorothea's face, and instantly regretted it. "Oh, Dory, I'm sorry."

Dorothea shook her head. "Don't worry. I know what you meant." She hastily buttoned her cardigan, and Hedy saw that her hands were trembling. "I'm going down to the market, see what I can find out."

"Be careful!" Hedy called after her. "The Jerries will be on edge today."

Hedy, washed and dressed, tried and failed to find something to distract her while she waited for Dorothea to return. The tick of the kitchen clock punctured the air as she paced the hallway; she could still hear the far-off hum of airplane engines and the crackle of German guns. She ached to switch on the wireless in the cupboard, but didn't dare. There was nothing for lunch, but she felt too nervous to eat.

Eventually, a little after four, Dorothea

returned, flushed with excitement. Hedy immediately dragged her into the kitchen and sat her down at the table.

"It's crazy out there!" Dorothea's voice was thick with agitation, and Hedy could hear her asthma bubbling underneath. "All the locals are smiling, some are even wearing red, white and blue rosettes! There are truckloads of Germans being driven out to man the gun emplacements and to guard billets. One man told me there are barbed-wire blockades across some roads in and out of town."

Hedy breathed deeply, trying to take it all in, attempting to picture the scene. "So Jerry thinks a full-scale Allied attack is on the way?"

"Must do. They were stopping lots of people, just ordinary pedestrians and cyclists, checking their papers." Dorothea's hands fidgeted in her lap. "There are so many rumors. Someone reported an American ship in St. Aubin's bay this morning, but it's nonsense. A woman told me she thought she'd seen Churchill himself in a car with the Field Commandant. I think she may be sick in the head," she added sadly.

Hedy reached out and patted Dorothea's hand; it was a mauve color, and the temperature of stone. "We need to stay calm. There

337

will be more news on the BBC tonight." She hesitated. "I don't suppose you saw Kurt?"

Dorothea shook her head. "I doubt he'll be able to visit for the next few days. They're all on high alert."

But a little before nine, just as they had finished their dinner of boiled macaroni, and Dorothea was about to pull the radio from its hiding place, Hedy heard Kurt's tap on the door. Gray-faced with dark rings beneath his eyes, he slumped at the kitchen table, throwing his cap onto the neighboring chair, while the two women stood around him, too nervous to settle.

"It's huge — I mean, massive. Thousands landing on the beaches in Normandy, vast air support. It's got to be the start of the end."

"So what happens now, I mean, here on the island?" Dorothea, beside the sink, was pushing up and down on her toes with excitement.

Kurt pulled a copy of the local evening paper from his inside pocket. "Read for yourself."

Hedy picked up the paper, and read aloud the proclamation dominating the front page: " 'Germany's enemy is on the point of attacking French soil. I expect the population of Jersey to keep its head, to remain calm, and to refrain from any acts of sabotage, and from hostile acts against the German forces, even should the fighting spread to Jersey. At the first sign of unrest or trouble, I will close the streets to every traffic and will secure hostages. Attacks against the German forces will be punished by death. Signed, the Commandant.' " Hedy shivered. "They sound scared. They really expect the locals to rebel?"

"God knows," Kurt replied. "They're taking some precautions — shipping out non-essential workers like nurses and canteen staff. And College House staff are sleeping on the premises in case of a night attack, though I don't see what good that will do."

"So they don't intend to surrender?"

"Most of the ordinary soldiers here would happily surrender, but the high-ups won't stand for it. With the defenses we've put up in the last two years, it could be a blood-bath." He rubbed his eyes, as if trying to press the images away. "But I suspect the Allies know that. Which is why I don't think —" He stopped abruptly.

Hedy felt her surge of hope ebbing away. "You don't think what?"

Kurt sighed deeply, from the gut. "The Allies will be looking to limit their losses. If

I were them, I would press on, try to gain ground on the Continent. The Channel Islands are tiny, after all. Plenty of time to come back for them later, when they've pushed the enemy line further."

Hedy, suddenly feeling a little unsteady, sank down onto the remaining chair. "You're saying they'll just . . . go around us?"

"Quite possibly."

"But if that happens, the islands will be completely cut off. There'll be no food or fuel from France or England. How will we survive?" She felt a painful lump form in her throat. "We'll all starve together."

Kurt squeezed her hand, but it brought no comfort. "Exactly."

"The public telephone system will remain suspended. A section of Gloucester Street jail is being set aside for casualties, and a Red Cross flag will be placed above it. Food stocks are to be removed from out-of-town depots and brought into stores in town . . ."

Baron von Aufsess paused, reading ahead down his list as if mentally sifting out some of the items. Kurt, standing a good six meters from him, swore he could hear the new chief administrator emit a small sigh. Then the baron coughed and continued, his clipped, aristocratic voice booming out across the hall. Something about potato supplies, and locals being warned away from the beaches. It was all the usual business: protect the garrison, override the populace, no surrender.

Kurt let his gaze wander. Beyond the windows of College House the sun was blazing, gulls were gliding on the summer breeze, and far above Allied planes continued to stream across the azure sky. Now and then came the dull boom of one of the giant cannons across the Channel; last night antiaircraft guns had brought down a British pilot at Les Landes, destroying two houses.

The baron continued to list instructions and priorities: all military were to use discretion, but come down hard on the smallest dissent; the deportation of all civilians to France could not be ruled out at this stage. Kurt looked at the haggard faces around the room, rigid with tension beneath a stoic veneer, and wondered who they believed they were fooling. It was just like the picturehouses where he'd watched Bela Lugosi films as a youth, when all the boys jutted out their chins and pretended not to be scared. Kurt's own stomach had been churning for days now, and the acrid scent

341

of sweat and sulfur in this room told him he was not alone.

Von Aufsess reached the end of his list and instructed his deputy to hand out new sectional orders. Kurt was charged with checking the working condition of every truck within his compound, maximizing transport potential should the need arise. Turning to leave, Kurt spotted Wildgrube at the back of the room. Like all the secret police, he was today dressed in military uniform, the first time Kurt had ever seen him so attired. From his strutting gait and the gleam in his eye, Kurt saw that the spy relished the opportunity to appear in public as a real soldier, and was forced to admit that it gave the little goon a genuine sense of authority. Hoping to avoid him in the crowd, Kurt pressed toward the door, but within a minute found Wildgrube at his shoulder.

"Kurt, my friend. How are you?"

"Just fine, Erich. Looking very smart today."

Wildgrube played with his cuffs. "We must all be on our best game to face what is before us." Kurt nodded, hoping that might be the end of the conversation. He'd seen little of Wildgrube since his attempt to intimidate him at the compound; Kurt had long hoped that a cold trail, combined with simple lack of manpower, had caused the investigation to be abandoned. Kurt had spotted the odd secret police minion outside his billet, and had twice curtailed a visit to West Park Avenue on the suspicion that he was being followed, but overall it seemed that Wildgrube had found other fish to fry. Kurt threw the spy a polite smile and went to move on, but felt a tug at his elbow. "Of course, recent events will necessitate a little . . . housekeeping."

"Housekeeping?"

"Old cases, unsolved problems. We need to reduce the burden of excess feeders on the island."

What kind of mind, Kurt thought, divided the human population up into such categories? "So?"

"So, we must make sure there are no ancient parasites lurking. One thing about me, Kurt . . ." He smirked, a cobra that had spotted a wounded mouse. "I am often commended for my scrupulous cleanliness." He patted Kurt on the shoulder then disappeared through the doorway and down the corridor, his blond head bobbing through the crowd.

Kurt watched him go with an indifferent sniff. Wildgrube had no more information about Hedy eight months on than he had in the week of her disappearance — he merely enjoyed the power of menace. If he had discovered anything new he'd have taken great delight in hauling Kurt into the notorious Silvertide building for questioning. Kurt decided there was enough to worry about this week — real, imminent dangers that far outweighed the niggling irritation of this idiot.

Kurt forced his way into the gray flannel mass of the corridor, pushing past the other officers, watching their reactions to the morning's briefing. Some were grimly silent; others opted for fake bravado, braying about finally seeing some action. He stuffed his hands into his pockets to imply endeavor and urgency, and instantly felt the lining of the right pocket, loose for some time, give way under the weight, allowing his hand to slip through to the inner layer. Glancing at the large mirror in the reception hallway to see if it was noticeable, he took in his whole reflection. Weight loss was causing the uniform to hang off him, like a schoolboy in his father's clothes. There was a grass stain on the knee of his trousers, picked up on an awkward repair job last week, which Mrs. Mezec's half-hearted laundering had not removed. And now he noticed a button missing from the front of his tunic, causing the fabric to gape instead of giving a crisp, smart line. The thousand-year Reich, he reflected with irony, was literally starting to fall apart at the seams.

"But my absolute favorite part . . ." Dorothea's eyes shone with excitement as she recalled the moment. Her palms ironed flat the open pages of the scrapbook on the table. ". . . is where she dumps Westley at the altar and rushes for her car. It's Peter she really loves, you see, and she realizes that true love is more important than anything."

"And her father approves?" Hedy traced the outline of Claudette Colbert's face with her finger. The edges were starting to curl for want of fresh paste, and her right ear had already disappeared.

"Her father is the one who tells her to go! He knows she doesn't really love Westley, you see, and he wants her to be happy." Dorothea turned the page. Shafts of golden-pink evening light slanted through the kitchen window and onto the table, creating patterns on the frayed paper and highlighting every line of Dorothea's face. "When all this is over, I'll take you to see it. It's my favorite movie."

"I'd like that. It sounds wonderful."

Hedy slowly gathered up the two plates and spoons they had used for their evening meal of unsalted potatoes, and carried them across to the draining board. The potatoes had been hard in the center, and sat heavy in her stomach; now that the gas supply was shut off and they were forced to rely on the communal bakehouse, it was potluck whether what Dorothea picked up at the end of the day was cooked through at all.

"Dorothea, do you ever think about your own parents?" The question was out of her mouth before she'd had time to weigh it, and she instantly regretted it. Dorothea always neatly sidestepped any reference to her family, making it clear that the subject was out of bounds. But Hedy had noticed, in recent weeks, they had both been voicing more direct, personal questions than they would have dreamed of asking six months ago. Perhaps it was the sense that the end to this bizarre, enforced marriage might not be far away, though neither of them dared to venture what that end might look like.

Dorothea kept her eyes on the scrapbook. "Sometimes."

"You ever think about going to see them?"

"Waste of time. My stepfather wouldn't allow it."

"Are you sure? It's been so long." A long silence. Dorothea slowly turned another page. Claudette Colbert gave way to Katharine Hepburn posing with a besuited Cary Grant. "Kurt says lots of older people are starting to get sick, with the shortage of food and medicines."

"I know." A strip of paper bearing the words Bringing Up Baby in curly, romantic lettering escaped completely from its ancient paste and fell to the bottom of the page. Dorothea caught it and stubbornly tried to force it back into position, to no avail.

Hedy returned to her chair. "Only . . . I know if I had the opportunity to see my parents just once more, no matter how painful —"

"Hedy, I tried, okay?" Dorothea slammed the book shut, her voice uncharacteristically loud. "I went up there in February, on my mother's birthday. My stepdad wouldn't come to the door, said if my mother didn't come back into the house he was done with her too." She shrank back, ashamed of her outburst. "My grandmother wrote to them, he tore the letter up. Like he said — I'm dead to them."

Hedy placed a hand on Dorothea's arm. "I'm sorry. You never said."

"You have enough problems of your own."

"It was brave to try."

Dorothea raised her finely plucked eyebrows, held the thought for a moment, and let them fall again. "I loved Anton so much, and I really believed that was all that mattered. But now . . ." She looked toward the window, and the last tips of the sun's rays colored her eyes an extraordinary blue. "Now I'm not so sure. Even if he does come back. At least you and Kurt have each other now. Sometimes, when I see the two of you together . . ."

"I'm sorry. We're not trying to —"

"Don't be silly. I know. You would never try to hurt me."

Hedy felt a flush of shame as a dozen memories rushed in: her resentment and dismissal of Dorothea at the start, her hope that she and Anton would cancel the wedding. Dorothea must have sensed at least some of it, yet in those wide, trusting eyes there was not a speck of resentment. Hedy had just begun to phrase some kind of apology in her head when Dorothea leaned back in her chair and began to cough.

"Do we have any mustard powder left?"

"I don't know, why?"

"I'm having trouble breathing."

Hedy rushed to the larder and scrabbled

through the shelves looking for the bottle. Sure enough, at the back was a small tin with a spoonful of mustard powder inside — she grabbed it and returned to Dorothea's side. "I've got it. Give me one minute."

Hedy shook out some of the powder onto a saucer. From the tap she added a few drops of water, dripping it in with her fingers, and stirred it into a yellow paste. Dorothea was by now leaning back in her chair, the wheezing of her breaths coming in short, strained gasps. Hedy pulled Dorothea's blouse open and smeared the paste onto her chest. Dorothea recoiled a little and began to whimper. "Burns!"

"I know." Hedy deliberately kept her voice low and steady. "But it will help. Try to keep your breaths regular. Count with me — in for five and out for five. One, two . . ." Her mind raced ahead. If Dorothea turned blue or began to lose consciousness, what was she to do? Kurt would not call till tomorrow at the earliest. Asking the neighbors was impossible — Hedy had never even seen them, far less judged whether they could be trusted with the sudden appearance of a foreigner on their street. ". . . And five. Now the same, going out. Come on, Dory, you can do it." She scrabbled for a plan. Perhaps she could drag Dorothea onto a neighbor's path, bang on the door then run back to the house before anyone saw her? The hospital was less than ten minutes away, surely someone would go for help? Though even there, the chances of them having any medication to help her were almost zero. "And again. You're doing well."

The breaths grew shorter and more tortuous. In the fading light of the kitchen, Hedy peered at Dorothea's features, and saw that the shade of lilac ash she most feared was now blooming on her lips. Her eyelids were drooping a little and she was starting to slump down on the tabletop. Hedy sat her back in her chair and held her upright to keep the airways open, all the while stroking her hair and keeping up a constant muttering of encouragement. But as the minutes crawled by and the hissing breaths grew weaker, Hedy knew she had to make a decision.

"Dory, I'm going to have to go for help. Just try to hang on." She turned to go, but felt a sudden clamp on her wrist. For a moment she barely believed it was Dorothea, so strong was the grip, but it pinned her where she stood. Then Dorothea, clinging to the struggling outbreaths as they fought their way through the fog of her lungs, pushed out the words: "No! Dangerous!"

"I know, but the hospital is the only place we have any chance of help."

Dorothea's hold, using only her thumb and forefinger, actually increased. "No! Not worth it!" She extended the fingers of her right hand and held it toward Hedy's face. "Five minutes."

Seeing that the suggestion was simply causing more stress, and afraid that Dorothea wouldn't survive her absence for longer than a few minutes, Hedy dropped back into her seat, dreading that she was making the wrong choice. Dorothea hauled in breath after breath, her face scrunched with concentration, each inhalation a private war with herself. The moments crawled by, the golden rays replaced with dim blue haze and purple shadows, and still Dorothea sat there, clay-faced, battling, until at last Hedy sensed the breaths grow fractionally looser, and the grip on her wrist released a little. Dorothea raised a finger from her limp hand on the table to indicate that change was afoot, and within a few minutes a little color returned to her lips and forehead.

"It's okay."

Relief bubbled up until it hurt Hedy's throat. "Thank God. But next time . . ."

Dorothea shook her head. "No! Never!

351

We've come this far. We must reach the end now." Then it was Dorothea's turn to comfort Hedy, as she dropped her chin to her chest and sobbed like a baby.

The spider crab, wrapped in newspaper and then in a torn pillowcase, was pressed so hard against the side of his body that Kurt could feel it wriggling. He had watched the fishmonger bind the claws tight with string, but it was still an unnerving experience to feel the creature strain and fight against the confines of its human prison. It had cost him a huge chunk of his wages and a proportion of his pitiful tobacco allowance, but none of that mattered. Kurt kept his arm firmly in place as he walked up Cheapside, imagining how Hedy's face would look when he presented her with it. There'd be no mayonnaise, of course, probably no bread either. But the ingenious contraption Kurt had set up on a recent visit, involving an old metal paint tin suspended over the fireplace, would enable them to boil the crab at home, provided they had enough wood, and eat it fresh from the shell. He thought about the two women cracking the claws, licking the delicious meat off their fingers, and smiled.

At the corner of the road, Kurt was forced

to admit to himself the suspicion that had been nibbling at the edge of his consciousness for several minutes. He was being followed. Glancing around as if checking for traffic, he scanned for a visible figure engaged in any kind of suspicious activity, and caught a glimpse of a man in a mac and trilby-style hat, fiddling pointlessly with a newspaper in a doorway. He couldn't tell from here whether or not it was Wildgrube — the hat suggested otherwise — but the behavior certainly suggested one of his henchmen. Either way, heading straight for West Park Avenue at this point was clearly out of the question. Kurt doubled back into the little park, following the tarmac path toward its center then suddenly swerving back toward the north end of Elizabeth Place. If this guy was following him, these twists and turns would surely force him out into the open. Kurt knew that he was clean — the crab had been legitimately bought and there was nothing about his person that couldn't be explained — and on that basis he felt confident about tackling the spy head-on. He began to prepare a stinging rebuke in his head, a righteous indignation at the waste of resources, snooping on German officers in their precious free time.

As he cleared the park and headed up the

street, he turned to look behind him. The man was still following, some distance away, but now making little attempt to hide his intent. He was moving slowly, and it occurred to Kurt that this might be a consequence of poor fitness, rather than incompetent subterfuge. Recent rations had been atrocious; perhaps the TB currently running rife through the local population was starting to infiltrate the sanctity of the secret police. Serve the bastards right, Kurt thought. But the thought gave him another option: to pick up his pace and make a clean getaway.

Kurt accelerated his stride until he was in a rapid march, his long legs moving like pistons across the paving stones. Reaching the corner of Parade Road, he took a speedy left and jogged past the row houses. He knew that coming up on the left was the entrance to the alley that ran parallel with the backyards of West Park Avenue. If he managed to put enough distance between them, he might be able to slip down there before his pursuer figured out where he'd gone. But as he was about to do just that, he glanced behind him and saw that the figure was still on his tail.

Kurt recalibrated. He was too close to the house now to take any chances. It wasn't beyond the power or will of Wildgrube's cronies to turn a whole street over, if they thought they might find something that would earn them credit or promotion. Kurt decided to return to his original plan and confront the spy — from here, he looked exhausted, giving Kurt an additional advantage. Pushing back his shoulders and stretching himself to his full height, Kurt walked back to where the man was now standing quite openly on the public pavement, his arm outstretched to the nearby wall for support, breathing heavily. His head was dropped in an attempt to recover, his face obscured beneath his hat.

Kurt assumed his most officious tone. "What the hell do you think you're playing at?" As the man raised his head, Kurt gasped. It was more than two years since he'd seen those craggy features, but even with the man's weight loss and significant aging, he recognized him instantly. "Doctor Maine!"

"I'm sorry . . ." The doctor waved his hand to indicate he needed an additional moment, then pulled himself upright. "I would have gone straight to Miss Le Brocq's — I mean Mrs. Weber's — house, but I was uncertain of the situation. One doesn't want to draw unnecessary attention to delicate circumstances, you understand?" Kurt nodded. "Then I recognized you walking up Cheapside, and suspected you might be on your way there."

"Has something happened?" Kurt glanced around, anxious; there was no one on the street, though he feared any number of eyes might be peering through twitching curtains at this very moment.

Maine nodded. "I'm afraid so." His exhausted brown eyes stared up at Kurt from beneath the brim of his hat. "Something very serious."

"But I don't know this man. I don't understand?"

Dorothea was on the edge of her seat, her fingers in her mouth, chewing at what was left of the fingernails. Hedy looked from her to Kurt, trying to control the violent thumping of her heart. The spider crab he'd donated lay forgotten in the kitchen sink, twitching and squirming through its stay of execution.

"Fintan Quinn was pulled in by the secret police last week for further questioning — part of Wildgrube's 'housekeeping' policy," Kurt explained. "They must have found a way to put pressure on him, because this time he offered up the doctor's name, link-ing him to the coupon theft. Next day they pulled Maine in for questioning too." Hedy thought of the gentle, exhausted doctor in an interrogation cell, and closed her eyes in horror. "Maine told them nothing, of course," Kurt went on, "and they have no evidence, so he's in the clear. But they checked his list of patients and found Dorothea's name. Now they're trying to join the dots, hoping it leads them to Hedy."

Hedy swallowed. "So they plan to search here?"

"Maine couldn't be sure — what he overheard was through a doorway into the corridor, and his German isn't that strong. But he thinks he heard the word 'Freitag.' "

"Friday! That's tonight!" Dorothea's eyes were liquid with panic.

"That's why there's no time to waste."

"Should we move Hedy into the attic?"

Hedy felt sick. The room was spinning a little. A cold toxicity seemed to be building in her veins. The moment had finally come. She had ceased to be a person; she was now a problem, a living liability to be discussed and hidden away like an illegal wireless or a pistol. She opened her mouth to speak, but nothing came out.

"The attic's far too dangerous for a targeted search," Kurt was saying. "It'll be the first place they look."

"But where else can she go? If Maine is under suspicion too —"

"I think I've got an idea," Kurt cut in. "First, we need to get the wireless set out of the house. Is there anyone you could leave it with?"

Dorothea nodded. "My grandmother. I could hide it in her garden shed."

Kurt nodded. "Take it around there now in the wheelbarrow. Make sure you cover it — leaves, an old blanket, anything. Go now, while the early shift is changing; the streets will be quiet." Then Kurt turned to Hedy and looked her dead in the eye. "And you — you, we need to get dressed."

"Dressed?"

"It's dangerous, but it's the best I can come up with. And it might work." He bent down and revealed a canvas satchel he had brought with him, undoing the straps as he spoke. "I want you to put this on."

Hedy watched as Kurt pulled out the bag's contents and laid the garments on the kitchen table. She heard Dorothea gasp, and felt her own legs grow weak.

"Kurt, you can't be serious? Have you lost your mind?"

On the table lay the drab gray woolen uniform of a Wehrmacht staff sergeant.

ELEVEN

"What do you think?"

Hedy glanced at Kurt, then at the jagged section of mirrored glass in front of her. It sat propped up on a stool, leaning against Dorothea's bedroom wall, and the angle made her look even shorter. She took in her new outfit — the heavy tunic with its neat metal buttons, the loose trousers with the tapered ankles and reinforced seat — and marveled at the imagined power that could be gleaned from a suit of clothes. She thought of the soldiers in the concentration camps, pulling on the same garments, believing themselves to be supermen, a superior species. All she saw was a stick-thin Jewish girl playing a tasteless game of dress-up. She pulled a face.

"It was the only one I could get — left behind by a sergeant at our billet a few months back. Luckily he was a small guy."

"Not small enough! No one is going to

take me for a soldier." She turned to him, choking back the simmering terror. "Kurt, this will never work."

He took her face in his hands. "It's our best chance. This administration becomes trapped by its own logic — if it decides something is impossible, it no longer views it as a threat. Hiding in plain sight is the one thing they won't be looking for." He kissed her lightly on the lips. "Put the field cap on, that will make all the difference."

Hedy took the cap and placed it on her head, tucking her hair up around the sides. "Better?"

"Still too much hair showing. Sorry, my love, but it's going to have to come off."

Hedy nodded without speaking. It was no occasion for time-wasting arguments. Within minutes Kurt returned with Dorothea's kitchen scissors, the only ones in the house, and began to chop. Hedy kept her eyes on his face as he worked, knowing his calm expression to be a lie. He worked his way methodically around her skull, occasionally giving her little smiles of reassurance. She thought back to this morning, when she had spent an hour over the kitchen sink, washing her beloved locks with a sliver of low-grade soap that lathered no more than pumice stone. How long ago that seemed.

Even the frantic scrabble around the house a mere two hours ago, trying to eliminate every sign of her presence by stuffing her remaining clothes into Dorothea's wardrobe and moving the mattress from the attic into the back bedroom, seemed like days away. Life could no longer be measured in days or weeks, but in minutes. It made her hypersensitive to every sight, sound and color, yet at the same time strangely numb.

She felt her tawny curls fall to her shoulders and slide to the floor, while Dorothea, still breathless from the sprint to her grandmother's house with the wireless, scurried around her feet, sweeping up the evidence into an old metal dustpan. Then Kurt wetted his razor from a bowl of cold water, and Hedy stood perfectly still as he scratched away at the nape of her neck and around her ears, until there was nothing left there but raw, prickly skin. Once or twice the razor nicked her and she flinched, but she never made a sound; Kurt pressed on the tiny wounds with his handkerchief until the bleeding stopped. When he was done, he tenderly kissed her forehead, placed the cap back on her head and turned her toward the mirror. Hedy took a sharp intake of breath. He was right: the loss of hair made all the difference. Before her stood a slight, undernourished boy soldier of the German army. The uniform was thick and warm, but she could feel her entire body trembling.

Kurt, standing behind her, wrapped his arms around her. "Good job you're so pretty to begin with, huh?"

Hedy forced a smile. "We should go."

Kurt placed a comforting hand on Dorothea's shoulder. "Leave us a sign by the back door. If it's open, we'll know they've not yet been, or are still in the house."

Dorothea nodded without flinching. "Good luck."

Stepping out into the yard, Hedy felt a sensory rush. The freshness of the late summer breeze, the luminosity of the approaching dusk and the smells drifting in from the street were overwhelming. Asphalt, horse droppings, distant pine, sea salt, diesel . . . They walked briskly down to the end of the alley and out onto the street. Immediately her head began to spin. The vastness of the sky, the seemingly endless length of the road — how had she ever coped with this degree of exposure? In the distance, barely visible, was St. Aubin's bay and the immense openness of the Channel. She thought about the depth of it, filled with rocks and creatures and armed ships. How did anyone navigate all this space, handle this amount of vulnerability? Her feet seemed planted where she stood, but Kurt gave her a firm push in the back, propelling her away from the house, and at that moment she gave in to the situation and allowed him to take control. The one thing she vowed was that, whatever happened, she would not let him down.

They walked down Parade Road. It felt exhilarating but exhausting to walk so far in a straight line, to feel her feet covering distance on a pavement again, especially in unfamiliar German boots. She had never worn trousers before, and the sensation of fabric between her legs was peculiar. She tried to relax into the uniform, to walk with weight and purpose, like a man. But now she was becoming aware of the sensations of noise around her, even though the evening was quiet. A distant engine, someone shouting from a window, birds in the trees, a far-off plane. What permanent damage had been done to her sensory organs, she wondered, by all those months shut away from the world? Would she ever be the same again?

"Where are we going?"

"We'll stick to the side roads," Kurt replied, "where it's quiet."

She yearned to look around her but kept her eyes down and let Kurt make the decisions. One or two locals returning home in time for curfew crossed the road in order not to get too close. Hedy fought her desire to peer at them, to take in the contours of a human face that did not belong to Kurt or Dorothea. Instead, she tried to focus on the effort of putting one foot in front of the other. Within a minute she was panting heavily.

"Kurt? I'm so tired." She sensed his tension straight away, a mixture of sympathy and frustration.

"I know. We're going to walk into the park, then we can sit down for a minute, but only a minute. All right?"

She glanced up at him from beneath her cap. His focus was firmly on the middle distance, his eyes noting every potential hazard.

"Kurt? You know that I love you?" A sense of dread was building inside her. If this plan were to fall apart, one thing was certain: it would happen in seconds, and she would never see Kurt again.

"I love you too, sweetheart. Now, no more talking."

They reached the Parade Park and found a bench. The sun had set, and the wind sent the first yellowing leaves bundling across the lawns. On the road opposite, German uniforms appeared around corners in twos and threes then disappeared, to be replaced by fresh ones. When Kurt spotted two young privates heading toward the park, he stood, indicating to Hedy that she must follow.

"Sitting down is an invitation to conversation," Kurt muttered. "We need to keep on the move."

"What if someone addresses me directly?"

"There's no reason why they should. Come on."

They set off down the Parade and turned into the little network of streets that crisscrossed this section of the town. Here, the front doors of the cottages opened directly onto the narrow pavement, so that they were no more than a couple of meters away from anyone sitting in their front room who chose to look out of the window. Their proximity was disturbing, and Hedy kept her chin pressed to her chest, but at least there was no one on the street itself. When they had completed a couple of circuits, Kurt looked anxiously about him.

"We need to move on. People will become suspicious if they see the same two soldiers walking by over and over again."

They marched purposelessly onward. As darkness fell, they cut through to Val Plaisant, crossed Rouge Bouillon and started up Trinity Hill, where the town petered out and gave way to winding, tree-lined roads.

Kurt brought them to a halt. "There's nothing up there — going on would look suspicious. We'll go back along the north side of the town."

Hedy's feet were throbbing. "How much longer?"

"They're likely to send the search party soon after curfew. Couple more hours at least."

Hedy sunk her teeth into her bottom lip. Don't let him down, she told herself over and over.

They walked on, over St. Saviours Hill, then back south toward the Howard Davis Park. The last glimmers of light had vanished now, and as the sky turned black the sound of planes in the sky grew louder and more numerous — night-bombing raids by the Allies, Hedy supposed. She strained to listen for return fire but heard none, just the distant sound of groups of Germans on exercises, practicing for a land assault. Her legs seemed to be moving independently, swinging below her like the string legs of a wooden doll. It will be all right, she told herself. Just a little longer.

As soon as they turned the corner of Colomberie, she saw them. Three NCOs, all in uniform, jostling each other on the pavement. She felt Kurt try to steer her to the other side, but just as he did so, one German's voice rang out across the quiet street.

"Haben Sie Feuer, Leutnant?"

They were close enough to sense that the men had been drinking. Hedy saw Kurt's shoulders stiffen inside his uniform, and absorbed every thought as if by osmosis. If he said no, no matter how cheerily, and walked on, the men were just drunk enough to make something of it. If he said yes and gave them a precious match, it would be impossible to avoid a conversation. She saw a flick of Kurt's fingers, indicating she should stay where she was, and watched him step forward, feeling in his pocket for his matches.

"These cost me three marks — better light it first time!" Kurt's relaxed smile and easy manner astonished her. He could be in any bar, on a night out with friends. She watched him strike the match and the three of them lean toward it with their hand-rolled cigarettes, shielding the flame from the breeze. Wisps of blue smoke rose into the air and they smiled their thanks. Then, as Kurt was about to pull away, it came.

"What are you and your pal up to tonight, sir?"

Kurt's answer was clear and confident. "Just out for a drink."

"Take us with you, would you, sir? We've finished our bottle, and all our usual places are closed."

Kurt faked a laugh. "Sorry, soldier! Can't help you there."

Hedy kept her eyes downward and distant, as if distracted by something more significant than the current conversation. But then the tallest of the three, a corporal, turned toward her. "How about you, Sergeant? Buy us a beer?"

Panic bubbled and spat in her stomach. She still had sufficient distance, perhaps five meters, to maintain the illusion in the darkness, but she knew that if she opened her mouth she was done for. They had had no time to prepare for this eventuality — now it was up to her to get them out of it. Her brain was spinning, a fruit machine with no controls. She thought of Roda. The smiles at the border, the confidence, the charm. It was all about creating a story and convincing others of its truth. At that second an idea popped into her head. She leaned to her right, hard enough to unbalance herself, and stumbled a little, praying to any god that might be watching that Kurt would take the hint. For a long, terrible moment she thought he'd missed it. Then she heard his voice. "I'm afraid the sergeant's already had quite enough. Can't take his drink."

Recalling images of her drunken cousin at old family parties, Hedy raised a hand toward the group as if in apology, then let it flop down by her side, allowing herself another sway and sidestep as she did so. The ensuing silence seemed to last eternally, hovering in the night air, and Hedy feared she'd overplayed it.

Then Kurt must have somehow given them permission to react, because the laughter came thick and fast, peppered with cackling remarks.

"Sarge, you look rough!"

"Going to feel bad tomorrow, Sarge!"

"Got the spins yet?"

Now the corporal was slapping his compatriots on their shoulders, the others returning with shoulder punches, throwing back their heads in enjoyment of the joke. Kurt marched back over to Hedy and gave her a hard thump on the shoulder. Maintaining character, Hedy stumbled again. This time Kurt grabbed hold of her upper arm as if to support her, and steered her away down the road, calling over his shoulder as he went,

"Have a good evening, gentlemen."

The punchy shouts of the soldiers' laughter, rising into the night sky, sang in her ears as they moved away. Kurt kept a viselike grip of her arm, and as the adrenaline drained from her and the realization of what had just happened began to sink in, Hedy knew that this buttressing was no longer part of the performance, but a physical necessity. They continued, past the shuttered shops and darkened windows of the town. Hedy's breath was coming in thick, irregular pants, Kurt's nervous energy fizzing through the layers of his uniform. It was several minutes before he spoke, making sure that no words would carry on the night breeze. When he did, they were the most thrilling words she had ever heard.

"Oh my God, sweetheart. Well done!"

By the time they reached the corner of West Park Avenue, it was gone midnight. Kurt signaled to her to stay back in the shadows of a shop doorway while he went into the alley to check ahead. A moment later, he returned and beckoned to her, and the two of them scampered up the passage and in through the back of the house.

Dorothea was standing in the front room, tears of frustration in her eyes. The house was a wreck. Chairs had been overturned, the contents of the attic and its hatch cover lay in a heap at the bottom of the stairs. Broken glass glittered everywhere.

Kurt put his arm around her. "How many of them were there? Did they do much damage?"

Dorothea nodded. "Four soldiers. They pulled everything out of the cupboards, upturned the beds. They broke my last teapot — I'll never be able to replace it."

Hedy held Dorothea close. "I'm so sorry, you must have been terrified. But we'll help you put everything back as it was. What matters is they didn't find anything." She felt Dorothea shrink, and pulled back. "They didn't, did they?"

Dorothea's fingers fluttered to her face, patting her skin to comfort herself. "I'm so sorry . . . I thought I'd swept everywhere, I thought I'd been so careful . . . It's my fault." Her words began to sputter as the tears quickened, choking her.

Hedy's bowels twisted and she felt an urgent need to use the lavatory. "What did they find?"

"A button, underneath the kitchen table. A button from a German uniform tunic."

Hedy looked toward Kurt, whose face had lost all its color.

"It's not your fault, Dorothea, it's mine. I

knew that button was missing, but I never thought it would be here. Scheisse!"

Hedy pulled the field cap from her head, stroking her shaven neck. "Would they not think it was Anton's?"

"That's what I told them, but I don't think they believed me. He's been gone for too long." She blinked up at him, grasping at straws. "It doesn't prove anything, though?"

Kurt pushed stray hair from his face. "No, but Wildgrube will be onto that in a flash. He's been searching for months for something connecting me to Hedy."

"You think they'll come back? Should we go back out?"

To her relief Kurt shook his head. "Not tonight, but they will be back — tomorrow, or the day after, or next week. And next time we'll get no warning. What we need is something to put the bastards off the scent for good. But I'm damned if I know how."

Hedy reached out and touched his arm. "There is one thing that might work."

The girl serving behind the bar was young, probably no more than seventeen, but she had the careworn face of a woman fifteen years older. Kurt, swirling the last drops of his brandy round the bottom of a grubby glass, wondered what the circumstances were that had forced her to take this job. Perhaps her father was out of work like so many local men, the family scraping together every penny to pay for black market food. Perhaps her parents were dead and she was trying to support herself and her siblings. Whatever it was, the girl was struggling to hide her contempt for the louche, loud officers who lounged around in here tonight, scraping their chair legs on the parquet floor and letting their cigarette butts burn holes in the soft furnishings. What was the French expression? Fin de siècle. Kurt watched them as they drank and laughed together at jokes they had repeated a hundred times before. The master race, he thought bitterly as he knocked back the remains of the brandy. What a joke.

Kurt surveyed the scene. Fischer was perched in a tub chair in the darkest corner, deep in conversation with two high-ranking officers from College House; their voices had dropped even lower once Fischer realized that Kurt was trying to catch snippets of their conversation. But those guys were not his focus tonight. Kurt's target was over by the window, drinking with some secret police cronies. Wildgrube had long ago given up any pretense about the true nature of his job, and now seemed to enjoy flaunting it. The presence of the other spies gave Kurt the confidence he needed — it would make his task that much easier.

Everyone was in this evening. This was the last remaining club for officers and "approved" clientele that still had a regular supply of French brandy, partly because the boss of the secret police, a notorious black marketeer, frequented the place. It was even still possible to get a crust of bread and a little cheese here sometimes, though the portions had more than halved. Kurt watched Wildgrube help himself to another drink, but noticed that he was displaying an unusual degree of decorum and control tonight, sipping instead of gulping, and occasionally throwing Kurt what he clearly considered to be subtle, scrutinizing glances. Kurt banged the glass down on the bar loud enough for Wildgrube to hear, edged his way across the room to the area where the spy was standing, and glared at him.

"Well, if it's not the big man himself."

Wildgrube looked Kurt up and down, getting the measure of his mood. "Lieutenant . . ."

"Made any good arrests lately?"

Wildgrube glanced around, already seething at this disrespect. "I beg your pardon?"

374

Kurt stepped closer, using the height difference to intimidate the spy. "Don't be coy, Erich. I thought you were proud of your work?"

Wildgrube delicately stepped backward a little, trying to gain some distance. "I'm sure we are all proud of how we serve the Reich."

"So, spit it out. Turned over any good houses? Smashed up anything? Because I know how much you guys love doing that."

Wildgrube's mouth set in a tight, thin line. His lips were too rosy pink for his pale face — it gave the impression he was wearing lipstick. "If you have some issue with my department, Lieutenant, I suggest you go through the proper channels."

"No, I think I'd rather say it to your face. Must be an exciting time for you, now that we're shut off from the rest of the world. Chance to get properly stuck into the locals. Doesn't really matter whether they've done anything, does it? We've got to show them who's boss, isn't that right?"

"I mean it, Kurt. This is not the time nor the place. I suggest you go home before you get yourself into real trouble."

Kurt leaned into his face, so close he could smell the man's pungent breath. "I'm going. Don't much like the atmosphere around here. But I'll be watching you, Erich

— very, very closely." And with that, Kurt spun on his heel and marched from the room, pushing a young officer out of the way as he went.

Once outside, Kurt took a deep breath of night air, then sneaked into a nearby doorway to light a cigarette. He waited another thirty seconds, then set off down the road at a moderate pace. At the corner, he looked both ways for traffic — there would be few official vehicles out at this time, but it gave him an excuse to glance backward. There, exactly where he knew he would be, was Wildgrube, cap jammed neatly under his arm, staying close to the shadow of the buildings to keep himself hidden. At his side were two heavily-built junior officers, all of them waiting for Kurt to get a little further down the road.

Kurt set off in the direction of Cheapside, resisting the temptation to look back again. His heart was hammering. Beneath his tunic, sweat was prickling his skin and running in itchy rivulets down his back. In his mind he felt calm and precise, but his body was taking delight in reminding him that when it came to abject fear, the body always gets the upper hand. He thought of Hedy, and allowed himself a small, black chuckle.

Love. The desperation it pushed you to. For this, without doubt, was true desperation.

Hedy closed her eyes, breathed in deeply, and tried to focus on a comforting thought. But choosing one was harder than she'd anticipated. The warm kitchen at her old family house was too painful a picture . . . the coastal walks she'd taken with Anton too harsh a reminder of what was lost. In the end she settled for her and Kurt tucked up together in a warm bed, in some vague, undefined room, sometime in the future, the smell of him in her nostrils, his arms scooping her into his body. If she could focus on that, she told herself, perhaps the physical pain and horror might fade into her subconscious.

She twisted her body a little, trying to ease the pressure. The space was cold and damp. There was little more than five centimeters above her head, the boards trapping her, coffin-like, in one position. Even the slightest movement caused a joist to press into her flesh, or a sharp splinter to push through her clothes into her skin; it also increased the risk of her falling straight through the plaster of the ceiling below. Stretching out a leg, or her spine even a little, was impossible. When Dorothea had announced that it was time, and had screwed the last floor-board into place over her head, the pitch black and confinement sent her into such a panic that for several moments Hedy truly thought she might die of fright. But she told herself over and over that it wasn't really that different from the darkness in the attic she'd learned to contend with for the last ten months; if she could control her breathing and keep the dust out of her nostrils, she would be all right.

There was one salvation: the tiny gaps between the floorboards allowed her to hear some of what was going on in the bedroom above. It gave her a sense of connection to the world, and calmed her claustrophobia. And she knew she would not have long to wait. Somewhere down on the ground floor, she heard the opening and closing of the front door. Then there were footsteps on the stairs, followed by the indistinguishable sounds of people moving around a room. A moment later, she heard the ancient springs of Dorothea's bed creak and groan as they contracted under the weight of a human body. There was some whispering — short nervous sentences exchanged in pops and crackles — then all went quiet again. Everyone, it seemed, was listening.

Hedy closed her eyes, trying to guess how

much time had passed. She used to play this game as a child in her schoolroom, forcing herself not to turn and look at the clock on the wall, betting with herself. If she guessed the right time within a five-minute margin, then Papa would take her for ice cream on Sunday; if she got it wrong by more than ten, she'd have to walk home through the nettle patch at the side of the school road. She'd got pretty good at it. Now she calculated that a good half hour had passed since the last discernible noise. Surely it couldn't be much longer? If this idea was going to work then they . . .

CRASH.

The sound was so shocking it caused Hedy to jump, jarring her body against the joists. Her heart pounding like a kettle drum, she squeezed her eyes even tighter shut. They were here.

The noise of the door being forced must have been audible four houses away. Kurt propped himself onto his elbows, his head against the bars at the top of the bedstead, and glanced across at Dorothea, whose ashen face was almost indistinguishable in color from the pillow behind it. Instinctively she pulled the blankets higher and tighter around her upper body, horrified at her own nakedness, her eyes huge with terror. Kurt checked that his trousers were correctly heaped in the center of the floor, then glanced down at the space between them. With an apologetic twist of his mouth he eased himself a little closer to her body, and Dorothea nodded her understanding. No point going this far and not making the final image realistic.

They lay perfectly still, listening to the thumping footsteps running through the downstairs then bounding up the staircase. Kurt closed his eyes for a second, and took a deep breath as the bedroom door burst open. Wildgrube was standing in the doorway, the shadows of his two huge assistants falling behind him. His cheeks, pink from the night air, highlighted the twinkling triumph in his eyes. How long had he dreamed of this moment, Kurt wondered — fantasized about clicking the cuffs around Kurt's wrists and dropping the completed file on his boss's desk. But even now those eyes were zooming in on Dorothea, comparing her to the photograph of Hedy that the spy carried in his head, and sensing that something had gone terribly wrong. His face reminded Kurt of a lip book he'd had as a child, where a visual story magically emerged by running the pictures together quickly with one's thumb; in the space of three seconds Kurt saw the shift from delight, to confusion, to disappointment, and finally, plain anger.

"You, whore! Where are your papers?" Dorothea, in a panic that Kurt knew was no act, whimpered and pointed to the chest of drawers in the bedroom alcove. "Get up and bring them to me." Dorothea obeyed, dragging the blanket from the bed to hold around herself, leaving Kurt naked on the mattress. Wildgrube made a performance of scanning Dorothea's identity card, but there was no doubt in Kurt's mind that the spy's subtle, involuntary peek at Kurt's exposed genitals, when he thought no one was looking, lasted a fraction longer than natural curiosity demanded.

"You, Lieutenant — put your clothes on!" Kurt silently did as he was told. "So, this is how you honor a fellow servant of the Reich, a soldier fighting for our country? You come into his house and screw his wife?" Kurt looked as ashamed as possible. "How long has this business been going on?"

Kurt sighed, as if reluctant to confess this final indignity. "Since her husband left." He risked a glance into Wildgrube's eyes, and knew that the spy was calculating backward, remembering some of Kurt's suspicious behavior, believing he was piecing it together. The man's face contorted into a sneer of repugnance, but not before Kurt had caught one more brief emotion upon it — admiration.

"If there were any law available to me," Wildgrube opined, "I would arrest you both now. As it stands, you will be amply judged when this war is won. You both disgust me," he added, before turning with what he clearly imagined to be dramatic effect and sweeping from the room. Kurt, wearing only his trousers, and Dorothea, still wrapped only in a blanket, remained motionless in the center of the room until the footsteps reached the front door, listening to it open and bang shut. Even then, it was another full minute before either of them dare make a sound.

Eventually Dorothea let out a nervous giggle. "I think it worked!"

Kurt nodded. "I think it did." Suddenly embarrassed, he took her dress from the bottom of the bed and passed it to her. "Put this on quickly, you must be freezing. I need to get this floorboard up quickly."

Hedy stooped over the bowl, soaking then squeezing the cloth, moving it carefully over her body. Trickles of water ran down her arms, her chest and in between her breasts, making tiny pathways through the dust and grime then vanishing beneath her slip. She was painfully aware of Kurt watching her, especially conscious of her scalp with its uneven tufts sprouting where her hair had once been and her body so thin she looked like a young boy. But when she looked across at him he was gazing at her with adoration.

"How are you feeling now?" he asked. She nodded, trying to indicate an improvement, though every joint in her body still ached, and it had taken her a full half hour to stop shaking after they'd pulled her out. "You were so brave, you know."

"You must have put on a pretty good show yourself. Tell me again what happened in the club?" He had already described the whole event to her twice over, but she felt like a child with a bedtime story.

He sat down on the chair opposite. "I knew it was the perfect night. He'd had a little to drink, but not too much, and he was virtually pawing the ground, desperate for a chance to catch us together, prove his theory. Like you said, all I had to do was convince him this was the perfect op-portunity."

She smiled at the thought. "You really shouted at him?"

"Just enough to humiliate him a little, stir his instinct for revenge. Not hard with men like that." The door clicked open, and Dorothea slipped in like a ghost. Hedy noticed that she avoided Kurt's eyes and kept her body turned away from him as she fussed around the kitchen, tipping more hot water into the bowl. Hedy threw Kurt a meaningful stare — it was going to be up to him to repair the damage. "And as for Dory," Kurt continued seamlessly, "that performance deserved an Oscar! I started to believe it myself!"

Dorothea blushed pink to her roots. "I just knew that it had to look good."

"I really didn't see anything, you know," Kurt assured her. "I kept my eyes shut as you were getting into bed."

Dorothea's cheeks were still flushed, but she managed a smile. "It's fine, honestly. I know that Anton would understand if he were here."

"More than that," Hedy assured her, "he'd be proud of what you did. Of all of us." Taking a small towel to dry herself, she turned to Kurt. "But is it enough to put the authorities permanently off the scent?"

Kurt nodded with genuine confidence. "It

would seem like a personal grudge for Wildgrube to continue pursuing me for such a private matter. He'd be made to look a fool. God knows there's enough going on in this island to keep him busy."

"So we're safer now?"

He pressed his lips together. "Safer, but not safe. We still need to be careful. Though to be honest, I don't think the secret police are our biggest problem anymore." Hedy and Dorothea both looked at him, willing him on. "The islands could face starvation in the next few months. Fischer was at the club with some officers, and I overheard them say that Churchill is refusing to permit the Red Cross to send relief."

Dorothea's eyes widened in horror. "But why?"

"Probably thinks the Germans would take the parcels for themselves. But from what they were saying, it might be revenge — a payback for what Churchill sees as collaboration."

"Collaboration?" Hedy stopped drying herself and threw the towel onto the back of a chair. "Why would he think that? Churchill has no idea what's gone on here!"

"Apparently the British Government is under the impression that we've all been scraping by, and that things haven't been too bad till now."

Hedy looked back toward Dorothea and watched the now familiar fury begin to rise.

"What were we islanders meant to do, fight the German army with our bare hands?"

"Just telling you what I heard."

Hedy's eyes slid automatically to the larder, calculating exactly what was in there to last her and Dorothea the rest of the week.

"How are we expected to survive, with no supplies and no outside help?"

"The garrison reckons it can hang on till January," Kurt replied, "if it takes control of all provisions. But it's going to be harder for me to get hold of anything for you. And if the Allies don't push across France quickly, then . . ."

Hedy went to the kitchen window, touching the blackout blind with her fingers, remembering the sights and smells of the outside world that she had tasted the other night. The kitchen suddenly seemed a great deal smaller.

Kurt rose and slipped his arms around her waist. "Don't worry, sweetheart. Churchill will have to relent if things get bad. We'll all get through this." But there was little conviction in his voice.

Hedy sighed with a deep resignation. "Who knows? Secret police or not — this winter may kill us after all."

The three of them sat down at the kitchen table, and after a while Dorothea brought out a packet of playing cards. They played for tiny pebbles from the back garden, sitting in silence, unable to think of anything else to say. Summer was over. The nights were cooling fast, and the sunsets were slowly creeping their way toward the afternoon. Far away across the Channel, the rumble of distant guns could be heard, occasionally rattling the windows in their ancient frames.

Tick-tick-tick. The kitchen clock ran on its hypnotic rhythm in the darkness. It would be another hour before the electricity supply returned, and the last candle had been used days ago. Now even reading, the last pleasurable activity left, was impossible after late afternoon. Rumors in town suggested that within two months there would be no electricity at all.

Hedy huddled by the kitchen fireplace, holding out her hands toward the warm ashes to extract the last heat. Next to the hearth, the log basket sat empty, nothing but tiny remnants of twigs and dried-up leaves scattered at the bottom. Dorothea had spent all the previous day "wooding" on Westmount, collecting any small sticks and kindling she could find, but every able-bodied person in town was doing the same, and the ones with proper, sharp saws were walking away with the lion's share. It didn't help that even the paltry bundle of twigs Dorothea did manage to bring back was soaking wet, and would take days to dry out in the cold, damp house.

Hedy sat back and listened to the rain beating on the windows and bouncing off the concrete in the yard. It had been raining for days, weeks. The wettest November for ten years, the locals were saying. She felt her stomach growl again, and the twinge of pain that she suspected was the start of an ulcer. Kurt had recently complained of the same thing — even officers were going hungry now. Last week he'd told her that a number of ordinary soldiers had been arrested for violent outbursts and theft from domestic properties. Hedy had wanted to put an additional bolt on the kitchen door, but Dorothea tried every hardware supplier in town and could find nothing. Perhaps, they reflected, it didn't matter that much — any burglar looking for food was far more likely to target the farmhouses of the country parishes, which sometimes still contained the carcasses of rabbits or a few homegrown vegetables. No point in breaking into a town property that had nothing in it.

Kurt's predictions had turned out to be true. Wildgrube and his cohorts had lost all interest in Kurt since the abortive house raid, and had evidently given up on finding Hedy too. The three of them had slowly gained confidence that the soldiers would not return, and in recent weeks Hedy had started sleeping in the spare room at the back of the house. It was wonderful to lie in a proper bed and be able to get up in the night if she needed to, though bizarrely she slept more fitfully there, having adapted over the months to the life of a bat in the attic. Truthfully, no one was sleeping well anymore. Who could sleep with a hunger so extreme it gnawed at your organs and pushed acid up your throat as soon as you lay down? Last night they had had absolutely nothing in the house to eat until Kurt had arrived with a tiny portion of German sausage and a crust of something no one would describe as bread. Two days before, Dorothea had fainted at the bottom of the stairs.

Hedy heard the latch turn on the front

door and Dorothea hurry in, slamming it behind her. Scrambling to her feet, Hedy went to meet her. They were so attuned to each other's sounds and movements now that any tiny change of mood was immediately obvious. Hedy watched her fold down her umbrella with the two broken spokes, spattering raindrops all over the floor, and stand dripping in the hallway. Dorothea's eyes were red and her mouth was pulled tight in a poor attempt to stem an outburst.

"What's happened?"

"I just saw Mrs. Le Cornu, the old lady down the road, crying in the street. Her cat's gone missing. She thinks the Germans took it."

"No!" Hedy's hand flew to her mouth.

"She says the same thing happened to her neighbor. They trap them and shoot them, apparently, then cook them at their barracks. I've noticed there are no dogs around lately, either."

"But that's horrible!" She remembered Hemingway's fluffy gray face nuzzling her cheek and prayed that he had escaped that fate.

"It's all horrible. Everything's horrible. I'm so sick of it." The tears began to run down her cheeks. "I was queuing outside the butcher's — there was a rumor that they had some rabbit, but it wasn't true — when this fight broke out between two women. A proper fight, they were hitting each other — all over a couple of rotten apples in the market."

She let out a strange little moan then slid down the wall until she was crouched on the floor, sobbing into her hands. Rainwater from her coat and hair pooled around her on the linoleum.

Hedy crouched down beside her and put an arm around her. "It's all right."

"No, it's not all right. It's happening all over," Dorothea wailed. "Everyone's so hungry and angry! There's nothing in any of the shops, and we can't even forage for limpets and winkles till the next low tide, and then everyone else will be doing the same."

"What about your cousin?" Hedy bit her lip. They both knew it was a stupid pointless question, but Dorothea pretended it was reasonable.

"The Germans are taking everything from the farms. I doubt he could feed his own children, never mind us." Words failed her for a while, crushed by the weight of her misery, then she took a deep breath. "I'm so stupid. You know, when Kurt said back in June that the Allies might not come for us, I didn't believe him. I pretended I did, but I was sure they'd come. My mother always loved King George — we always stood for the national anthem — but I never thought he'd let this happen. I thought they would send a ship, something . . ."

Hedy hugged her close. "If they had, the Germans would have fought back — it would have been a bloodbath. We might all be dead now."

"Perhaps that would be better!" In the darkness of the hallway, her pale skin was almost translucent, and Hedy could clearly see the blue veins beneath the surface. "Perhaps it's better to die quickly, fighting, than to sit around helpless, waiting for it."

"But we're still here." Hedy drew her closer. "We've survived so long, Dory, against the worst odds. We've fought back in the only way we could. We can't give up now."

Dorothea was still crying, but it was a different kind of weeping now, quiet, resigned. "I'm not sure I have the strength, Hedy. I'm so tired, and everything hurts all the time. Sometimes" — she wiped a dollop of snot from her nose — "sometimes I wish I'd just have an asthma attack in the night and not wake up."

"Don't say that!" Hedy heard her voice, shrill and desperate. "I need you, and so will Anton. We just have to hang on. Kurt will always bring us whatever he can. And it can't be much longer. It just can't."

Dorothea shook her head. "I don't know . . ."

"I know! Belgium is liberated now. The Americans are already crossing parts of the Rhine. The Allies will win, Dory, everyone knows it. We just have to get through the next few" — she couldn't bring herself to say months, though that was what she was thinking — "weeks."

"I'm just so tired. So, so tired."

Hedy pressed her face against Dorothea's downturned head and closed her eyes. The rainwater on the floor was soaking up through the hem of her dress, adding a new layer of cold, but she took no notice. There was nowhere to go and nothing to do, but sit there, rocking gently on the hall floor, watching their own breath steam in the cold air, and listening to the relentless tick-tick-tick of the kitchen clock.

TWELVE

1945
Evening Post
8th May, 1945

I appeal to you to maintain your calm and dignity in the hours that lie ahead, and to refrain from all forms of demonstration.

. . . I feel that the conclusion of the Prime Minister's speech this afternoon will be the appropriate moment for the hoisting of flags, and I make the strongest appeal to you, in the interests of public order, not to fly flags before that time.

I was present last evening at the release from custody of the majority of political prisoners, and I am doing all in my power to obtain the immediate release of the remainder of them.

I shall make known to you immediately any further developments.

A. M. Coutanche, Bailiff

This was a new smell, Kurt thought, as he shuffled into the main hall of College House with the other officers. Not the usual mixed scents of damp uniforms, body odor and leather. Not even the stink of fear that had pervaded in the early days of the land invasion. He couldn't place it at first, but the answer lay in the expressions on his colleagues' faces, the dejected slope of their shoulders, and especially in the undisguised curses and questions skimming through the room. Questions no longer muttered in corners or the silent corridors of officers' clubs, but spat forcefully with rage and resentment. It was defeat.

He gazed through the same leaded window he had looked through so often before, struck by the precious blue sky and bouncing white clouds, and mentally repeated some phrases on a loop, trying to make the news real to himself. It was all over. Hitler was dead, Germany was finished, the great dream of the Fatherland was no more. Millions of lives lost or wrecked, all for the fever dream of a nation too consumed with fury and ideology to see its own reflection. All for a mirage. All for nothing. Kurt tried to figure out what he was feeling, but all he could identify was a sense of relief.

The day of reckoning was no longer a possibility somewhere in the future. Within days — perhaps hours — British troops would be landing on these shores, and every man in this room would be going to jail. Some of them would be put to death. With a strange detachment, Kurt wondered if he would be one of them. How tragic, he thought, to have survived this long, to have kept alive the woman he loved, only to be snatched from the earth now, when happiness was finally possible. But he felt no fear or self-pity, just an eerie calmness. Nothing was any longer within his control — all his responsibilities were in the past. Perhaps that was part of the odd aroma in this room today — the passive pleasure of release from duty. The future was out of their hands.

Baron von Aufsess, standing on a desk at the end of the room, spoke in a confident voice as if dispatching notices for any normal day. "I have been informed," he said, "that Mr. Churchill will address the British nation via the BBC at three o'clock this afternoon. I have received orders that we are to prevent the public from hearing any such illegal broadcast . . ." He hesitated here, and gave a little cough that seemed to Kurt more about punctuation than clearing his throat. "However, as we also have it on good authority that British naval ships are already on their way to the islands carrying orders for our immediate surrender, I have given permission for the broadcast to be available to any of the local population in possession of a wireless." A soft murmur went quickly around the room. Everyone knew that at least half the locals on the island either had their original radios or an illegal crystal set. "Meanwhile," von Aufsess continued, "you will be aware that I will be speaking with the Bailiff today regarding the release of ration stores, and that the Bailiff has urged the islanders to act with restraint, and not get any foolish ideas of retribution."

Kurt grimaced, on the edge of laughter. Even now, they couldn't shake off that underlying assumption of superiority! What a shock the coming days would be.

The baron dismissed his officers, and minions passed around instructions on hastily handwritten cards. Kurt skim-read his orders and tucked them into his breast pocket. Moving slowly through the crush toward the door, he managed a quick glance at some of the other orders handed out. Remove . . . destroy . . . dismantle. It was clear that the Area Command's priority now was an island-wide concealment of what had been going on here for the last five years. Mountains of paperwork, private German food stores, anything that could be viewed by the Allies as contrary to the Hague Convention. Kurt buttoned his tunic and set off from College House with the rest, but instead of heading to the compound to bonfire stock lists as instructed, he turned at the bottom of the hill and headed for West Park Avenue. To hell with them — what could they do to him now? And at this moment he needed to see Hedy more than anything.

The streets were buzzing with locals, many of whom had clearly abandoned work for the day. Some grinned at him as he passed, filled with vengeful glee. Others shouted insults. Several women had gathered to watch four German privates desperately whitewashing over the giant red cross that had been painted on the wall of the officers' club nine months earlier, in a desperate attempt to save it from bombing. The whitewash turned the cross pink, but its outline remained stubbornly visible, to the growing panic of the paint-spattered soldiers. Kurt snorted at the pertinence of the image. Not enough whitewash in the world, he thought to himself.

In defiance of the appeal, many Union Jacks and Jersey flags were already being openly displayed in private windows. They had appeared from nowhere, after years stashed away in attics and cellars, or hidden in the storage rooms of shops. Crossing Val Plaisant, he spotted a beaming old gentleman placing speakers on his windowsill, ready to broadcast further news to all and sundry that afternoon. Kurt felt the man's joy and couldn't help smiling. It felt strange to be surrounded by so much happiness and to know that your own demise was the cause of it.

At Dorothea's house, he tapped his usual coded knock and was quickly shown inside. Dorothea was resplendent in the dress she had worn for her wedding but rarely worn since. Hedy was wearing the gray floral cotton frock and ancient cardigan she had been in most days for the last eighteen months, but Kurt's heart dissolved when he looked at her. There was a gleam in her eye he hadn't seen in months, and the featheriness of her movements as she skipped around the house reminded him of illustrations in fairy stories. Her hair, though still not back to its original length, was now curling around her jawline, its rich tawny color as beguiling as ever.

"We had a whole tin of salmon between us for dinner last night!" Hedy bubbled. "It was the last thing left in the April Red Cross box, but apparently the British ships are bringing relief parcels, so we decided to give ourselves a treat!"

"Quite right too." Kurt reached out and touched that hair, marveling at its softness. "Do you have somewhere to listen to the speech at three o'clock?"

"Dory fetched the wireless back from her grandmother's house. She walked right by a German soldier at the top of the road, pushing it in the wheelbarrow, and he didn't even ask to look under the blanket! That's when we knew, when we really understood that it was all over."

He wound her tresses around his fingers. "The British boats will be here tomorrow. You should go down to the harbor to greet the Tommies — it'll be quite a day."

"Come with us?" Dorothea suggested, peering at her reflection in the mirror of her empty powder compact.

Kurt glanced toward Hedy. The look between them said everything.

"I think I may be required elsewhere."

Hedy took his hand from her hair and led him into the privacy of the front room. "I've got a plan. As soon as I'm certain it's safe, I'm going to go to the Jersey States offices to tell them everything. I'm going to tell them about you, and how you helped me."

Kurt tried to look pleased and grateful. "Well, I appreciate that —"

"I'm sure that the British will have to round you all up initially. But they can't treat you all the same. They'll want to identify the leaders. But I'm living proof that you're in a different category."

"Hedy, I'm an officer." He tried to speak gently. "That has certain implications."

"At first, yes, but the British judicial system is very fair. Once they know the whole story, I'm certain they'll make exceptions. I mean, they might decide not to imprison you at all."

Unwilling to snatch this moment from her, Kurt indulged himself, falling into those sea-green eyes one more time. As sunlight poured in from the window, bathing them both, he pulled her toward him and held her, relishing the warmth of her body, the softness of her breasts through his tunic, the security of those skinny arms around his neck. Then he kissed her, long and deep, and took a deep sniff of her neck, breathing in the natural perfume of her skin. Finally, he pulled back and forced a beaming smile.

"I need to go, sweetheart. I have so much

to do. Enjoy Churchill's speech." And with that, he set off toward the east and his billet.

Hedy and Dorothea gazed at the crowds around the harbor in astonishment. The shouting, singing and cheering seemed to fill the sky. Like a giant, chaotic whirlpool of humanity, eddies and swirls of faces circled in different directions, all trying to reach the next vantage point, or reach a friend lost in the melee. The greatest surge of people was on the West Park side, where streams of British soldiers were now pouring off the troop carriers in the bay and trudging their slow, shambolic path through the thousands of well-wishers. Old farmers stretched out their arms to shake hands with them, women young and old threw themselves at the newcomers, showering them with kisses. Eager fingers reached across every gap, begging for the cigarettes and sweets in every soldier's pocket.

Hedy's eyes darted from one extraordinary sight to another. "Look, Dory — the hotel!"

The Pomme d'Or, home of the German Naval headquarters for the duration of the war, was now filled with British uniforms, military men brimming over its front balcony. The raising of the Union Jack from its flagpole drew another roar from the crowd, and a spontaneous chorus of "God Save The King" burst out and spread right down to the quayside. Everywhere she looked, Hedy saw faces creased with emotion — women cuddling children, husbands kissing wives, old men wiping tears of joy.

"Isn't it wonderful?" Dorothea's voice was high and bright, but when Hedy turned to her she saw only a fixed mask of theatrical joy. She knew that her own face projected the same lie. In fact she was finding the whole experience terrifying. The closeness of strangers pressed against her, the dozens of unknown hands touching her arms and back — it felt revolting. Less like celebration, more like defilement. Her breath was coming in uneven bursts, and she wondered how Dorothea's asthma would fare with the emotion of the day.

At that moment, as if conjured by her own thoughts, she spotted a familiar figure on the far side of the Weighbridge, a man in an old brown mackintosh being carried along by a river of people toward the landing area. As Hedy looked toward him, Oliver Maine turned his head and miraculously caught sight of her, immediately taking the hat from his head and waving frantically in affection and triumph. Hedy waved back, gesticulating that to try and reach him now would be hopeless, and the doctor laughed in agreement before disappearing into the crowd. Hedy felt her heart swell, and promised herself that her first visit when this madness was over would be to the hospital. Perhaps, she considered, in a week or two she might be able to get hold of a few eggs and a little sugar. If so, she would make him an apple cake to take home for his wife.

Hedy realized that Dorothea was pulling her by the arm.

"There's two soldiers over there. I want to find out what they know about the war in Europe."

"What do you mean? Know what?"

But Dorothea was already pulling her toward two young Tommies, shouting at them for attention. As they reached the men Dorothea reached out and grabbed one of them by the arm. He was little more than twenty, pasty-faced and chubby by island standards. Dorothea pressed her face close to his. "Could I ask you something? I'm trying to get news of my husband. Last I heard he was fighting in East Prussia. Don't suppose you know what happened to the soldiers out there?"

The Tommy looked at her with confusion. Hedy pulled at her dress, but Dorothea's eyes were fixed on the young man and she refused to budge.

"No Brits out there, love. Russkies pushed Jerry back over that side. Which regiment was your old man with?"

Again, Hedy pulled; again Dorothea resisted.

"He's Austrian, he was forced to fight with the Germans. Do you know if the Russians took many prisoners? How do I find out if he's alive?"

The Tommy was now backing away from them, as was his friend. "Your husband fought for the Jerries?"

"He didn't want to, he was conscripted. I just wondered if you could tell me how to find out what happened to him?"

"Dory," Hedy muttered, "let's go. This isn't the right time."

Hearing Hedy's voice, the Tommy whipped around to look at her. "Here, that accent! You a Jerry too?"

"No, I'm not German." Hedy felt her heart bang in her chest. "I'm . . . I've been . . ."

The Tommies looked them both up and down, then pushed onward through the crowd.

Hedy watched their uniforms disappear into the throng, then turned to a deflated Dorothea. "It's just not the right day, Dory.

Those men aren't from here, they don't understand. Why don't we go up to Fort Regent? That must be where they're going to hoist the Union Jack."

But Dorothea was no longer looking at Hedy, or at the departing soldiers. Her eyes were focused on a fast-moving rabble on the Esplanade side of the crowd. A pack of half a dozen men, young and in shirtsleeves, was moving at speed, running as fast as the crowd allowed, apparently chasing something or someone. The rumble of their collective feet parted the hordes, and as a space appeared, the object of their pursuit suddenly became visible. For a moment Hedy thought it was a youth wearing some kind of pale, tight-fitting overall, then to her horror she realized that it was actually a young girl. Her hair had been roughly cut down to the skull and she was entirely naked. The girl was running as fast as she could in desperation to escape her pursuers, and her intermittent squeals of terror carried across the heads of the throng, causing everyone to turn and stare. A second later, the girl escaped up a side street and two of her hunters were stopped by a local policeman.

Hedy turned to look at Dorothea, whose face was now completely colorless.

"Oh my God, Hedy . . . was that what I

think it is?"

Hedy scrabbled for words, but found none. She nodded.

"Is this what it's going to be like? Is this how they're going to treat us? What was it all for?"

Hedy took Dorothea's hand in her own. "Come on. Let's get down to the collection depot, pick up our Red Cross parcels. Then we'll just go home."

Dorothea meekly followed Hedy through the heaving streets, the collective frenzy of the day still ringing in their ears. As they forced their way against the current of revelers, Hedy watched Dorothea's eyes constantly flick back to the lengthening line of Tommies snaking into the town center, redrawing each face with Anton's thick dark hair and smiling eyes. They had talked so often of this day, dreamed about it, pinned a picture of it in their minds for years. Now all Hedy could think about was returning to the peace and sanity of Dorothea's little kitchen and keeping this feverish world at a safe, manageable distance.

"Neumann, his name is Lieutenant Kurt Neumann. He's an engineer. He's been based at the Lager Hühnlein compound since 1941."

Hedy crossed her legs and deliberately added a touch of iron to her gaze. This office hadn't changed an iota in five years. The same leather-topped desk, the same oversize chandelier, same neatly stacked files on the shelves. She remembered every detail, of both the room and the conversation, and she wanted Clifford Orange to know that she did. Given the expression on his face, she was pretty confident that he knew what she was thinking.

She peered at him as he made his notes with agonizing slowness, holding his fountain pen in red flaky fingers. He had lost weight, of course, and more of his hair. The crimson flush that once bloomed across his cheeks, presumably the result of too much drink, had now been replaced by malnourishment eczema. But the biggest difference, evident to Hedy as soon as she entered the office, was a visible loss of authority. He seemed smaller, not merely in bulk but in character, as if someone had scooped out all his arrogance with a spoon, leaving only a husk of desiccated obedience. Hedy wanted to leer, to let him know that she saw his decline and was glad. But she thought of Kurt, and kept her face expressionless.

The news was out now. Photographs of the liberation of Bergen-Belsen, where a Jerseyman had miraculously been found alive, had been placed in the window of the town post office. News reels had been shown in the local cinema, to the audible screams and tears of the audience. No one, not even Orange, could now pretend that the consequence of classing any person a Jew was not fully understood. Hedy wondered if it was guilt that had shrunk this man so much, whether he acknowledged any aspect of his wretched role in history. But Orange gave no hint of it as he finished his notes and raised his face to her. He focused, she noted, not on her eyes but on a space a little lower, around her top lip.

"Well, Miss Bercu, it seems that, thanks to your clever concealment at the home of Mrs. Weber, you have had an extraordinary escape. Might I offer you my congratulations, and express relief that you have emerged from this experience no worse for wear. No harm done, it seems."

Hedy thought of her parents behind fences of barbed wire, being herded toward gas chambers. She wondered how many other people had sat in this chair, listening to Orange's trite, mindless phrases, taut with perfect grammar and devoid of meaning. But the truth was, even now, the power still lay with these gray-suited men, and she was still required to beg for favors at their door.

"And Lieutenant Neumann?"

Orange replaced the cap of his pen with precision. "I will pass this information on to the appropriate department, of course. But in all honesty, I doubt it will make any difference."

Hedy shifted in her seat. "He saved my life. He risked his own to keep me safe and bring me food. Do you understand what the Germans would have done to him if they'd discovered he was protecting a Jew? An officer of his rank?" She heard her volume increase and tried to rein herself back. "What I'm saying is, he's not a Nazi. He hated the German authorities here as much as" — she paused, knowing her meaning would not be missed, but no longer caring — "any decent person. And to my mind, that should be taken into account."

Orange smoothed down his spiky gray mustache with two fingers. "As I've said, Miss Bercu, the information will be forwarded. But Lieutenant Neumann was — indeed is — a serving officer of the German military and, as such, will be subject to the laws and decisions of the British legal system. I'm sorry that I can't help you further."

The door swung open. Hedy looked up,

surprised to see two British officers enter the room without waiting for permission. The senior of the two, a captain, jerked his head toward Orange. "The major would like to see you in his office, please, sir."

Orange's hand went instantly to his collar, pulling it away from his throat. "I am, as you can see, in the middle of an interview."

Hedy stood up and addressed the captain directly. "Actually, Mr. Orange has just informed me that he's unable to help me further. So I think this interview is over."

"Thank you, ma'am." The captain turned back to Orange. "After you, sir."

Orange rose slowly from his desk chair, hoping to give the impression of moving at his own speed, though Hedy suspected it was more that he was feeling a little faint. He walked deliberately to the door and allowed the officers to escort him out.

Hedy picked up her bag and turned to leave the office when another Jersey official entered the room, bustling in a way that suggested frantic activity. Hedy recognized him at once. "Excuse me, Deputy Le Quesne?"

The man turned to her with a weary smile. "May I help you?"

"I just wondered . . ." Hedy hesitated; this was probably a waste of time. But there was something about this tired old politician that she trusted. "Why do those officers want to speak to Mr. Orange?"

"All local representatives are being interviewed by British intelligence," Le Quesne replied, "for debriefing and assessment."

"Assessment?"

"To make sure that we exercised our duties correctly. It's been asserted that certain public servants" — he hesitated just long enough to make his inference clear to her — "were somewhat overzealous in the execution of German orders. Should that be proven, there will be consequences."

Hedy gave him the smallest smile, then nodded. "Thank you, Deputy. Good day to you."

Kurt stuffed his toothbrush into the pocket of his rucksack and buckled it up. It had taken him all of five minutes to pack. Five minutes for five years. He looked around the pretty room that had been his bedroom for so long. The little casement window, the Edwardian washstand in the corner, with its china washbowl and jug. That cream-painted plaster ceiling with the hundred little cracks he knew by heart. How many nights had he lain awake till dawn, staring at them and fretting about Hedy — if she

412

was safe, if she had enough to eat, when he would be able to see her again. Now the tables would be turned, and it would be Hedy's turn to lie in a comfortable bed, her mind twisting with imagined nightmares. He threw the rucksack over his shoulder and was preparing to go downstairs when he heard Hedy's voice from the hallway.

By the time he was halfway down, Kurt could see Hedy remonstrating with the harassed British sergeant who had been standing in the billet hallway since early that morning, ticking off names and serial numbers of German officers on his clipboard.

"You don't understand," Hedy was shouting. "I am not trying to prevent you doing anything. I just want a private moment with Lieutenant Neumann."

"I'm sorry, ma'am," the sergeant replied, "but these men are now prisoners of war. There is an armored truck outside that needs to leave in five minutes to deliver them to their assembly point."

Another five minutes, Kurt thought. Years of clockwatching and waiting, and now everything is happening in five minutes.

"It's all right, Sergeant." Kurt used his most polished English accent for maximum impact. "I'm aware of your schedule and I give you my personal guarantee that all offi-

413

cers from this billet will be on that truck at the correct time. If you could just give me a moment?"

The sergeant gave Kurt a doubtful look, and Hedy an even more doubtful one, then stepped out onto the porch to give them privacy. Kurt dumped his rucksack on the parquet floor and looked at her. She looked as lovely as ever, but there was a look about her that startled him, a determination. It was the same look he'd seen the day she'd first arrived at the compound to apply for the translator's job. He stood before her, waiting.

"I saw them lining the soldiers up on the beach. I didn't know if you'd already been taken away."

"You heard the man. Five minutes."

"Were you not going to come and say goodbye?"

"I've not been allowed to leave this house since yesterday. And to be honest I wasn't sure . . ." To his horror, he felt a lump in his throat and had to swallow hard. "I wasn't sure either of us could stand it."

Hedy nodded. "But you've forgotten something."

"Have I?"

"You told me you were with the Jungen-

414

schaft. You're meant to remember your manners."

"Have I offended you?" He sensed laughter building inside, but he couldn't be certain it wouldn't convert to tears on its way out, and swallowed again.

"A little. I'm still waiting, you see."

That jutting little chin, that stubbornness. He wanted to tear her clothes from her and take her right then and there on the parquet floor. "Waiting for what?"

"For my engagement ring."

A little snort escaped from his nose. "You're right. Forgive me. These last few days, there hasn't been much opportunity for shopping." They both giggled a little at this. Then Kurt had an idea. "Wait there."

Kurt hurried out to the porch and approached the British sergeant, who was still clutching the clipboard and glancing repeatedly at his watch as if he couldn't make its information stick.

"Excuse me, Sergeant, may I ask you one more favor? That rubber band holding together your notes — may I have it?" The sergeant leaned back a little, anticipating some kind of trickery. "I need to give it to my girlfriend." The man looked puzzled for a moment, then seemed to understand. Without a word, he removed the thick brown band from his clipboard and gave it to Kurt, who smiled his gratitude then hurried back to the hallway.

Taking Hedy's left hand, he gently placed the rubber band on her third finger, doubling it over until it fitted. "It's not exactly what I had in mind, but it's something until I can get to a jeweler's. Which might be a while," he added.

Hedy splayed out her hand and touched the rubber band with affection. "I don't mind waiting. This one will always be my favorite."

He stared at her, still clinging to the tips of her fingers. He wanted to hold her, but was frightened that if he did, he would be unable to let go. He saw himself being dragged from the room like a screaming toddler, wailing and flailing. The humiliation was almost as unbearable as the sense of loss. He groped for something to say, and opted for a lousy joke. "Summer or winter wedding?"

"The day after you're released."

"You know that could be years?"

"Of course I know."

"There's a public outcry over the concentration camps. People will want revenge, and the politicians may provide it."

"I know that too."

He continued to massage the ends of her fingers, as if trying to press all the emotions of his body into the smallest possible area. "What are you going to do now?"

Hedy shrugged. "Stay here for a while, try to find out what happened to my parents, to Roda and my other siblings. Europe is a mess; it will probably take a while."

"How will you live?"

"I'll get another job. I hear lots of evacuees are planning to return — perhaps the Mitchells will come back." She smiled with sadness. "Of course, they might not need me anymore."

"I can't see anyone not needing you anymore."

"I'll be fine. I'm tougher than I look."

"That I know."

"I'll be like King Canute — letting the waves roll over me, knowing there's nothing I can do to stop them."

He grabbed her and kissed her, then he pulled back and threw his rucksack back over his shoulder. "I have to go. Don't wait to watch the boat. Go home and see Dorothea."

She blinked her agreement and bit her lip. "Auf Wiedersehen."

She shook her head. "Bis bald."

He nodded, walked quickly out through

the porch to the waiting armored truck, and slumped down onto the bench without waiting to be asked. He knew the dam was about to burst, and that when it did, he would be out of control for some time. It was almost a relief when the door crunched shut and delivered him to the dark, chill metal interior of his future.

She waited to watch the boat, of course. She knew that she would, even when she promised not to. Standing by the sea wall, shivering in the stiff spring breeze for two hours, even though she knew full well that even if Kurt was one of those on the beach below, she would never be able to make him out. Not among those vast snakes of tiny toy soldiers that stretched across the West Park sand, some in straight lines and some in odd curled shapes, as though the hundreds of figures down there were attempting to spell out a giant message across the shore. The men were peaceful, as far as she could make out — sitting or standing, muttering to their neighbors, smoking if they had any tobacco, or simply staring at the horizon.

Strange, Hedy contemplated, what terror these figures had once stirred in her. Today they were nothing but numb, exhausted boys in grubby wool tunics, all longing to go home, yet knowing that that dream, too, had vanished, along with all the others. She almost felt sorry for them. There must have been others like Kurt, youngsters forced into a movement they never believed in. But perhaps there were just as many who still believed, who still held that filthy doctrine dear. Right now, she didn't have the energy to figure it out, or even to care. An exhaustion of monstrous proportion was slowly gripping her, and had it not been for the cold and the freshness of the air, she felt she might fall asleep on her feet.

Out in the bay, the landing craft sat waiting on the flat silver sea for their human cargo. By evening they would all be gone, and only the low silhouette of Elizabeth Castle would be left against the pearly sky. Normality was rapidly returning to the island. Trucks filled with coal rumbled through the streets, shops made window displays of goods that would be available to buy in a matter of days — shoes, children's clothes, cooking pots. Last night's Evening Post had announced that the postal service would be operational again from today. Tonight, Hedy and Dorothea would sit down to a delicious tuna casserole that would swell their bellies to bursting, while

Kurt would be halfway across a rolling English Channel, on a share of prisoners' rations.

Hedy stood watching the landing craft swallow load after load, until the wind bit through her thin coat and into her bones, and she finally accepted it was time to go. Slowly she made her way along the Esplanade through crowds of smiling locals, trying to respond to each joyful greeting with something appropriate. But as she grew closer to West Park Avenue, a sense of foreboding grew in her. She told herself it was just the misery of losing Kurt and the massive emotional adjustment of returning to a forgotten life. But by the time she reached the house she knew that something bad was going to happen. Pushing open the front door — everyone had now stopped locking their doors, as they had before the Occupation — she heard voices in the kitchen and hurried through to investigate.

Dorothea was standing with her back to the kitchen sink. At the table sat a man of about forty, wearing a British uniform with the two white stripes of a corporal.

Hedy stared from one to the other. "What's going on?"

Dorothea's voice was tight and croaky. "This gentleman has brought a message from the German War Office. Apparently it arrived a week ago, but with all the mayhem, nothing was sent on. So the British Commander ordered it to be delivered by hand." She held up a small piece of creamy-brown paper. It was years since Hedy had seen one, but she instantly recognized it as a telegram, and froze. "Anton?"

Dorothea nodded, and handed the paper to her. "It's in German, but the meaning's pretty clear."

Hedy read the typewritten words on the white strips of paper several times before they made any sense: "Regret to inform you Lance Corporal Anton Weber 734659 24th Infantry Division died in service of his country 14th October, 1944."

Hedy rushed to Dorothea and put her arms around her, waiting for the outpouring, but nothing happened. They both just stood silently together in the kitchen for what felt like a long time, holding each other. Perhaps the probability of Anton's death had lived with them for so long that its reality no longer shocked them. Or perhaps neither of them had any emotion left to expend. In her mind, Hedy reached out for Anton's face: the day outside the cinema when he had first introduced her to Dorothea; the day they had searched for limpets down at Seymour Tower. But all she felt was a hollowness. Only when the corporal awkwardly scraped his chair on the kitchen floor did she recall there was anyone else in the room.

"Sorry to interrupt," he broke in, embarrassed, "but is there anything else I can do?"

Hedy went across to shake the man's hand. "No, thank you. It was good of you to come."

He nodded. "They're never good news. I got a similar one last year — sister and her family all killed by a V2. Nothing prepares you."

"I'm so sorry." Hedy noticed that his eyes, which were warm and hazel, were set against a tan, leathery skin, suggesting he'd spent part of the war in North Africa. "The Occupation has been very hard . . . but at least we didn't suffer the Blitz."

"We all fought our own war," the corporal replied. "I'm very sorry for your loss, Mrs. Weber."

"Are you?" Dorothea spat. Hedy held up her hand, indicating this was the wrong moment and target for bitterness, but Dorothea couldn't stop herself. "He died fighting for Hitler. I wouldn't want you to waste your precious sympathy."

The corporal turned to her. "I mean it. I

came across a ton of different nationalities fighting on both sides. Only thing they had in common was not one bugger actually wanted to be there — pardon my French."

Dorothea's scowl faded. "Thank you for saying that, sir."

"Please" — he held up a palm — "Frank, Frank Flanagan. Sick to death of being a number, to be honest. Just want to get back to Cheshire."

Hedy caught the affection in his voice and felt sick with envy; to have a home to return to, a community still filled with familiar faces.

Flanagan picked up his cap from the table, then turned back to Dorothea. "Anyway, you've had a shock, so I'll leave you to it, now your friend's here."

He slipped quietly down the hall and let himself out, leaving Hedy still holding the telegram in her hand and Dorothea standing in the middle of the kitchen as if she had no idea what to do next.

"Is Kurt gone?"

Hedy nodded.

"So that's that." Dorothea pushed the hair from her eyes and gave herself a tiny shake. "I suppose I should make dinner."

"Let me."

"No, I'd rather have something to do."

Dorothea busied herself in the kitchen, and at six o'clock the women sat down at a kitchen table laid for two, spooning out generous portions of tuna casserole. In the corner stood the wireless; human voices and music filled the room, connecting them to a distant, rejoicing world. While they ate, the newscaster informed them that the last unrepentant Axis forces had been beaten back in Yugoslavia by local partisans, supported by British troops, and that Nagoya had been bombed heavily, bringing victory in Japan ever closer. Then Tommy Handley evoked gales of laughter from his audience by his rendition of the Minister of Aggravation and Mysteries at the Office of Twerps. Dorothea offered Hedy another portion of casserole, but she declined. Neither of them had yet eaten half of what was on their plate.

The delivery of the evening paper caused a brief hiatus. Hedy flicked through the proclamations of the Bailiff and notices about the restoration of sterling, until her eye was caught by a smaller headline on an inside page. The report described attempts by some senior Germans to escape capture by dressing as civilians and trying to pass as locals. British army officials, it reported, had discovered one such coward on an abandoned farm property, hiding in an outhouse.

He had "offered no resistance," but had wept "hysterically" on his arrest. He was named as Erich Gerhard Wildgrube, formerly of the Geheime Feldpolizei.

After dinner the women washed up together, using baking soda and vinegar. From the open window, they could hear the shouting and singing of a party going on next door; children were running in and out of the garden wearing cooking pots for German helmets and firing finger guns at each other, while the adults inside were belting out rousing choruses of "All The Nice Girls Love A Sailor" and "Bill Bailey." As the songs came to their loud, chaotic climaxes, Hedy and Dorothea couldn't help smiling at each other.

The plates were put away. The sun was dipping, and shafts of golden light peeped down the hallway. Dorothea switched off the radio and lit a small coal fire as the chill of the evening began to bite. They sat back down at the table; Dorothea with some mending, Hedy with a book. Over two hours, Dorothea sewed one button, while Hedy read two pages. Neither of them spoke. The party next door gradually fizzled to an end and they heard the door bang as people left. The clock ticked on the wall and the light dimmed. There were two new candles in the larder but neither of them suggested lighting one. Night fell, and Dorothea went to bed.

It was the end of the Occupation. It was over. They were both alive and free.

Hedy sat for another hour in the dark kitchen, staring at nothing. Then she, too, went to bed.

EPILOGUE

1946

The suitcase was simply not going to close. She tried sitting on it, bouncing her bottom on it, then leaning heavily on one end while trying to push one of the chrome hasps into its slot. Eventually Hedy gave in to the inevitable and removed one cardigan and the slippers she'd been given at Christmas. She had other woolens, she told herself, and she could buy another pair of slippers with her first wages, once her ration card had been reissued. The case instantly closed without difficulty, and satisfied that it wasn't going to pop open again, she dragged it off the bed and down the stairs, being careful not to scratch the polished wood at the side of the runner carpet. Mrs. Mitchell was extremely proud of her staircase.

She was glad that the family was all out at this hour. The thought of another goodbye was more than she could take. The farewell party they'd given her last night had been sweet and moving, with thoughtful gifts of handkerchiefs and lavender soap, and a handmade card from their daughter. She knew that she would miss them horribly, and had made them promise to write every week. All that supervised homework and the trips to the beach hadn't felt like work at all; even the housework had been no burden, as she reveled in the scent of freshly laundered sheets and furniture polish, and she'd taken great pleasure in lining up the family's rubber boots in order of size in the hall. But at other times, walking alone on her day off or lying in her solitary bed, the gap between the family's coziness and her personal situation tugged at her soul, and in recent weeks she'd known for certain that it was time to go.

She pulled on her thick brown winter coat and its matching hat with the pink trim; it was mid-December, and the frost was already thick on the grass. At the hall mirror she had only time to apply some lipstick and dab a little extra powder on her nose before she heard the honk of the car horn outside. Taking a last look around the elegant, gleaming hallway, she picked up her case and walked out into the winter afternoon.

Dorothea waved at her from the passenger seat of the old Austin. Frank Flanagan, after heaving himself out of the driver's seat, helped her with the suitcase, making a joke about how light it was.

"This all you've got?"

"My worldly possessions," Hedy confessed with a wry smile. "Do you think I need to start making a trousseau?"

"Well, Dory never had one, and I weren't bothered. And I don't imagine it's your linens your fiancé will be interested in when he gets out."

Hedy laughed and climbed into the back seat while Frank restarted the car. Soon they were heading down St. Saviours Road toward the harbor. Dorothea stretched her hand over the back of her seat toward Hedy, twisted around in her seat like a schoolgirl. "Oh, Hedy, I'm so excited for you! What time does the boat get to Weymouth?"

"We dock at six tomorrow morning. Then I have to catch a train — three trains actually — to get to Plumpton."

Dorothea raised her hand to her cheek. "Goodness! You'll be exhausted. I should have brought some sandwiches for you. Didn't I say, Frank, I should have made her some sandwiches?"

"Certainly did — woke me up to say it

too." Frank grinned at Hedy in the mirror and gave her a wink.

"And when will you get to see Kurt?"

"If the paperwork comes through, next Thursday. He looks good in the photo he sent me — he's been working outside most days since he was moved again."

"You'll give him my love, won't you? You two are going to be so happy." She turned to face the front, and Hedy sat back to take in her last views of the island. The roads where Kurt had walked her weak, failing body in a German uniform . . . Mr. Reis's bakery, now owned by someone else . . . the jail where Kurt served his time. Memories galloped in, images forming and evaporating. By the time the car pulled up at the end of the quay, her head was spinning.

Frank went off to park the car, while Dorothea stood at Hedy's side, looking up at the ship. The stripes of its giant funnel stood sharp against the darkening sky, and shiny blue cranes swung cargo across its bows to the hold. Far below, the water, closing in on its high-tide mark, slapped against the ancient blackened stone of the quay and hinted at the swell beyond. Hedy looked at Dorothea, remembering the last time they had both stood in this spot.

"Anton would be happy for you, you

know," Hedy said, reading her thoughts.

Dorothea nodded. "I know. Frank's been so kind, and it's made such a difference. Everyone at my new office only knows me as Mrs. Flanagan. Sometimes I wish I could tell them about Anton — tell them how wonderful he was — but . . ."

Hedy nodded. "Sometimes it's best to let things be."

"Anyway, we're moving to Cheshire in the summer. Frank wants to start a new business — all his contacts are there. Be a fresh start for us both."

"Don't forget to write."

"Silly! Why would I not write to my best friend?"

Hedy held her close for a moment, the brims of their hats rubbing against each other. Frank arrived with Hedy's suitcase, and the three of them huddled together in the cold, speaking over each other with their wishes of good luck and promises to visit each other soon. When there was no more to say, Hedy gave them both a final kiss and made her way up the gangplank, turning twice to wave until she saw them turn and head back to their car. She walked down two enclosed staircases to her reserved seat where she stowed her case, then returned to the stern of the top deck and found a quiet section of rail to wait for departure. Soon the engines were thundering beneath her, sending vibrations pulsating up through her feet and knees. The water below fizzed white and foamy, and with creaking slowness, the ship pulled away from the quayside and headed for the harbor mouth.

For a while Hedy stood watching the departing shore, marveling at the light reflections skipping across the blackness of the water. Then she reached into her bag and took out her most precious possession — the beribboned brown envelope containing all her recent letters. She took the one from the top, smiling at Roda's curly, girlish hand; she thought about the day it had flopped onto the doormat of the Mitchells' hallway and her employers' excitement when they saw her reaction. Now her eyes, as always, jumped to her favorite section:

. . . and now find myself living by the sea in Hadera. So can you imagine my delight when I found out that our darling baby brother was less than fifty kilometers away in Tel Aviv? Daniel is doing so well, and writes regularly to Golda in London now the post is working again. Chana and her husband love Australia and plan to stay. We are all agreed, and very determined, that no matter how long it takes, we will find out what happened to Mama and Papa. We believe the Red Cross may be able to help.

Hedy tucked the letter back into place with a sigh. In truth, she knew there would be little to discover. Dates and precise locations wouldn't change what they already knew. Perhaps, though, the information would bring a little closure, maybe eventually acceptance, after all the years of uncertainty. Her fingers slid back into the envelope, this time drawing out the sheet with the words HMP Ford printed at the top.

Sweetheart, I can't believe this new job means you will be only a few miles from my new placement. I'm enjoying farm work, and there's talk of release within the next six months. As soon as I have a date, you must choose a wedding ring, and start saving for your ticket to Germany! Being without you has been the only unbearable part of this. Can't wait to see you. All my love, K.

She pressed the thin, translucent paper to her chest before placing it carefully back in her bag. And at the same time, she smiled at the brown rubber band on her third finger and kissed it.

The harbor began to fade, and the sea grew choppier as the ship chugged toward the open sea. It looked so small from here, this tiny prison of an island. She knew she was one of the lucky ones. So many had perished here at the invaders' hands, so many others would never see these shores again. It was hard to think about them without a furious desire for revenge. How easy it was to access hate, Hedy pondered. How close to the surface that putrid emotion always floated, waiting for a target, biding its time to find a focus and bloom like a poisonous algae, while forgiveness lay limp and impotent at the bottom of the soul, guiltily aware that duty called, but without the energy to do its job. Would she and Kurt have the strength to resist that temptation? "Even if you forget the past, it will remember you," her mother had been fond of saying. Only in the years to come, Hedy supposed, would she discover if that were true.

The waves were fierce now, and the ship rolled back and forth as it plowed across the southern bay of the island and prepared to round Noirmont Point. Hedy gripped hard to the rail, sensing the unseen forces that were pushing and pulling at the hull, battering it below the surface. The currents of the Channel would try to drag the ship west as it pressed on toward the English coast; only the strength of the steel pistons beneath would keep it true.

Hedy closed her eyes as the freezing wind sucked at her skin, and smiled into the dark. She and Kurt would be all right, she decided. They would find a way to discard their past, seek out different lands and create new adventures. Europe was broken, but already thousands were coming together with tools, ideas and laws with which to mend it. A hundred miles away at this very moment there were young, scrub-faced children being informed of Hedy's imminent arrival, and a fresh bed being made up for her in a pretty country bedroom. In a few months Kurt would be a free man. And somewhere beyond that invisible horizon lay the fresh allure of Weymouth harbor, working farms and scattered villages, firm plowed fields of winter wheat and the crisp golden light of the morning.

ACKNOWLEDGMENTS

In accessing the factual material on which this novel is based, I would like to thank Dr. Gilly Carr, Senior Lecturer at the University of Cambridge, and author of numerous books, journals and papers on Occupation history. Her submission to the Yad Vashem World Holocaust Remembrance Center for the acceptance of Dorothea Weber (née Le Brocq) of Righteous Among the Nations status did much to bring that extraordinary piece of history to public attention, and her contribution to a wider understanding of Channel Islands history is to be applauded.

Thanks are due to Bob Le Sueur and Bruce Scott Dalgleish for sharing their personal memories; to Susannah Waters and Julie Corbin for their substantial assistance in my transition from screenwriting to prose; to Maurice Gran, Jo Briggs and Gabbie Asher for their scrutiny of Jewish issues

437

and phrases; to the brilliant George Aboud who did more than anyone to help shape this project, all out of the kindness of her writer's heart; to my late grandmother Grace Lecoat for passing on to me the "Beautiful Swedes" song (originally from an amateur Green Room Club production of the period).

Thanks also to Sean McTernan, my book agent John Beaton for showing faith, and to my incredibly supportive editor Alison Rae.

Finally, to my fantastic husband, who dealt with my frequent tantrums and insistence that this project was impossible to complete with his usual stoicism, humor and love.

■ ■ ■ ■

THE GIRL FROM THE CHANNEL ISLANDS

JENNY LECOAT

■ ■ ■ ■

READER'S GUIDE

A CONVERSATION
WITH THE AUTHOR

Q: It's a bit of a cliché to ask a writer what her inspiration was, but in this case, the book is inspired by a true story. Can you tell the readers more about it?

A: The story is based on documented history. The real Hedy arrived in Jersey in 1938, having fled the Nazis in her native Austria, only to find herself trapped once more by the Channel Island invasion of 1940. We know that despite being racially classified as Jewish, she found work with the German authorities and, despite the risks, exploited that position to help her community. At some point she began a relationship with a German officer named Kurt, and when Hedy was forced into hiding with local woman Dorothea, Kurt visited and supplied food, at tremendous personal risk.

441

Q: How did you find out about Hedy's story?

A: A local historian, who researched the story in order to procure a posthumous Yad Vashem Righteous Among the Nations award for Dorothea, sent me some news links in 2016. These showed a plaque being unveiled outside the house where the women lived, and also revealed some old newspaper clippings. The story is also mentioned in several Occupation history books.

Q: Were any of the other characters based on real people?

A: Hedy, Kurt, Dorothea and Anton were all real people, although only basic facts about them during these years are known, so how they met and how the relationships between them came about is fictionalized in the novel. The Jersey politicians Orange and Le Quesne are also real historical figures.

Q: What's your family's connection to the story?

A: I was born in Jersey to an island family. Both sides of the family were involved in what might be termed "resistance activity" during the Occupation years. My paternal grand-

father made illegal crystal radio sets, and my mother's family hid two Russian slave workers who had been captured to build Hitler's Atlantic wall defenses, but who escaped from their camps. My great aunt Louisa sheltered a young man she called "Bill" for two years in her own home, but was betrayed. Consequently several of the family were arrested, Louisa was deported to the camps and died at Ravensbrück. Her brother Harold was the only British survivor of Belsen.

Q: What were some of the unexpected realities of living under Occupation?

A: The loss of liberty and fear of arrest for trivial offences must have been horrifying enough, but the confiscation of radios in 1942, cutting the population off from real news, and the near starvation as the war progressed were the worst aspects for many.

Q: The Channel Islands were the only part of Britain to be Occupied during WWII. Younger readers or those unfamiliar with this part of the war may be wondering why Britain allowed them to be captured. Why did it happen?

A: In 1940 the Allies had been pushed back by Hitler's forces, and the evacuation of

Dunkirk had occurred just weeks earlier. Britain was in no position to defend the Channel Islands, which, although part of the British Isles, are geographically far closer to France. Britain withdrew its military from the islands to save manpower and resources, but did not inform the enemy they had done so, which caused the Germans to bomb what they assumed to be a defended territory.

Hitler was fanatical about his acquisition of the islands, which were not only a useful strategic gain but, as a British territory, a morale boost for the Third Reich, whose generals assumed the conquest of the British mainland was a simple next step.

Q: What was it like growing up on Jersey? Can you tell us more about island life? How is it different from growing up in more central UK? What is it like to visit the Channel Islands in the present day — do they see a lot of tourism, and if so, is any of that tourism related to their WWII history?

A: Jersey, although the largest of the Channel Islands, is only nine by five miles. As France and England can only be reached by boat or plane, it was expensive to travel, and it often felt restrictive growing up there, especially as a teenager. But it is a profoundly beautiful island with beaches that rival any in Europe, and that is where I spent most of my child-hood summers. In the '60s and '70s the islands were flooded with tourists every July and August; tourism is quieter now, but the island still attracts visitors who come for the scenery, food and history. The island's Oc-cupation past has become a major part of its cultural draw, with the abandoned bunkers and War Tunnels Museum attracting thou-sands every year.

Q: You have a background in many dif-ferent areas, including screenwriting. How does writing a film differ from writing a novel? How did it prepare you for writing a novel?

A: It's a vastly different format and the transi-tion wasn't easy. Film is a very collaborative process, with much of the final work done by others — the director, designer, actors. A novel is entirely the work of the author, includ-ing descriptions and characters' thought processes. But screenwriters get used to structuring a story carefully, over three acts, and I found that a useful transferable skill. Never commit to a word until you know your direction of travel!

Q: Here's another question writers always get asked! What's next for you?

A: *I'm undecided as yet. But I'm considering another book set in Jersey, perhaps in a different period.*

QUESIONS FOR DISCUSSION

1. Hedy is based on a real person, but her life bears a resemblance to the realities of some people's present-day lives. What parallels can you draw between Occupied Jersey and some regions of the world today? Or between Hedy's life as a refugee and a displaced person?

2. What are your thoughts on the friendship between Hedy and Anton?

3. Hedy's friends and community risked their own lives to protect her. Even if we aren't living in a country at war or an extreme situation, what responsibilities do we have to each other as neighbors and citizens? What does doing the right thing look like in your life?

4. What are some ways that ordinary people

can stand up to injustice in the present day?

5. Kurt and Hedy shared a powerful relationship in an incredibly stressful situation. What other books (or movies, or TV shows) can you think of in which love flourishes under impossible circumstances?

6. What aspects of Hedy's story might you be able to relate to?

7. Kurt is a man who realizes he's fighting on the wrong side of the war, for a leader whose actions he cannot accept. How do you feel about his decisions? What would you have done in his place? How easy do you think it is to fight against injustice in a position like Kurt's?

8. What did you make of Dorothea? Of her relationship with Hedy?

9. What was the most exciting part of the story for you?

10. What are your thoughts on the novel's ending?

ABOUT THE AUTHOR

Jenny Lecoat was born in Jersey, Channel Islands, where her parents were raised under German Occupation and were involved in resistance activity. Lecoat moved to England at 18, where, after earning a drama degree, she spent a decade on the alternative comedy circuit as a feminist stand-up. She also wrote for newspapers and women's magazines (*Cosmopolitan, Observer*) and worked as a TV and radio presenter, before focusing on screenwriting from sitcom to sketch shows. A love of history and factual stories, as well as a return to her island roots, brought about her feature film *Another Mother's Son* (2017). She is married to television writer Gary Lawson and now lives in East Sussex. *The Girl from the Channel Islands* is her first novel.

